AF207243

THE TRUE LIFE ADVENTURES
OF SPARROW DRINKWATER

60 YEARS IN CANADA
1933
1993
HarperCollins

Novels by Trevor Ferguson

High Water Chants
Onyx John
The Kinkajou
The True Life Adventures of Sparrow Drinkwater

TREVOR FERGUSON

The

TRUE LIFE

ADVENTURES

of

SPARROW

DRINKWATER

HarperCollins*Publishers*Ltd

THE TRUE LIFE ADVENTURES OF SPARROW DRINKWATER.
Copyright © 1993 by Trevor Ferguson. All rights reserved. No part of
this book may be used or reproduced in any manner whatsoever without
prior written permission except in the case of brief quotations embodied
in reviews. For information address HarperCollins Publishers Ltd,
Suite 2900, 55 Avenue Road, Toronto, Canada M5R 3L2.

First Edition

Canadian Cataloguing in Publication Data

Ferguson, Trevor, 1947-
    The true life adventures of Sparrow Drinkwater

ISBN 0-00-223891-8

I. Title.

PS8561.E74T78 1993   C813'.54   C92-095379-4
PR9199.3.F47T78 1993

---

93 94 95 96 97 98 99 ❖ RRD 10 9 8 7 6 5 4 3 2 1

§

In memory of my father
the Rev. P.A. Ferguson
and for Rod, Joan, Judy, and Jamie
for Freya and Jamie
for my mother, Jo,
and for Lynne, for everything.

§

But let us never forget that not everyone who has not lost his senses thereby proves conclusively that he is in possession of them.

–The Journals of Kierkegaard, 1834-1854
Sören Kierkegaard

"No, no! The adventures first," said the Gryphon in an impatient tone: "explanations take such a dreadful time."

–Alice's Adventures in Wonderland
Lewis Carroll

This is a work of fiction. All characters and events are fictitious. Any resemblance to persons living or dead is purely coincidental.

ACKNOWLEDGEMENTS

The author wishes to thank the Canada Council, the Ontario Arts Council, and the Ministère des Affaires culturelles, Gouvernement du Québec, for support during the writing of this book.

Chapter one, *Floating Hearts*, was published in slightly different form in The Malahat Review, No. 89.

The two anecdotes in Chapter Five concerning the holocaust are factual, although related here by fictitious characters and altered slightly. For the use of his story, the author thanks the late Mr. Herman Hubscher, who survived the massacre at Stanislov, Galitzia, on October 12, 1941. His account was originally published in "Forewards," New York, February 13th and 14th, 1947; the English translation is deposited in the Archives of the Montreal Holocaust Memorial Centre. The events were also recounted to Mr. Ronald Headland, author of *Messages of Murder, A Study of the Reports of the Einsatzgruppen of the Security Police and the Security Service, 1941-1943*, (Associated University Presses, Cranbury, New Jersey, 1992) who relayed them to the author. Thanks also to Gabrielle Tyrnauer, author of *Bibliography: Gypsies and the Holocaust, a Bibliography and Introductory Essay* (Interuniversity Centre for European Studies, and The Montreal Institute for Genocide Studies, 1989) for relating the 'telephone' anecdote, again relayed through Mr. Headland.

The OIS financial scandal of this book bears marked similarity to the IOS scandal of the early 1970s. The author found three articles particularly useful in unravelling that episode, so that it could then be subject to fictional creation. One appeared in *Maclean's*, August, 1973, "The Sweet Smell of Norman LeBlanc"; and another in *The Financial Post*, November 16, 1974, "The inside story of the looting of IOS"; both written by Robert A. Hutchison, author of a book related to the subject, *Vesco*. The third was published in *The Toronto Star*, October 1, 1977, "$224-million fugitive fears for his life," by Roger Croft. Useful for other purposes was my correspondence with former Park Extension neighbour and later a fugitive, Norman LeBlanc. In undergoing a reexamination of his life, Mr. Leblanc found the burdens of his past too much to bear, and took his own life in the summer of 1991.

THE TRUE LIFE ADVENTURES

OF SPARROW DRINKWATER

one

1940–1957

UNDER THE WORLD

1.

Floating Hearts

Is it true that human life ascended from a swamp? After eons did amoebae, weary of the muck and slime, yearn for a succulent breath above the fetid air, desire a new address? I wonder. Did life among the scum and scuzzies prove too stressful for certain sensitive souls, whose attraction to an esoteric realm quickened them to embark upon an overland passage through time? A faithful search, let's say, for heaven? Or, as measured on a different scale, is all human endeavour ultimately a quarrel about real estate? Are we to assume that life's true meaning is resident with the upwardly mobile? Can any quest be more significant than the scramble for power, fame, possessions, at the very least a photo-opportunity? I'm asking the question, can we honestly accept that human life ascended from the swamp?

Mine did. What more can I say for certain about the origins of my species? I emerged from a swamp. Most days, I let it go at that.

*

Darkness is her patron. Night affords safe passage.

My mother, who is fourteen, less than a year before my birth, steps softly through the shadows. Her fingertips explore a map of cracks splayed across the walls. Shards of moonlight gash her skin. A lithe girl, she escapes first the dormitory of her school, then slips along the penumbra of the quadrangle toward the fleeting emancipation of the field. My mother goes over the wall. Like bed-wetting, a frequent nocturnal habit.

And no one knows. Nor sees. Nor hears her speak to demons boisterous in the field, run terrified as spirits mock from seats high among the trees. It is not the branches that frighten her, silly girl, a sudden hurtling swish or crack. The wind and its pranks do not propel her across field and meadow down into the sanctuary of woods sloping into a swamp. Don't blame demons who, offended by their own ugliness and wretchedness, conceal themselves. Rather, point a finger at those benign spirits pleading deliverance for themselves. Spirits stained by tree-bark and arrowroot, weighted by despair, who shine like tarnished silver in the moonlight. In particular, those are the ones who scare her. They call her by name, claim her as a friend. Whisper words, actual words, and as she flees they shout, and she must run stopping her ears. My mother must flee to the soft woods and down into the swamp where the trees and the demons in the trees and the blessed wind curry a racket, develop a stench, deliver her from this compact of strangers, fiends, and friends.

Panting, she breathes awhile, knows a moment's peace.

She has come to her place.

My mother, like a cat, digs herself a small hollow in the wet earth, and under the augury of a crescent moon squats to piddle in the grim depth of night.

Then she returns to the private boarding school. We know that the school was situated in the south of Georgia, most likely in Clinch County, on a sandy rise overlooking Okefinokee Swamp. (Indigenous Indians believed that human life first emerged from that swamp. Refutable, but in any case, mine did.) Nobody found out about my mother's habit, which indicates some guile, some intelligent planning and execution on her part. All we know is that she escaped each night and raced through a gauntlet of phantoms to piss among alligators, snapping turtles, and moccasin snakes.

We do not know when the practice started or for how long it continued. Nor do we know whether she was courting madness, or whether she was already insane. Based on the evidence, we are left to assume that on one of those nights, or more often, she was met, and we must also conclude that it was neither a spook nor a reptile who caressed her, but a man.

It is also fair to speculate that my mother might not have known the difference.

My mother could not have been more than fourteen when she lost her shadow for good.

First she heard a demon whirring in her ears. She attributed the sound to being a demon's noise because she had never heard it before.

Then her shadow sailed across the grass. She felt torn, ripped in the way that paper rips, and watched her shadow scale the walls of her school. Last seen sliding out of sight above the roof.

My mother expressed her torment by screaming.

A rhythmic, high-pitched squeal. She wanted to block out the hard sound of the demon's whirring. She screamed for her shadow to return although instinctively she knew that shadows are like flowers, that the torn petal can never be reattached. Her classmates had ceased their play. Some were watching my mother scream, others were gazing at the sky where the demon was whirring. Still others had seen the flight of her shadow and searched the direction where it had vanished.

Three teachers came running. My mother saw Miss Grayson, the stoic elderly lady who taught Pure and Applied Science, and out the corner of her eye she saw wee Miss Fitzpatrick, who taught French, Latin, and took the girls on picnics and nature walks. She did not see Mrs. Gruenwald, who was a toad, who wore a green dress like a frog, who taught Arithmetic and Health, and who was also the Assistant Principal. Mrs. Gruenwald caught hold of my mother from behind, spun her around, and gave her a royal shake. When my mother screamed louder, Mrs. Gruenwald slapped her face.

My mother stopped the dreadful sound she was making. She merely sobbed. When she looked down she thought she saw her shadow once again, and Miss Fitzpatrick led her away. Docile, Mother spent the afternoon on a cot in the infirmary.

The room was kept dark, with the shades of the tall windows drawn. Thinking that the girl might have been affected by the heat, a nurse placed a cool compress on my mother's brow. She was a fair girl, hers a complexion not suitable to sunlight. Free from a class, Miss Fitzpatrick dropped by for a visit, lightly touching my mother's palm and wrist. "Didn't you give us a scare, dear? Such blither! Don't fret now. Too much sun, that's all it was."

My mother believed that the sun could properly be blamed. She only felt safe after dusk. Often the sun disoriented her. Miss Fitzpatrick replaced the compress with a fresh one and under that soothing darkness my mother witnessed suns swirling, phantoms burning.

Led outside again she thought she saw her shadow. But it was fat and long and bent across the cypress tree. And then she saw Mrs. Gruenwald, the toad, laughing under the spotlight of the quadrangle with a small and lively shadow. *Mrs. Gruenwald had stolen hers!* Mrs. Gruenwald had stuck her own fat and distorted shadow to my mother's feet!

This time, even Mrs. Gruenwald assailing her face could not prevent my mother from making a scene.

And in the months that followed her stomach grew. The big shadow attached to her feet shrank, and my mother believed that Mrs. Gruenwald's huge shadow was sliding inside her, engorging her tummy. Making her sick.

But that was me. I was the shadow inflating inside her.

Miss Fitzpatrick took four girls on a field trip into the swamp in a flat-bottomed *bateau* effortlessly propelled by leaning on a long pole. Parents had come to visit their daughters at the school. Those whose families were not able to make it (which automatically included my mother every time) were taken off the grounds so as not to feel neglected. Miss Fitzpatrick preferred her girls to feel privileged. Everyone had something to look for, some treasure to seize and bring back with them to balance the gifts likely to be left behind by the parents visiting daughters.

Wild orchids, snipped from sandy knolls rising from the swamp, were a great prize. Two of the girls gathered these. Pine forests gave way to thicker woods of cypress and black gum, and the *bateau* gently glided deeper into the morass of swamp and antediluvian sanctuary. One girl, my mother's best friend, was determined to catch a male and a female lizard, and mate them. She had brought along a cage for their nuptials. My mother let her hand glide through the lilies and Miss Fitzpatrick whispered warning. "Careful, dear." Alligators. Snapping turtles. Day-time demons. Curled on a limb, a moccasin snake. A bear waddling down to the shore excited the girls. Except my mother. Accustomed to behemoths, she kept her eyes peeled on the water instead. The flat calm of the water. Miss Fitzpatrick had given her something to search for and so my mother remained alert.

Deeper into the humidity and harmony of the swamp. Deep into lost places. Bird cry and barter. Alligators perused their *bateau* and the girls, except my mother, giggled as though they were being courted for the first time. Deeper into recesses and dream, and the girls were silent, still, the flat calm of the water and the flat blue of the sky a threshold, the darker woods whispering, watching, surrounding them, moving in behind them. Opening ahead, then closing in behind.

Standing at the back of the boat above the girls, Miss Fitzpatrick raised the long pole and pushed it down into the mysterious brackish water. The quiet girls would watch her shadow turn to the other side of the craft. The pole extend, reach down into the murky depths. Find bottom. Push.

Turn, lift, and push.

Eyelids drooped. Temples perspired. The girls fanned themselves and felt stifled. A lack of air. A failure to navigate.

My mother disrupted that pristine, erotic stillness. She bounded into the water, nearly capsizing the boat. Suddenly desperate, she plunged forward, frantic, half-swimming, a wild, vigorous splash, and those left behind called out and the girls helped paddle, sinking bare hands into the alligator pool, crying with fear, expecting with each stroke to lose fingers. My mother fell upon her prize, clutching her flowers and holding them desperately to herself. Alligators lazing in the sun slid from the mud to vanish into the depths of the murky swamp. The girls pulled her back aboard and she lay in the *bateau* with everyone hysterical and angry, and with Miss Fitzpatrick cross and equally amazed. My mother just lay there. Soaking. Her white dress a ruin. Presenting her prize.

My mother had been attracted to the flowers by their name. She valued them to replace her missing, inchoate shadow. Miss Fitzpatrick would show her how to dry them between the pages of a book. Keep them forever that way.

The crimson flowers my mother had rescued from the swamp were called floating hearts.

Mother believed that I had been sired by a bird. She remembers the night it happened. She had been peeing in the woods behind the school when a huge raven drifted out of the sky, blotting the moon. The raven put its claws on her hips, so that she was pinned, and used its long beak to pick off her night-clothes. She knew it was a raven because it was all black with an impressive wing-span.

(I suspect a priest in his robes. Or a travelling monk. An ecclesiastic. I suspect a man.)

After my mother was told that it was not Mrs. Gruenwald's shadow that was growing inside her, she was informed that she was going to have a baby. Teachers and the nurse took turns explaining how that worked. A baby would be born out of her stomach. She was told that the baby was put there by the same person who had entered her there, between the legs, there.

- Where?

- Right here. Miss Fitzpatrick showed her.

- A big black raven, my mother said. A big black raven, or maybe it was a crow, he put me on the ground. His big claws were on my hips. He hurt me there. Every night he put me on the ground, pushing into me there.

The revelation astounded the women. That a schoolgirl had become pregnant when no man worked nearby and none lived within four miles upset their traditional southern decorum.

- Where? Miss Scott, the Principal, asked.

- Here.

- How did you know that the big black bird was male? the Principal asked her. You keep saying 'he', and 'his'.

- He had a deep voice, a man's voice, my mother explained with an unusual eagerness. She felt no need to curtail her excitement. Except that he talked like a bird.

- How does a bird talk? Miss Fitzpatrick wanted to know.

- A bird has its own language, my mother explained. The teachers had never seen her quite so animated. She was usually reserved and shy. And she imitated the language of huge ravens, a deep bellowing, a kind of retching, followed by a rapid series of guttural grunts.

My mother expected to give birth to a bird.

When I emerged from her womb instead, and was so tiny, she named me Sparrow.

She must have put up a stink, because that's the name that appears on my birth certificate.

Sparrow.

Drinkwater.

She always called me her little bird. Apparently her main disappointment in life has been that I never learned to fly particularly high.

*

Details are sketchy, some of the stories are bound to be apocryphal, but I do remember the asylum in which I was raised. My mother and I share pleasant memories of Lougain, Mississippi, where we convalesced following the trauma of my birth. The town's two principal sources of commerce were the nuthouse and the military firing range on the opposite side of the highway. Some people were sent to Lougain for peace and quiet, others to make a racket. What the soldiers and the inmates of the nuthouse did have in common was that none had volunteered to be there, and the majority of both kooks and paratroopers would have preferred being somewhere else.

No one has ever been invited to visit Lougain. It is a place where people are consigned. Much like being born.

I didn't mind it so much. It was all that I knew the world to be. Lazy days in the heat. Old men and women in rocking chairs. The slow shuffle down white corridors. In the morning, breakfast and gunfire. Grenade practice after lunch. I was lulled to sleep each evening by my mother humming against a backdrop of exploding mortars.

During the hours after my birth, my mother called me her little bird. Her Sparrow. Terms of endearment, quite possibly. It also must be realized that through her eyes—given her mental state, and what she had just been through—she might actually have seen me with feathers, a beak, wings, and perspicacious black eyes.

For days at a time the nurses kept us separated. My mother had had to be dissuaded from feeding me worms pinched from the flower beds.

While the world was all new to me, my mother had more trouble adjusting to the change of locale. She had less freedom in the asylum than she had enjoyed at school. Escaping the locked building to slip over the wall at night proved impossible. The walls were too high. Complicating the issue, her interior geography was changing. A regular dosage of drugs glazed her eyes and kept her calm. Most of her old companions, the spooks and demons and polychromatic spirits, steered clear of her whenever she was on her medication.

Blessed with many visions while pregnant, she had overheard the most wonderful oratory. Often she had been strapped to the bed as delusions overwhelmed her. After giving birth, perhaps as a punishment for having me, a doctor devised her dosage. She needed the tranquillizers to be herself, he explained, to deter her from behaving as a crazy person. Pills would grant her back her dignity. The doctor told my mother that they had waited until the baby was born to prevent me from being affected by the drugs. She had been allowed to hallucinate and to revel in her visions so that I could remain whole and healthy.

(Thanks, Doc. Due to your kind intervention, I came into the world without an addiction to opiates prescribed to suppress schizophrenia. Instead, I was brought into a world snared by lucid dreams, with a propensity for mirage and nightmare. Everything's a trade-off.)

My mother missed her friends, even the fiends, and the grey world under the mist of drugs lacked colour and vivacity. She inferred from this that the only way to stop ingesting pills every day was to get pregnant again. That was a problem. On drugs, she could not communicate with giant ravens, none visited her, and anyway she could not escape the grounds at night. So she invited the caretaker, whose skin was as black as a raven's and smoother, to do as he wished under the shade of the bougainvillaea.

My mother suggested to him that he use the handle of his mop, but the caretaker had something else in mind.

We do not know for how long this practice went on, but when it was discovered, the caretaker vanished, much like my raven-father before him.

How well I remember the day the paratroopers attacked!

Soldiers thundered out of the sky, raining down upon the asylum. I was old enough then, about five-and-a-half, to fight back. With a contented grin on her face, and a blithe light in her eyes that pierced her customary glaze, my mother lovingly welcomed the specks tumbling from the darkened clouds. She believed her demons had returned—she recognized the whirring in the air. I did what she did, picked up a croquet mallet. We were off to charge the shadow-thieves.

Sky-jumpers landed on the lawn and in the trees. Pounded down on the rooftops, and their heavy boots cracked cabbages in the vegetable patch. One soldier seriously pranged himself on the weather vane, the rooster's comb gouging his thigh. Another careened off the sloped tin roof of the tool shed and landed in the compost heap. When they hit the ground the troopers wrestled with their enormous chutes, trying to keep themselves from blowing away. And after the chutes were scrunched up, the men had to defend themselves against my mother and me.

We clobbered them with our mallets. Mom broke a guy's nose, and he ran off yowling. The other patients who had been outside that day joined in the spree, and at first the battle was going our way. A paratrooper dangling from a tree had to keep his feet up or have them walloped by residents taking turns at the sport. And still the soldiers were gliding down out of the sky, at the mercy of the stiff breeze and the maniacal guerilla forces assembling on the ground.

A few young recruits, unaware that they had landed on the wrong target, dug up the lawn to bury their chutes.

Another was intimidated by Mother's vicious mallet. Weary of having his backside pummelled, he ran away, spun around, and fired a burst over our heads. That stopped us.

The shots incited other recruits to open fire on the buildings while they were still in mid-air. They thought they were blasting an abandoned barracks. Thinking they heard hail on the roof, residents on the upper floor peered out their windows. Others wandered outside to learn why the gunfire sounded so near today. Spying their peers assailing the paratroopers, most of them joined the fray.

Bullets ricocheted off brick. Windows shattered.

Frantically running around, nurses and orderlies tried to instill calm, although they themselves had panicked.

Mother and me were stalking a man with a radio. Mom probably was interested in him because he was behaving like a lunatic. He had rank—a corporal, let's say—and was yelling into the sky, "Hold your fire! Hold your fire!" He was screaming into his field telephone to abort the drop, a message he was never able to wholly transmit because Mom had raised her mallet on high—a mighty swing crunched the phone into a sad tangle of wires and battered metal. Then she stood, leaning on her weapon, her small child beside her, both of us quite pleased with ourselves.

The corporal just kept looking from his smashed phone and then up at us, gaping, his mouth ajar as though he wanted to say something but couldn't find the words. Which was how half the Lougain inmates prospered through their days. Had he kept that pose for too long he might have been admitted.

Moments later, the corporal was sidetracked by the explosion of a grenade blowing out the backside of the dining hall. He raced away, met by a confused band of casualties basking in the glory of this dream, delighted that their friends were participating in it too.

Feeling like we had just won a war, Mom and I shook hands.

Only a few of the patients truly believed that the enemy dropping from the sky was a battalion of demons. Most thought they were paratroopers. Specifically—the nuisances who woke them every morning with machine-gun fire and disrupted blissful afternoons with tank manoeuvres while their neighbours across the way were attempting to nap. Motivated, the inmates were tenacious fighters. When the soldiers finally realized that they had not landed at the designated front, but had in fact been blown behind enemy lines, they reorganized themselves, rescued comrades from the trees and rooftops, and signalled a full retreat. They would not return until the nurses and orderlies had pacified everyone, and then, once a truce was declared, they shuffled back into the compound like whipped dogs to whimper pathetic apologies.

A jostle of soldiers paid as much attention to my mother as others did to the few who were bleeding. One guy shook her hand, then raised it to his lips to kiss. My mom seemed to like that. The next G.I., pointing to the welt on his chin, forgave her, and proved his change of heart by giving her a hug. She enjoyed that too. The next in line pecked her cheek. He breathed in deeply, as if filling himself with the scent of her. Eight or ten soldiers had surrounded my mother and me, laughing and making jokes. The nurses failed to shoo them away. Shrieking commands, a sergeant got them moving, but he was not in any hurry to leave himself. Tipping his helmet toward my mother, he said, "'Scuse us, ma'm. We won't be bothering you no more." He took another step backwards. "Pardon me, ma'm?"

"Mmm?"

"My name is Sergeant Driver? Me and the men were wondering if, you know, we might be privileged to learn what's yours."

"What?"

"What's your name, sugar?"

"It's not sugar."

"But you have a name."

She giggled at his foolishness. "Everybody has a name."

"What's yours then, sweet cakes?"

"No. It's Sheilagh."

"You're a live one, Sheilagh." He was walking away backwards. Either he appreciated the woman in front of him, and wanted a longer look, or he was wary of her smoking mallet.

Battle-weary, we were obliged to lick our wounds as well as our chops. Change is a boon to institutional life. Disruption nudges nirvana, and we were fortunate to have shared a taste of heaven. Yet war wreaks havoc in its aftermath, and the ensuing subtle reforms were not appreciated.

Outsiders have trouble getting a handle on this—being the youngest child in an asylum is a nifty place to be. An appropriate introduction to life, perhaps, but the home was also a wonderful playground, lush with greenery and bright flowers, a setting vivid with imagination and wonder. Apparently our Eden. Aloof from frenzy, the ordered, cultivated community segregated itself from whatever planetary malaise happened to be in vogue.

World War Two, for instance, had just passed us by unnoticed.

I'd been adopted by a maze of friends. Having the run of such a big place is a special privilege for a tot. How many kids enjoy access to forty rooms and receive the attention of fifty parents? Like any child, I was counted among the needy, yet nurses preferred an hour of make-believe with me to force-feeding the infantile, or to buoying the spirits of a manic-depressive. Driving a dump truck in my sandbox beat changing bedpans any day.

Not every inmate was friendly, of course. After all, most were there for a reason. Several women sought to claim me as their own, pressing me to their bosoms at each opportunity, and I had to be quick to dodge an old man who lurked around corridors and shot out after me in his wheelchair. What he planned to do if he managed to snatch me was a constant worry, the only clue to his intent being the frustrated gnashing of his teeth as I made my escape.

Really, my closest pal in those days was my mother. We'd stroll around the grounds, and in the afternoons she'd nap beside me in the shade while I shaped plasticine into grotesque and merry little friends. Whenever it rained she snuck me outside to splash in the puddles, me in my little boots, her in her bare feet. We loved building ditches and dams to move the water around. She was especially fond of creating an artificial swamp. We ate together and slept in the same room that had immaculate white walls and a revolving squeaky fan on the high ceiling. We washed our hands together in the same sink and before tucking me in at night she'd recite fairy tales. She was a good storyteller because she believed all the old favourites implicitly.

Being packed off to different classes following the raid, then, was distressing to us both.

In my class, the first thing I had to learn was how to tie my own shoes. I had been following my mother's example, which was to kick them off and tug them on again already tied. Loops and knots were an endless struggle. The close scrutiny of a nurse aggravated the chore. I could not comprehend why this had suddenly become necessary. Growing up in an asylum, I suppose, had instilled a sense of letting others do the work. You would think that I had been born to a manor with a passel of servants. Everything was provided for, and I presumed that that was how the world would ever be. Each morning after breakfast my mother and I returned to find that our room had mysteriously been cleaned. Three square meals a day landed warm before us on the dining-table. Raw carrots were an unknown quantity to me, I figured a magic garden grew them hot and peeled, limp and sliced. It took me ages to accept that the sandy potatoes I helped dig from our field had any relationship to the steaming baked spuds on my plate. Faithfully, egged on by my tutors, I learned to tie my shoes. Secretly, however, I was spiteful. Such labour was beneath my dignity.

Kitchen duty blossomed on the curriculum. Mom and I continued to take separate classes, and we had to develop a certain proficiency before we were allowed to slice onions together, bawling our eyes out. In the afternoons we were shown photograph albums, the world in black and white. At night we were allowed to listen to the radio, and on Wednesday mornings we were forced to study picture books. Especially, we were to learn about cities. Drilled into us was the radical notion that we were not the few inhabitants of a minuscule planet. A whole world lay out there. And apparently, that whole world was lying in wait for us.

We were being primed to face it.

A scary prospect. Worrying about it kept me up late some nights. I could not figure out what we had done wrong. I could not understand how the doctors and the nurses could be so cruel to have plotted to kick us out. Could we not have a second chance?

On one of those sleepless evenings, I heard the wind calling my mother's name. "Sheeee-laghhh! Sheilagh!" murmured the air. For the first time, I appreciated the existence of her demons. I had thought that she had made them up, in the way that I invented my clay pals. I remember feeling relieved that they were calling *her* name, and not mine, because I really did not desire demons of my own.

"Sheeeee-laggghhhh! Sheeee-laghhhh!"

My mother could not hear or respond to her demons in the wind because she had been put to sleep by her medication.

The next day when we were doing up the breakfast dishes, I told her about the voices. (This was something new—not only doing the dishes, but working. All of a sudden we had to support ourselves.) My mother was excited by the news, and that very night she played a trick. The nurse watched her take her night pill, but after she had left the room I saw her spit the red capsule out. She winked at me. Her demons were calling her! And she needed to be awake to greet them.

"Sheee-laghhh!" summoned the demon in the black stillness of night. Not the wind this time, because there was no wind. Only that melodious voice, enticing her, beckoning to her. "Sheee-laghhh!"

Putting on her night-dress, my mother slipped out of the room. She bid me quiet with a finger to her lips, and sneaked away.

I watched from the window. Rooting for her.

Moonlight filtered into my room through the bullet holes plugged with plastic in the roof. That same light shone on my mother's back.

Dashing across the lawn, her night-clothes aflutter, she seemed angelic to me. Radiant. Possessed by joy. The damaged wall in the dining room remained under construction, and Mom had used that cavity to escape. I could feel her freedom, sense her pleasure in her run. I wanted to be out galloping beside her. On the edge of the moonlight, where the lawn darkened into the trees, my mother was welcomed into the arms of her demon who took her down into the underbrush, where he spoke the words of a loving raven. Fast breathing. Guttural grunts. And yet, I must confess that from my aerie I saw no wings. And after my mother ran back, I observed no beast ascend into the night sky.

(You know whom I suspect. A soldier. You know I suspect a sergeant. Someone with rank.)

Returning, my mother was giddy and light-headed. She danced around our room, she could not stop talking. Euphoric, she laughed and kissed the top of my head. By breakfast time she had not slowed down, while I was exhausted, and her high spirits displeased the morning intern. He took her aside before she could polish off her eggs, which she had described as glowing on the plate like twin suns in love with one another. She wanted to gobble them up quickly, so that their light would manifest inside her.

Dragging along behind my mother and the intern, I could scarcely keep my eyes open. My mother had worn me out. Examining her closely, the intern apparently did not appreciate the radiance of life emitting from her. He wished to see instead the dull glaze of defeat and sadness.

I was sent back to the table, and my mother was taken away. When she returned to my side to help with the breakfast dishes, her eyes had resumed their customary glaze, as though she wore thick lenses. A visionary, she once again looked myopic. A seer with cataracts. She was subdued.

Stashing her pills under the bed sheet, my mother made several forays into the night. Competing voices counselled her under our window. Mending the dining room wall could not thwart her for very long. Mysteriously, exterior locks would bust apart. Windows pried themselves ajar. Blame thieves, but what was missing? My mother could tiptoe from her room and, like a wisp, be downstairs where the voices of her demons guided her to freedom. She'd wrestle them in the woods. When they were spent, she would graft herself to the walls and steal back inside. She had learned a new trick. Safely

ensconced in our room, she would take her pill. That way, no one
had cause to accuse her.

Tired one evening, she ingested her pill as instructed, tumbling into
a fast sleep. I alone heard the voices outside after the moon rose. My
mother could not reply. Glass shattered, and the choir of voices continued, "Sheilagh! Come on out! Sheeee-lagh!"

I crept from the room, tracing their sound. I slinked through the
kitchen where glass had broken into the sink. Outside the window the
voices were persistent.

- Sheilagh! Don't keep us out here all night, girl!
- Go 'way, I said to my mother's demons.

Quiet awhile.

- Then, Who's that?
- My mother's sleeping, I said. I hid myself in the dark, crouching
below the level of the window.
- Not tonight, she ain't. You tell your ma to haul ass down here,
kid, or there'll be shit to pay. Go tell her.

I didn't know what he meant by any of that, so I left.

Soon, two figures appeared in our room, standing at the foot of my
mother's bed.

- Go 'way, I whispered.
- Face the wall, kid. This ain't no business of yourn.

I knew that these were real demons because they smelled funny.
Besides that, they were wobbly on their feet.

- This between your momma and us.

They found out that she was limp when they tried to wake her up.
Dead to the world. That's when they tore off her top. I attacked. Bit my
teeth right into a demon's wrist. He had real flesh and bone, felt pain just
like a person. His fluid tasted like human blood. The other demon pulled
me off and both of them took turns smacking me open-handed across the
face. Going down I hit the corner of my bedspring. Felt so funny. Lost and
hurt and when I touched my forehead it was all wet. I just lay on the floor,
whimpering, rocking myself, I couldn't stop shaking, and the demons on
the bed tore at my mother and she just lay there. They laboured over her
emitting the demon grunts of a raven. Just like my mother had described
them. Then they went away, without making another sound.

Early in the morning a nurse overheard my soft mewing. She came
into the room and heaven knows what she thought. Me, bleeding on
the floor, shivering like I was cold, my mother naked on the bed,
sprawled out, legs akimbo, looking barely alive.

Because I was hurt, because I was disoriented and frightened, I was allowed to attend one of my mother's classes. At the beginning of the lesson a young doctor came in with an officer from the Base. The soldier expressed an apology, and assured my mother that the incident would not be repeated.

"There, my Sparrow, no one will come and hit you any more," Mom promised.

She shook the soldier's hand as he was leaving. He and I saluted.

The doctor wanted her to understand that this was what came from doing with men whatever they wanted. My mother didn't understand what she had been doing with men. As far as she was concerned she had been corresponding with spirits.

"Sheilagh," the doctor explained, "those were soldiers who have been coming to your window at night."

My mother looked down at me, at my black eye and puffy nose, as if to contemplate whose side she was on. She lifted her head up, and spoke in a way that was proud, almost defiant.

"I wanted to be having one more baby."

"Why, Sheilagh?" the doctor asked her. "You have Sparrow. Why do you want another?"

"Because, when I'm having a baby you take me off my medication. Too strong a dose! I don't want my medication no more!"

The doctor sighed and rubbed his hands together. He asked us to wait in the room, walked out, and returned with an easel. Then he left the room again, and this time carried back a coloured map of something. Some strange country. "Might as well listen to this too, Sparrow," he said to me. "Lord knows you won't ever hear it from your mom." He used a pointer to show us where the seed of a man journeyed through an underworld of tunnels to where the egg of a woman dropped into a cavern. If the seed of the man found the egg of the woman and stuck to it, then a baby would begin to grow.

"What happens," my mother questioned, "if the seed of a man is swallowed by the woman, will it still find the egg?"

"No." The doctor flushed, shot a glance at me, and coughed. "No," he repeated. "The seed of a man has to go in there."

"So only if it goes in there," my mother wanted to make sure. I couldn't figure out where this cavern began or ended. In rock? In upholstery? She seemed to understand.

"That's right."

"Okay. So now I know how."

The doctor stood up again. "This can't happen again with you," he said.

"What?"

"Sparrow, lend me your shoelace."

My mother seemed quite amazed that I could untie my shoelace. "Now," he explained, "let's pretend that this shoelace is your inside. After you had Sparrow, a doctor, who was only thinking of your best interest, Sheilagh, took your Fallopian tubes, which you see here in the diagram, he took them like this, and tied them in a knot, like this. We wanted to protect you from having any more babies. So you see, Sheilagh, you must not run outside to meet spirits or soldiers at night, because they cannot make you pregnant. Your insides are tied in a knot."

The doctor handed me back the shoelace. I slipped my mother's Fallopian tubes through the eyelets of my shoe. Tying a bow, I felt that I was knotting the mysterious canals and tunnels that wove inside my mother. When I had finished, I looked up, and I can remember as clearly as though I possess a photograph of the moment the quarter-smile and half-grimace crippling her mouth. What made the look peculiar to me was the way that she held her head, chin high, when normally she was so evasive and shy. The doctor sighed and mumbled something to himself. He seemed upset. He bowed his head and ran his fingers through the thin thatch of his hair. He would not look at my mother. Smiling sadly, my mother looked over at me.

"When did you learn to tie your own shoes, Sparrow?"

I looked down at my shoe. At my mother's knotted inside. "Last week," I told her, feeling as though I had committed a crime.

"Now you can show me how," she said.

My mother wanted to become adept at fashioning knots.

She needed practice untying them as well.

*

Miss Fitzpatrick from Georgia, mother's former teacher, visited on a dull, humid day. A cause for both celebration and panic. Discovering that we had a friend in the mythical outside world was very curious to me. Mom was glad to see her, I noticed, and became as excited as her medication would allow. I could tell that her emotions were battling the restraints of the drug, that she was trying to see her guest with her mind and heart, bring her into focus. She was doing her best to fathom this occurrence.

Early on, my mother squandered a few tears, so delighted and amazed was she by the encounter. I was impressed by the fuss that the new arrival had provoked. We were each served pink drinks in tall glasses, with straws and ice-cubes. We were given a private room for our party where the women nattered. Miss Fitzpatrick fanned herself, and laughed, reminiscing. She told me about the day my mother had gone swimming in the swamp for the floating hearts. My mother left the room and came back with the dried flowers between the pages of a book. She was keeping them. Miss Fitzpatrick smiled and wept and gave her a squeeze. Then she came to the point. She had been chosen by the people of Lougain to deliver the hard news. By the end of their conversation, it was Miss Fitzpatrick who had to stifle tears while my mother had grown more stiff and quiet. On parting, the two women held one another. They hugged for the longest time while I looked up from the floor. I knew that something was going to happen.

Miss Fitzpatrick wore purple glasses with sequins, and when she knelt to say goodbye to me, I noticed them more than her advice. Her sequins, her sparkling tears, and the woodsy scent of her perfume. She did not smell like a nurse or a patient, scrubbed with lye soap and pampered with talcum. She smelled like a stranger from an alien country. From a swamp. She smelled like the whole wide world. "You take good care of your momma now, Sparrow. You will have to be the strong little man."

Her words had an echo. Over the next few weeks, they would be repeated by others suggesting that I become the head of our fledgling family. I had recently turned six, my mother twenty-one. One of us was now considered old enough to leave Lougain in the company of the other. Whether it was her or me was never made clear to either of us.

Not knowing who was at fault, we would walk through the wide gate together. Hand in hand. Cast out of the garden.

And the question mutates. Seriously, it makes me wonder. Did humankind ascend from the swamp? For me, what has become the crux of the issue is this—if so, if we have all arisen from the clay, pursued by alligators and humans and a disorder of demons, why did we do it? What was the point of that crusade?

2.

Mardi Gras

"Chidrens! Chidrens! Listen me up, y'hear! Follow that freedom road, li'l' chidrens! Follow that North Staaaarrr to freedom!"

Arrangements had been made. Mother and me were deposited on a bus destined for New Orleans. We had said goodbye to our friends, and my last memory of Lougain is of a tearful bunch waving to us while an old man in his wheelchair whirled about the perimeter of our gathering snapping nastily. Derek was his name, I think, although I may be putting that on him—down through the years 'Derek' has become a generic appellation for many of my foes. He advertised that he didn't want me to escape without first gnawing on my ribs for brunch.

The moment we boarded a gritty pick-up truck to take us to the highway where we could flag a bus, Derek busted loose from the pack. He gave chase as we began moving. The truck gained speed and he braked his wheelchair to offer a contorted two-handed wave. Curious about that, thinking that he might want to make friends at last, I didn't take my eyes off him. I almost waved back. Then I saw what he was up to. Derek had removed his false teeth. Holding both halves aloft, he was grinding them together in a lascivious chew.

So there was that to be said about getting out of Lougain.

My duties had been impressed upon me. Before I boarded the bus, an envelope containing my mother's prescriptions, tickets, and a letter addressed to the world at large, had been ceremoniously pinned to the inside of my jacket. References to my manhood and responsibilities were repeated, and for the first time on that hard day my mother had the sniffles. Sad to be leaving Lougain, it frightened her to trespass upon the outside world under the critical eye of sunlight.

We may also speculate on her dismay at having her six-year-old son, and not herself, entrusted with our important documents.

My mother was not unwise. Once we were on the bus I removed the pin and passed her the envelope. She smiled, hugged me to her side, and declined to accept our papers. "Keep them, Sparrow. Sometimes I don't know what I'm not doing. I don't know why I'm not doing it. Dr. Coslet says, he says if it wasn't glued on I'd forget my head. I'd get up in the morning and it would still be sleeping on the pillow. How do I have my breakfast when I don't have my mouth? Or maybe my head rolled away in the night and my hands can't find it because my eyes are in my head and my head's not attached to my hands no more. That'd be a terrible thing. Dr. Coslet said, he said don't worry about that. He promised me my glue'll stick good for one hundred more years. I hope I die first before I lose my head. So you hang onto everything for now, Sparrow. You be keeping your momma safe that way."

We were sliding down the highway. So many cars and trucks and people! At a rest stop we refused to get out. The next time the bus bumped to a halt, Mom disappeared into the bushes. I had my doubts about whether I'd see her again. I chose to do my business in a more civilized manner, and stood in line for the men's room. All those men, lined up to do number one in bowls hanging on a wall. A man had to hoist me up so that my thing could reach. It was hard to pee with my feet dangling and these strange hands under my armpits, but I managed. "Shake it," the man said, "before you put it away." That's how I learned that sort of thing. Mom flagged down the bus just as it was pulling out, climbed aboard, and I was glad of that too.

Then we were crossing Lake Pontchartrain. We had never seen such water. The land was disappearing and I jumped between sides of the bus and reported back to my mother that there was no land in sight, only water and this bridge to nowhere.

We stared ahead like Columbus's sailors wondering if we would fall off the edge of the world, half-believing that we were being shipped to the rim of the earth for disposal.

Then, *land ho!* A sighting.

Shortly we are in New Orleans, and we don't know what that is, or how we can make this nutty journey stop.

"'Yo' sending me white chidrens,' I says to the man. 'White chidrens. What's wrong with 'em,' I says, 'thet no white folks'll take 'em?'"

Our hostess in the city, on Franklin Street, a block above Basin, was Sally Rawlins. She spoke only with passion. A zealot, everything to

Sally became her life's mission. "I'm goin' to the bakery, *now!* I'm goin' t'buy bread. Right *now!*" My mother and I trusted her perception of things, for we considered a trip to the bakery to be fraught with alarm. We had never heard of such a thing. That she would actually return, alive, with bread, enlarged our scope of the world.

The horizontal view staggered us. Our lack of containment put us both out of kilter. Limits had not been set. There were no locked doors, no high walls. Imprisoned in school or at the asylum, my mother had plotted periodic and temporary escape. Free at last, she needed to be enclosed. Sally met us at the depot, and having made it to her house in a cab, neither of us was brave enough to venture outside.

"Man says, 'They need special treatment. Yo' gotta handle 'em wit' care. They's comin' from the nuthouse.' I says, 'So what's wrong wit' thet? They's more nuts 'round here than in any house.' He says thet's right, but thet white folks won' take 'em. 'Thet's there look-out,' I says. 'They can sleep here any time they wants. Go crazy anytime they wants. Go as crazy as they wants t'be at Sally Rawlins' house.' Thet's what I told the man. Thet's what I said. So what does he go and do? He sends me two sweeeeeeeet li'l' chidrens, sweeeet li'l' darlin's, and there ain't nobody walkin' down Basin nor Bourbon neither ain't crazier than ten of these two put together."

"Myself, I'm not crazy right now," my mother pointed out with pride. The words were a declaration, a manifesto.

"I can see thet, honey-chil'. Yo' a *sweeeet* li'l' thing."

"On my medication. I'm not a crazy person on my medication."

"Honey, they got yo' wrapped and twisted more ways than a kitty's ball a string."

I chose to expand on that theme. "My mom has her insides tied up. They're knotted."

Sally Rawlins gave me a good look. She seemed astonished.

"Sparrow is never crazy," my mother intervened.

Heavy footsteps mounted the stairs. In our state of continuous bedazzlement my mother and I waited to see whom would be revealed.

"Sturgess! Sturgess! Come in here, my man! I got two nuts I want yo' t'meet."

Sally's husband was a quiet man who spoke rarely, and usually in pronouncements. The first time we met he did not say hello. He simply sat down facing us, crossed his ankles, rapped the arm of his chair, and decreed, "New Orleans is the armpit of America. Don't believe me? Then look at any map. The Mississippi River draws the sweat off the shoulder of America, off the hard-working back of America, perspires across the delta. That's why the delta stinks. It's an honest stink. A hard-working-man stink. The delta smells just like America."

"We come from Mississippi," I said, wanting to impress upon him my knowledge of geography. Wanting to be located.

"We come from Lougain," Mother added.

"Then what you doing here?" Sturgess asked. My mother and I glanced each other's way, hoping to think of something. I remembered my envelope—a premonition told me to keep it tucked inside my coat. That letter felt dangerous to me. "I'm an oysterman," Sturgess announced. "I fish oysters and crayfish from the delta. Tomorrow, boy, me and you going oystering."

"Oysterin'. Thet's all thet man know. Ain't no wonder we never had no li'l' chidrens t'call our own."

"I went to school in Georgia," mother spoke up. "Away from Florida, a little bit. Nearby was Okefinokee Swamp where I went to school."

"Florida is the limp prick of America," Sturgess intoned, "pissing on Brazil. Look at any map."

"They have big ravens there," I mentioned. "Bigger than any man. My father was a huge raven with wings out to here."

"My shadow sailed away to Florida," Mother elaborated. "It broke off and flew across the ground. Another woman stuck her shadow to me but it's not my real shadow. It's a dumb shadow, a stupid shadow, it shrinks and squeezes inside me and sometimes it bleeds."

"Clarisse! Clarisse!" Sally hollered down onto Franklin Street. She stuck her head out the window to bellow the good news. "Come on up here! I got two crazy people up here I want yo' t'meet!"

"Sparrow's not a crazy person," my mother repeated, a stickler for that detail.

"I said *two* crazy people." Sally pulled her head back inside. A kind of apology. At least she didn't rouse the rest of the street. "Didn' say three."

"Chicago is the asshole of America," Sturgess lectured. "California is the pussy of America. Look at any map."

Each of us was learning to navigate the zone.

Sturgess woke me before the sun had risen and I dressed in a jiff. We ate Kellogg's Corn Flakes for breakfast—my first familiar food in New Orleans—and walked out onto the vacant streets. We travelled a long way through that emptiness, the odd derelict slumped in a corner, a window-cleaner, and a policeman among the few who observed our stroll. I kept my head up, amazed by the congestion of buildings. We arrived at Lake Pontchartrain where Sturgess sucked the dawn's clear air, and said, "Ain't it a fine morning on the delta, Sparrow?"

"Yes, mister. It's a fine morning on the delta."

"A grand-daddy morning for oystering and crabbing, don't you think so, boy?"

"It's a good morning for that, I think." My enthusiasms were genuine.

"With luck, with a good breeze, maybe we'll sail onto the Gulf of Mexico. Are you game, my Sparrow?"

I was ready for anything. "Sure," I said.

"Maybe fish tuna."

"Right. Fish. Tuna. What's tuna?"

We walked along the bank of the lake. I was wondering where he kept his boat. We walked until the city began to look small, and came upon a rock jetty where rowboats docked. Some were half-filled with water, others were holed. One showed only the tip of its bow above the surface of the lake. A number of black men were hanging around. More men than boats, I noticed. They stopped whatever they were doing or talking about to watch us.

Sturgess threw his lunch bag in a rowboat and told me to step in and sit in the stern while he held her steady. He followed and we cast off onto Lake Pontchartrain. But I didn't know that then. I didn't know where we were. Sturgess told me we were sailing on the Gulf of Mexico. He also told me we were fishing, and I believed that, too.

By noon, I gave up hope of catching anything. All we ever did was drift under the sun. Whenever the shore loomed close, Sturgess rowed us away. Then we'd just sit there, languid on the water. Sturgess lay back with his head in the bow, his rump down in the water that flooded the floorboards, and for intervals he would snore.

I lay sideways across the stern. My job was to bail once in awhile.

After lunch, Sturgess grew more talkative. "We're having a good day."

"Yes, mister."

"Catching ourselves a heap of crayfish."

"Yeah?"

"Got my weather eye on that storm coming too. Can't head back yet though. Promised my wife I'd do some oystering today, that has to be done, hurry-cane or no hurry-cane."

I searched the waters for our heap of crayfish. The little blue line dangling from the bow looked frayed, and too short to be dragging a heap of crayfish. Were they stuck to the bottom of the boat? That must be it. I didn't know what crayfish were or how they behaved.

We lazed around under the sun. My mother would die out there. The sunlight would drive her crazy. When the "hurry-cane" hit, the sky was blue and the breeze was down to nothing. The water was dead calm. Sturgess rocked the boat from side to side and I hung on. "Hold the boat! Hold the boat!" Sturgess hollered. "This ol' goddamn hurry-cane can't last forever. Look out, Sparrow! Look out for that big wave! Hold on!" And he rocked the boat and water slipped in over the gun-wales so that whenever I wasn't holding on I was bailing like mad. I knew I had to, even at age six, or we'd sink.

Then the storm passed.

Just like that. Sturgess rowed us ashore.

He pressed his hand to the back of my neck. "That was some mean bitchin' storm, Sparrow, my bird. You been initiated now. You a real sailor and fisherman now, boy."

"Yes, mister," I said.

"Never seen a storm so big hit so fast," Sturgess mentioned as we walked back along the shore toward New Orleans.

"Me neither," I agreed.

"I ain't never seen nothing like it, Sparrow. You?"

I swore it was the worst storm I had ever seen.

"That boat was a-shaking and a-rocking. Good thing she's a sound ol' boat. We had a good day of fishing, too. Lots of crayfish, loads of oysters."

We seemed to have left them behind.

Sturgess did not take me straight home. I knew this because I had established the St. Louis Cathedral as a landmark close to our home, and we had walked past it. Ended up in a fishmarket. Sturgess bought a few crayfish and plenty of oysters for our dinner, then we walked back to his house.

"You tell your Momma what you been doing today, Sparrow."

"We went oystering!" I held up the bag to my mother.

Mom was really thrilled. She said that she had never done anything like that in her life. Sturgess said he wished he could take her, but that it was men's work. "It's a man's life and you never know when a big storm might hit. Women aren't lucky on a boat, that's a known fact."

"You can't get out of the sun," I told my mother. "You wouldn't like it."

"Watch out no oysters steal your shadow," she warned me.

"See you done some crayfishin' too," Sally bellowed.

"Told you I would, didn't I? Didn't I promise you that?"

"What's it like?" Mother wanted to know. "Where did you go?"

"We were sailing on the Gulf of Mexico!" I told her. "We were fishing on the delta of the Mississippi River!"

"Going again tomorrow," Sturgess told us.

"Don' wear out thet poor boy," Sally recommended.

"He's a good worker." Receiving the man's praise, I grinned widely. "I need help handling the big catch."

Exhausted from my day of labour in the sun, I went to bed that night preparing for tomorrow's storm at sea.

The world orbits around the child, the infant knows. All in due course, the growing child will be cast to the perimeter by life's spin. A simple adage of physics related to centrifugal force. That night I slept soundly, my ear rapt at the mouth of a conch shell, and dreamed of whales and dolphins, pictures from a book. Fishes swam around me, and beyond them shone starfish amid schooners bobbing as crescent moons. I slept because I was a child, and as a child I could not imagine how my mother's day might have gone.

Could not imagine it back then.

Now I can.

Picture those women. With swagger and trill, this is Saturday. This the weekend, girl. Preparation day. Get-ready-to-party time. In Sally Rawlins' house they meet to sew, to gab, and to sing. Mad with noise, Clarisse plods up the stairs. Irma, Ottilie, and, of course, Sally and my mother, already are there. "Have you heard the news, people? Have you heard that story goin' 'round?"

"Jesus Christ is risen t'day!" Sally chipped in.

"Hallelujah!" Ottilie responded with a whoop.

"Did I say the good news, people? No I didn'. I'm sayin', have you heard that baaaaddd news?" Clarisse, who my mother had met the day before, gained the top of the stairs. While she was in good voice and vigour, the triumph of her climb had to be commemorated with a moment's rest. She mopped her damp brow and huffed for breath. Broad of beam and top-heavy, Clarisse was both the most substantial of these large women, and the most adorned. Flowering plants swung from her ear-lobes. Her hair shot up from her scalp as a small cannon, and the dress she had on today, fuchsia and mauve and florentine, clashed with most of the world.

"How bad is it?" Ottilie put in while separating fabrics for her dress by colour. She had decided to compete with rainbows. Constantly humming under her breath, Ottilie had aroused my mother's interest. She wore thick lenses and her eyes seemed faraway. Familiar. Like her own in a mirror.

"The worst! Rosaline come home last night, come home from singing in the choir."

"Oh, what's thet girl been up to now?" Sally begged.

"Choir let out early from practice, 'cause of Deacon Jones comin' down with tonsillitis and various other affections too pers'nal to mention." To emphasize the last few words, Clarisse resorted to a thumping rhythm, and humped her hips to the same beat. My mother had never heard people talk like this, or seen them move their bodies this way. They communicated with their hands and their hips as much as with words. The women scared her because they were saying things which she did not understand.

"That man's always sick with affections," was Ottilie's opinion of him, which convulsed the friends with laughter and the giggles. My mother sat in the corner and watched them. She was supposed to be doing something with her bolt of blue cloth, but she didn't know what. She was wondering how many more women would be coming up those stairs into the room that already seemed past its bursting point. She could not imagine the room or her own senses accommodating any more women or much more of the sing-song chat.

Sally said, "Thet's not fair now, girl. He mi' heft jest the sore throat and nuthin' mo'."

"His throat's sore mebbe, but other parts of him are wore out," Irma made known.

"You should know," Ottilie implied.

"Let me speak!" Clarisse was accustomed to continuous bubble and interruption, but today's news was too itchy to keep close to her skin for long.

"Speak."

"She come home and her man, I mean her man, he is inside the bed, I mean he is under the sheets—you *knoooow* what I'm talkin' 'bout."

"No!"

"He ain't alone!" Ottilie hollers, giving my mom a start. "Tell me he ain't alone, girl."

"Honey, he ain't alone," Clarisse confirms.

Although Sally rarely looks up from her needlework, she shouts with such abandon that it is hard to understand how she can be concentrating on her task. "He so ugly. He the ugliest man I know. He the ugliest man I ever seed. I ain't never seed no picture a no critter more ugly than thet there man. Who'd get into bed with thet man excepting maybe Rosaline herself and herself she admitted it one time right here in this room—she did—that she's wanting the lights turned out and it ain't 'cause she's anyway shy."

"Let me tell you who was wit' him in that bed."

"Who? Or should I ask, what? What besides a lovesick crocodile's gonna crawl under sheets with thet ugly man? He's ugly!"

"Undine."

Everybody looked up. Everybody put down their work. Everybody was quiet at once. My mother glanced around the room at the women's stricken faces. Ottilie was trying to look over her glasses, as if the thick lenses somehow had interfered with her hearing. Sally was stopped with her mouth open, sucking air like a vacuum. Irma put both her hands to the sides of her cheeks and held her face up, fearful that it might come crashing down and splatter on the floor. Only Clarisse was smiling. She had the great double-pleasure of not only telling these friends something that they didn't know, but she had accomplished the impossible as well. She had told them something they could not believe.

"Undine!" Sally Rawlins cried out at last. "Undine fussed wit' that ugly man? I don' believe it. Yo' lyin' to us, Clarisse."

"You know I don' tell no lies."

"Yo' are now. What you doin' that fo', girl?"

"She can have any man she wants," Irma says. "What she want wit' Earl?"

"Undine says he made her do it."

"What? She went up all those stairs, she got off all those clothes and corsets, she crawled into thet bed and got under them sheets, and she says he made her do all thet?"

"You know how it is," Clarisse informed them, privy to secret information gained from her walk along Bourbon Street. "That's what she told Rosaline, who by this time was a-hittin' on her and a-hittin' on him too and she's sayin' just what you're sayin', Sal. She's sayin', 'He's a ugly man! I got a ugly man so all you tramp womens will leave my man alone. What you doing in bed with my ugly man, Undine?' Hittin' her all the time she goin' on like this."

"It's a good question," Irma noted.

"So Undine says he made her. Dragged her up off the street and made her do it. She puts all the blame on Earl, as if any man in his circumstances could resist. As if any man so ugly as Earl could resist a woman like Undine if she ever throwed herself at him."

"Dragged her up them three floors," Sally said directly to my mother, filling her in on the details as though her boarder had not been in the room until that moment, "and not a soul heard a sound."

"That's right! And she wasn't exactly screamin' 'Help' when Rosaline found them in there, and she wasn't exactly quiet neither. Know what I mean?" Clarisse asked my mother, following Sally's cue to include her. My mother did not have an inkling as to what they were talking about, although she was fascinated by the constant blather. "Rosaline come walking in that door and Undine wasn't tryin' to be quiet, but what she hears is sounds under the sheets and those sounds ain't 'Help!' And those sounds ain't 'Rape!'"

"I hear you," Ottilie says. My mother could not understand how she could not.

"You hear me, and Rosaline, she heard Undine."

"What happened after that?" Irma was anxious to find out.

"What you think happened, that's what happened. Rosaline belted Undine all the way down the stairs nekid and kept a-hittin' her in the street nekid and it was Earl who throwed down her clothes from the third floor, except her brassiere got wrapped up in the balcony below and it's still there right now like a flag. It's wavin' in the breeze right this minute, Undine's blue underwear, flappin' in the wind like Missus Ol' Glory."

"Why'd she do it? That's what I'd like to know," Sally pondered some more. "She wantin' a fast start on Mardi Gras?"

"Maybe Earl," Ottilie considered, and she was the thinker among them, "did find a way to make her do it. Make her walk up the stairs and take them corsets off one by one."

"She wasn't yellin' for help," Clarisse reminded her.

"Maybe Earl's got somethin' none of us has heard tell about befo'."

Although they laughed at that, Sally remained the most sceptical. "Rosaline never mentioned it, if he does."

"She took him for some reason. Can't only be 'cause he's so ugly."

Conversation was not the lone peril my mother would have to face that day while I was off oystering. When Ottilie erupted into song, and the others joined in with a sympathetic dirge, my mother felt the scant security of her world begin to quake.

Boisterous sound. The women rocked as they sewed, their bodies swayed, and Mom had to be rhythmic herself just to stay clear of Sally's bulk leaning into her from one side, and Irma's head bobbing on the other. Dishes rattled in their traces, and the power of Ottilie's naturally mournful voice thumped within my mother's heart like blows to the chest.

"Jeee-sus!" rollicked that high, triumphant voice. *"Jeee-sus!"*

"Amen, brothers!" rolled the response. *"I say, Amen, sisters!"*

"Come down and walk with me here!"

"Amen, brothers! I say, Amen, sisters!"

"Come down and talk with me nee-ear!"

"Amen, brothers! I say, Amen, sisters!"

And the music went on, harmonious at times, or disjointed, bluesy sacred carnal comic sad. One song grafted onto the next, one lead singer giving way to another who'd change the tempo and the tune, and the friends rocked with their back-up vocals. Only hunger lowered the curtain for an intermission, and the women abruptly were busy preparing a feast.

"For a crazy-woman," Ottilie surmised, speaking directly to my mother for the first time, "yo' sho' is quiet."

It puzzled them. A crazy-person in their minds was someone out of control, someone ranting, or wielding a weapon. Crazy people were scary, they were either doing damage to their neighbours, or were a danger to themselves. Decorous in a corner and keeping to herself seemed normal behaviour, to them, for a white woman. My mother hardly contributed at all to their enterprise, except to hold things on command or help pull fabric taut. This uselessness they also considered normal—she was white.

"She on a drug t'keep her quiet," Sally explained. "She ain't herself, thet drug don't let her be herself."

"That how come she ain't got nothin' to say?" Irma asked.

"She talks when she gets her mind made up. And when she talks, she make her own sense. Ain't no kind of sense fo' yo' and me."

That got the women interested. Ottilie encouraged my mother to, "Say something, ma'm."

"Favour us with yo' point-a-view," Clarisse pressed her.

"Tell us anything you want to, honey," Irma agreed. "We's all girls. Ain't no nasty folks in this house."

My mother looked each one of them in the eye as best as she was able. Focusing at close range was always difficult. She told them her secret dream. "When my Sparrow learns to fly, we will go to Florida. He can fly and catch my shadow for me."

She looked around the room once more, hoping to make friends. The women stared back, glanced at one another, and it was Ottilie who summed up, "Yep, she's crazy all right. Ain't no doubt about it now."

Irma tapped her on the knee. "You should feel right at home here. Sally and Sturgess Rawlins be the two biggest nuts I know." And as each of the women laughed and their heavy flesh bounced, and as Sally broke into song while shredding onions for the salad, my mother smiled too, almost feeling as though she was a part of this crew.

"So how long yo' stayin' here, chil'?" Ottilie wanted to know.

"That was never made clear 'nough," Sally said. "They said they let me know."

"Don' you know?" Ottilie asked my mother.

"Honey, she don' know nuthin' 'bout nuthin'. She don't know her own face in the mirror. She don't know who's payin' the bills. She don't know nuthin' today."

"Who payin' the bills?" Clarisse piped up.

"Her people is. But she don' know her people."

"Honey, is that true?" Ottilie inquired, but my mother was looking at Sally, who seemed to have quite a few answers about things. People? What people?

"Course it's true," Sally chimed. "Her people ain't never revealed themselves to this po' chil'. Mabbe they reckon she's a crazy-girl and they don't want no crazy chidrens in their high-society house. She has a rich daddy who keeped her locked up in that nuthouse in Lougain, Mississippi."

"So how come she's out? Did she escape?"

"Folks in a nuthouse too crazy to escape. Somebody musta said, 'What about thet boy? What about thet boy Sparrow? Can't let a boy grow up inside a nuthouse. She got to live a regular life among ordinary people,' somebody said, 'if he gonna get any kind a chance for hisself.'"

"So they sent her here? That's crazy."

"Ain't permanent. Is only for a li'l' while. You don' know your mommy nor your daddy, chil'," Sally reiterated to my mother as she placed her lunch of spicy chicken, and salad with hot peppers, in front of her. "But from what I study on the matter, yo' the lucky one fo' it."

"How long she stayin' then?"

"I told you, Ottilie. I don' know why you ain't listenin'. She stayin' here a spell, but don' nobody know when she's leavin' or where she's

gonna get sent from here. This a po' lost chil', and we her only friends
in this cruel world."

"All I want to know is, is she or ain't she gonna be comin' wit' us
fo' Mardi Gras? That's all I'm askin' in plain language, Sally Rawlins."

"We ain't gonna give her up, are we? She only got a week to go, we
ain't gonna let her get away wit'out Mardi Gras."

"Glory hallelujah!" Irma intoned.

"Jesus be praised!" Clarisse announced. "And send down His love
upon this po' sinner-chil'."

"If she stayin' for Mardi Gras," Ottilie mentioned, "all I'm sayin' is,
we got 'nough t'read and 'nough cloth leftover from all our dresses
t'make sure Sheilagh got a dress too for her first Mardi Gras."

"And I got a extra mask!" Sally shouted out.

Amid the uproar, my mother understood that she was going to
Mardi Gras, whatever that was, in a new dress fabricated from vibrant
leftover scraps, and while this news was both bewildering and enticing
to her, it paled when juxtaposed against something Sally had mentioned. Sally believed that she had people. Isn't that what she said?
And weren't these unknown people looking after her? Taking care of
her from a distance, from beyond some looking-glass, some screen?

That night my mother contemplated whether or not she should take
her pill. For my benefit, she did. And as she rolled into sleep, she fought
back against the cloud, wanting to think, to ponder, to understand.
Drifting off, she concluded, through deduction of her own, that her
people lived in the sky, high above the clouds, where they kept watch
over her. Someday, perhaps when the world was safe for them, they
would reappear, and my mother would be united at last with her family.

I was sleeping beside her. But I was a child, and did not know what
thoughts fomented within that mind.

*

The black line of the squall rose up out of the southwest. Looking over
Sturgess's shoulders, I saw it coming, while he remained unaware of our
peril. His weather-eye was out of focus today. "Leastways, we don' have
t'fight no hurry-canes this afternoon," Sturgess believed. I was not convinced. The storm looked like it had potential to me, muscled with
menace. My skipper snoozed wedged in the bow while I trolled for
tuna. We had had a successful day, had sweated and strained our backs
reeling in five-hundred pounders, but the big one, the champion fish,

still eluded us. "That last one was a real fighter," Sturgess reminisced. "It plain tuckered me out."

Four tuna swam strapped to the side of our dingy. Before nodding off, Sturgess gave strict instructions for me to wake him up if sharks attacked.

The wind kicked up, pushing us farther out. The shore disappeared.

"Sturgess," I said. Nudged his boot with my foot.

"Sharks attacking?"

"I don't see any. But I think maybe there's another hurry-cane coming."

"Naw. Ain't no hurry-canes crossing the Gulf today. All I heard was maybe Lake Pontchartrain might catch a storm."

"Maybe it changed its mind and came here instead." I could see the bridge I had crossed with my mother on the bus. The storm was going to pound across that bridge then swoop down upon us. We were going to get wet, that was one thing for sure. "It's getting darker," I prodded him timidly.

Sturgess opened one eye from his nap, but he was facing the sun. "Keep watch," was his only advice to me.

So I did.

When the raindrops hit like machine-gun fire, Sturgess woke up. The wind, which had been stiff all day, gusted with fresh ferocity.

Sturgess jumped upright in his seat and the boat began to rock and this time it wasn't my companion instigating the unpleasantness. In the choppy water our stout dingy, with its holes, cracks, and low freeboard, took a wave over the side. We both bailed like mad.

"Might have to cut them tuna loose!" Sturgess yelled at me. "It'll give us more buoyancy." He paused from his bailing to evaluate the sky and the wild water. "I know. You're right. We'll wait to see how it goes." We rolled once hard and I let out a yelp. For the first time I was afraid. This was getting to be more than I could handle. Sturgess commanded me to "Hang on, Sparrow! It might get nasty." His eyes scanned an horizon that had disappeared. "What's your bearings, mate?" he hollered through the torrent of rain while lashing our ark together with twine.

"What?"

"Which way's south?"

"I don't know! I can't see anything! Where's the land, Sturgess?" New Orleans had vanished beneath the churlish sea.

"Storm come out of the southwest, I reckon," he deciphered, "heading northeast. Means we gotta head this-away to get to where we're going. You follow me?"

We took another wave over the side, and I helped bail with my bare hands. Scooping water and throwing it up into the driving wind.

Sturgess stopped at one point. "Sorry, mate. We can't make it dragging them tuna. Can't risk attracting sharks in case we go overboard ourselves. We got to cut them loose, Sparrow, I don't care what you say."

I said, "Okay!"

"No use arguing with me!" he bellowed. "I've made up my mind and I'm the captain of this ship!" After his lecture, I worked extra hard to cut our tuna loose into the Gulf of Mexico. Each of us laboured off one side of the vessel, while our boat filled with water, and Sturgess seemed quite satisfied. "There we go, that gives us some buoyancy. What we need. She lying in the water better now. I can do some rowing."

It's strange, but taking time to cut away the imaginary fish made me feel better, more calm. If Sturgess was not willing to give up the game, then things could not be as bad as they seemed.

I had worked my way down to the middle of the boat. Sturgess hoisted me aloft in his strong hands and transferred me to the stern again, then he took command of the oars. The rain would not abate, but the wind had eased a notch. We were rowing with the waves abeam, so that each roll of the water carried us up and we had to be sure of our stability. I learned fast how to use my weight to counterbalance the sea. A big motorboat cut across our bow and the crossing wave swamped us again, and low in the water we were hit a second time, so that now the water completely filled our little dingy. "Bail!"

I think I was screaming the whole time that my hands worked with remarkable speed. Dying was not my first consideration, I guess I was too young to be fully cognizant of that likelihood. Two other worries eclipsed death. In the first place, I did not know how to swim. Had never, in fact, been swimming. Right at that moment, I was ashamed to admit to the frailty. More importantly, as I chose to articulate to Sturgess, "I got a letter! I can't get my letter wet, Sturgess!"

"You got a what?"

"A letter!"

"Who's the letter from, boy?"

"I don't know!"

"Then who's it for?" As hard as we were bailing, we were lucky to stay afloat. Lying low in the water allowed the lake access through large leaks in the topsides, and waves more easily splashed over the gunwale.

"It's to the whole world!" I yelled back at him. And remembered some of the envelope's important contents. "It's got my mother's medicine in it. And tickets."

"Tickets to where?" Sturgess wanted to know.

"I don't know!"

"Bail!" he shouted out. "Don't worry, boy, we'll keep your letter dry."

Within the minute it was obvious that we were sinking.

"I'm getting out of the boat," Sturgess shouted in my ear. "You keep bailing. Don't matter how tired you get, you keep bailing!"

"Are we sinking, Sturgess?"

"Damn right we are. But listen to me, boy, we ain't sunk."

Sturgess removed his boots and socks, then he leapt out of the boat. For awhile I feared that I had lost him in the dark, his black skin invisible beneath the surface. He reappeared at the bow with the frayed rope clamped between his teeth. He started swimming. The water was cold. I continued bailing. It was easier with him out of the boat. The dingy floated higher, so whatever water I threw out of the boat, stayed out.

Sturgess kept on swimming, toward shore I hoped.

The squall went on through, the sun emerged again, the day was suddenly warm and calm, the shoreline emerged into view, and Sturgess continued swimming in the water with the rope between his teeth. A few motorboats puttered around us, curious, before one offered help. We took it. Our dingy was towed ashore and Sturgess profusely thanked our rescuers. "You can always count upon a mariner to help a man in some distress," he announced, but one of our rescuers clucked his tongue. The other one said that we had no business being out so far in such a small boat—and with a white kid. Sturgess acted like he never heard the admonishment. "Thank God for you brave men in your hearty little ship."

Ashore, dripping wet, we walked up the rise that put us on the road back to New Orleans. "One hurry-cane after another," Sturgess said, his left hand clamped to the back of my neck. "Ain't seen nothing like it. We sure been through it, Sparrow."

"It's been terrible!" I agreed.

"Too bad we had to cut them tuna loose."

"That's too bad," I said.

"We'll have to go out and get more tomorrow."

I didn't say anything to that.

Sturgess waited until we reached the house on Franklin Street before saying to me, "Now, I think I should read this here letter you been jabbering about. If it's been writ to the whole world, then it must be writ to me too. Because I'm a man who's part of this world. I knowed this world, how it is and how it works. I knowed how the world is shaped. If it's addressed to the whole world, then it must be addressed to me, too. Look on any map, Sparrow. You will find me there. I'll be around there some-place. If I ain't been there yet, then you got to believe I'm coming."

No mere letter to the editor, the Magna Charta had both guts and impact. By nailing his thesis to the door of the Cathedral, Luther shook up his times. The Declaration of Independence, basted by the Gettys-burg Address, was a new bird in the oven of history. Public correspon-dences—fuelled by partisan need, the light of radical ideas forging identity, demanding currency. While we failed to fully appreciate its significance at the time, within the private history of my family that letter was similarly pivotal.

Selecting a pair of reading glasses from the cupboard above the dishes, Sturgess Rawlins sat down at the kitchen table. (We may safely infer that he took exception to the necessity of corrective lenses, and expressed his resentment by keeping them beyond easy reach.) With the horn-rimmed glasses precariously propped on the tip of his nose, Sturgess found support for the ear-hooks high off his temples amid a thatch of thick, crinkly hair. I studied his face and salt-and-pepper beard, observing him in that avid manner native to children. The fin-gers of the mind twist and turn the view around, ratify its nature, absorb the wonder. Inside my head, I played croquet with Sturgess's.

"Let me see here," the ageing, kindly man began as he leaned over the cracked white table. He shot a scornful glance across at the standing lamp, and I was unprepared for his sudden pique. "It's a wonder a man has eyes in his head when he's got to live out his days in this dim darkness!" He spoke with the passion of a prophet while I, appropriately, trembled.

"Don' go bellyachin' t'me," Sally ignited. "Yo' have some com-plaint, take it up wit' the landlord, not wit' me."

"All I want is to read this here letter," Sturgess fought back. "I don't want to be picking no fight. Woman, I'm a tired man. All that shrimp-ing and crabbing. All that tuna-fishing and dodging hurry-canes. I don't have the strength to be fighting with you no more tonight."

Clearly sceptical, Sally questioned, "Who send yo' a letter?"

"Not writ to me, woman. Is writ to the whole wide world. I just happen to be living at the present time in that particular world. This here be Sparrow's letter."

Sally glanced up from her sewing for a moment, clear proof that she was interested. "Sparrow's?"

"I do believe it will say who he is and what he's about."

"Maybe where he's goin'," Sally added.

"Maybe."

"Sheilagh! Sheilagh-girl!" Sally put down her sewing. "Come out here one minute, chil'."

As though on a pitching deck, my mother voyaged from our room, a ponderous shuffle drowsy with sleep. She was stretching her body and rubbing her eyes at the same time, looking funny in Sal's oversized, fluffy, blue robe.

"Did yo' know thet Sparrow's got a letter?" Sally asked her.

"Yes'm," my mother said. Like me, feeling accused.

"Does yo' know what it say? Who it fo'?"

"No, ma'm Sally."

"We's goin' to find out right now. Clear up thet mystery. Sit down, chil', sit. Maybe yo' will learn who yo' are and where yo' is goin'."

Yet the letter proved stingy with information. Each line created more mysteries than it solved and broadened existing puzzles. I would have to grow up and learn about the world before I could attempt to decode that document. A controlled and deliberate reader, Sturgess spoke with authority and with his customary dramatic inflection, as if issuing official decree.

> To whom it may concern:
> This letter which you hold in your hands is the property of Sheilagh Drinkwater and her small son, Sparrow Drinkwater.

"Glory be! We knowed thet part, Sturgess." Sally was never one to mind her peace for long. Every line deserved comment.

"I'm reading the letter. You want to read it yourself?"

(We may assume, with some assurance of accuracy, that Sally's reluctance to accept the challenge stemmed from the likelihood that she was illiterate.)

"Get on wit' it then," she urged him.

> Please look with kindness upon these two souls, as they mean no one harm. The mother does suffer from a medical condition

"A medical condition!" Sally brayed, as if the rest of us were deaf.

She gave Sturgess a look, his signal to carry on.

a medical condition which requires a pre-scription for her treatment. The boy is a normal, healthy child.

"We can see thet!"

They are travelling to Canada.

"Canada!" Sally whooped. "Thet's all the way up north!"
"That's right." Sturgess always had time for geographic digression. "A long, long ways up."
"Read the letter."
Sitting primly at the table, my mother folded her hands in her lap and bowed her head. From the set of her chin, I could tell that she was secretly interested, for she had inclined an ear to pick up Mr. Rawlins' every word.

Should the woman be exhibiting any signs of strange behaviour, please assure that she ingests one of her pills. After that, she'll be fine, and in no way bothersome. Should her medication be exhausted or lost, a prescription is enclosed.

"There yo' go, honey-chil'. Yo' all set."

Also enclosed, please find train tickets for travel from New Orleans to New York via St. Louis,

"The train! To Saint Loo!"

and to Montreal, Canada from New York aboard the bus.

"The bus! From Nnneeeeww York! You're goin' to Broadway, honey!"

On the following pages please find the itin-

Sturgess tried again.

itin-ner-ary, itinerary, for their trip. Please select the page corresponding to the locale where you have encountered these two

desti-tute souls. We ask your kindness to fa-cil-i-tate their travel to
their ultimate destination.

"Go t'where it says what t'do here," Sally instructed.

Sturgess pulled out the appropriate page, reciting aloud, "New
Orleans."

"That's us."

Informed that they would be compensated mid-week for the care of
their guests for twelve days, Sturgess and Sal nodded between themselves. A fair arrangement. They seemed honoured—their shoulders
had straightened, chins lifted—to have been addressed by name.
According to the epistle, the purpose of the sojourn in New Orleans
was to acquaint the son and mother with life in a city among common
people, so that the two of them would learn to fend for themselves
when eventually "left to their own devices." The Rawlins' job was to
feed them (us), see to their comfort, show them the city, and put them
on the seven o'clock train bound for St. Louis on a specified date.

"Day after Mardi Gras," Sally noted. "I guess when thet letter says
'common people' it mean people who don' have a 'medical condition'."

"If they want them to see how ordinary folks live, how come they
sent them here for Mardi Gras?" Sturgess's question was neither easily
answered nor readily dismissed.

(Questions raised by the letter scoured deeper than that. My life and
my mother's were being plotted by an invisible power. Bank drafts drawn
against different accounts were included in the envelope's contents—we
were bound to the letter by economic manipulation. Complicating matters, we had to present ourselves to particular officers at certain financial
institutions at specified times if we wished to remain solvent. A tight
schedule for an organized person—for us, an impossibility. An itinerary
had been mapped out. Amid the glut of information was the explanation that we were being sent north on our own, rather than in the company of an escort, to test and develop our ability to cope in the real
world. We were an experiment in someone's warped mind. Governed by
persons and forces unseen, our lives were being put at grave risk for no
other purpose than to see if we could make it. For a mentally-troubled,
young, inexperienced woman and her six-year old son to cross the continent from south to north on their own recognizance more closely resembled a prescription for disaster than it did a support system.)

What struck home at the time was not the inherent cruelty of
the treatment we were receiving but the simple fact that someone,

somewhere, somehow was guiding our lives. We were known. We had a connection in this world. I curled up against my mother's arm, and she held me until it hurt. Sometimes she forgot what she was squeezing. Mystifying news, that letter, and we didn't know how to cope with it, or what it would portend.

"Po' li'l' chidrens," lamented Sal.

"Canada's America's hat," Sturgess observed. "On that hat is snow and frozen ice. White snow and frozen ice. Don't believe me? Look at any map."

That would be his final word on the subject.

Monday morning. Sturgess woke me later than usual, and we buzzed off. Today's clothes were not those he had soaked on Sunday, which was understandable, except that this time his outfit resembled a uniform. Pressed grey trousers and an ironed shirt the same bland colour with a trim red tie. The chunky workboots appeared inappropriate to me for a leaky dingy. I worried that he'd sink to the bottom of the Gulf of Mexico if he happened to slip over the side. Where would that leave me? Vigilant, hoping for an absence of hurry-canes, I kept my mouth shut and my eyes open. Welcomed the new route which had lots of neat stuff to look at, sights never previously imagined.

On this trip we didn't bother to fetch our boat.

Other things were different. Being Monday, and later in the morning, New Orleans was bustling with people and traffic. Sturgess paid our fares onto a bus on Canal Street and I had no idea where we were headed. Just prayed it wasn't back to Lougain. Daymares about Derek's snapping incisors made that a grim prospect. One bus let us off onto another, and then we took a third. We were really going far. Maybe, I began to hope, and soon believed, we might do some real fishing.

While travelling, Sturgess said nothing about his plans, but he had a job to do that day. Honest work. So he was only a fisherman on the weekends, although he did not admit that to me either. I figured it out. Sturgess was employed by the Bonnet Carré Floodway and Spillway. He looked after the grounds along a navigation system connecting the Mississippi River with Lake Pontchartrain. I walked around with him, picking up bits of paper in the morning, trimming hedges in the afternoon. Playing by myself but mostly being a nuisance underfoot. "Tomorrow," he promised, "we cut grass."

I believed him.

Sturgess was my babysitter that week, and I spent every hour with him, keeping tabs on him, or, knowing that I was within his eye, romping free along the banks of the canal. An old man sunning himself explained to me one day what was happening to the water, that it was being moved to and fro by an impressive system of dams, gates, and canals. As soon as I had a grasp of this knowledge in my own terms, I begged Sturgess to let my mother come along the following day, a Friday. I wanted to show her, and ran ahead, shouting with a newly acquired confidence and glee, "Here! The water gets lifted up." And farther along, "Here it spills out." Mom caught on. Big people were making puddles just like we used to do in Lougain, only on a much larger scale. Once she made the connection, I believe that she was alternately thrilled and disappointed. Moving water around was a tremendous wonder for her. She was only saddened, it is fair to speculate, because the people in charge of the project had nowhere succeeded in creating a swamp.

"Tomorrow," Sturgess decreed, with a steady, determined kind of violence, "we go shrimping and crabbing."

*

My mother cannot, must not, stand stunned by any mob for too long. Fatal, to absorb the impact of such mysteriousness whole. Whenever a maze of colour, or racket of sound, or conflagration of movement knocks her silly, she is all but lost. To protect herself, she must disrupt her concentration, seize control, and focus upon individuals instead, although even this exercise is bound to bog down. At Mardi Gras, the motion of hips and the weave of disembodied heads does not confound and distract her nearly so much as the shock of costume. The man speaking to her is dressed as a skeleton. His skintight black garment displays white fluorescent ribs. She finds herself drawn to any man who, demonlike, wears his bones on the outside. Large bat-shaped wings float from his shoulder blades. As he stretches his arms overhead and brings them down to engulf her, his cape has the wing-span of an albatross.

But she is not free to explore costumes. She is not at ease to decipher what is real or who's a demon. She is compelled by the masks. My mother revels in hidden faces. The man next to her swirls in a rhythm foreign to the clap of tambourines and drums. He wears a devil's red mask over his sweaty black silk skin. Nor can she wholly let go and appreciate the onslaught of masks, not while she is overpowered by eyes compatible with ice and fire. They flicker and flame and, combustible, freeze her within their cubes.

The man who dances with my mother on the streets of New Orleans in the midst of a fever called Mardi Gras has told her that his name is Earl.

"My name is Sheilagh."

"I know that."

"I know about you, too."

"What do you know?"

Uncertain, although she is convinced that she has heard something, my mother hesitates. "I learned some things," she answers, as though with guile.

"Make sure he keeps thet mask on, honey-chil'," Sally warns. "It's an improvement. A mask works wonders wit' yo' appearance, Earl. Yo' such a ugly man, I don' know why yo' don' wear masks the rest a the year and only show us yo' ugly bare face at Mardi Gras when nobody know no diff'rence."

Shuffle on down the street to the sway and hectic rhythm, the percussion of music altering heartbeat, liquor swimming in the bloodstream. Night will eclipse her medication. Up later than her bedtime, she has passed her medicine-taking hour, and my mother will emerge from the vapour of her days into the familiar anarchy of night. Moves among the spooks of these streets with confidence and yearning, strangely legitimate, her awkward physical prowess saucy with promise. Kissed by demons, she hugs them right back, and dances amid their carnival stew. Her shuffle shall evolve into a high-step, her walk sanction style, and she will brush and bump her body against the flanks of elaborate, flamboyant suitors, especially against the muscled, black-robed, bat-winged demon whose bones glow.

When Sally Rawlins and her friends had donned their masks for Mardi Gras, my mother recognized immediately that she was among friends. Given a mask of her own and made to look in the mirror, she recognized herself. This was real. She understood these faces. And in the streets of the old town where the music and bedlam and dancing travels on through the night, she feels her spirit rekindle.

I learned about her mood when she brought Earl home. My mother and I shared a bed in Sally's house, and the arrival in the room of the two revellers woke me from a calm sleep. In the distance I heard the sounds of the continuing street party, and in the light of the window saw the silhouette of a demon peeling off his bones. He rested his wings on the back of a chair. My mother too was slithering out of her clothes, and the two of them tumbled onto the bed beside me.

I bounce with the concussion of their fall, and hang on.

"What's that?" Next to me now, Earl is startled, surprised by the resident lump. Perhaps, for an instant, he worries that I might prove to be a sleeping husband.

"He's my boy, Sparrow," my mother thinks to mention as she pulls the big black demon on top of her. I peek. Neither have bothered to remove their masks, and my mother twists on the bed beneath the black body with the red face and the nub of horns protruding from his forehead. My mom makes sounds like she's dying, releases deep long sighs, and the demon's own noise is reminiscent of giant ravens. To keep myself from sliding into the depression they've burrowed in the bed, I move over and clutch the edge of the mattress. Cling to it. Yet I sink back, we rub together, and I have to hold onto the mattress while the bedsprings yelp and the surface heaves and my mother issues long awful moans and the beast is grunting like he can't catch a breath and the bedsprings jounce and everything is crazy and getting faster and his elbow is in my back and my mother keeps lashing out with her foot, bruising my calf, and it takes all my strength just to hang on, by my fingernails, just to hang on.

I'm thinking about biting the demon to see if he bleeds when I hear Sally and Sturgess on the stairs.

Sally calls out, "Sheilagh! Yo' in this house?" The demon on my bed delivers a long, low groan, like he's been sucked up by the earth and drawn back down into the hot furnace of its core. He seems ready to expire. But we all survive. The demon lies quietly for a few seconds, then stands up and puts his bones and wings back on. He adjusts his cape which tucks up under the wing-straps.

Sally busts in. "Earl. What yo' doin' here wit' this po' sick chil'?"

"She a healthy womans, Sal. I knowed that."

"Get out my house, yo' ugly man. Go back to yo' own good woman."

"Is Mardi Gras, Sal. A man can play the fool on Mardi Gras."

"Not in my house he can't. Anyhow, it ain't Mardi Gras no mo'. Sun's up."

"I'm on my way home, Sal. I just leaving."

Wriggling on the bed, my mother places her hands above her head and stretches herself right out.

"First, you take off thet mask. I wan' yo' to show this po' chil' what a ugly man yo' is, so she won' hold no feelings for yo'."

Earl does what he's told, and that is my first close-up view of what a demon looks like. I'm queasy with revelation. The way the forehead flops down over the eyes, the way the eyes are set apart. The shift of the jaw and the dents in the cheekbones. The mush of lips. Everything's distorted and oversized or undersized. The way the maladroit features fuse together. Demons are sordid and ugly creatures, I can attest to that. Adjusting his wings once more, embracing himself and covering his exposed bones with his cape, Earl leaves the room and the house.

"There now, chil', you just get yo'self some sleep. Yo' got a train to catch later t'day."

My mother fights Sally off, proclaims, "I want to stay alive." She stands up on the bouncy bed, scampers across it, and leaps onto the floor. She tries to dress herself in the drapes.

"Look at yo', chil'." The transformation has Sally enthralled. "Yo' a diff'rent chil' this morning."

Faking it, I stir. Sally decides we should all have breakfast, and while we're waiting for the eggs to fry my mother experiments with munching on a candlestick.

"Ain't she a diff'rent girl, Sturgess?" Sally's impressed, although her concern comes to the fore when my mother starts kissing her own image in the mirror. "Mabbe it's time yo' take yo' pill, dear. We got to get yo' on thet train by seven."

"Look! An angel!" Mom cries out, but no one else can distinguish the features. I try hard, but can't make her out. Either the angel is on the other side of the window or she's shimmering in the glass, yet the sighting goes unconfirmed. Even Mom must keep herself at a certain angle to the morning rays of sunlight to behold the being clearly.

"Yo' got to take yo' pill," Sally reiterates, with me ducking behind her skirts. Sal holds up both a glass of water and the medicine, and my mother remains naked in the centre of the room. Still wearing her blue mask with the silvery sequins.

"Let me stay alive. Just a few minutes more."

Sturgess and Sally let her, and Mom twirls around, spinning herself, her hair flying. When she spots me, she comes over and cups my face in her hands. I think to myself that she smells funny, she smells like the soldiers who slapped my face, but I know it's her.

"Sparrow, my precious," she says so quietly. Her luminous, quixotic eyes seem to flex and go soft under her sequined brow, flex and surrender. "My beautiful little birdie." I feel mildly uncomfortable. Then she binds me tightly to her bare skin, squeezing me so hard that the air blows out of me and Sally has to pry us apart. Sally helps my mother to sit down, and holds out the pill and the glass of water.

My mother accepts her medicine. "Goodbye, Sparrow," she says, and swallows the pill, and drinks from the glass.

*

Sturgess kept a hand firmly clamped on my shoulder while we waited to board the train. "You keep those tickets in your hand."

"I will."

"Show them only to men in uniform."

"Okay. I hope you have good fishing, Sturgess."

"I don't really go fishing," Sturgess said. He lifted his chin. "I just pretend."

"When I grow up," I told him, "I want to do what you do."

"You better off doing something. I only pretend."

"No," I said, "I want to move the water around."

Sturgess thought about that. "I just cut the grass and take out the garbage," he reminded me.

"Don't you help move the water around?"

He thought about it further. "I guess so. But that ain't nothing."

"It's what I want to do," I told him.

Sally waddled over after my mother climbed onto the train. "Yo' take care of your momma," she ordered me.

"Okay," I said. I was accustomed to that sort of direction, although the force behind her words indicated trouble if I disobeyed. Probably Sally would appear and give me a spank. I followed my mother onto the train and we found seats. Leaning out the window we both touched Sally's hand, although my mother's had a leafy quality, the fingers just seemed to hang there, suspended, as if unattached.

"Chidrens! Chidrens! Listen me up, y'hear! Follow that freedom road, li'l' chidrens! Follow that North Staaaarrr to freedom!"

Sally-talk, and as usual I did not know what she was hollering about. Yet her words stuck to me. The train lurched out of the station and I was terrified, all that screech and crank, whistle and sway. I was certain that this massive hulk of metal and wood was doomed to crash, or fall off a bridge into a very real abyss. My mother seemed undisturbed by the train, which helped me to calm down, although after the conductor had punched our tickets she did say something to indicate that she was not wholly cognizant of her circumstances.

"Where are we, Sparrow?" she asked in that slow speech. "Where's Sal? Is this house moving, or am I just being a crazy person again?"

How could I answer her? What could I say? I guess I was growing up without knowing it, because I leaned forward like the responsible little man everybody was asking me to be, and told her, "You took your pill, Mom. You go to sleep now."

"Okay," my mother complied, and I helped adjust my jacket for her to use as a pillow, placed her coat across her lap to keep her cosy, then nestled in against her warmth to draw a measure of it back.

Pell-mell, the train ricocheted through the night into the distant, dark, unknown future of our lives.

3.

Night Flights

Bastards are obliged to invent their own beginnings, a knack learned early and I'm no exception. These days, single mothers proliferate, which ought to change things, but it was my lot to be raised without the benefit of being in vogue. So go ahead, pronounce me tainted, not merely a bastard but a fibber to boot, and save me the last waltz at the Liar's Ball. (God knows, I attend most years.) Just remember, at the best of times, fabrication is merely an ornament for the truth, not its mask. A form of costume jewellery. And who can know for certain that the fake rubies, pearls, and diamonds have been left at home and the real rocks withdrawn from the vault?

Where's the grief? Either it happened, or it did not. Either I was awake or I was asleep, and what anyone believes will depend on the resources of that person's own knowledge and understanding. (Or gullibility, perhaps.) I won't argue the issue, or make a case. Allow me to state the facts as simply as I remember them. I flew when I was six. Lifting above my seat I hovered in mid-air, enjoying the sensation. My body tingled all over. Were it not for the immense effort of flapping my wings and the fact that I tired easily, I would gladly have made a spectacle of myself, buzzing about the coach like a busy bee. (Take note, bumblebees also defy the laws of physics.)

How necessary is it that my story be believed? In all honesty, I don't care. I have no reason to be scouring the countryside for converts. What's important here is that *I* believed that I had flown, and that I have trouble denying the memory now. And flying, being airborne on wings of angelic design, has had serious repercussions upon my life. The event has played havoc with my comprehension of this and other worlds.

Bear in mind that I have had to fortify my imagination as a means of survival. It's a honed facility, one not bereft of guile. How else do I dispel my mother's clearly dubious recollections? Perhaps my father was an actual gigantic crow—prehistoric or, more likely, extraterrestrial—and I have come by my name honestly. In which case my doubts, and I clutch a few, profane a curious heritage. (Not to mention, an arcane species.) Yet, honestly now, who in this world would nix my desire to proclaim myself human and not a hybrid fowl, one of the boys, with only my class, worth, and legitimacy up for grabs?

The moment my feet rose from the floor and a hectic flapping of wings had me airborne a scant few inches above my seat, I was on the night train to St. Louis. A mere child, of course, lightest-feather division. By fluttering my feet, I discovered that I had the ability to hover, free-float in the air, and I basked in the appreciation of my mother's eyes. She's my key witness. "You fly just like your father used to do,"—then whispering—"when he descended from the moon!" Mom applauded. By easing up on my wing flaps (the invisible ones, which had unfolded from nubs on my shoulder blades which, come to think of it now, had been irritating me for weeks) and by drawing my arms tightly to my body, I could descend without a hard thunk. Nestle into the comforting embrace of my mother's arms.

Which was nice. She was weary and, drugged, struggled to keep her eyes open. "Wake me," she said, "if you want to test your wings again. You might hurt yourself flying on a train." I promised. Eyes closed, I slept to the rhythm of her breathing, the scent of her body, and the syncopated percussion of the tracks. Waking, and I don't know whether hours or mere minutes had passed, I discovered that we were surrounded by a band of dwarfs.

It's not possible that they also had been fabricated in a dream sequence. How awake was I? That may be the nub of the question for some, but not for me. The wee men politely introduced themselves, and each had a common name, such as Harry and George and Michael, although the leader of the bunch was known as Deputy. Over his heart and pinned to his vest he wore a silver shield. "I been given the power to arrest children," he informed me. Less a declaration of pride than a manifesto of judicious intent. He wanted youngsters to understand in advance that he had the edge in any quarrel.

Brian, red-bearded and jolly, the most elfin of the bunch, looked me in the eye and swore that, "Deputy would only arrest his mother. Anybody else, he just shoots them between the eyes." I felt under threat, and curled my feet up under me.

"We have it in for children," Robert informed me. He looked authoritative in his three-piece, pin-striped suit. C.E.O. material.

"Especially we got it in for teasers," George qualified. "If you want to tease us, Deputy will shoot you."

"And if he misses, we'll hang you," promised Harry.

"We get a kick out of lynching children," said a feminine voice from the back of the huddle.

"And if we can't find a rope we'll drag you behind the train until your fingers fall out of your hands, and then we'll wave goodbye while you're left crying for your mommy on the tracks."

I curled in more tightly against her.

"So?" Harry wanted to know.

Michael asked me, "Are you going to tease us?"

Solemnly, I vowed that I would not. That I would not even think of doing such a thing.

"Not even when we read our poetry?" Deputy pressed on.

That was a tough one, but I consented to their demands. "I won't tease you," I swore, and the timbre of my voice, laced with my abundant fear, convinced them. Deputy and Michael slid off the facing seat and joined in the procession out of our coach into the next. We may speculate that they had been to New Orleans to participate in Mardi Gras as a comic or freak act, and that they were wandering through the train to hunt children before any molested them first. The dwarfs were clearing the way for a comfortable and incident-free journey, a lesson that I should have taken to heart.

A stop-and-go junket, a bump 'n' grind that slandered sleep, contorted limbs, made muscles sore, and agitated normally placid tempers. My bones ached. Waking up beside me, Mother surfaced from both her dreams and her medication, a lethal combination on this trip, so perhaps she was prepped for the pair of cowboys who had sat down in the seat facing us. Each in turn tipped his Stetson in a mannered salute.

"You armed?" the bigger of the two asked me. His limbs were of legendary proportions. He sat with his knees wide apart to accommodate within the narrow gap between benches legs that could service a giant. With his sleeves rolled up, the great lengths of his arms lounged at his side like a pair of napping lions, and I found the protuberance of muscles and veins fascinating. His pinkie stretched further than my entire hand, the diameter of his biceps equalled my girth. Like stars erupting from a galaxy, freckles formed his other astonishing characteristic. They scattered from the density of his nose and fled down his neck, entering a negative universe under his shirt to reappear on those elongated arms. He was clad in jeans, cowboy boots, and a black shirt, and his smile habitually hung on him in the way that lopsided old gates swing from broken-down fences.

Neither my mother nor I could comprehend his meaning. Both of us glanced down at our arms. We seemed to possess the appropriate pair.

The second cowboy helped out. A foot shorter, he was stocky and looked powerful. Neck muscles bulged beyond the width of his head. Blonde hair curled out from under his hat and his eyes were strange, the pupils tiny, the whites immense. I remember bulky lips that protruded beyond the extension of his nose, although he was not an ugly man, merely odd. "Your momma's such a pretty lady, you havta pr'tect her, boy. D'y'carry a gun?"

"I don't," I professed. The only weapon that I concealed as secretly as any robber might tote a revolver was my envelope of documents.

"A boy's gotta pr'tect his momma," the first reiterated.

"He has sharp teeth," my mother pointed out. "Once a man come into my room? An army man? My boy bit his hand right off nearly. Didn't you do that, Sparrow?"

Curling their fingers safely out of chomping range, the men edged back in their seats slightly.

"Glad to hear that, ma'm. 'Cause a pretty woman like you needs pr'tection."

"What did I hear you call your boy?" the stocky one asked.

"Sparrow." Mother slid her hand up the nape of my neck, fluffing my hair.

That would be the first time, and perhaps the most painful moment, when I was obliged to endure serious abuse about my name. The two cowpokes, who probably could not bust a bronco or rope a steer if their lives were at stake, they'd be bucked from a horse the moment it had a mind to gallop, had the gall to laugh out loud. "Sparrow! That's a good one. Are you a boy or a bird?" the short, dumpy rustler sputtered.

"You can't go through life wit' a name like that and expect to defend your momma." This clown was not only tall enough, he was dumb enough to mate with giraffes. Come to think of it, that may account for his splotchy skin colouring.

"What's he doing with a name like that, ma'm, if you don't mind my asking?"

We mind your asking.

"I can fly," I put in sharply, capable of fighting my own battles.

"I seen him," Mother confirmed.

"He can fly!" the second man announced, not only to his friend but to the Pullman car in general. Fortunately his outburst attracted the attention of the conductor, who wandered by as a watchful chaperon.

"This boy can fly," the first cowboy, leery of the uniform, of the accouterments of authority, declared to the black man.

"I'm sure of that. Why not? I seen stranger things than a boy that flies. In my time I've seen stranger things than that." Pleased with this intermediary, I was delighted by his confidence in me.

"Hey, kid. Maybe you'd care to give us a demonstration?"

"Yeah, flap your wings, sonny."

"You can't see them," I shot back, miffed. "They're invisible!" Didn't these people know anything?

"I think I saw youse flying a little while ago," the conductor put in. He was my star witness, and one of my regrets in life was that I never learned his last name. "I said to myself, look at that little boy, he's walkin' on air!" The man turned away from my happy grin to tangle with the cowboys' scowl. "Were youse two gentlemen invited into this seat, or were youse just helping yerself?"

"Little lady here," the first cowboy assured him, "begged us to sit down." The pockets of his black shirt were decorated with a red filigree. Strange, that that detail should survive the transgression of time, one of those fleeting memories that has stuck. His pal backed him up, claiming that, "She's a lonesome gal who appreciates good comp'ny." A team (I guess they were young, between twenty-five and thirty) the men were quick to parlay each other's words into an elaborate agreement. "She seemed real hot 'n' bothered," the first one said, and the second finished his sentence, "like she ain't been with a man in some long while."

Requiring no coaching from us, the conductor smoothly contradicted their testimony. "The lady was having a peaceful nap. Can't youse see she's wore down from Mardi Gras?" He had an expert way of being both diplomatic and hard-nosed at the same time.

As things worked out, my mother was drifting through a fade-away moment, and the cowboys noticed. Concluding that little action was happening here, they acquiesced to return to their own coach, and the conductor smiled, patted my head, and went off down the aisle. Before the gangly cowboy struggled out of his seat, he took a moment to show me his gun. Reaching into the back of his pants he took out a black pistol that I found to be both beautiful and scary. "This is what you need, boy. You ain't always gonna have niggras 'round pr'tecting you and your momma. You need one of these here to shoot the bastards gonna be comin' 'round. Sharp teeth are good, sharp teeth are real good, I like that, but they ain't good enough." He slid the gun out of view, gave me a big wink, and joined his friend. The men returned the same way as had the dwarfs before them, which made me wonder what was going on in the car up front.

The conductor who had punched our ticket and seen to our welfare was a jocular black man with a massive waist. He didn't forget about us. He returned with a bagful of candies intended for kids, and I said, "Thank you," when he handed me a mint as clear and as shiny as a diamond. My mother held out her hand too. He laughed merrily at first, before he had the chance to study her more intently. Then, with hardly a hitch to his motion, he dug deeply for a candy the colour of forest jade. "Don't you worry about nothing now," the man said, "everything gonna be all right." My mother sucked on her jewel while I shut my eyes and did the same. Enthralled by the sounds on board, by the cars bumping behind the locomotive, the squeal of the brakes, the comforting clatter as we rolled over the rails, I was lulled asleep by the holy whistle—long-long-short-long—signalling crossings, alerting the world to our progress.

I decided at that moment, and profoundly, that I liked living on a train. I enjoyed being in motion. Travel suited me better than landing in strange places. I preferred movement to keeping still. Standing in one place I'm aware of cross-hairs focusing. Living in a house, to this day, I feel quartered, backed up against the wall of leaky faucets, invasions of vermin. I expect paratroopers to drift out of the sky at any moment. It's strange, but I have never been able to kick that yen to be on the move.

(Hey, piano man. You want to keep me happy? Want to see another big bill in the snifter? Sing me those railway tunes, man. You know the ones I mean.

The Rock Island Line.
The Wabash Cannonball.
Let's hear it for The Orange Blossom Special.
A Train They Call the City of New Orleans.
Be aware It Takes a Lot to Laugh, It Takes a Train to Cry.

Know what I mean? Honestly, do you hear what I'm saying? Sing me those railway tunes and I'm left weeping for another spot in time. I break down. The whistle blows and listen to my stomach growl. I'm riding the rails, breathing soot, hopping freights. A guy told me one time, an honest-to-God hobo deserving of the name, told me one time never to ride the New York Central, because the bulls there break your back before they sweep you out the door. I was young enough then to believe that that was genuine occult knowledge, that I knew something of importance still a mystery to the rest of the world. I believed that this was the only part of my education that had much worth. Know what I mean? Sure you do. I know you do. Sing me those railway tunes for all they're worth. Mix in a few bluesy chords if you feel so inclined, let's hear that mouth-harp wail.)

Fears eroded as my mother and me succumbed to the rhythm of the rails. Danger lay at the beginning and at the end of a journey, the actual business of being in motion assured us that we were both safe for the nonce. On the train, people trying to make their way down the aisle tumbled into surprised laps. I'd laugh and kick my feet. Then look away, my noise met by the scornful glance of a sourpuss.

On the whole I think I was a pretty good kid, for a kid. But allow my mother to nod off to sleep again, let the conductor settle down into an empty seat and close his eyes for a few minutes, then tickle my curiosity about what was going on in other parts of the train, and I was soon afoot, rampant, pulling with all my might to open the door that would lead me into the forward coach.

That was scary. I tried to keep my balance between the two cars on a curve, and the sudden onslaught of noise, the hard clacking rails, the scrape of brake-shoes, the banging joint was terrifying as I was knocked about the vestibule against steel walls. Such mysterious smells—burnt metal and oil, soot from the coal-fired smoke stack—I thought I couldn't breathe, and solid footing was too elusive for me to firmly grip the forward door. Trapped.

A crying jag might be appropriate, except no one was around to notice.

I had to wait for someone to be walking through the train as I had been trying to do, and the moment that the guarded door lurched open I was quick to squiggle loose into the cryptic realm.

Perhaps that was my first true disappointment with the world as it was being presented to me. Up until that moment I had journeyed without expectations. Misgivings, yes, but I really had no idea of what to look for, and I'd developed no concepts of what I should expect to find. Given the encounters in my coach, my imagination had fashioned a wayward carnival of sorts, a kind of Mardi Gras in motion, at the very least one populated with pistol-packing cowboy giants and swarms of dwarfs stringing up children by their necks. Instead, I was the daring one in a Pullman populated by the somnambulant. Every seat offered travellers contorted into uncomfortable shapes, as if their passions had stalled at an awkward moment and had atrophied in time. They were wedged into corners and they pressed against one another for warmth. Couples sought the cushioning effect of bones, breasts, and muscle. I was disappointed that the scary dwarfs were not to be found. Had I made them up, like I used to do with my clay chums? Or had they climbed onto the luggage racks and fallen asleep up there? The cowboys had also vanished, and it finally occurred to me that the many cars I had seen upon boarding remained connected to this train. Despite my interest in exploration, I was not game to take on the heavy doors one more time, nor was I willing to walk through another frightening vestibule. I waited for the chance to return to my mother's side and would have done so had I not suddenly been clamped by a hand clutching the back of my shirt collar and lifting me up onto my tiptoes.

"Are you Ssssssparrow?" the disembodied voice demanded. Then my interloper spun me around to scold me with his look.

"No, mister." Like any child, my first instinct was to deny everything, including my very existence if necessary. I was too startled by his treatment to say much else, and to this day fantasize that I had been the type of boy who would have reared back and powdered this weasel-faced sap with a punch in the mouth. I appreciated neither his rough handling nor the sibilant pronunciation of my name. Pow! Right on the kisser. Violence had never been a trained reflex in me, yet his manner sponsored abuse. He was a man and I was a boy, but I thought of him as being nearly as short as me and just as narrow, for my recent brush with Paul Bunyan's clone had set him apart as diminutive. Some adults command authority, yet I was learning that others beg to be defied.

"I sssaid, are you Ssssssparrow or are you deaf?"

Spray spit from his lips. I twisted my head away. I had had enough time now to comprehend the question, and knew what my answer ought to be. That I hesitated may be credited to my shyness, although I prefer to think that certain natural instincts also were operating. An ingrained wisdom made me leery about confessing my name to any stranger. How had he known it? Had the cowboys already strolled through the train ridiculing my name, mocking my mother and me both?

"Cat got your tongue?" It's a cute expression, inherently harmless, though for a frightened child who is hearing the remark for the first time without comprehending the line, it can be spooky. To confirm that it was still there, I waggled my tongue inside my mouth, and frantically searched about for the feline prowling for a meal.

"Sssspeak up! Are you Sssssparrow or not?"

"Not." Valiantly, I defended myself against this inquisition.

Suddenly worried that he might have confiscated the wrong boy, my interloper let me go. I hadn't realized that the thrust of his pull had stretched me taut, and the sudden drop jarred my heels. "What's your name then?" This time, his tone was reasonably civil.

Too young to be aware of my options, or to have devised skilful lies, I whispered, "Drinkwater, mister."

That hand again, coming around behind my neck, gripping my collar, pinning me up like a shirt on a line. This time the man positively snarled, "You're Sssssparrow!" Wetting my cheeks and eyelids with the spittle of his indignation.

"I'm sorry!" Staggered, I searched around the Pullman for help. Everywhere, sleeping adults conveniently ignored my strife.

I had told the truth, I was released from further physical interrogation and invited to participate in a more benign form of mind-control. "Good for you, young man. I can sssee that you are a fine young fellow. A fine ssssstrapping lad! Come, sssit down beside me. I know your mother well. We're old friends. Ssssit down beside me, Sssssparrow. Tell me about yourself in great detail. What wonders have you ssssseen?"

I had been outside the Lougain asylum for only a short time. The whole wide world was strange to me and becoming increasingly odd. I was suspicious of much of the world, and certainly I was sufficiently experienced to foster reservations about this man. Yet he had known my name. Since I had never been taught how to hold my own with adults, nor had I been counselled in subversion, I answered his questions truthfully, and before long he had me talking freely. It's a reasonable speculation that confiding so much of my own and my mother's life to him derived from the presumption that he was acquainted with us. He had known my name. He had told me that he knew my mom. When he asked about New Orleans my doubts were reborn and I was quick to counter, "How did you know I was in New Orleans?" You'd think I was training to become a child-detective. Smiling, he explained casually that New Orleans was where the train had originated, so everyone aboard had spent time in that city. Finally. A logic I could assimilate.

Later he said, "And your mother, Ssshhheilagh, how is ssshe?"

I asked him pointblank how he knew my mother's name. He scooted around the issue in that clumsy way endemic to adults when they're being harassed by children to explain themselves. He planted an elbow in his opposite hand, cupped his chin, and surmised, "You'll make a fine lawyer sssome day, Ssssparrow. Indeedy yes, I sssee a future for you in the legal profession."

"I don't know what that is," I stated honestly.

"Nothing gets by you. That's all I'm ssssaying. Nothing gets by you and I'm positive that we can find a use for that talent."

"I want to go back to Mom," I beseeched him, feeling captive. "Please open the doors for me, mister. They're heavy."

"That didn't sssstop you coming through, did it? No, you sssit down right where you are. And don't ssssquirm. We'll have a nice long chat, you and me. If you insist on wandering about on trains, learn to pay the consequences. Tell me sssomething, Ssssparrow," and here his interrogation took an odd turn. He spoke to me about the world. "Tell me if you disagree." He held up a pillow and said, "This is a pillow." He opened his coat and proselytized, "This is my coat." With the acuity of a prophet he pointed to the overhead rack. "That is my bag." Across the aisle. "That is a woman." I had no reason to dispute any of these claims, nor could I comprehend why they were being proposed. During the spree I gazed at him closely in that carnivorous, uncompromising way that children have, as though understanding might be revealed in his facial characteristics. What made me fearful of the man was his nostril hair. Large, black, wiry bristles grew from his small nose, virtually mingling with his moustache. His glasses were of the wire-rimmed variety popular at the time, and the hair on his head was slicked back, greased, every strand in place. His chin was as knobby as a kneecap, his cheeks had collapsed into a sallow, concave formation as though he was accustomed to being ill, and his eyes confided a weary look, as if he was perpetually bored with standing outside of himself manipulating a puppet of his likeness. Naturally, not all these impressions occurred to me at the same time—I was six years old—and I am adding information that could only accumulate in later years (which is to say that I would come to know this man, that we were destined to draft a history together) but at the time I was distinctly repelled by his nostril tresses. I suppose it had to do with the fact that he was a man. I was accustomed to the company of my mother and facial fur was more common among my mother's nocturnal spooks than to people that I knew well.

Having defined the furniture, the man began to see if I would deny his point of view. "Ssssometimes, Ssssparrow, when you are looking at an object, at anything, sssay a ssseat or a cushion, does it begin to grow? Do flowers emerge? Does it ssssuddenly look like food to you, sssomething you can eat? Or does it change into sssomething else, sssomething beautiful, or sssomething ugly, sssomething that grows big teeth and fangs and ssssnarls at you like a big ferocious doggie? Does that ever happen, Ssssparrow, and then, just like that"—he snapped his fingers— "the thing goes back to being what it was? Does that happen to you very often or just once in awhile?"

I thought this man was crazy. Once again, asking to see my mother, I was denied. So I started to cry. I decided that he must be the kind of person I feared the most, neither a demon nor a bad man, worse than any of those, a doctor. Didn't he talk like one? For me, my mother had difficulty sometimes because doctors warned her that if she didn't do this or that she'd be in trouble. Physicians had the power of self-fulfilling prophecy. If this doctor-man told me I was crazy, wouldn't it become true? I would have to take medication like my mom. I levelled the cruel accusation.

"I am not a doctor," my inquisitor laughed. "Why do you ask? I wish I was a doctor, I'd be a rich man. I wouldn't be on this train doing another man's business. I am a bookkeeper, Ssssparrow. Do you know what that is? Indisputably a profession more honourable than being a doctor. Doctors are thieves. I know. I have done their books. A bookkeeper is the arbitrator of truth in the modern world. That's me. Truth's henchman. Figures never lie, Ssssparrow, though I'll admit they are ssssubject to manipulation. Me, I'm the one who determines the honesty of others, my Ssssparrow, a noble duty. In the final analysis, I'm poor but I'm noble. Don't forget that."

"Oh." In my own way I was impressed, and my tone probably reflected my wonderment.

"Does the world sssometimes ssseem like a dream to you, Ssssparrow, only you are wide awake?"

"A pillow is a pillow." That's what I said, aged six, as God is my witness. "It's never anything else." I kept to myself the knowledge that I could fly, which I figured was none of his business.

This time when he cupped my shirt collar, his touch was gentle, his hold less firm. A hard black candy, like a smoothed chunk of coal, appeared in the gentleman's paw. My due. I popped it into my mouth, and immediately understood that the consequence of accepting the payment was that I had to endure his company a while longer. He put on a shiny smile, washed his lower lip with his upper, wiggled his brush moustache as if cleaning house, and poked his fingers about the corners of my mouth to entice me to emulate his goofy grin. Then he began beating his palms against his stomach. "Ssssolid," he postured, "like rock. I might be a book-keeper but I am prepared to go to war again. Sssstand me in the trenches, ssson, that's where I belong. Ssshhhoulders back!" he commanded and gave my nearest one a slap. "Tummy in, ssshhhoulders back! Sssay sssolid sssoldiers' sssshoulders. Ssssay that fast."

I couldn't say it slow.

"Tuck in that chin, like this." The gyration formed half a dozen chins, and he sat as stiff as a dummy without its grin. What broke him from his trance was a shout from the forward end of the car. A dwarf was running through the Pullman shouting gibberish, and I jumped up to hear what he had to announce.

Deputy was trying to hide under seats, but each time he squirrelled himself away, unfriendly feet kicked him back out again. I finally deciphered his news. "Hide your money! Hide your jewels! Hide away your diamond rings! Robbers and thieves! Robbers and thieves!"

"Deputy," I said when he had been forced to the back near me, "where's your badge?"

"He took it! The cowboy! Said he'd shoot me through the heart unless I gave it up. He'd steal the gold out of a poor man's tooth."

With that, our oracle dropped to the floor and hid under the seat in front of mine. He had finally found a use for children—my legs were too short to kick him. Ruthlessly, my companion tried to pull him out, but Deputy held fast to the cast-iron leg of the seat and fought to keep his position. The bigger man quit the tug-of-war when a sonorous voice bellowed from the front of the coach.

"Your money," and it was the cowboy, the gargantuan one, his consecrated black revolver pointing in the air, "or your life. That's the deal. Take it or leave it." He aimed his pistol at the temple of a large woman who had immediately gone into hysterics. "Stop that squealing or you're one dead sow."

The woman sobbed on in silence.

I noticed that the big cowboy was wearing Deputy's badge.

"I want my mother," I said to the man beside me, who was equally as stiff as when he had demonstrated a soldierly manner. This time his temples perspired, and when he spoke he opened but one side of his mouth to snarl, "Sssssit down. Don't move. Be sssssstill."

Children are accustomed to that sort of instruction. We rarely obey.

The second cowboy was mingling among the people carrying a pillowcase, collecting offerings for Santa's bag. I waved when he reached my seat.

"This your old man?" the smaller cowboy wanted to know. "Kinda old and spindly for your momma, ain't he?"

I did not think that my companion was my "old man," so I didn't answer. The tallest cowboy pressed the barrel of his pistol against the man's cheek, deflecting it out of shape. "You married to that sweet young tulip?"

"No, ssssssir," the man squeaked, or squawked. His voice now had a harsh resonance that scarcely seemed human.

"Heyyup!" hollered the smaller robber when he noticed Deputy hiding under the seat. "Look who's here. It's one of them squirts." He began kicking at him. "Get out of there, you little varmint."

The giant got down on his knees for a closer inspection of the hidden dwarf. He bent way over so that his face was also on the floor. "Which one're you?" he snarled. "Are you Dopey?"

"No!" Deputy denied being a friend of Snow White's.

"Are you Bashful? Grumpy? Are you Happy, you shrunken freak? Are you Sleepy? Or Sneezy? Which one of you sawed-off runts are you?"

A proud man, the little fellow refused to answer to any of the famous nicknames.

"His name is Deputy," I helped out.

"I shoot deputies. I'm a robber. If he's a cop I'll shoot him. Right between the eyeballs." He aimed the gun elsewhere, wedging it firmly into the little man's soft, plump rear. "Which one are you, varmint?"

"I'm Doc," a faint voice admitted.

"That's not what I heard," the cowboy brayed. He left the matter up to me. Standing on his knees, his head at my level now, he asked, "Who is he, kid? Tell me the little guy's name once and for all. You decide."

"Umm," I said, accepting the responsibility with appropriate seriousness. "I think his name is Doc," was my final decision. The cowboy stood up, his head grazing the ceiling of the Pullman so that he had to keep his neck kinked.

"Okay, if you say so, I won't blow his ass off." Then he began to kick at the wee fellow again. Demanding, "Sing Hi-ho! Hi-ho! for me. Sing it, Doc."

"Hi-ho! Hi-ho!

"It's off to work we go!"

The faint, humiliated voice continued as the two cowboys finished cleaning everybody out. The man beside me, whose face was as wet as if he had taken a shower, dropped his wallet into the pillowcase. I worried about my secret envelope, but the cowboys did not ask for it, concentrating on the earrings of the lady across the aisle.

"Keep singing, Doc," the giant directed as he backed out of the car to enter the next one, where my mother was waiting.

"Hi-ho! Hi-ho! Hi-ho!"

In my first home, in Lougain, Mississippi, in the asylum there, an unfortunate number of the residents were beguiled by the shakes. A palsy that for some was constant and uncontrollable, bodies stuttering between time and space, out of sync with the blessings of this world as if rotating on a contrary, wobbly axis. Triggered by stress or a rapacious chemical folly, the affliction hit others periodically, often when they expected it the least. The man beside me on the night train to St. Louis now began to shake like that. Developing rapidly, the quiver was rampant through his limbs. Even the thick black bristles in his nostrils trembled, and his moustache stepped into motion like a caterpillar's walk. The gentleman's left arm encircled my shoulders to give me the comfort of a hug—or was he hoping to anchor his hand, did he expect that clinging to whatever seemed to be still might calm the calamity of nerves? Pressed against his rib-cage, I felt that man's bony body quake.

"Hot damn!" he was whispering to himself. In waves, the shakes would vacate his extremities, move upward through his torso, and erupt across his face. While his lower lip twitched, the moustache would begin to gyrate like a squiggly night-crawler on a hook. "Hot damn!" Where the pressure of the pistol had left a circular, red impression like a clandestine kiss, the skin on his cheek flexed and jumped.

Deputy burrowed backwards out of his hiding-place. "Whew! That was a close call. He damned near blowed my arse off."

"You get away from me." As taut as a bass string, the man spoke with a deep-voiced fury. "You're trouble."

"Me?" The dwarf slapped his chest in disbelief. "I'm trouble? Didn't you see what just walked out the door? That was trouble."

"He might be back. I want you away from me, you little freak! He might come back looking for you—I don't want you near me." His body had coiled forward, as if the sudden release of a latch would cause him to rebound like a spring.

Not particularly interested in this dispute, I slid off my seat and scampered to the front of the coach.

"How come you only talk tough to midgets?" Deputy countered. "How come you didn't tell that giant to take a hike? He's a bigger freak than me. Just 'cause we don't play basketball, that don't mean you can push us around. See this?" He held out his hand on a level plane. "Not shaking one bit. Hold out yours. Let's everybody see."

"Sssscram, sssssshrimp!"

"We're all interested. Hold out your hand, mister. Let's see if you're a man or a pansy."

Frantic, I ran back and tugged on his jacket. "Deputy!" Throughout the coach, men and women had gotten sidetracked, raising their hands to test the status of their own nerves. Deputy, it must be conceded, was the most steady, and perhaps that was why I had run to him. "Help me open the doors! Let me save my mom!"

My plea was interrupted by the other dwarfs entering the coach from the opposite end. They spied Deputy, and rushed to greet him. "Dep! Thank God you're safe!"

"That boy saved my skin!" my new pal proclaimed.

"A kid?"

"He's a hero. He let me hide. He kept that giant from blowing my arse off!"

Precious time to revel in this praise. "Open the doors for me, Deputy! I have to save Mom!"

"Open the doors!" Deputy commanded.

"Open the doors!" shouted Michael.

The man with the twitching moustache was sitting on his hands to keep them concealed.

"Open the doors!" reiterated George, and finally three dwarfs acceded to the will of the pack, and opened the doors. Too timid, or too wise, to come through with me to rescue my mother, they remained safe in the car behind, keeping company with the man who, out of a sense of obligation or duty, had planned to follow me. Upon standing the bookkeeper with the wiggly moustache had discovered that his knees were as wobbly as his hands were spastic, and he was obliged to slump down into his seat again.

Seeing me again, my mother welcomed this verification that I was alive and not lost forever. She was standing in the aisle, facing me, wrapped in the arms of the elongated cowboy who was preoccupied with the black conductor. The trainman sat crouched on the floor, a ready-to-pounce fat panther staring into the cowboy's pistol.

"Back off, Sambo," the robber warned.

"Sparrow," my mother said, and I can vouch for her choice of words. "Fly away."

"Let the lady go free," the conductor advised in an even voice. "Then we'll talk about this."

"What for? You got sumpin t'say t'me, black face, let's hear it." He cocked the hammer of his gun.

In trying to squeeze past the hefty cat of a man, I was stymied by his massive rump. So I slipped under his legs and eluded his grip like a greased piglet, and scooted up to my mother. Pressed my face flush against her thigh. My wee voice, muffled by her dress, pleaded with the giant, "Don't hurt her."

"Stretch!" Wallets and pocket watches, earrings, diamond rings, and gold wedding bands. This was an era when the well-to-do travelled by train, and the giant's partner continued collecting a king's ransom from the passengers. Unfortunately for him, his pillowcase was now over-stuffed, and the process of trying to pack more and more items into the swollen sack was slowing him down. He had just now realized the time. "Shake a leg. Time's running out." Both images befuddled me. Why was it necessary to shake someone's leg? And whose would they choose? And for the first time in my life I was beset by the curious idea that time might stop, that suddenly we'd be immobile, held in our places for eternity.

Peering around Mom's legs to glance at the second bandit, I spotted him comparing several of the stolen watches. Apparently they provided him with contradictory information. "Which one of these is ackrit?" he demanded of his victims, sparking a heated debate over whose time-piece was the most reliable. "Any which way," the robber deduced, "we're 'bout ready."

Stretch, the gangly cowboy whose head bumped the ceiling with the motion of the train, gestured with his pistol. "You do it, nigra," he indicated.

"Do what, sir?" The conductor shifted his weight on the floor.

"Pull the switch."

The black man hesitated and the cowboy took aim.

As if counselling a friend, my mother, who I guess understood about guns ever since we'd been attacked by paratroopers in Lougain, said to him, "Don't shoot the nicest man."

"Maybe just in the hip," Stretch negotiated.

"He give me yummy-good green candy."

"Then you pull it," the giraffe among cowboys invited.

"Pull what?"

"Stretch! Don't fart around. It's time." Behind us, the shorter cowboy had averaged out the time on six different watches, calculating that he and Stretch had pushed their schedule to the limit.

"Let me do it," I volunteered. Compared to my mother I was smart, and I didn't want to see her embarrassed. Mounting a seat, I pulled the bright red handle of the emergency brake. It's true that this was my first ride on a train, but either some thing's are instinctive, or I had followed the line of the cowboy's motion.

Dynamiting a train, is railroad parlance. Not only do the wheels screech to a stop, their direction is actually reversed. The cowboy used his great reach to break the glass that protected the switch with the butt end of his pistol. Then he clucked his tongue at me. I smiled. At the instant of pulling the lever for the conductor's use only, the effect of literally being dynamited could not have been more severe. I catapulted forward, a flight witnessed by many. My invisible wings never got going, and I bounded onto the lap of an elderly matron recently relieved of a family heirloom, a broach, and now in mourning. Comically dumped onto his behind, the conductor offered substantial bulk to cushion my mother's fall. Stretch hung tightly to an overhead strap. Behind him the contents of the pillowcase spilled down the length of the aisle.

The train slammed to a riotous stop.

Bedlam transformed the coach into a trolley for the damned. People moaned and called out. Grovelling on his knees, the shorter cowboy reclaimed his plunder, while several passengers also helped themselves to the spilled loot, recouping losses, and in one case turning a profit. The frantic cowboy hollered to his partner to lift his feet, he was standing on a prized necklace. They argued back and forth, and I looked about at the people with split lips and hurt noses, mesmerized by the blood dripping down their chins. I'd lost track of my mom.

Pulling herself out of the grasp of the conductor, she stood again. My mother wore a strange, dreamy expression, and in the narrow aisle congested with debris and jewels and tossed bodies, she began to dance. Her hips swayed to an imagined music. My mother celebrated the beautiful destruction of the coach, the chaos of bodies, the passengers' stupefied shock. She had returned to her Mardi Gras life, waiting for a demon who wore his skin beneath his bones.

The frustrated short cowboy blew a gasket. Goods that had previously been compacted into his sack now spilled over the brim. The scavenger had a difficult time hoisting the bag over his shoulder without once again spilling his valuables. The stress was too much for him. He released a wild spiel of foul language.

My mother danced to his words, and to the percussion of moans and cries, as if hearing an orchestra.

I wailed, "Mom!" Stumbled over seats and capsized bodies until I was back at her side. She made me her waltzing partner. She spun me around.

"Guess we take the kid, too," Stretch decided.

"I got enuffofa load to lug."

"He's got two good feet." The giant smiled down at me, virtually a paternal look. "Not to mention sharp teeth."

"Fly, Sparrow," my mother instructed me, although she seemed adrift and not really connected to what was going on. She held my hands and made me dance. "Fly."

"Robbery is one thing," went the gist of the conductor's case while seated on his fanny. Hemmed down by his own considerable ballast and low centre of gravity, he probably could not move without assistance. "Kidnapping, if you think about it, that's something else."

"Yeah, and shooting darkies, that must be sumpin else again, right?"

"Don't shoot," my mother advised, still here. Still doing a two-step.

"Leave the boy." The conductor was bargaining for my life but whose side was he on? I wanted to be a part of this, I did not want to be separated from my mother. Had I not just stopped the train? Didn't that prove I could be useful? I was six years old, I had forced a zillion tons of steel to a ruthless halt. Didn't I deserve consideration for that?

Before I could present my side of the quarrel, the engineer and a pair of brakemen (dressed in traditional railroader's garb, they looked like convicts who had escaped from a prison farm) bolted into the car, searching for the cause of the abrupt stop. On their knees behind them, scarcely visible, crowded seven brave and curious dwarfs. My mother looked for a foxtrot partner among these new recruits.

"Back off!" Stretch aimed his weapon at the interlopers. "Hank," he called to his partner, "move it!" Accompanied by my dancing mother and me, the two bandits shuffled toward the rear of the coach. We had to step over strewn, stunned ladies. My mother stayed in rhythm. "Sambo!" Stretch commanded. "Up off your ass!"

Three dwarfs and the engineer helped hoist the conductor onto his feet again.

"Open the door for us, Sambo."

I caught the engineer's wink when he issued his advice. "Take care, Bartholomew. That first step is kinda steep."

Waddling down the aisle to obey the robber's command, the conductor opened the door of the Pullman and put down a small stepping stool for our convenience. Such service. He came back inside and Stretch was the first one down the short ladder of stairs.

That's when the conductor grabbed my mother's arm.

"Stand back!" he shouted.

He had her, for an instant. Then Mom spun in rhythm to some song, she did a twirl, and Stretch used his extraordinary reach to grasp her around the waist and tug her down. Together they stumbled from the Pullman and vanished from the dance floor.

I couldn't see her anymore.

Only darkness.

Heard only the startled wail of the bandit falling into the void.

Hank burst past the conductor and me to have a look for himself. "Stretch!" he hollered into the silence now. "Stretch!"

Beside me, the conductor was breathing rapidly, as though he might expire.

"Goddamnit, Stretch!"

"Maybe youse checked watches," the conductor pointed out. "But youse never asked me if the train's running on time."

As though his whole body was being constrained by invisible hands and straps, Hank turned to face us both. He stared in our approximate direction with a mixture of bewilderment and rage. "What you tryin' t'say?" he begged to know.

"We're behind schedule. Yer friend just stepped off the Wataminga River Bridge."

Now I could tell that that robber was jammed up even before the brakeman took my hand and guided me aside. The brakeman had figured out that something had to shake loose, and he was astute enough to want the child out of the way. The bandit continued standing there dazed, as though he could not move, could not react, while his eyes showed the dark temper of a midwest twister on the descent. In the very next instant he leapt at the conductor's throat, I yelped, and it is possible that that was the sound of my stricken heart leaping off the Wataminga River Bridge.

Choked by those violent hands, the portly conductor was gagging, making hoarse, ugly noises. A brakeman, the engineer, and finally half-a-dozen dwarfs hurling themselves at the cowboy were my black friend's salvation. The bandit was driven back, he tumbled down the stairs, stood again, tripped, and he, too, fell into the night. Just like his friend, he signalled his free-fall into the grim abyss with a long and desolate cry.

Deputy would be the only one to comment on his end. Under his breath he muttered, simply, "Freak."

I trusted my hands to the black, pudgy, soft fingers of the conductor. He sat me on his knee and rummaged in his pockets for his bag of candies.

This one time I was not in the mood for a sweet. I could not understand. My mother had merged with the shadows. She had been reclaimed by the spirits who occupy the darkness. My mother had stepped again into her native realm of spooks and wraiths and demons and spirits, a place where I could not easily follow. She had forgotten, or neglected, to take me along.

"Little boy, do you know where your father is?" the conductor asked. Perhaps his large and comfortable hands, and their blackness, touched off the memory.

"I don't have a father like that," I implied. "My father was a bird. A big black bird who flew out of the sky down from the moon and put my mother on the ground."

That provoked a few curious glances.

"What's he talking about?" The engineer was leaning over the back of our seat. His question would have to go unanswered. The man in the forward coach who had accosted me, the man with the squiggly moustache, dropped his hand onto my shoulder once again and staked a claim.

"Excuse me, gentlemen. This boy is my responsibility now," he informed us all. "I will sssssee to his welfare."

His point was not immediately conceded, least of all by me, and yet he would emerge from hushed conversations with the railroad men with his status approved. The conductor told me that, for now, this man would be my guardian. One by one, I hugged each of the dwarfs, and Deputy kissed my forehead. They guessed that I was too young to comprehend all that had transpired, that the best that I could do was sense my mother's absence. But I knew more than they thought I did. My mother, I realized, had leapt off the bridge into the wretched spirit-world of night.

My new guardian had turned tender as well. He touched my chin, he patted my hair into place, and tears in the corners of his eyes sparkled. "Ssssparrow," he said, his stiff upper lip trembling, "I'm very sssssorry."

That tone of voice made me sad.

4.

Black Feathers

The train staggered off the bridge and cars banged once, twice, jangling loose what few coins and splintered nerves had not already been looted by thieves. Feeling bumped out of my own life I kicked and fussed about the move. To the relief of those forced to endure my caterwaul we were not going far, the locomotive hawed onto a siding where I took solace from the misery of passengers complaining about the ongoing delay.

"Nothing can be done for her now, am I right?"

"Accidents happen. It's tragic."

"Nobody can expect the whole world to stop turning for one missing bandit and his floozy."

"We have to move on."

"I got appointments. You got appointments. Sure, it's a tragedy, but excuse me, busy people on the move do not have time for this right now."

Midgets warned me not to listen. They were the ones offering comfort.

And yet, even the wee folk would be expelled. Cars were shunted about the siding, my own went back and forth frequently, and by the time the railroaders had finished my Pullman had been segregated from the rest. I waved goodbye to Deputy and his companions, their hands and faces pressed up against the glass of the windows, the romping roar of the train shaking my bones. Myself, the conductor, the man who had interrogated me, and a few interested passengers including a physician and a small-town cop, waited for dawn as the train bore into the night.

From a great distance, from the other side of the world, a melancholy whistle blew. That plaintive voice.

Dwarfs or midgets—whatever my friends had been—they bore an uncanny resemblance to the paunchy pals I used to carve in plasticine. I missed them. Someone arrived with a blanket and I nodded off listening to talk. Everybody criticized themselves at the same time that they offered excuses. The cop admitted, "I should've done something." And then revised his position. "How could I shoot? Innocent people would've been killed." Bandying together, the men came to a consensus—blame the crooks.

(For years I would agree. Only much later did I think—blame whoever put on us on that train, whoever shipped us down the tracks.)

In the morning, police and officials stormed our garrison, a search party scoured the riverbank, and the conductor accompanied me outside for a closer look. The shorter cowboy had not drifted far. From the height of the bridge I watched him being fished from an eddy that had rotated him, like the minute hand of a clock, in slow, precise circles throughout the night. He was reeled ashore where a volunteer snared his ankle with a gaff hook. The conductor's face was oddly contorted as he led me beyond viewing range, but not before I'd glimpsed the sheared off top of the cowboy's head.

His brains had spilled loose.

Both sides of the riverbank were being combed. I preferred to look the other way, upriver, where no one searched, imagining that Mom had flown or swum in that direction. "She's in a tree top, that-a-way," I pointed, "eating Corn Flakes." I sang her usual wake-up call, "Cockadoodledoooo!"

The conductor kindly explained about the natural world. The water would have carried her downstream. Whatever cereal she had spooned from her pockets would, by now, be soggy. What did I know? I was six years old and my mother had jumped off a bridge in the middle of the night and nobody could find her or the missing cowboy or the missing lid to the other cowboy's skull.

They did locate his hat, or somebody's hat. That image remains vivid enough. I see the cowboy lying on the bank where they had dragged him out, a snoozing swimmer toasting in the sun, his legs bowed, his hollowed-out scalp shaded by a Stetson.

Then volunteers started dragging the river.

They trolled for my mother under the surging water while I watched from above. An eel-faced old-timer, surfacing up top for more cables, suggested, "Somebody oughta take thet kid 'way from there."

"He's curious." Count on the conductor to stick up for me.

"What if we drug up a body? Is'e curious 'bout thet too?"

"Is my mother in the river?" I asked the man. Skin the texture of fish scales.

He didn't want to say, fudging, "I's hoping not, kid."

Failing a proper grasp of the situation, I believed that my mother might be better off in the water. I thought that the man with the eel's puss and the fishy protruding lips had said something cruel. But I was mixed up about many things.

"We've been sssssearching for a day and a half." Bending at the waist the man lowered himself to my height. "As you can plainly ssseee we can't find hide nor hair of your mom. I have to take you home now, Ssssparrow, and when these people find her, they'll sssend her to you. Guaranteed. Does that ssssound fine?"

I was confused. "What does that mean what you said?"

"What did I sssay?"

"Hide nor hair."

"It means we can't find her."

But I was still perplexed. "What home?" I asked him.

He straightened himself up, resting a hand on my shoulder. "I sssaid it before, I'll ssssay it again, there's a lot of the lawyer in you, laddie. Come along." Solitary on the siding, the Pullman resembled a lonely frontier fort. The man carried me into the car and dropped me onto the big bouncy seat I had been using for my bed. Sitting across from me, he announced, "My name's Mr. Boisvert. Can you ssssay that? It's French. Mr. Bois-vert. *Bois* means wood, *vert* means green. Try it. Mr. Boisvert."

"Mr. ..." Speaking those syllables was like talking with a mouthful of slippery raspberry Jello.

"Mr. Boisvert," he repeated. "Do your best."

"Mr. ... Butter."

"It's a hard name to ssssay." He laughed for the first time since I had known him. "Holy moly. Mr. Butter! There's one for the books." Dabbed at one of his laughing tears. "I have to tell you ssssomething, Ssssparrow, and I want you to listen very, very carefully, all right?"

"Okay," I said.

"Okay. Ssssparrow, I don't travel on trains for fun. I had a purpose to be on this trip. My job is to keep an eye out for you and your mom. It's my responsibility to keep you ssssafe. How could I do that with ssso many restrictions?" He was looking out the window now, a worried hand saluting from his brow. "How do I protect people and at the sssame time keep my distance? 'Hands off', that's the rule. 'No interference unless ssssituation critical'. What kind of orders are those? I was sssssupposed to observe but if I'm observing how do I catch a woman who goes flying out the door? *Whoosh!* Sssshe's gone. Men with guns. Cowboys and sssshrimps. Nobody warned me about those." He cupped my chin, looked at me, and I was watching the way his eyebrows arched into a tent under the threatening dark cloud of wrinkles on his brow. "It's a tragedy, but Ssssparrow, it's by the wayside. Life goes on. Water under the bridge. I know you understand."

I did not.

The water under the bridge nearby was being dragged with grappling hooks big enough to snag a whale. That I understood.

"It's my duty to take care of you, my responsibility to make sssure that you find your way home to Montreal."

"I can go there by myself."

"Think sssso? How will your mom find you? Sssssomeday, Ssssparrow, when your mom sssshows up around here, I'll come back and fetch her. That's a promise. After that, you and your mom can live happily ever after, or until you become a teenager, whichever comes first."

"What's that?"

"A teenager? Little boys are afraid of bogeymen. Big people fear teenagers. I've thought it over, Ssssparrow, and I've decided to ssship you home. But wait. That's not the best part. I have an excellent idea. A sssstupendous idea. A gem of a notion! You will come to live with me. In my house. Would you like that? Be part of my family? I'll take care of you as if you were a child of my own. I will. It's my job."

"I want to wait here for Mommy."

"I don't sssee her walking down the tracks, do you? Listen, a few matters have to be arranged. Ssso you will go to Sssssst. Louis, that's not far, until I can validate my authority in this case. Sssssshouldn't take more than a few days. Aw, Sssssparrow, ssstop sssssnivelling. I ran out of tissue hours ago."

"I'm not snivelling."

"Then call a plumber to fix that nose."

"Fix you in the behind first!"

"Hush that foul mouth!"

Who would he hire for that job, a carpenter?

"Ssssssparrow! Sssstop kicking my sssshins!"

"I want to!"

He paddled my bottom. I refused to cry for him and when he released me I thrashed him right back. To my dismay, my return volley delighted this stranger.

"That's the ssstuff! Sssstiff upper lip! That's what the Brits sssay, sss-
standing in the trenches. Be a man, Ssssssparrow. Be a ssssoldier.
Ssssshoulders back! Tummy in! Look ssssmart! Now, my Ssssssparrow,
wait here. I ssshall sssee to the details of our retreat."

Apparently, I was on my way to Ssssst. Louis.

*

On a sunny afternoon, in the quiet hour before nap-time, I was plough-
ing roads in the orphanage sandbox in St. Louis when a shoe flattened
the hill I had created around a make-believe swamp a minute before. I
looked up. The criminal foot was connected to Mr. Butter who was
wearing a colossal grin instead of his usual grim reaper's face. Before he
spoke I knew what he had to announce. "Pack your duffel, ssssoldier,
we're sssshipping out!" All the way to Montreal, via New York, the
stranger repeated, with a smile, with a nod, sometimes with a clap of his
hands, that at long last I was his responsibility. "Entrusted to my custody. I'm a bookkeeper, Ssssssparrow. Above all others I am the man
people trust. With their money. With their tax returns. Now, now with
their children. This is a particularly distinguished honour."

We ate together, we slept in the same rooms, we trundled off to
public urinals in tandem. Accustomed mainly to women's washrooms
with my mom, where we did our business behind closed doors, men's
rooms were often strange territory. I'd sneak a peek down the line of men
pissing, their ugly hanging scrotums and lumpy penises springing from
briar patches like pale, soggy vegetables. I had a hard time identifying
myself as one of the species. In the mornings, Mr. Boisvert dressed on the
sly, turning his back to me, displaying a set of puckered buttocks like
deflated balloons. I laughed at his nakedness and that made him sore.

"I'm a ssssoldier. Ssstraight and true. Ssssshoulders back! Tummy in!"

In New York, instead of getting mad, the bastard got even. He confiscated my secret letter and the envelope's contents which I had successfully guarded for so long. He had known about it from the beginning, so
he said, he didn't have to read the letter to study its contents. I didn't
kick his shins just for the fun of it this time. I railed at him, "I hate you!
Hate you! Hate you!" Kicking him to drive home that point.

Sadly, the outburst went for naught. He had convinced himself that
we were getting along famously. "You and me, Ssssssparrow, and my ssss-
son, Barclay, we ssshall conquer the world. And that—" waving his
forefinger prophetically in the air, "—will be only the beginning."

I was supposed to be impressed by such a fate.

The best way to rattle him whenever he spouted that sort of non-sense was to demand, "Where's my mother?"

He'd stop. Usually he'd chronicle a sigh. That time in our New York hotel, high above the city, many weeks after my mother's disappearance, he reacted under his breath, "I didn't lose her, Sssssparrow. Sssshe jumped on her own accord."

"She didn't jump off the bridge!" I retorted.

"All right then, fell," he acknowledged.

"She didn't fall!" I hurled back at him.

"Okay. Sssshe was pushed. Pulled. Ssssshe was yanked off the bridge and that's too bad."

"She flew off!" I wailed. "She flew off the bridge! She flew all the way to where I'm going! She's there by now!"

"Sssssparrow, what kind of an argument is that for a good lawyer? You have to make ssssense. You have to be convincing if you expect to win cases."

If he wasn't calling me a lawyer he was referring to me as a little soldier. When I behaved as an undisciplined civilian I was dubbed a dreamer, which prompted his most serious rebuke. "Name one person who ever made money dreaming? Mmmm? Just one. Even Jesus Christ died broke. If it wasn't for his rich friends he'd've been forgotten by now. Sssssstick to the law, Ssssssparrow. If you ssstick to the law and change your name, you've got a future, guaranteed."

What was he talking about?

I vowed, "I won't change my name. You can't make me." That was the one thing in life that I knew for sure.

As I stepped down from the bus in Montreal strange voices puzzled my ears. Sturgess Rawlins had warned me that Canada would be covered in snow and frozen ice. Mentally I had cultivated a landscape similar to vanilla ice cream. Instead, the flavour was grey. Worse, the people spoke gibberish. Mr. Butter was one of them, he spoke gobbledegook. Which he called French. I slid further under his influence. How could I beg help from strangers now? How would I publicly infuriate my patron as I liked to do when nobody could understand my words? Who was around to listen to my tantrums? In the station, I clasped Mr. Butter's stiff, dry fingers, with the thick whorls of black hair above the knuckles, tightly.

The bustle of the depot yielded to docile traffic, a fraternal mingling of automobiles and horse-drawn buggies, electric streetcars and backfiring trucks. We crossed the shallow slope of a mountain where children ran on the grass and families strolled. Young women trotted horses. Along the street that we were following, clothes hung on sidewalk racks and plucked dead chickens dangled in windows. Mr. Butter called the avenue Park, not that I noticed an abundance of playgrounds.

Suddenly, rain collapsed in torrents. We could scarcely see out. Merchants—murky spirits through the windows—fled to the curbs to salvage their wares on display. Elated, Mr. Butter snapped, "It's a cloudburst."

Here, in this strange land where people talked funny, clouds burst.

The sun came out and the car veered onto another busy street. "Park Avenue ends right where we turned. Welcome to Park Extension, Ssssparrow. This is where we live."

Details were invested with the enormity of this news. Washed by the heavy rain, storefronts seemed glazed, candy huts in a dream. Spewed from the volcano of my dormant imagination, people flew by me like sparks, like schizophrenic flames. As lava the pavement moved, big banks swayed.

Chasing a red-white-and-blue ball, children played a game on the street with sticks, digging it free from under parked cars, then slashing at it with their weapons. Most houses were two stories high, with outdoor staircases serving each level. When we entered a block of single homes the taxi slowed down. Mr. Butter said, "The one with the yellow door," and we lurched to a stop. Paying the cabby, he switched to that gibberish language. Then he said something so very peculiar and foreboding. "Let's go, Ssssparrow. We're home."

I was not convinced.

Had my mother been waiting at the door with a timid smile, her wonky, crazed eyes seeking me out, I might have been disposed to accepting this place. That we were observed from the sidewalk by quiet children, and met by a dumpling of a woman who tucked me into her soft round belly and squeezed the daylights out of me, struck me as menacing. I was on my guard. The woman wore a red kerchief in her hair. Her hands were covered with a fine white dust as though her skin flecked off. The scent of fresh bread emanated from inside the house. The couple exchanged perfunctory kisses and the woman swarmed over me once again, hugging incessantly, murmuring, "You poor child, you poor, poor baby! You must be exhausted."

"Is my mother here?" Those were the first words I uttered in my new home.

Mrs. Butter's response was to flee the room. A moment later she returned with white powder sticking to her tears. She offered me a pan of fresh buns lathered with a bright red jam.

"They're bleeding," I joked, one of my mother's. She used to say it about jam on toast and both of us would break into howls and giggles in the communal dining hall. These two proved to be a tougher audience. I detected their knowing glances, intercepted and interpreted their conclusion. "I'm never crazy," I reminded them both. "Not me."

What a weird asylum. To find my room I had to heave on a rope. The ceiling opened upward at the same time that a ladder slid down. I climbed into this turret. Wood chips for insulation covered the floor between the jousts, and a narrow strip of loose boards had been laid for me to walk upon. At the far end of the attic under a wee, round, window that resembled the entrance to a birdhouse, a small pallet had been fitted. Reached by walking a plank. In the opposite corner my mother's belongings had been stored. The cedar chips made the room smell like a forest, and outside my window a branch rhythmically tapped against the roof. Perhaps I believed otherwise, but I agreed that I was tired and needed to rest. I would have preferred going outside to explore, or to flee, but a nap was the option Mrs. Butter was promoting, so I complied. I lay down on the bed, a mattress supported by boards made level by bricks. Raising the ladder closed the hatch, which prevented escape, and I lay on my bunk with my ears attuned to every whisper and nuance, my eyes wholly concentrated on the floor, hoping that one day it might spring open again.

Long after I realized that more than two voices were talking in the house below, I fell asleep in my nest. According to the intents and purposes of strangers and fates, I had arrived all the way home.

*

One problem I had to sort out among many was that I had not been initiated into the lives of children. My temporary stay at the orphanage in St. Louis while Uncle Butter had convinced others to let him be my guardian, had been marked by my despondency and withdrawal. I had not made friends. Normal kids who lived typical lives were a foreign nationality to me. A knock on the hatch disrupted my dreams and, groggy, I had to watch my balance crossing on the boards. Take time to figure out the pulley system. With luck, the floor opened. Gazing up at me between my knees smiled the cheery plump face of a boy who put down the broom handle he had used to batter the ceiling.

"Hello up there!" he sang out. "Can I pay you a visit?"

Without waiting for permission, he scampered up the ladder into my loft.

"Hello!" he cried again. "I'm Barclay. Barc, if you want to make it shorter. Do you like living up here?"

In the same way that genetic diseases are sadly inherent in some children, formality was instilled in Barclay Butter. His manner was insufferably adult as he extended his hand. I was familiar with the manoeuvre, I had shaken hands before, yet his insistence on the greeting struck me as irregular. No kid at the orphanage had done this. He had to initiate the action, lifting my right arm before giving my palm a pump, executing a slight officious bow as he did so.

"I am honoured and pleased to make your acquaintance, little Sparrow. Mother and I have been waiting for you for so long. Father told us everything about your travels. You've had an adventure. Me, I'm nine. How old are you?"

Ah, now I was acquainted with this ploy. In St. Louis I had learned to lump all children into the same age bracket in order not to be viewed as the youngest and, therefore, the least privileged. Older kids boasted about their ages, younger kids lied. Here, in this small house, with just the two of us, age would be a difficult criteria to avoid. I said nothing.

"You're six," he announced on my behalf. "I think you should be comfortable in the attic, don't you?" His survey of the tower made it seem palatial. "Don't you?" he asked again, suddenly conscious of my silence. "What's the matter, Sparrow? Cat got your tongue?"

A cat was in here? Where? Another predator amid the throng? His father had made the same remark on the train. Like any jittery sparrow, I was wary of felines.

"Can't you talk?" he asked me more directly. "Say something."

"I talk when I want to," I let him know.

"That's a relief. I wouldn't want a dumb friend. I'm sorry your mother jumped off the train—"

"She flew," I muttered.

"Pardon me? You're mumbling."

"She flew off the train. She flew up into the sky. She landed in a tree somewhere safe."

"Really? Do you think so? I had an imagination once, a long time ago, but I don't need it any more. Father says you can't live in a dream world and be a success in this one. Do you think he's right? I'm precocious. Did Father tell you? You're not precocious."

Did that mean he had a disease? But he seemed proud of himself. "It depends," I warned him.

"No it doesn't," he insisted. "You are or you aren't. You aren't. But that's okay. I'm the only one around who is. Would you like to come downstairs," were his precise words, "where my family lives?"

An invitation to join the household. With a shrug I stipulated that, "I don't care."

"I could show you around the neighbourhood."

"Okay!" I tried to contain my pleasure with the offer. Having been cooped up in the attic after days of trains, buses, and hotel rooms, and after weeks of confinement at the orphanage, a walk outside sounded suspiciously like freedom. "I'll come down with you."

"Great," my new pal decreed. Then he spilled a confidence. I'm amazed that any child could have kept it to himself for so long. "Can you keep a secret?" (Why is it that that question is always posed by someone who can't?) "We might become brothers. I heard Dad tell Mom. He wants to make so-and-so feel better. Won't that be advantageous, Sparrow? Me and you. Brothers!"

What, I wanted to ask him, was brothers?

But I minded my peace.

A new home. A fearful destination. I explored the streets with an inquisitive left eye and a carnivorous right one. What harm might come to me here? How could I find my way amid this ludicrous congestion? (Circumventing the common pattern, the district was going to seed before it had ever been planted. Lacking the patience for the cycle of growth, prosperity, decay, and regeneration, Park Ex was jumping from its history as farmland to embrace its destiny as an urban ghetto.

[That's nothing. Within two months I had bounded from the Eden of Lougain into the catastrophe of the modern world.])

Slapped together with inferior wartime materials, the Butter house enjoyed the distinction of being a single-family dwelling guarded by a moat of scruffy yard. Flowerbeds lined the foundation in the front and back. Throughout the rest of the district, most dwellings were multiple-units, and my walk with Barclay led me past great craters gouged out for a summer of active construction. Like walking on the moon during a building boom. Houses were being erected in great haste for the immigrant poor, hordes of disenfranchised Europeans were sailing the North Atlantic, and I was merely a forerunner of this throng.

Dirt roads were being paved by huge asphalt machines laying smooth, black, smoking surfaces. Like Pied Piper's tribe of kids and rodents, children lagged behind the crews. Their favourite pastime was chewing tar. Bulbous wads of the gum were wound onto sticks, masticated, then the children displayed their black lips, teeth, and tongues. The game was fun because it was daring, but Barclay tugged me away to ramble off by ourselves in search of new land and fresh adventures.

Open fields still flourished, tangled and rough, with rabbit warrens and fox dens and paths tramped flat by children released from their winter harness. Dogs romped freely and so did we. Under skies rapidly clearing following the morning rains, we trespassed onto a magical land of small forests spotted here and there across majestic green lawns. By heaven's rim, we ducked down among the bramble and trees.

Familiar, this sport played by men. The mallets were longer, the ball smaller, and I could see no hoops, but the game looked remarkably similar to croquet. "What're they trying to do?" I asked my trail guide.

"They're rich," Barclay Butter explained. "They have stacks of cash."

Under cover of bracken and woods, we ventured along trails native only to children. I fell into step behind Barc's leadership, impressed by his knowledge of the world. Once, when a gruff voice snapped at me, I thought that the tree had talked. Barclay yanked me clear. "They're kissing!" he hissed. Looking over my shoulder, I was prepared to spy maples in an embrace. "Try not to step on people when they're necking in the woods." That was the thing about Barclay, the advice he dispensed would never go out-of-date. I searched back into the shadows again. People were hidden away in there. Maybe they lived there, concealed from view, doing something with their necks. Were these rich people, too? Did they also have stacks of cash? I presumed so. "This is my favourite spot," Barc confided to me.

Scratched by branches, nipped by thorns, I was a contented little boy, muddied and sullied in the forbidden woods. I followed Barclay up a knoll overlooking a still pond. Next to the water, an orange pennant flapped gently on a spindly flagpole imbedded in the greenest, shortest grass I had ever seen. Someone had gotten down on hands and knees to snip that lawn with scissors. Was this the kind of terrain Mom called a swamp? No wonder she enjoyed bogs so much. "That's a funny place to put a flag," I pointed out.

Barc sneered. "Don't you know anything? It's called a pin."

"I know lots of things," I retaliated.

"Like what?"

I had to think fast, and got lucky when I looked around. "There's goldfish in that swamp." A matron at the asylum, and several patients, had kept goldfish.

"Swamp?" Clearly, my choice of word offended him.

"In the lake."

"It's a water trap, dodo bird."

"There's goldfish in it. Lookit!"

"What did you expect to find in a water trap, squirrels? Do you think squirrels live underwater, Sparrow?" Faking a delirious laugh, he hung onto the trunk of a birch to hold himself upright. "Do fish fly and birds go swimming? Are you as crazy as your mother's supposed to be?"

The whip-crack of my voice. "My mother's not crazy!" Mmm, wait a second. Even I knew that that statement had to be modified. "Not when she takes her medication."

Barclay's fake mirth came to a herky-jerky, halting stop, a job he made look more difficult than suppressing hiccups. Slowly he caught his breath. "That's true, Sparrow." For a second I believed that we were forming a friendship. We might become pals. "She's not crazy."

"You're telling me."

"How can she be crazy when she's already dead?" Barclay jack-knifed into his aggressive belly-laugh once more.

I heard what he said, I took it in, I weighed and measured the remark. No one had broached the possibility with me before. My mother, dead. Her good parts, such as her smile and her warmth and her scent, vanished into heaven. Leftover parts, such as her body, assembled in a box in the ground. Maybe, like the cowboy Hank, her brains had spilled loose. I mulled these things over, and when I was done I curled my hands into brave little fists and flailed them against Barclay's ribs.

"My mother's not dead! She flew into the sky."

"Dummy. People can't fly."

"They can too! I can fly. My mother can fly if she wants. My father flew down from the moon."

"You're crazy too. You should be locked up in the loony bin."

"Better than living at your house."

"Take that back!"

"Never!"

Barclay worked his greater size and the superior coordination that comes with being nine years old to frustrate my attack. As I grew tiresome, he neatly avoided my lunge, tripped me up, rolled me over on the ground, and plopped his fat ass down on my chest. The shame of it. My shoulders were bolted down by his knees. My wrists shackled by his hands. Worse, he leered into my face and demanded that I say, "Uncle." So I said, "Uncle." The moment he let me up I immediately resumed thrashing him again, this time provoking his ire and he sat on my chest with his face scrunched up in a devilish mask of contempt. "You said Uncle! You said Uncle! That means you quit. That means you give up. Say it again. Say Uncle!"

An impasse. Barclay could not trust my sincerity when finally I did—consent to repeat "Uncle" ten times. Out of respect for my innate fury he was disinclined to let me go. Tears sprang up, and really, I had much to lament. My father had spread his wings and drifted down from the moon, only to disappear without so much as a card on my birthdays. My mother had unfurled secret wings of her own and leapt into the sanctuary of night accompanied by a giant cowboy thief. I had been lured into a foreign country so that a peer, a boy, one of my own, potentially a brother, could berate me while sitting on my chest and pinning my shoulders against bare rock. I had plenty of complaints to cry about. As a child can best decipher in a fit of insight and stupor, the earth is a weird and terrifying place to be obliged to spend time. Barclay's knees convinced me that I had no way out. I was trapped, weighted by excessive gravity to the planet floor.

Nothing less than a miracle could revive my grim spirits.

Sat upon, riveted by my own demise, I was growing accustomed to the condition when out of the brightness of the sky, through the branches and early foliage, dropped a minuscule chip of the sun. My miracle. A pocked white ball hit the ground. Bouncing off a patch of soft earth, it decoratively imbedded itself in a salad of old leaves and dried twigs. Although the ball had landed slightly beyond our reach, both Barclay and I perceived it as a signal to end our ritual of torment and aggravation. This was more important. The appropriate reaction to any heavenly portent is to cease all shenanigans at once and get on with something neat.

My life had just been altered by divine intervention, and in keeping with someone in such a heightened state of consciousness, I uttered the first sensible words since the beginning of our debacle. "Get off me," I told Barc, and he did. Complying with my request indicated that he was equally affected by the miraculous occurrence.

Some boys wait the whole of their lives for a golf ball to plummet into their vicinity, or for a foul ball or a hockey puck to streak toward them in the stands. Such events are rare and, as a consequence, some boys never grow up. Had our foreheads been etched by angels declaring that we were the elect of God, Barclay and I could not have felt more fortunate or victorious. One of God's eggs had been spirited to us out of the sky, and it hadn't cracked. One egg, to be divided between the two of us. Initially, we blunted the issue of ownership to focus on our options.

"What're we going to do with it?" was the quiz that I broached to my older and wiser companion. As any child can appreciate, the one thing we could not do was leave it alone. This was the fisherman's pearl in the oyster, the farmer's wife's needle in the haystack, the child's lucky penny. This was the teenager's lay in the back seat of a DeSoto. This was our shot in the dark and we had to fire the trigger. Buckled with awe, neither of us had yet dared to touch the marvel.

"If we keep it," Barclay proffered, "at the end of the day we can sell it for a dime. That's one nickel each." Not having learned about money—cash hadn't been legal currency at Lougain—the prospect struck me as daring and extravagant. Real money! Fortunately, while I was easily converted, Barclay's precocious mind continued to spin. "If we leave it right where it is, and we go tell the golfer, he might give us a tip."

"What's a tip?"

"Where've you been living, on Jupiter? On Saturn? On Mars?"

"Lougain. My mom and me, we had a room there."

"Where was that, the nuthouse?"

I couldn't deny it.

"We might get a quarter for a tip," Barc explained, turning friendly again. "It's a gamble. A cheapskate golfer, we wind up with horse's manure."

What use we had for manure was beyond my ken. "We could keep it," I bravely ventured.

"What for?" Barclay emphasized his disapproval with a scowl.

"We could play with it." I was thinking, we could find a stick and whack it, and see what that did. And I was thinking, we could make hoops out of branches and bang the ball through them, as I had done in Lougain, and I wondered what my mother was doing right at that moment. Was she in the breeze, flying? Was she sailing through heaven? If she was looking for me she might have a better chance of spotting me if I was playing a game of croquet. The sound of an airplane brought my attention to the sky, and I searched for soldiers tumbling in the air. As I glanced down, the shadow of the plane floated across the fairway and at that precise instant I seemed to understand something, I didn't know exactly what. My knowledge of the world had suddenly transcended its usual parameters. I had achieved a rich new plateau of awareness. What a vista! How I wished that my mother could be there so I could tell her the good news. Mom, your shadow didn't fly away! It was an airplane's shadow. You still got your own good shadow attached to your feet. Flush with wisdom, I wanted to pluck the ball off the ground and stow it away as a child from another time might pocket a talisman, because I had been enriched and enlightened by its magic.

"I have a better idea," Barc said. We were still getting acquainted, still sparring, and I did not know then that it was intrinsic to Barclay's nature to always have a better idea. Snatching the ball, he ran through the bracken, shouting his favourite manifesto, "Follow me!"

Our foray intercepted carefree golfers' voices, a mix of lyrical cursing, jibing, and good-natured chuckles. "Hub's looking for his ball," one straggler joked to the other, "because he knows there's nothing in those woods but teenage pussy."

"That's one putt he'd like to sink."

"Take the penalty, Hub. Muck around in there too long you'll catch a disease."

In advance of the others, a man was using his club like a machete, thrashing the bushes. "Maybe it hit a tree! Maybe it ricocheted!"

"That's right. And maybe Betty Grable is in my waiting room right now, complaining that she has this itch." The largest of the men groped his crotch, hoisting loose paraphernalia before letting it all flop.

"Here," Barc let me know. We had emerged at the edge of the magnificent green fairway overlooking the water-trap stocked with goldfish. The men remained out of sight around the jut of woods. Delicately, Barc arranged the ball on a tuft of grass, it looked like a boiled egg in an egg cup, standard morning fare at Lougain. "Wait here, Sparrow. When I come back with the man, keep your ears wide open."

I laughed. "How'm I supposed to close them?"

"Don't get smart. If you hear me say, 'Isn't it a nice day?', pick up the ball and run like a house on fire. If I don't say that, leave the ball right where it is. Don't touch it. Get me?"

"A house on fire?"

"Isn't it a nice day? If you hear that, run."

"Okay."

"Wait here and don't touch the ball."

Is sneakiness inherited? The son of a mother who slipped over walls at night, I kept Barc in sight and followed him, remaining concealed. I was careful not to step on any rich people kissing on their stacks of cash. Barc jumped out at the golfer with the machete. My view of the man, as I hunkered down in the bushes, was from the bottom up. He was decked out in spiked white shoes, white socks, garish plaid trousers, a pink long-sleeved shirt and a light blue cardigan. Unlike the comic prop sported by Mr. Butter, this man's moustache, which was white, served him as a badge of status and authority. He was taller than most, and he had a nervous habit of removing his white peaked cap to wax the shine on his bald pate.

I didn't know it then, but the caddie who lumbered in the man's footsteps must have hailed from our district. A ruffian, his hair was greased back, he wore a rash of pimples across his chin and a cigarette dangled from the corner of his lips. The collar was turned up on his black leather jacket and he wore blue jeans in contrast to the white and paisley golfers. Later in my education I would learn that he was called a "rock." If he was really tough, he might be labelled a "hard rock." As a hard rock, the greatest effort he would extend in search of the missing ball was to bend back the leaf of a fern with his motorcycle boots, the sort useful for kicking. The bag of clubs across his shoulders was an undue burden for this boy, he had to readjust the load several times, snorting like a donkey.

"Mister!" Barc shouted, virtually in his face. "I found your ball."

Startled by this Puck who had leapt from the woods, the man was less swift than his friends to recover.

"Go ahead, Hub. Bang it out of there. Make the green in under ten strokes, I buy you a beer."

"Where is it, son?" the golfer asked quietly. Grateful for the respite, the caddie slid the bag from his sagging shoulders.

"I can show you where it landed, mister," Barclay told him, imitating the quiet voice. "Or I can show you where it bounced."

The man looked back at his partners, who had finally taken an interest in analysing their own shots. "Bounced?" he repeated.

"My friend's looking after it. If you want I can show everybody where it really landed. If you want." A mirror of the caddie, Barclay slouched, shrugged, and demonstrated that the outcome made no difference to him.

"This is my lucky day," the man mentioned. Reaching into his pockets he slid a dollar from his wallet and passed it to Barclay. "You know, a boy like you can go a long way if you put your mind to it. Take me. I'm a self-made man. I wasn't always a rich sonofabitch."

Some men made themselves? First he made himself one thing and then he made himself something else? First he was one thing and now he was a rich sonofabitch?

"Yes, sir," Barclay agreed. He crushed the bill in his fist. "The ball's over here. Follow me!"

"The damn ball bounced in my favour," the golfer announced.

"Bullshit."

"That's what the boy says. Come see for yourself."

I raced back to our secret nest. The men and their caddies came along to observe our magic egg. Barclay never mentioned that it was a nice day. Instead, he regaled the golfer with a version of how the ball "binged" off trees and "zinged" off rocks, "I had to duck it three times before it pooped out on the grass."

The golfer spit in his hands before giving them a vigorous wash. "It's a fucking three wood." He strode right up to the ball, asked me to stand back, and gave it a whack. It soared, it sailed up to the sun, veering close to heaven where my mother might catch it, then curved back down again. It bounced where the grass was greenest and rolled near the pin. That made the other men throw their clubs on the ground and curse him. I wasn't used to that kind of language, it reminded me of the soldiers who visited my mother at night. After the angry men had left, the happy golfer said, "What's your name, sonny?"

"Barclay, sir. This is my friend, Sparrow, sir."

"Mr. Hubble. Pleased to meet you, Barclay. You're my kind of kid. Grow a little, then come around the clubhouse. Ask for me. You can be my caddie any day." Immediately he spun, swatting the back of his current caddie's head. "What're you waiting for, Christmas? Get moving!"

"Thank you, sir," Barclay said, whether for the offer or for belting the caddie I wasn't sure.

"Good luck to you, son." A dozen steps away, the man turned around and looked directly at me. "Half-pint. You. What did he say your name was?"

"Sparrow."

"Say, 'sir'," Barclay hissed at me.

"Sir."

"That's your nickname."

"That's his real name, sir," Barclay attested. "Honest-to-God, Sparrow's his real name, like the bird."

"I see." The sage Mr. Hubble nodded several times. "Good luck to you too, son. You might need it."

On our walk back through the woods, Barclay slipped me a dime. "Take it. It's your share." Real money. The coin in my pocket signalled a victory of sorts, a private triumph. Blissful in my ignorance, I accepted the token with pleasure, knowing only that I had survived the day and that somehow I had prospered. The money was my proof. It's too bad, really, that the past must be contaminated by the knowledge of more recent events. In light of his current notoriety, it was quite a distinction to have been one of the first rooked out of his money by Barclay Boisvert. Handing me the dime bonded our friendship, I felt fraternal with him, and even today boast that that was probably the first and the last time that Barclay Butter would allow anyone to take ten per cent of his earnings.

*

"You cannot go through life calling me Mr. Butter," Mr. Butter said.

"I can't say your name."

"Maybe so. I have decided that you ssshall call Mother, 'Aunt', and you sssshall call me, 'Uncle'. Can you ssssay 'Uncle'?"

Barclay had taught me a secret scripture. To say Uncle means to quit. It means to give up.

"Sssssay Uncle," Mr. Butter insisted.

I sat with my head down.

"Goodness gravy, child, I know you aren't sssstupid. Sssay my name."

"Mr. Butter."

"No. Uncle. Now say it."

Mrs. Butter stepped softly into the room with her wide smile and skin as flaky as pie crust. "Can you call me Aunt, dear, or Auntie?"

"Aunt," I said. "Auntie."

"All right. Once more from the top. *Uncle!*"

I would not call him that, I would never call him that until I knew exactly what I would have to give up.

Four people for dinner, what kind of an asylum was this? In such a small group I was too exposed, too closely evaluated. Mrs. Butter would walk through the living room, pause to give me a hug and a kiss, and by osmosis my skin would be dusted with flour. She prepped me for baking. Every time she called me into the kitchen I half-expected to be stuffed in the oven. I sat down at the table, put my napkin on my lap, and bowed my head for the prayer.

"The Chinese are warring among themselves—"

"Gerald," Mrs. Butter stopped him. "Grace."

"We thank thee for this food amen." We could lift our heads up now. "The Chinese are fighting it out, Ssssparrow. Looks like the Reds'll win. Imagine that. Communist China. If they get organized they'll land on our doorstep by Monday noon."

"Sparrow and me, we'll mow them down," Barc reassured his father. He had handled me, yet I felt that his confidence in our fighting ability was misplaced. "We'll beat them back with hockey sticks!"

"A-bombs, and plenty of them, while they ssssleep, that's our best bet. That's our only hope. Do it fast, and while the Yanks are at it, sssspare a few for the Ruskies. Obliterate Moscow, wipe it off the map, then we can get ssssome sssense in the world."

"Stop that," Aunt objected. "You'll frighten Sparrow."

"Ssssparrow's a sssssoldier, Mother. He's been through the wars. He won't frighten easily."

"What wars?" Barclay was legitimately intrigued, and so was I.

"The war of life, ssson. He's been to battle and back again. Did you tell him all about it, Sssssparrow?"

My swift elevation to noble warrior would have been more fully appreciated had I known what he was talking about. Confounded by his reference, I nodded in the negative.

"A giant bandit,"—Mr. Butter put down his fork—"ssshoved his pistol right into my cheek. He threatened to sssssshoot. An elbow in the gut, a punch in the jaw, he dropped like a whore's drawers."

"Gerald," Aunt fumed.

"Ssssorry, kids, you're too young to know what that means. He hit the floor. Thank God I was able to kick his gun away. That's when he ssssscrambled to his feet and ran away. The sssad part of it is, he was ssso ssscared of me he took Ssssparrow's mom hostage and jumped off the train. Once he found out there was a sssssoldier on board, he panicked. Didn't even look, just jumped off the bridge. Isn't that right, Ssssparrow?"

I consented to paint my friend's father as a hero. Over my head loomed the attic, and the prospect for banishment beyond the common geography of this family, not to mention the rest of humankind. Barclay repeatedly pestered his dad for exploits. He wanted suspense, danger, fist-fights. As—the evening lapsed into night, Mr. Butter provided his son with a shoot-out. By the children's bedtime, as he sipped his port, Mr. Butter confessed that he had had to fire on one of the cowboys. Pulled from the river, the man's scalp had been creased by a bullet.

"Where'd you get the gun, Dad?"

"It belonged to a policeman, one of the passengers. I picked it up after he was wounded."

"Is that true? Is that true?"

"Sssssparrow? You must remember?" Mr. Butter prompted me.

Threat may not have been intended, but I felt under seige. My silence had already bolstered his lies, and I did not know what punishment might be doled out in this asylum if I spoke up now. Travelling, I had battled him mile by mile on neutral turf. Now that I was held captive in his house, I believed that I was at his mercy. "Deputy was hiding under the seat," I admitted. I told Barc, "The man they pulled out of the water had no top to his head."

"Oh, puke!"

"I said the Deputy was wounded, but you're right, Sssssparrow, he was hiding. Sssssomebody had to fight that battle, ssso I took the pistol right out of his holster. Didn't want to sssay that part, wanted to protect the good man's reputation."

"Come along now, Sparrow," Aunt invited, "story-hour is over. It's time for beddybyes."

Decked out in colourful pyjamas, Barclay's hand-me-downs, I was escorted into the attic by Mrs. Butter. She taught me the easiest way to use the pulley, "in case you have to go toity in the middle of the night," and she bequeathed a hug garnished with talcum powder as well as flour. I was tucked into my lonely pallet on the floor like dough left alone to rise at night. "Sleep tight, Sparrow."

"What?"

"Sleep tight. Don't let the bugs bite."

"What bugs?" I jerked upright.

Tears dampened the tea biscuits of her cheeks. "You poor child. You poor brave little boy. There aren't any bugs. That's only a saying. Sometimes we say things just to make fun. Sometimes we don't mean exactly what we say. Have a good night's sleep, Sparrow."

"Okay."

In that dark, more strongly than I had since her disappearance, I sensed my mother's presence. And by extension, her absence. I breathed her scent and looked into the zany mystery of her eyes. I got up and looked through her stuff. Smelled her in her clothes. Opening a book, I came upon her floating hearts. The book had been on top. I placed it in the middle of her things to keep the dried flowers, the emblems of her youth, very safe.

In the years before my birth, my mother used to pee outside at night, a story that had had something to do with my being born. The impulse, then, came to me through a worthy line of descent. I chose a quiet hour and rose a second time from my bed like a phantom, creeping on my hands and knees across the planks. I worked the hatch with a minimal number of squeaks, crawled down the ladder and slipped through the kitchen, stepping outside into the night's quiet.

Under a lopsided cradle of moon, I peed on Mrs. Butter's flowerbeds.

Listen to the sounds awhile. Cats do battle, a distant drunk brays at a siren miles off. Look for my mother across the lonesome breadth of sky, listen for her in the percussion of philandering footsteps on the street. Below the awesome canopy of dark, terrified by the spooky trees, by the disconsolate tintinnabulation of leaves, my childhood is put at risk. This covert adventure proves my heritage, less an act of defiance than a necessary ritual of confirmation. Outside, I connect to the memory of my mother, I affirm my closeness to her, an affection and allegiance that supersedes these new and imposed circumstances. I take time to verify who I am and where I have lived before. This is not my place, I tell myself, this is somebody else's place. Peeing in the outback of night enforces the impression that this must not be my home. I must not belong here. Wanting me to stay here means people want me to become somebody else. Peeing, below dark, I am not that other person. I'm ... me, my mother's Sparrow. And in my bed again I know a token peace for the first time in a multitude of tumultuous days.

In the weeks, months, indeed years, to come, this nocturnal escapade became my habit, and I eluded detection, remarkable for my age. I peed on the flowerbeds. Each morning before going downstairs I made sure to pull on my socks to disguise the muddy, grass-stained soles of my feet.

*

Barclay's tour had transcribed the boundaries of my district for me while unveiling a flea market of prospects. Railway tracks limited Park Extension on two sides, east and south, and only the daring recalcitrant adolescents Mr. Butter was fond of cursing crossed into the nether, and French-speaking, regions beyond. To the north, Crémazie Street, the extension of a dirt highway thick with traffic, barricaded our settlement from wild and boundless fields and scruffy woods. The west side was restricted by the golf course. While the fairways were considered a natural adjunct to our range, the affluent town beyond it—called the Town of Mount Royal, commonly referred to as "The Town"—was inherently hostile to our ragamuffin presence. (In time, I would learn that I was a bad influence on any child from that privileged locality, a danger to the security of every home, and a leech, for reasons that remain unknown. Over time, I would ascertain that I was a Park Extension Bum, and there was no use arguing my southern heritage and birthplace because everybody here came from somewhere else. We were all a bunch of D.P.'s.) Brave adolescents might search the world in three directions, but a citizen of Park Ex, a "bum," normally would wait for a civilized age of adulthood before venturing into that western kingdom. This was the domain of the rich, the horizon to which Barclay routinely cast his eyes. He had kindly defined the limits for me, but, as his gaze remained attentive across those prominent borders, it was left to his father to initiate me into the district's core.

True to his claim, Mr. Butter was a bookkeeper, maintaining a modest business out of cramped quarters on Blair Avenue above the Laurentian Bank. I enjoyed dropping by whenever Barc took me along to mooch a nickel or a dime, delighting in the rhythm of the secretaries' typing and Mr. Butter's wrenching of the manual adding machine. I enjoyed the magical order amid the chaos of papers. The drudgery of business and computations is rarely an admissible realm to a child, for that reason I treasured my visits to the hot, stuffy rooms.

Air-conditioning in those days was Kleenex, rubbed languorously across damp brows. The senior secretary, a remarkably skinny, faintly ill-humoured woman, filled her waste-basket daily. On the scorching afternoons of summer, fans came down from the roofs of the filing cabinets to blast gale-force winds across the room. Witnessing the ensuing paper chase was a delightful form of cheap entertainment.

Apart from his prosperous little business, Mr. Butter's job was to deliver his wife's home-baked pies, buns, and pastries twice a day to three restaurants on busy rue Jean Talon. He left too early on his first round for me to go along, but a second run late in the afternoon, shortly before the supper hour, was convenient. Raisin. Cherry. Apple. Lemon meringue. Each pie was handled like an ancient feudal crown and placed securely on a slab of wood, with fiddles, fitted across the back seat of his trusty black Ford. Going with him I sat up front, and while I was never permitted to carry a pie, Mr. Butter prided himself on introducing me around. The entire excursion could be accomplished in under twenty minutes, although he usually extended our itinerary to include chats with business clients. Everybody knew Mr. Butter and treated him with courtesy. And yet, perhaps because I was sensitive to that sort of thing, I noted that his presence was not always welcome. People were polite. Genuine friendliness was reserved for customers or others who had wandered into the store to pass the time. In the course of my childhood, and from Mr. Butter's own pronouncements, I came to realize that he had made it his mission in life to keep everybody honest. "Better to go bankrupt," he would preach to the unconverted with an infuriating wag of his forefinger, "than to cheat on your taxes." Among all creditors, governments came first, and he had many feuds with clients by insisting on depleting their coffers with a tax bill while refuting their arguments for fresh inventory. He bullied people. Ethics were his weapons. He adopted a righteous tone and vocabulary. If he could not burden someone with a lesson on fiscal responsibility, he inflicted a war report, elaborating on his exploits in Europe. When the past failed him, he terrorized listeners with prophecies of horror and degradation, the imminent triumph of Communism and the subsequent disintegration of the West.

On my first trip in his company, the range of his power and influence impressed me. Comfortable, successful merchants were chided for the inadequacy of their window displays, the dourness of their personnel. "Ssssshopping ssshould be an experience, not a chore. Make it exciting. Make it fun. And for God's sssssake, ssssweep the floor. Is this a barnyard or a haberdashery?" Store owners who cited a cash shortage that precluded renovation, or who sighed that their loyal customers liked things done a certain way, were mercilessly chastised.

"Have they been given a choice? Times are changing fast. Don't get left behind in a cloud of dust."

The pet-store owner received a tongue-lashing for a sale on mutts. "If you sssee a nice car, do you go out and buy a bicycle? No. Never. You sssave, you borrow, you purchase a car. Educate your customers. The sss-mart money is in pure-breds. Go after it."

"This is poor neighbourhood, Mr. Bo'vert. Who wants buy pure-bred dog? I sell kittens, me, a turtle, a budgie on a good day. Lots of hamsters."

"Drabinski, wake up! You are right next door to one of the most affluent communities in the country. Where do you think the rich buy pets, Outer Mongolia? Sssshake a leg, Drabinski! Get cracking! Think big! If you can't think big, at least think bigger! Think breeding!"

Every business person visited was convicted of malfeasance, and after we were on our way he railed against their general incompetence. "Sssmall-timers! Pea-brains! Are they allergic to money? Does it make them sssssneeze? They'd rather indulge petty quarrels and petty ambitions and petty, petty ssssssales. Would you rather ssssell a Rolls Royce or an ice cream cone, Ssssparrow? Answer me!"

"I don't know what a Rolls Royce is," I admitted, timidly, not wishing to be catalogued among the legions subject to his rebuke.

"Exactly. Neither do any of these petrified numskulls. It's a car, Ssssparrow. It's a big, beautiful, wonderful car."

After deep thought, I decided, "I think I'd like to keep the car. I don't think I'd sell it." Which started him chuckling to himself and broke his truculent mood.

How did Mr. Butter keep his clients? That was one mystery I would investigate in time. People didn't appreciate being badgered by him, nor did they value being told how to run their businesses. These were scrappy, proud, tough people who silently submitted to his rebuke. He was no great entrepreneur himself. What I would decide, over my first ten years in his household, was that he was cheap, and low prices can sometimes purchase a modicum of loyalty. Not being a Chartered Accountant, his fees lagged behind the going rate. As well, his moral integrity eclipsed reproach. He was unyielding with figures and appropriate fiscal principle. He would never cook anybody's books, would not so much as allow a ledger to simmer, and he used that reputation to browbeat clients with his own high and mighty ethical stature. Shop-keepers, I believed—and I was onto something even though I was unfamiliar with the whole story—subjected themselves to his florid rants because they were afraid of him.

Still, it remained a mystery. He wielded power over those who thought of him as a fly among men, eminently swattable. They took his insults, and they took them again. If he had been anybody else, shop-keepers would have given him the boot, but they listened to Mr. Butter's verbal abuse without fighting back. A conundrum not easily deciphered.

Not that he was universally feared. On one of our excursions that first summer he quickly grabbed my hand and ushered me across Jean Talon, dangerously dodging traffic. No way to teach a six-year-old how to cross the street. I heard catcalls in our wake. On the other side, at the curb we had just abandoned, men in coveralls coming out of the tavern were mocking him, slinging curses at us with sibilant *esses*. I repeatedly looked over my shoulder at the small mob, fascinated, and Mr. Butter yanked me away, furious with my interest in the men.

"Commies!" Mr. Butter muttered once we were safely beyond their range. And he confessed, "They didn't like the result. Sssso what? Is life fair? They sssssay I ssssold them down the river. That was their favourite phrase, I ssssold them down the river. Sssso what? Can't they ssssswim? Bunch of commies. None of them was brought to this country to go on ssssstrike. They're here to work! I ssssaved them money by getting them back on the job. Do they appreciate that? Do they acknowledge that? Nossssirreebob, they want that extra nickel an hour. A nickel an hour! It would've taken another three weeks, minimum, to get that paltry nickel, and the money lost in three weeks would've taken a year and a half to make back. Commie ssscum don't understand that. They talk about sssaving face. They'd rather go broke themselves just sssso their boss sssuffers too. I did what I could for the pink finks. They don't understand the figures. They won't listen to reason. And that's what I am, Ssssparrow. That's what I ssstand for. If nothing else, know that I am the voice of reason in this sssssstupid ssssssstupid world."

He had his fingers in many pies, including his wife's. He was prone to dipping a digit through a whole in the crust to sample the filling. He'd lick the delinquent finger with great sucking noises and never offer me a bite, while pontificating on the decline of civilization as we knew it. "The whole kit and caboodle, Sssssparrow, will come crashing down ssssoon. Believe you me."

I did.

*

Beset by urges to pat, grab, tug, tickle and poke, Mrs. Butter could asphyxiate me within her snug embrace and not be aware of the death for hours. I was not distressed. My mother and I used to lather one another with an abundance of hugs and an assortment of kisses, so this was nothing new. My uneasiness developed when I noticed that I was the sole recipient of her affections. Apart from a welcoming kiss reserved for her husband upon our arrival, she rarely touched the man. Of greater significance to me, Barclay was long overdue for a hug, while I was repeatedly starched to his mother's apron, sprinkled with flour, and baked in the rotisserie of her embrace.

Watching.

Alert.

Every gesture observed.

Every movement traced.

They balanced my life in their hands, these people. Whenever I was juggled between their palms, I had to be nimble, I had to be quick. I had to consider scurrying up a candlestick.

Mrs. Butter reached across to flick stray dirt from her son's forehead. Barclay's response was worthy of a martial arts expert. Lightning fast, he routed her attack. "Don't touch me! I told you that before!" Aunt meekly explained about the smudge above his eye. "Maybe I want it there," he told her, "maybe I don't. Who hired you to remove it? I am quite capable, dearest Mother, of scrubbing my own face. Do I look like an imbecile to you? Some kind of monkey? We're human beings. Mother. Guess what? We talk! If something's on my face, say so, that's all you have to do. Speak up. Speak English."

"Of course, dear," Aunt acknowledged, and retreated. "Sorry, dear."

Instinctively, I feared that my condition was tentative, so I did not fend against Aunt's advances. One mistake and someone might toss me out the door among the yowling tom-cats. This home did not possess a hierarchy, there were no institutional guardians, no nurses bent on sympathy, no doctors willing to hear your case, no fellow inmates anxious to underscore your gripes. My role was to pretend that I was an integral part of the family, an act foreign to my experience. Instinctively, I knew that I had to take things as they came, observe, calculate, and play along.

Aunt was there to tuck me in and give me hugs. I liked her, and relied upon her mercy. Unlike Barclay, I permitted Aunt to wash my face, and presumed that this meant I looked like an imbecile to her, like some kind of monkey. But that was okay. The tactics of compromise are not easily learned, but I was an adept student.

*

School!

What did it mean? A place where children were mailed for the day? Did that make it an asylum for small-fry? Being dispatched to an institution sounded like a keen idea, what I couldn't understand was the anxiety of others. Especially Auntie's.

Registering my name, apparently, had proven difficult. Twice I went down to the school to be seen—and once, prodded and poked—by officials who needed to confirm that I was human. Questions of parentage were uttered, matters of legal guardianship discussed. The issue of citizenship was raised, my intelligence quotient tested. Perhaps I was more popular than expected, and various institutions, including asylums, were vying for the privilege of my attendance. In the end, the argument that swayed opinion was that I ought to be attending the same school as Barclay, and on one fine, warm morning, mere weeks before the summer holidays, Aunt, beset by the sniffles, marched me hand in hand off to Barclay School.

"Barclay's School?"

"That's right. It's called Barclay School."

That was impressive.

"Uncle wanted Barc to have a head start in life," Aunt explained. "He wanted him to have a strong English name. He wanted him to know where he was going in life. So he named him after the school."

Built penitentiary-style, in brick, three stories up with barred windows and a macadam school yard and a huge ball field inundated with thousands of maniacal screaming children, Barclay's Barclay School looked like a real institution to me, which was a comfort. Lining up double-file with the Grade Ones, Aunt adjusted my clothing while solemnly delivering her advice. "Keep your head up, Sparrow."

What a strange thing to say. How will I see if I'm watching the sky?

"Don't shuffle your feet."

I liked the sound of that. What's shuffle?

"Work hard."

Work?

"Don't fight."

With whom?

"Barclay will bring you home for lunch."

That's a relief.

"And remember, whatever you do ..."

Yes?

"...don't tell anyone you know how to fly. Children will tease you if they hear that, because children can be very nasty."

Got it.

She started to weep as I marched inside. And I thought, *Barclay squealed!* Because I had never told Auntie about my ability to fly.

Aunt had prepared me for the wrong experience. Whatever incidents jogged sour reminders in her, whatever grim fears denuded her perception of school, her wisdom did not conform to the experience. In her mind, sending me through the huge doors was tantamount to putting me on a troop ship destined for battle. Two of her brothers had sailed off to war never to return and she feared a similar fate for me. She had instilled such a high level of trepidation in me that it took a couple of days to slough it off. When I finally relaxed I ascended to an alternate reality—*I loved school!* The regimentation was wonderful. Ordered into disciplined lines, marched from the school yard up the stairs to class, made to sit with our hands folded on the desk and both feet on the floor—what could be more fun? In my case, what could be more reassuring? The Principal had a strap and the Vice-Principal used it. Anyone who misbehaved had to stand in the corner, or if they were really wicked, stand out in the hall where they trembled at the sound of the Vice-Principal's heels.

School was great. The routine was an improvement on asylum-life because school was populated with children. What a neat idea. Kids to play with. Girls and boys of every colour and hue, of every personality and character. Tough kids, mean kids, great kids, cherubs. Kids my age. In gym class I caught my first ball—no one had thrown me one before—and I became addicted to baseball. On Field Day I ran my first dash and skinned my knees tripping over the finish line. I was commanded to "run like crazy" then leap as far as I could across a dirt pit. I was airborne. Landing on my fanny did not earn me a scolding, only praise for the extraordinary length of my flight. "The sparrow flies," a teacher noted to a colleague.

Recess was a gas, we played tag and marbles and "pops." Striking the curve where the cement base of the school yielded to the brick with a tennis ball caused it to "pop" into the air. I got a few pops the first time I tried when I was six—a hundred in a row one time when I was ten. In class, we were taught all kinds of stuff—how to read and write words and we were told about boys and girls just like us who lived in the Congo and on the steppes of Lapland. Friday afternoons the teacher read us a story. *I liked school!*

Every day the bell at three-fifteen rang with regret, and my greatest concern in those early days was the rumour about summer holidays.

Kids warned me that the school would be locked and the teachers would stay home. I thought they were teasing me. I had been through hard times before, yet I couldn't accept that such a dreadful occurrence might befall me again.

Mrs. Butter's nightly tutoring failed to teach me otherwise. She asked if I ever got into fights, and I said, "Sure!", unable to censure my enthusiasm for scraps. She squeezed me against her side. In a quiet voice, she wanted to know how mean were my teachers, commiserating with me when I was obviously too sick at heart to even discuss it. All the teachers I had met were nice. Teary-eyed, she wondered if the bullies were making life miserable for me. I didn't tell her that the only person who pushed me around was her son.

In the days to come, whenever she did detect that I enjoyed the crass and difficult world of school and play and having friends, that I revelled in the tumult and hand-to-hand combat and the shenanigans and shouting, I could tell that she was offended, and I guessed that her disappointment in me was not trivial.

Children make the best of things. Open fields were being lost to housing, so kids quickly fashioned a new sport. The playgrounds were empty—parents, look for your children hanging around construction sites. We watched steam shovels excavate the earth, and later romped through the frames of apartment buildings, balancing on beams when there was no floor, climbing scaffolding as if ascending magic rungs into the sky.

I loved tottering on the roof beams to claim a throne.

I'm the King of the Castle!
And you're the dirty rascal!

Great entertainment, risky, and fraught with incidents. Nails sliced palms. Legs were broken in falls. Barclay was dumped inside a small cement-mixer one time and would have suffocated had I not come along and heard his clamour. He came away from that experience brittle and angry, with ruthless eyes. He didn't liked being picked on. But he never retaliated, coddling his venom within.

The best game was being chased about the timbers by one of the roving supervisors who would catch sight of trespassing kids during off-hours. Being only six, I was captured several times. Before I could be hung and garrotted, or whatever they did to children, other kids would taunt the man into giving up on me and pursuing more vitriolic game. Usually the man would be beer-bellied and slow, no match for the monkeys luring him up to the fourth floor only to slither back down with elan. Huffing and puffing, fending against a heart attack, the supervisor would descend into the net of our ridicule, then we'd run away, merry in our mischief, looking for a witch or a feeble grandfather to mock.

I was finding friends my age, I was fitting in. Adults with their eyes on me probably reported that I was adjusting. Life at school was great, and apart from my nocturnal habit of pissing on the flowers, life with the Butters was going well too.

And so I lurched off to the final day of school and my classmates were giddy and I was morose. Perhaps I was prescient. We overwhelmed our teacher with useless gifts. Aunt had wrapped a box of bubble-bath crystals, the most wondrous present of all, I believed. Our class photograph was snapped on the front stairs, each of us grotesquely squinting into a brilliant sun. The ringing of the noon bell was greeted by a roar, signalling summer, that rattled windows miles away.

Walking home, my gang followed a ragman and his horse-drawn cart of junk. I was impressed by his appearance and performance, the fearsome bray of his voice, "Rrrrraaaagggs! Rrrrrraaaaggags!" Given his beard and craggy face and heavy black clothes, the old man's look was not dissimilar to that of my mother's midnight demons, or so I imagined.

Then someone in our pack invented a new game. Work had stopped on the construction sites for lunch. The men slaked their thirst with large bottles of Kik Cola. They opened their lunch pails and checked under the top slice before biting into their sandwiches. Our new sport was to race through the unfinished buildings under the salacious eyes of the foremen and their crews. Sometimes we were chased, which was neat and frightening, and sometimes we were scolded in loud, boisterous Italian. One crew cheered us on while the foreman tried tackling us. Another row of men, perched above us on a rafter, tossed down the ingredients of their sandwiches.

Maybe summer wouldn't be so bad after all.

Making our escape from our last building, we noticed that a crowd had formed at the end of the block, at the corner of d'Anvers and de l'Epée. Me and Barclay went along with the others, it was more or less on our way home. Getting closer, the loud laughter quickened our pace into a run. Barclay must have been taking it easy, because I remember looking for him and he was way behind. Then he wedged himself through to the front row of the throng. The instant he saw what was going on, he was as stricken as me.

Mr. Butter was walking through the gauntlet of onlookers. His clothing had been stripped off, and he had been lathered in the gooey black tar intended for paving. He was dressed as well in chicken feathers. Actually, he was not walking, he was marching, a forthright military gait with a deliberate high swing to his arms. I could hardly look at him. I noticed his penis, unsheathed from its holster, dangling like a black pistol in the noon sun. Higher—eyes white with rage. He didn't seem to see me, or anyone. As he passed us, bits of feather floated up behind him, and his rubbery rear was graced with a thatch of feathers like an Indian chief's headdress.

His bare feet left black tracks along the sidewalk.

Barclay did not follow the trail, he did not accompany his father home. He ran off instead, aimlessly drifting through the open fields. I lagged behind him. He shied away from the well-travelled paths, preferring to stomp through the wild underbrush. Thistles scratched his ankles. Burrs clung to our pants. Eventually we crossed McEachren and slipped under the fence, trespassing onto the golf course. Barclay spent that afternoon sitting in the crook of a tree. I sat underneath him, too small to climb up beside him, too young to know what to say. The only time he spoke that afternoon, he said, "Look out below," and I dodged a stream of urine. Then he settled back into the crook again.

I wanted to say to him, "Cat got your tongue?" Pleased with myself for being able to use trick language. But I chose to mind my peace.

As the sun was setting Barclay climbed down, and silently we marched home, striding with our arms waving forward and back. Soldiers on parade. Shoulders back! Tummy in! Chests thrust forward like proud little warriors. We found Mr. Butter in his kitchen.

"There you are!" he bellowed, probably to Barclay although he may have intended to include me. "Come in here. Take a good look at your old man." Mr. Butter had not bothered to clean himself up. Or dress. He had prohibited his wife from scraping his skin. Sitting belligerently in his chair with the tar dried into a parched, cracked earth, and the feathers sticking out like those of a frazzled, angry grouse, he could easily be mistaken for a gigantic black rooster ready to crow.

Weeping, his wife stood against the stove. The smell of burnt pastry. Her posture was slumped forward and to one side, as though she had not been off her feet in hours. Sobs sputtered out of her as Mr. Butter stood up to expose his naked bestiality, and he did seem huge to me, a figure greater than any demon my mother had witnessed, a pterodactyl from the dawn of time. Black and feathered, he did bear a passing resemblance to my mythical dad, and perhaps that is what provoked such strong sympathy in me.

"Why am I disgraced before men?" he asked us. And answered, "Because I represent moral authority! I am the voice of reason against the unscrupulous mob, I am the voice of integrity that defies the anarchy of the human ssssoul. I am a proud man this day, gentlemen. Every feather on this sssskin I have earned, and I've earned this new sssskin. I ssstand before you with the ssstrength of the world's just men. Know this! I am true to my word. If I were a weak man, if I compromised my principles, if I knuckled under to sssscoundrels, and sssscum, then I would walk in tailored sssuits. Only because I have remained righteous and true, only because of that am I honoured by this hide. Do not be ashamed of your father's sssskin. Be proud of it. I've earned it. It's my badge of honour. I wear it with dignity. It's a sssuit of armour."

Speech over, he sat down. Poured himself another shot of rye.

Impressed by his performance, that night I did not sneak downstairs to piss on the geraniums. He was down there. Solitary in the kitchen. His eyes furled, his righteous anger, like Barc's, volcanic without a place to erupt. I knew that he was down there, braced at the table in the dark in the middle of the night, drinking whisky.

He was down there.

Dressed in my real father's clothes.

And in the morning, the three of us, Barclay and Mrs. Butter and me, plucked his blackened feathers while he slept.

After that, I agreed to call him 'Uncle'.

5.

Tunnelling

I looked for my mother on the streets and down the lanes. I looked for her in Aunt Butter's garden, at night, as the earth turned its stubborn back on the moon. I looked for her on the golf course and at the corner grocer's, and on the way to church each Sunday morning. In the ascending and descending colons of the earth, the tunnels beneath Park Extension, I dug for my mother. I hoped to catch a trace of her in the faces and minds of lunatics. Where was she? Would she make it to Canada? to Montreal? to Park Extension? How would she find Bloomfield Street? How would she find her way when I had been in possession of the map, and even that map and the letter proclaiming our legitimacy had been confiscated? I wandered grungy streets and searched the eyes of destitute women, not expecting to find her but striving to rekindle her look and appearance. Nothing terrified me more than the prospect of forgetting her. To forget her would be to abandon her, and I would never do that.

As snow fell—confirming Sturgess Rawlins' oracle—and the city retreated beneath a winter shell of parkas and ice, I worried that she had been left out in the cold. On baseball diamonds in summer, shading my eyes to catch an infield pop, I glimpsed images of her above the clouds. On canals carved in a municipal sandbox that I had flooded with water, impressions of her floated so distinctly I could cup them in my palms and hold them until the water drained through my fingers. Slippery images. I thought of her when I learned to swim in a northern lake, and swung from a rope to hurtle through the open air—fly, fly, with my wings spread wide—splashing down beside my friend and house-brother, Barclay Butter.

Where was she?

How was she?

Would we meet again?

I yearned for contact with her the first time I dated. The afternoon I brought home a report card clean of failures, I willed signs of her approval. My eyes scanned the spectators any time I slugged a fast ball over the right field fence. (A short fence, fortunately, and I batted left, although I threw right. That odd configuration I credited, illogically, to being my mother's son.) In school I attached myself to female teachers at the risk of being labelled their pet, and scuffled in the school yard to uphold the honour of their good names. I regretted testing myself as a thief the day I shoplifted candy, and swore that I was sorry the first time I woke up feeling rocky from guzzling Molson Ex.

Tying my shoelaces every morning reminded me that I had once enjoyed the company of a real mother. In the attic I reflected upon our nights together in Lougain. Depressed one day, I visited a cemetery and planted dandelions on a grave so old and decrepid the name of the tenant had been rubbed out. Growing up, I warned myself that nobody can tumble off a bridge and survive. And yet, death remained the more difficult adjunct. At an early age I had hitched myself to the notion that once upon a time in Neverneverland I had flown, and if I could fly, even for a split second, then she might have drifted down from the sky. Mom could have saved herself. It was possible. Love for her child—that alone, somehow—would be reason enough to accomplish the impossible.

I looked for my mother, and the years went by.

Early in life I started working. Which is not to invoke some Dickensian child-labour horror, I merely suffered from various boyhood diseases, most notably a virus of independence and a strain of entrepreneurial flu. The remedy was to accept a position in Ludmilla Cherkova's basement.

Her home served as a depot for carriers of *The Montreal Star*, our city's afternoon newspaper, now defunct, and my duties there would include counting out the papers for each route and keeping things tidy. Day one on the payroll—Uncle Butter followed me into the dank, dim basement, resting a protective hand upon my shoulder. Loathe to relinquish me to the commerce of the city, he had come to insist upon a job description.

"Vhat's dis?" my boss asked. She had not meant to hire us both.

"Ludmilla Cherkova, I understand that you have commissioned young Ssssparrow Drinkwater into your sssservice."

The woman was unaccustomed to Uncle's level of formality. Never did she tame her stringy grey hair, she had big lips and a massive nose and her eyes were soft and tiny. Hefty, she preferred to wear men's clothes. Boys admired her gruff demeanour. "He vant job. I give it him job. Vhat's problem?"

"We need to know, Mrs. Cherkova, precisely what are his duties."

"Verk. He vill verk."

"We understand that much, Ludmilla Cherkova. Sssurely you can accept, that before we can allow an eight-year old to be indentured into your modest enterprise, we must become acquainted with his tasks. In precise detail. We must reach agreement concerning his ssssstarting sssalary. What will be his hours?"

"He vill clean."

"Ahh. Sssparrow keeps his attic very neat. He will do a good job of cleaning up."

"He vill unpack bundles, ya? He vill count papers."

"You've chosen wisely. His arithmetic sssskills are excellent."

"Not so important, 'rithlemetic. Need courage, ya?"

"Pardon me?"

"Stop boys cheatink, dat's his job."

"Ssssparrow? You didn't tell me. You're following in my footsteps!"

A coded phrase for adults.

"What will the lad's ssstarting ssssalary be, Ludmilla Cherkova?"

Actually, this was one question that intrigued me as well.

"Vhat is startink celery?" Mrs. Cherkova complained. "Vhat you mean *startink*? He vill startink fifteen cents hour, he vill finishink fifteen cents hour."

Satisfactory to me.

"Will he have a job-title? Work that carries sssso much responsibility ought to have a name."

"Vhy sure! I call him Bigshot. Me, I call him President." She laughed.

Nonplussed by sarcasm, unbowed by humour, Uncle pressed on. "Does your enterprise have an assistant manager, for instance?"

"Husband, he assist."

"Then how about Assistant to the Assistant Manager? Would that be fine? It'll look good on his C.V."

"Fine wit' me."

Fine wit' me too.

Uncle took me aside. "Ssso Ssssparrow, what a sssurprise! You are to be the one who prevents cheating! A great responsibility. You sssshould feel honoured that Ludmilla Cherkova has chosen you for this task. Ssshe must feel that you are a person of great integrity, sssomeone who can be trusted. As do I. Sssome of us must keep this sssssociety honest, and if that obligation has fallen upon me, it makes me proud that you, too, are willing to accept the sssame charge. This is a good job, Sssspar- row. Perform your tasks with honour and with dispatch."

Admittedly, a momentary dread did drift through me. Would I be tarred and feathered too, was that the cost of being responsible for the world? The foreboding passed as I basked in the pleasure of his praise. "Okay, Uncle," I told him, hoping he would never be obliged to pluck my hide.

Left alone with Ludmilla Cherkova in the basement of her house, I snooped around for something to do while she kept an eye on me. The sprinkle of a smile dampened the brutish, chronic suffering on her face. "Ve vait," she directed at last. "You vould drink milk, ya?" Side by side, while she sipped her tea and I downed my milk, we anticipated delivery of the afternoon edition.

I *knew* it! Barclay put up a stink. The rise in my station as a working man-of-the-world carried implications—he would not tolerate the change. Curling himself in his arms while sitting in a kitchen chair, he rhythmically banged his heels against the linoleum floor. He could have patented that tantrum. Nobody's rube, Barclay could predict, as could I, that the immediate effect of his performance would be my banishment to the attic.

I was summarily dismissed up the ladder.

From my aerie—the trap door raised a crack—I listened to the family quarrel.

"Barclay," his father pleaded, and I could rely upon him to keep faith with logic, "Sssparrow ssssolicited that job on his own initiative. The boy ssshowed gumption. I wasn't involved. I was not playing favourites."

"Last year *I* wanted a newspaper route—*you* said I couldn't have one."

"I never said anything of the sssort."

"Liar! Liar! Pants on fire!"

I had learned from my years in this family that in the midst of a tantrum Barclay Boisvert had the edge. As a tactic, losing control worked beautifully. Uncle's whine of a voice was both defensive and sub- missive, although he never relinquished the high ground of pure reason.

"I distinctly remember sssaying that a newspaper route was not up to your sssstandards."

"That's the same thing as saying no."

"There's a distinction. Listen, if you want a newspaper route," Uncle offered, "go out and get one."

While Barclay mulled over his decision, I lifted the trap-door wider, poking my head down to yell, "There aren't any positions! Mrs. Cherkova doesn't have any openings!" I was anxious to help Barclay understand his options.

"Ssssparrow!" my guardian called out. "Sssshut that hatch!"

The family wanted to protect me from Barclay's tantrums, that's how Aunt had explained it. He was not a good role model whenever he worked himself into a state. Perhaps Aunt and Uncle feared that I might emulate his techniques.

"Tell him there's no positions, Uncle!"

Armed with this untoward information, Barclay chose to be defiant, demanding, "I want a paper route!"

"He can't—"

"Sssssssshut that hatch!"

"I want a paper route!" Barclay emphasized his point by kicking his heels. As these episodes always occurred in the kitchen in the same chair, Barc's chair, the linoleum had crazed where his feet had thrashed damage.

"Sparrow," the quiet voice of Aunt Butter dictated directly below me, "close the hatch. It's not polite to listen in." I had no weapons to combat her gentle voice.

"Yes, Auntie." I shut it for a second before springing it open again. "Tell Barc there's no openings!"

"Now there's no openings!" the boy shrieked with criminal despair. "I could've signed up last year. Now Sparrow has a job first! He's younger than me. I'm supposed to be your real boy. He's not even adopted."

I closed the hatch. Barc's loud voice carried through the floor. I could not hear Uncle any more, and guessed that he was placating his son, doing his best to soothe him into silence. Uncle and Aunt had learned over time to strike a bargain whenever Barclay pulverized the floor. They had also figured out that their best tactic was to sell me down the river. On my bed, listening, I wondered what the deal would be this time, how far and how swiftly I'd be washed away.

Eventually the voices were too still for me to detect, a sure sign that negotiations had begun in earnest. Once concluded, Aunt popped her head up through the trap, smiled sweetly, and invited me to climb downstairs. Should I ever be executed at dawn, at least I'll be accustomed to that last, lonely walk. Though my heart might flutter, my knees won't fail me.

I made the descent down the ladder. Subdued at last, Barclay continued to occupy his temper-tantrum-chair in the kitchen, rubbing his red and swollen eyes.

"Ssssparrow!" Uncle announced, delighted to see me. "Barclay and me've been talking."

"I won't quit my job," making my position clear from the outset.

Uncle enjoyed a quiet chuckle to himself, stopping when he noticed that his good humour only provoked my ire. He assured me that quitting wouldn't be necessary. "It's not on the agenda. Barclay wants to put his name on the list to be a paperboy. That's all. Isn't that great?"

"He'll be number four. My name's already on the list. I'm number three. Mrs. Cherkova told me so."

Blubbering at this news for a bit, Barc slowly manoeuvred himself under control.

"What we've decided," Uncle informed me, simultaneously gesturing for me to come over and lean against his knee, "is that, sssince you have a job, you could let Barclay take your place on the waiting list."

For the first time, Barc chose to monitor my reaction as I assessed this news.

"Do you mean," I needed to verify, "he'll make paperboy before me?"

"Barclay's older." Uncle tried to win me over by holding his arm around my shoulders and giving me a squeeze. My disaffection, he hoped, might squirt free like toothpaste from a tube.

This time, I was the one who shed a few tears. "My name's already on the list," I pointed out.

"That's true. Then again, Barclay sssshould have had his name on the list a year ago, he misunderstood sssomething that I sssaid. Sssso it really would be fair if he went ahead of you, don't you think?" He wiggled his moustache. "Besides, you have a job. A very important job. You keep the other boys honest. It might be a long time before a route comes open. This way, you and Barclay can work together sssssooner. Isn't that great?"

I looked at Barc, who was watching me through teary eyes. I felt sorry for him, and sympathized with his point of view. How could he have a boy younger than him living in his own house and earning more money than he did? Under the light of that wisdom I would concede my place in line. One of the recent lessons in Sunday School had been about Jacob and Esau. I had had a hard time figuring out who was supposed to be the good son in that tale and who was the bad—wasn't every story supposed to have good guys and bad guys? Jacob had bullied

Esau out of his birthright, and subsequently he had tricked him out of their father's blessing, and that's where things got complicated. Esau seemed like the bad one, he ate venison and went hunting and he was hairy and his mother didn't like him much, but Jacob had done the tricky deed. His mother dressed him up in a goat's skin. Our teacher had tried to explain that doing the tricky deed had been good, because Jacob loved God but that's where things stopped making sense. Barc, like Esau, had a birthright, and he ought to be smarter than to sell it to me for a bowl of porridge. Okay. I could accept that. Barc was protecting his birthright—in everything, he was in line ahead of me—and he was making sure that I didn't trick him out of his blessing. Not wanting to be sneaky like Jacob, or to walk around in a hairy animal skin, I let Barc keep his allotted place in line.

"Sssshake on it," Uncle asked us to do.

This was the part I hated the most. You had to take your foe's hand and really give it a good thump, which sealed the pact for life. If you fought your enemy again you had to find an alternative grievance. What I resented about enforced handshakes with Barc was that they sealed his triumph and my defeat, every time, and having shaken his hand there was nothing that I could do about it or even say about it "in this world or the next." At times like these I'd wish I'd jumped into the river after my mom.

I shook.

Aunt cried, "Who's for a slice of cherry pie?"

"Me!" Barc sang out.

Losers are reluctant to celebrate defeat. I felt more reticent.

Aunt arched her left eyebrow. "With vanilla ice cream?"

"Me, too," I consented.

Perhaps the thought slipped into my mind at another time, when Barc and I were both much older, but I do remember thinking, "At least I don't have to eat his mushy porridge."

*

In Ludmilla Cherkova's basement, things happen.

Things you don't want to happen, happen.

My initiation to the world.

Pink, rat-faced Derek Mahoney pins Neil Abrahamson's arms behind his back and his girlfriend screams, "Hold him! Hold the little kyke!" She's fumbling in her purse. Her name is Maureen but Derek calls her Mo. She finds her butane lighter and the flame shoots six-inches high. Maureen is a tall girl with incredibly lush black hair they say makes all the boys go wild. She's thin and she wears mean jeans. She waves the flame as though burning down the house is a considera-tion and Neil gets a crazed look. He wants to spit in her eye, then his anger turns to fear, he's stricken, he's panicked, he's lost it. Mo holds him by the hair as she flaunts the flame closer to his nose.

Neil cries, "Maureen! Please! Don't do it to me!"

The flame warms one side of his cheek. "Kiss my ass."

"Why do I have to?" he wails, a lament that echoes off the walls of heaven. In the corner under the stairs I am counting out forty-four papers for Derek's route, forty-seven for Neil's, and I know what it means to have fear implode on the heart.

"Because I said so. Kiss my ass or I burn the hook out of your nose." Bringing the flame nearer to demonstrate.

"All right already I'll do it!" Through his tears.

"Do what?" He had to do it, and he had to say it first.

Quietly, the voice of humiliation, "Kiss your ass."

"Don't I have a name?"

"Maureen."

"Say all of it."

"Kiss your ass, Maureen."

"Say *please! Beg me!*" She waved the torch under his eyes.

"Why don't you leave me alone?"

"You wanna get toasted?" Flame singed his hair.

"Please, Maureen, can I kiss your ass, please?" His voice quaking with sobs. "All right I said it."

"I didn't hear you. Speak up."

"Let me kiss your ass, Maureen, please. Now are you satisfied?"

"Almost." Mo snuffed the flame. "On your knees, kyke." Neil did so, his arms pinned behind his back. Mo turned around and Derek shoved Neil's face into the crevice of the girl's jeans.

I'm thinking, I'm glad I'm not Neil. I'll sub for him, I'll do his route for him and let him go home. My gratitude for not being Neil is immense.

They force him to make slurping noises.

Other things happen.

Patty Correlli asks me if I'd like to look at her muffin. I'm not inter-ested in somebody's leftover lunch. Ten years old, I say no thanks.

Other things. Derek makes Neil pull down his pants. The boy's underwear has been bleached white. Neil must pull down his underwear too and he stands there, shivering. His prick huddles in the mat of hair like a scared white mouse in a medical lab. I'm counting papers. I'm concentrating hard. Losing track, I have to start over several times. Derek knees him in the groin and it hurts Neil so much tears are running down my cheeks.

He's moaning on the floor.

Derek takes off, whistling.

I will sub for Neil again.

He's crying and Ludmilla's husband, the Assistant Manager who never assists, happens to come downstairs and he figures out that everything is not sunshine and lollipops. So he invites us into his furnace room to show us an excavation he's begun. The hole is about six feet high and goes through the wall for about four feet. I ask if he plans to put a workbench in there, or a washing machine, but I don't believe he answers. Instead, Mr. Cherkova picks up a shovel and resumes digging.

That's his idea of keeping us entertained. That's his idea of offering comfort. Shovelling.

Ludmilla teaches me to drink tea. I have a cup with her every day. We talk and we drink tea and we wait for the late afternoon edition.

When I'm twelve, Patty Correlli asks me if I would like to pet her. She pulls her sweater out from the top and I peer down at her breasts. Two lovely plump breasts. My tongue has bonded to my teeth. My saliva feels like glue. Sweat steeps in my socks. I put my hand down her sweater and she says, "Don't get any ideas. Keep your fingers outside the bra." That's the deal. The material is slippery smooth. I rub the outer stitching with my thumb. Patty slips a stick of gum in her mouth while I do this and afterwards I help her deliver her papers.

The police come over one afternoon to have a cup of tea with Ludmilla and me, and we talk. When Derek Mahoney shows up they take him away and I have to do his route that day and again the next. We hear he's been sent to reform school. Derek's mother shows up at the depot and she's crying. She has a cup of tea. She says please don't punish Derek any more, he's just rambunctious, he's been through enough, please let him keep his route, he loves his paper route, it's the one thing in life he's got going for himself, he's proud of his paper route, that boy, he's not a juvenile delinquent or anything like that, he's just rambunctious. So I do his route, plus my own job, until Derek's rehabilitated.

Neil has a smile on his face for three months. "I'm going to get that guy," he lets me know. "I got something cooking. A surprise. He better not pick on me again."

So I'm curious. "Judo?" I ask him.

"Better than judo," he swears. "My uncle's in construction."

Patty Correlli shows me her muffin when I'm not looking. I'm on my knees counting papers when I glance up, and there it is. It looks furry and pleasant only there isn't much to see. Her muffin gives me lockjaw and blocks my sinuses. She never asked my permission to show it to me. Two years had passed since I had touched the outside of her bra and she had never given me another chance. I turn around and she displays it for me, with one stipulation. "Tomorrow, you show me what you got."

Mo drops in. She's anxious to do me a favour because I've been kind enough to take Derek's route for him. She will do the collecting. I deliver the papers, she collects the money. Sound fair? I don't say a word. She puts a cig in her mouth and flicks the butane lighter and the flame has got to be a good eight inches high. So I say okay.

I let Patty examine what I've got. She's never had a close-up look before. Outside Ludmilla's basement she's a nice girl. I don't know what she thinks but she seems more surprised than impressed.

Other things happen. Things I can't figure out. Ludmilla has friends who visit from time to time. If they're present when the papers arrive they carry their tea downstairs. One old fogy stares at me, and sometimes he weeps. I ask Mr. Cherkova about this and he explains that it was the war. "Oh," I'm saying, "the war. Did he have a boy like me?"

Mr. Cherkova looks at me curiously, as though I'm stupid, and he blows out a gust of air. His breath smells like a clogged drain pipe. Dirt is impacted under his fingernails and ground into his skin from the constant digging. He says to me, "He *was* a boy like you."

But not in the war, I'm thinking. He had not been a boy in the war.

Derek comes back from Shawbridge—the boys' farm—rehabilitated. He thanks me for looking after his paper route. He says, "Thank you, Sparrow. You're a pal." I say it's okay, that I know it means a lot to him. He asks me for the three months collections he missed. "Should come out to around forty-five bucks, with tips." He even wants me to hand over the tips. I'm looking at the floor. Possibly trembling. "Pay me," he says, and then, because he's been rehabilitated, he adds, "please." I tell him Mo has the money, that she's been doing the collecting. Derek says he'll look her up. Neil comes in the door just then and Derek shouts, "Hi!" and slaps the boy's back. "How're you doing, Neil? How you been?"

I found out that getting my own paper route wouldn't be easy. Walter Fishman quit, but his route didn't go to the next name on the list. Walter's younger brother Gordon got it. Ludmilla consoled me. She explained, "Dat happen sometime. Ve allow route stay in fam'ly. Customer like it dis vay. Paperboy like it ve revard good servicink. Valter vas good boy. Fishmans poor peoples, dat's one think keep in mind, you."

"That bitch stole my money!" Mo has run away from home, that's Derek's report. What a relief. He doesn't expect me to pay him. Derek is definitely different than he used to be. Since he's been back he hasn't kneed anybody in the groin.

Mr. Cherkova shows me his excavation again. This time it's sixteen feet long, and at the end there's a ladder heading down. "What's it going to be?" I wonder out loud.

"What it is, is what it's going to be." That's his philosophy.

I stare, I worry that the walls will crumble and we'll be buried. "So what is it?" I have to ask him. I have no choice. I can't figure it out. He laughs as merrily as I have heard him, tickled by my dumbness.

Then he reveals his secret. "It's a tunnel."

Derek is lingering at the depot later than usual—unnecessarily, I think. His customers will be waiting. Neil always arrives late to avoid bumping into Derek and today he walks in and his enemy is right there, waiting for him. Derek, who is older—he turned sixteen while Neil is two years younger—claps him on the shoulder and shouts, "Neil! See you around!" Then he takes off to deliver his papers.

After packing his *Montreal Stars*, Neil carries the first bag out to his wagon. Before hoisting the second bag, he asks me, "Why's he being nice to me already?"

"He's reformed. I don't know. Maybe he's scared about going back to the boys' farm. Don't forget, he's almost old enough for Bordeaux Jail."

Neil hopes that what I say is true. "He better not bother me again, the creep."

"You're telling me. He better watch out. I heard your Uncle's in construction."

Things keep happening in Ludmilla Cherkova's basement.

*

Mother, you'd have been proud of me. The thermometer on our back porch reached the lowest level on its scale, minus forty Fahrenheit, scrunching down there out of sight for three days. Out west where the air is dry a man can survive in weather like that, or so I'm told. In the humid east, the cold seizes joints and burns the skin. At our depot the tough guy was supposed to be Derek Mahoney, he was the bully we feared the most, our psychopath earning credits toward an institution. He stayed home to play Monopoly, walloping opponents with nooggies on their biceps if they made an aggressive move. Our tough guy had called in sick. The "hard rock" couldn't take the cold. Four years his junior, I was obliged to assume the task of delivering Derek's *Stars*.

Wind out of the Arctic stung like a pirate's cat-o'-nine-tails across my nose and chin.

Bundled up by Mrs. Butter to resemble a polar bear cub (its fur dyed red), I peered out at the hostile earth through a narrow gap in the layers of wrapped scarf. Moisture crystallized on the mask as delicate glass sculpture. Each breath tasted of wool and ice. Agony, pulling the sled. Three pairs of mitts did not prevent the rope feeling as heavy and as cold as frozen chain. Not knowing Derek's route by heart, I had to flip subscribers' cards attached to a metal ring—try that wearing layers of big mitts like boxing gloves, the thumbs padded as though they'd been wound in thick surgical gauze. Sometimes I had to remove my mitts and, with my bare fingers exposed to the cold, nudge the top card over. Then jump around, trying to rout the pain from my hand as though it had caught fire.

I loitered in apartment buildings, stomping my dead feet and punching my shoulders with the boxing gloves. I hoped somebody would come along and steal the newspapers from my sled, or steal the sled. A good enough excuse to go home. Unfortunately, when it's forty-two below in the dark on a January evening—and it was soon dark, for my progress was slow—thieves are too stiff and too cold to stoop for a *Montreal Star*. Be proud of your tyke, Momma, it might have taken awhile, but he delivered every paper.

On the first night of the cold snap, as I arrived home, Mrs. Butter fell upon me in her usual flurry of flour. "I'm okay. Don't worry. I'm tough as nails, Auntie."

"You're frozen!"

She meant it literally. Patches of my skin had been scorched white. Cheeks, fingertips, and toes had succumbed to the preliminary stages of frostbite.

"It's okay, Auntie. I can't feel them at all."

"Oh my God. Sparrow! That's the trouble."

Freezing's great, it saves us from the agony of the north wind. Thawing out, as I would discover, is hell.

Aunt dipped my digits in cold water, gradually increasing the temperature. My sense of touch returned as an excruciating pain. *Stop it! I don't want to be warm! Freeze me!* I considered the logistics of locking myself in the fridge. I never would have believed how painful it is to live at room temperature.

In the midst of my delirium I did catch sight of Barclay slouching in the doorway to the kitchen, which was strange. Upright Barclay never slouched. Watching me, he took stock of his desire for a paper route of his own.

My ordeal led to an evening of coddling. Under a mountain of blankets I was made cosy on the sofa. Even with the electric heater blazing red, the attic had tumbled below fifty degrees. Outside, the

radio reported, the nighttime low would be minus fifty-four. Add the
wind-chill to that. Families were being urged to keep their pets indoors.
Cold enough to kill a collie, the weather was sufficiently extreme to
allow me to sleep downstairs.

Such privilege.

And I dreamed that many years ago I had lived in a warmer clime.
Woke up in a sweat. Where was I? Displaced again. I reoriented myself,
the room came into focus. Rearranging my bearings, I collapsed into a
sub-tropical slumber.

What had saved many of the newspaper carriers was a parent, usually a
father arriving home from work and taking his child around in the family
sedan, exactly the form of salvation I was banking on for myself that
second day of the deep-freeze. No such luck. I settled for Vaseline smeared
across exposed skin, one more pair of mittens suitable for a lumberjack's
hands, and huge hockey socks pulled over the *outside* of my boots. Aunt
stuffed newspapers down the legs of my trousers and wrapped my middle
with magazines supported by a belt. If I had resembled a red polar bear cub
on my first day out, I now moved across a landscape of ice and snow with
the dexterity of a baby walrus. Walking was treachery. My socks slipped on
frozen wood stairs, and the extra ballast made scaling snowbanks as weary-
ing an expedition as a jaunt up Everest. The one blessing on that second
day was that the wind had lessened, allowing me to withstand the cold
despite needing an extra hour to complete my rounds.

Homeward bound, dragging the empty sled behind me, I glimpsed
Uncle's grey Rambler parking against the curb farther down the block.
Had he come to pick me up? As best as I was able, I ran, a kind of rolly-
polly waddle. Uncle left the engine running and stepped out of his car.
Pulling the hood of his duffle across his face, he kept his back to the
light wind and climbed a short flight of stairs to ring a doorbell.

Uncle was quickly admitted inside.

I skidded on my socks, hit an icy patch, and my hide of coats,
sweaters and newsprint collapsed into a snowbank. Weighted by the
blubber of magazines, getting upright was a struggle. I went as far as the
house that Uncle had entered, and stopped. What the weather could
not accomplish, Uncle had. Frozen solid by astonishment and disbelief,
I stared at the closed door.

Like cops and garbagemen, physicians and vendors, every neighbourhood keeps witches on call. Children designate who those witches are.

First they pick on someone who's strange, then they test her. Kids liked to climb an oak tree that grew in the middle of the fence behind the house that Uncle had just entered. Its branches spread across the lane. Ensconced in these bleacher seats, they'd launch acorns at the back door until a woman sallied forth with a broom, which officially confirmed her status as a shrew. Uneasy about attacking lonely, odd women, I'd walk away from such scenes conscious of an absence, of a dull ache resident in my memory, of a yearning to be found again, to be located.

I looked for my mother everywhere. Never finding her.

On Hallowe'en, no child dared ring the doorbell of this dark, brooding house. No one had ever been seen to visit. *Now Uncle had gone inside! Right inside and he had closed the door!*

I feared for his life.

He might fall under a spell!

The woman who lived alone in the house was seldom spotted. Groceries were delivered to her door by van, and she never indulged in a walk. News of her existence was either hearsay or provoked by the guerilla tactics deployed by children. Now Uncle was in that terrible place. In the midst of my fright, I'd spy an occasional shadow pass the curtained window. Not brave enough to attempt a closer look, I blamed my walrus-suit because it prevented me from easily sneaking around, and I also blamed the cold.

The witch, I guessed, had to be one of Uncle's many clients. He didn't plan to stay long, as he had left his car running in the cold. I deposited my sled across the floor of the back seat, and established a vigil on the passenger side of the front where the car's relative warmth made me sleepy. What woke me up was the plumber's truck backing into the gap in the snowbank behind me, and within a minute the man to fix the furnace parked across the street. Both tradesmen scrounged around in their vehicles awhile, then went up the steps to the witch's lair together.

So that was it. Her furnace had conked out, the pipes had frozen, her own black magic had let her down, and Uncle was the person to call in an emergency. Having put the tradesmen to work, Uncle returned outside and hurried through the frigid air—startled by my bulky presence in the car.

"Ssssparrow—"

"Hi."

"What are you doing here?" His tone surprised me. I was made to feel that I had done something wrong.

"Warming up."

He sat with his hands frozen to the steering wheel. "Yes," he conceded at last. "Of course. You gave me a sssshock." When he slipped on his esses in this weather, it sounded like he was shivering. "You don't look yourself in all those duds. I thought sssomething had happened to you. Are you frozen sssstiff? Did the paper route go well today?"

"I'm okay. Is that lady's furnace broke?"

"What lady?" he shot back at me.

"The lady in the spook house."

"Sssspook house? Sssparrow, do you know the lady who lives there?"

"Everybody calls her a witch."

He gazed at me awhile, before squeezing my knee. *Sports Illustrateds* and *Chatelaines* scrunched up under the pressure of his hand. "That's not very nice," he told me. "I hope you never call her names like that. Ssshe's a very sssweet lady. Ssshe's just a poor lost sssoul, that's all."

I was surprised. Usually Uncle spoke harshly of people.

Uncle put the car in gear and moved the Rambler off the curb and the crisp crunch of snow under the tires made my spine tingle. "I'm her accountant," he explained to me, and guided the car into Bloomfield's icy ruts. "The poor sssoul cannot manage her own affairs. It's a good thing ssshe telephoned. Another day of this weather and sssssshe'd've frozen to death."

A proud feeling, to know that Uncle was the person people called in their hour of need. Uncle was a bony man with a soft centre. Strict with his clients and his friends, he was equally severe with himself, with me, and especially with Barclay. When it came to Barclay's studies he could be a tyrant. And yet, that crusty surface, I had discovered over time, was not a harbinger of cruelty or meanness. Uncle Butter was a kind man at heart, and on that winter's drive home I felt as safe and as cosy with him as any child might with a decent and loving father.

Barclay helped me deliver the papers on the third day of our bitter cold. That was great. The two of us finished in record time, and the next day was much milder and Derek Mahoney returned to the depot. He pretended to cough as though recuperating from an illness, and Ludmilla Cherkova passed him a slip of paper. "Dis vhat you owink Sparrow for t'ree days."

"Sure," Derek confirmed. "You bet."

After she left, he tore up the I.O.U. before my eyes. No surprise. I swept the remnants into the dust bin. I forked over Barclay's share, letting him think that I had been paid. No big deal. I was glad to do it. He had behaved like a brother and the favour was not only appreciated, it has been remembered to this day.

*

The depot had become my second home, the Cherkovas my parents in an extended family. With the Butters I slept in the attic. At the Cherkovas I burrowed underground. Over the years Mr. Cherkova's tunnel sank deeper, splitting into tributaries. Until blocked by rock, soft sand, or water, each new shaft was extended as far as he could dig, in whatever direction was accessible. A network of elaborate and interconnected trails was being spawned beneath the surface of Park Extension.

A damp, murky realm. Early along, burrowers clasped hooks and handles fashioned by tree roots to pull themselves through the mud slurping at their boots. Shine a light, and the tunnel telescoped narrower. The bending whorls of the earth resembled the innards of winding intestinal track, and the black hole ahead could not be penetrated by an ordinary beam. Water perpetually dribbled from the side walls and ceiling, and anyone brave enough and foolish enough to continue had first to crouch, then crawl forward on hands and knees like a gopher.

I mapped the maze. I knew my way around down there. Warning Mr. Cherkova never made a difference. He would dig one shaft right into another, then embark upon a stray direction. Once he missed when I had expected two lines to intersect, which made me realize that we had gone above or below the other burrow. That taught me to devise a map in three dimensions. The tunnels were a magical place to go, the poor boy's Disneyland, which I entered whenever I felt blue or adventuresome. Later I would descend into the maze because it had become both my habit and my haven.

Wanting to prove my bravery, to take advantage of my access to the weird and the wonderful (and hoping to swipe a kiss in the dark), I took girls into the tunnels when I was older. "Chicks" who were distant or ornery on the surface were willing to be petted underground. I also escorted Neil Abrahamson down there the day he schemed—and failed—to murder Derek Mahoney.

Neil had found out that he wasn't much of a killer. He didn't have it in him, or, at least, not yet. He had been amazed and flattered by

Derek's gestures of friendship, until the Sunday morning that Derek took Neil for a ride with a group of men. "A nature trip," he called it. The men had expressed a carnal interest in young boys. Neil escaped that scene, walked miles home, and came to the depot the following day to stand quietly in a corner, sheltered by the furnace. Derek arrived. He packed his papers and left. Neil hadn't moved. When I walked by him, he was shaking, staring dead ahead. A kitchen knife dangled in his right hand. Now that Derek was off doing his route, it occurred to me that Neil had no one left to kill but himself, or me, so I invited him down to the tunnels where we could talk.

The labyrinth was not as intricate then as it would become, yet the tunnels soothed him. The grotto gave him strength. To be submerged in the bowels of the earth, like warm stools in a body as cold as a corpse, granted us power. To know that another kingdom, another world of streets and houses and yards and sidewalks, lay directly above us while we inhabited a retreat as exclusive as anybody's notion of heaven, gave us a keen sense of privilege. Clandestine knowledge fortifies the soul. Down below, Neil needed to weep, but his tears were stymied by shame. I offered him a self-conscious arm around his shoulders. He had a problem with that, so I let him go. Neil was frustrated and angry and afraid of the dark and afraid of himself and the only cure I could prescribe was to lead him through the maze. I deliberately frightened him, as I had done with girls to break down their ordinary defenses. Neil was claustrophobic and panicky, convinced that we were lost, he shouted out that the walls were caving in, and I said, "This way. Grab hold of me." And we climbed up and I showed him the secret hatch with the trick latch which even Mr. Cherkova did not know that I knew about. Now Neil was the third person in all the world to know and he breathed the air deeply, he calmed himself down, he relaxed in the late afternoon light, and I gave him a choice. "You can climb out right here, or come back down with me. Either way, you have to swear to God not to tell."

Having failed once that day in what he considered to be a test of courage, having yielded to the rational side of his nature in his feud with Derek, Neil returned to the grotto and together we found a comfortable place to sit. I shone the flashlight on our wallpaper of crawling worms and centipedes. On the shiny eyes of a rodent. We were being observed by an inquisitive rat taking a shortcut between sewers. The tunnels were affecting Neil as they had affected me. Some people are driven batty by solitude, others are restored. To be below the earth's skin, segregated from the world, spared from enemies and contests and troubles, saved Neil. He got the chance to recuperate.

"I'll talk to Ludmilla," I promised. "She trusts me. I'll coax her to fire Derek."

"He'll freak out."

"So what? She'll make up some excuse. She's been looking for a reason to get rid of him for a long time. Derek's such a prick. He's too old to be a paperboy anymore. Don't worry. We can count on Ludmilla. Derek won't suspect it was us."

The tunnels could do that. In the depths of Mr. Cherkova's irrational puzzle, common sense staggered to the surface. Master plans emerged devoid of glitches. Like rubber, ideas could be moulded, and like pucks, dropped into play. The tunnels focused concentration, they helped us to unravel the vagaries of the world above, they showed us how to negotiate the dark, the fearful, and the unknown. The tunnels demonstrated ways to subdue our fears, to form pacts with our closest allies, and to seal agreements with a cryptic double-handed shake. Our lives in the tunnels demonstrated that anytime things got really bad, we could always burrow.

Throughout Park Extension, rumours about the tunnels were rife, probably instigated by my ex-girlfriends. Adults, naturally, discredited the tales, and I had made a point of confusing the girls about where they had visited, having brought them below only after dark. Neil and I never told anybody else, and Mr. Cherkova maintained few confidants.

Barclay was never told. Instinctively I knew that this place had to remain my private asylum, where I could dwell as cosily as shit before being evacuated into the world.

Above ground it was raining, on a day when Neil and me were wandering through a section that had to be broached on hands and knees. At the end of the long corridor we found Mr. Cherkova busily shovelling, dumping his earth and clay onto a plastic sheet. Hauling away the loaded sheets was always an onerous, back-breaking chore. What had at one time been a cavity in Mr. Cherkova's back yard was now a mound, and these days the excess had to be carted away in the bed of his best friend's pickup. The friend was the man given to staring at me and weeping. He was down below, talking quietly to Mr. Cherkova. His name was Mr. Kershner.

Mr. Kershner asked Neil, "So, you're Jewish?" Neil said yes. I had not known this man to talk, only to weep, and to haul away Mr. Cherkova's dirt. "Listen to me. You must know. You are man now. I want tell you what happening to the Jews." Being Neil's friend, I was allowed to listen in, while Mr. Cherkova quietly persisted with his excavation nearby. Mr. Kershner told us many things, and eventually he told us about the holocaust—in particular, about the Jews in the town of Stanislov, Galitzia, who had been rounded up, marched out of town, and gunned down. His sister and mother had rushed into the hail of bullets. Taking her cue from a book that she had read, his sister had pinned her dress to her thigh, the needle driven through her flesh, so that when her corpse was dragged away she would not be immodest. In the depths of the tunnels, listening to the tale, riveted by the misery and horror, Neil and I learned that the world could be a vile place, that human debasement was rampant. We had had no warning, for in the fifties the holocaust had been suppressed news. "On that day there, fifteen thousand Jews killed, dead, murdered," he told us. "Slaughtered. Five thousand—Nazi machineguns. Ten thousand suffocate, you know, lose breath, can't breathe, they die, we are squashed in one place. Then whistle blows, whistle blows, Germans, they send us everybody home. Go home, they saying to me. Save that person, saying to me, carry that child. Whistle blows, they saying go away. They kill families, one minute ago they shoot my mother, my sister, I waiting my turn. After they doing this thing they say go home. I am wishing that whistle do not blow, I am wishing they kill me like my mother."

Down in the tunnels we ingested the fury of the tale. Mr. Kershner could not have repeated his story to children on the earth's surface, he had had to be sequestered in the semidark, under a blanket of rock, whispering his terrifying words in the silence of the subterranean cavity. The ambient mystery of the tunnels evoked the confidence to share his story, and perhaps the wonder of the tunnels allowed us to be quiet and to listen to an old man's tale. On that afternoon, we absorbed it whole. I could scarcely conceive of such a massacre. My comprehension of the world did not accommodate atrocity. The image of the young girl sticking a pin through the flesh of her thigh to hold down her dress pricked my mind. I could see the dot of blood on her leg, watched her run, her body berserk with bullets. Down in the tunnels, I could not be immune to that pain, I believed her to be down there with us, near us, abiding in her unmarked mass grave.

Perhaps Mr. Cherkova had been digging for her bones?

He himself did not talk about the war in the beginning. The labyrinth fostered plain and wondrous talk, but his only statement was to dig. For ten years he had done nothing but dig, deeper, further, in more intricate patterns, dig. I was surprised, then, on another occasion, when he ceased his relentless activity to have a chat.

"I got map," he informed me. Under the dim glow of his flashlight he showed me an official roadmap of the streets of Montreal. Over the past few years, he often became lost in the maze of his own making, he relied upon me to know which tunnels were interconnected and which were not. He had devoted his life to excavating the tunnels, yet he rarely used them for recreational purposes. He left that up to me. Having a map, a destination, was something new.

"Where do you want to go?" I asked him.

"Remember, Sparrow? You tell to me about witch? Her house I want go. Make trapdoor her back yard. You tell to me Bloomfield Street, here?"

"This might not be such a good idea, Mr. Cherkova. Shouldn't you keep your tunnels underground?"

"She alone, you said. She troubled womans. She understand the need many tunnels. You tell to me, Sparrow, exactly where to go. Measure space—distance—for me on ground."

From his point of view, he was sending me up to the moon, but how could I refuse? Neil and I would use Neil's father's tape measure to figure out how Mr. Cherkova could dig his way into the witch's backyard. Part of our survey had to be done after dark, as the shorter route passed under homes and lawns. We snooped around on private property, taking measurements, deciding on directions. In the past, whenever Mr. Cherkova hit a problem, such as solid rock or water, he simply dug somewhere else on a whim. Now, when stymied, he had to shift his course, and I was called upon to recalibrate the path. The new extension was going to be his longest and most ambitious tunnel. I measured the distance at a hundred and fourteen yards, to be lengthened every time he had to dodge water or rock. Complicating the project, he had to sideswipe storm drains along the way to ventilate the tunnels, which tested my map-making skills. Mr. Cherkova claimed he wanted to finish digging before he died. I was betting that the job would kill him. I had finally conceded that he was mad.

Mr. Cherkova was crazy. Of course, in my cosmology crazies were benign. They were family. For me, the man's looniness was the best possible excuse to support him.

*

From an early age, not wanting to lose connection to my mother, I
carefully reconnoitred the past. Out of that discipline I enjoy a focused
and fruitful memory for particular incidents. Even if I allow for the
intrusion of time, which surely must deflect and inform my perceptions
of many things, I remain convinced that the weekend of our Canadian
Thanksgiving, in 1957, is remembered with neither embellishment nor
alteration.

Above ground, October's chilly winds routed summer debris, ransacked leaves in the gutters. I chose to drop down below the surface. In
Ludmilla Cherkova's basement I was pulling on my overalls to descend
into the underground maze. Flashlight in hand, I filled my lungs with a
last gulp of decent air, then strode through the fetid muck.

That time of year, the tunnels mirrored the ambience of dark antediluvian swamp.

To cross a pool I shimmied on a board.

Intruders were challenged by a narrow orifice, it was a struggle to
squeeze through the grip of rock. Those who panicked would feel the
earth's unforgiving vise tighten. Once through, sufficient headroom
allowed the explorer to stand and contemplate his next move. Tunnels
extended in various directions. A few were illuminated by stark bulbs
that fossilized shadows. Carved in circles, two would return burrowing
guests to their starting point. Others intersected feeder tunnels, or
merged into bore-holes that offered no escape other than retreat. As
the map-maker of this realm, I generally did not get lost.

Shaped as an ellipsis, the tunnel I entered had a smooth flat surface, a floor of sand over clay. Upon mastering a four-legged motion I
travelled swiftly, careful not to dislodge the structural timbers. I ignored
tributaries until I had reached a shaft steeping to a forty-degree angle,
which delivered me to another subterranean trail.

Continued along, bearing right.

A sharp descent made controlling momentum difficult.

Eventually I entered onto a smooth and gradual incline. At its
end, the tunnel evacuated into a hollowed-out waiting station. Above
lay the roof of the earth. I had calculated and recalculated this position. All my expertise and a fortune in sixteen-year-old worry put me
directly beneath the witch's backyard. The shaft up had not been completed, although Mr. Cherkova had punctured the surface with twin
aluminium air ducts—narrow holes—so at least we knew that we had
arrived beneath soil, that we were not stationed directly under a
house, street, or paved lane.

It was Thanksgiving, I was expected home, but I had had to come
here to sit in the privilege of this place, to fret about my calculations,
and to brood upon the nature of the enterprise. Perhaps Mr. Cherkova
was right. I hoped so. If I was wrong about our position he'd just dig
more tunnels, but if he had erred in his assessment of human nature his
life's work would be rendered futile. According to the man who had
excavated this tunnel, to knock on the front door of a witch's house
and expect a welcome was folly. People such as her had to be
approached on terms they could understand. Rise up like an ogre out of
the earth, he told me, in effect, like a demon forged from muck. Offer
her the use of private tunnels for her refuge and escape. Then she will
be glad to see you, then she will rejoice.

Witches worth knowing, to translate and paraphrase Mr.
Cherkova, appreciate opportunities to vanish under the earth's crust
whenever they please.

The pursuit of the witch from below had finally engaged my imagination. I had begun to speculate on her true identity. Was it possible that I
had reached the termination of my life-long quest? Her reputation
evolved from the cruel fun of the streets—I was too old to believe that she
was a legitimate sorceress. On the other hand, the seminal signs indicated
that she was mentally dislocated. Was it possible? God! Could it be that
the witch—the woman—in the house above my head ... was my mother?

While the turkey was cooking, Barclay and I ran pass patterns over the
furniture, tossing a hefty Red Delicious apple across the living-room in
football spirals. Aunt shouted from the kitchen to take our game outside, but it was rainy and cold, and she was not being supported by
Uncle. He was seated on the sofa basking in the pleasure of his sons.

"And the C.E.O., I mean, he's getting into this chauffeur-driven
stretch Mercedes—do you have any idea what they cost?"

"Big bucks," Uncle imagined.

Barc faked the pass as I leapt over the coffee table and hit me with
a bullet as I cut back inside the hanging lamp. Avoiding a hit from the
ottoman, I turned upfield before being forced out of bounds by the wall.
Uncle beamed. Barc, at nineteen, was enjoying an extraordinary academic career. He was being avidly recruited. He was able to pick and
choose from among the top accounting firms in the city for apprentice
employment. "Anyway, he says to me, 'Keep up the good work,
Boisvert. Some day every skyscraper in this city will bow down as you

pass by. Not everybody will see it, but you'll feel it. That's the day you'll know you've arrived.' That's what he said."

"Get thee behind me, Satan," I kidded.

"People of his calibre don't make those sssstatements unless they're ssssincere," Uncle wanted to have noted for the record.

"Banana right!" I hollered, and pretended to take a snap out of the back of the armchair before lofting a perfect spiral to Barclay who was headed for the end zone beyond the upright piano.

Where he was tackled by Aunt.

"You'll wreck the place! Now take your game outside. Both of you."

We'd been going at it for so long that I was mildly out of breath and perspiring. On the radio, the Montreal Alouettes had been thoroughly drubbed in the first half by the Ottawa Rough Riders, putting me in the mood for a scrimmage to exact revenge. Dropping down into a three-point stance, I lined up Aunt like a tight end taking umbrage with a linebacker.

"Hup one!" Barc cried out.

Aunt eyed me warily.

"Hup two!" Uncle hollered.

She attempted to retreat into the sanity and sanctuary of her kitchen.

"Hike!" shouted Barc and his father together.

I plunged into Aunt's midriff, blocking off her escape. She was snared further by Barclay, my pulling guard. Uncle sliced off-tackle behind us, remarking, "I think I'll help myself to a piece of pumpkin pie."

Whooping, hooting, flustered and dismayed, Aunt threw off our blocks like Sam Huff going after Jim Brown. She clothes-lined her husband, hoisted him up by his starched collar, and laid down her own game plan. "Unless you want to be tarred and turkey-feathered once again, Gerald Boisvert, you stay where you are."

Often, in our home, we had good times like these.

Barc and I tossed a football around the backyard without much enthusiasm. The game wasn't his sport, and he generally loathed holidays and idle afternoons on principle. After dropping an easy toss, he confided, "I better get some work done."

"It's Thanksgiving," I reminded him, the shard of petulance intentional. Still, I understood. I had learned to exhibit happiness for his great success. Barclay paid a premium for being a notable student. He had endured considerable abuse through High School and on the streets of Park Extension for his life as a prodigy. Our peers adhered to that curious schizophrenia loose in the world, in which excellence and striving were mocked, while sloth, laziness, and contempt for success were applauded. At McGill, where he moved through a different milieu, Barclay was admired and emulated. Leave it to him to set the standard. At home, my job was to support his ambitions and to fortify his mania for hard work.

"Things are heating up at school." He twirled the football up and down. Bored running pass patterns, Barc preferred to run his fingers down a ledger.

"Mind if I tag along?" He was wrecking my day by being such a boob and I wanted him to know it. The trouble with Barclay, he figured that that was his due.

"Course not. I'll get Dad's keys." As teenagers, walking contravened our nature. Uncle's office was a short sprint away, but my house-brother requisitioned the family Buick.

Our supernova student maintained a desk at Uncle's office. Moon-lighting paid for the modest rent (Uncle charged him rent) and he was on hand to assist the old man whenever he was vexed by tough prob-lems. Neither father nor son laboured under the assumption that Bar-clay would join the firm after he became a Chartered Accountant. They both shared his aspirations for the big time, for the complex multinational deal, the Buy-out and the Takeover, for seats on high-powered boards. Uncle was convinced that his son had a mission to clean up the nation's business, revamp its ethics, and signal a new age of prosperity-with-a-conscience. His boy's biggest booster, Uncle had no intention of confining him to neighbourhood economics.

Tunnelling, constructing dams and irrigation systems, and design-ing bridges were the possibilities that had snared my imagination. Yet I continued to hear talk of a law degree. My fault. I hadn't found the gumption to impress upon Uncle my inclination to be an engineer. With an accountant and a lawyer in the family, Uncle anticipated managing a handsome chunk of the world. Mine was the lesser vision—I wanted to rebuild it. Worse than not speaking to Uncle about my plans, I had not seriously broached the subject with myself. My Geometry marks were fine, Algebra was okay, but my Trig failed to get close to an engineer's scratch.

Slide-rules baffled me.

Barclay stopped on Bloomfield at the corner of d'Anvers, where we waited for Patty Correlli to cross the street. Eighteen, Patty boiled boys' blood with her extravagant figure and pimple-free skin. Not that she tried. Either she inherited or she had developed a predilection for convent colours, and that day she was bundled up in weighty tweeds. "Watch this," recklessly, I boasted to Barc. "Bet you I can make her run."

Too dim to be luminous in his galaxy, I sometimes tried to better him with my worldliness. Barc was a virgin. So was I, but being three years younger granted me a waiver. I treated my condition as an ailment in desperate need of radical cure. Barclay considered virginity to be an asset that looked impressive on his C.V. Ascending the belfry of his ego, he asserted that sex was put upon this earth to test the moral fibre of respectable men. Under the flag of his complex, befuddled standards, only people who sweated for a living could claim a legitimate right to rut.

Day by day he sounded more like his father.

Rolling down the window, I idiotically shouted out, "How're you doing, Pats?"

Like a sprinter bursting from the blocks, she picked up speed. Within a few strides Patty had shifted into a shuffle-run. She resembled an upright dolphin, chest forward, head back, propelled along by rapid-fire flipper-feet.

"Wait! Pats! Hey, it's me, Sparrow. I'm starving for a muffin."

Poor Patty. Somewhere along the line she had been mortified by the flesh. Privileged to know about her precocious talent to show-and-not-tell, I had made it my job in life to embarrass her. Patty ran. Cruelly, I culled pleasure from her torment, and gloated at Barc.

Stern-faced, versed, stable, decorous, serious, the penultimate Chartered Accountant, the lad was not amused. I kept forgetting—Barclay was in-training to become a community pillar. "Leave her alone," he scoffed gently. "When did you get so obscene, Sparrow?"

A nick. A flesh wound. No big deal. "Shitting is obscene," I told him. "Plumbing and porcelain make it sanitary, that don't necessarily make it clean." Like Mr. Cherkova in his tunnels gouging rock, I kept scratching at Barc's nineteen-year-old surface. Inevitably, Mr. Cherkova ran up against a wall. I perpetually uncovered a personality cast as a fifty-year-old. Same thing. Poor Barc. He suffered youth as an indignity.

Watching Patty run, I conjured a fantasy of her down in the tunnels. Ludmilla's basement, to my mind, had instigated the earlier bouts of exhibitionism. I imagined Patty's secret instincts being provoked way down in the maze. Subterranean geography agitated a complementary region of mind. I carried Patty down, deeper into the dungeons, deeper into the mysteries, into the contradictions of her own mind and desires, deeper into the labyrinth of the world where she was free to become the wanton animal of my desires—hot-stuff. I shuddered. Chickening out. Couldn't even think about it. Patty's excavated passion was scary, and I had to wrench myself free from her dissolute grasp.

At rue Jarry, formally Blair Street, my own blood ran frigid. Barc yielded to crossing traffic, which included a faded cerulean Ford. I spotted the passenger first, Neil Abrahamson, but the impulse to honk a greeting was stymied by a glimpse of the driver. Derek? Our cars passed and I could not believe the slanderous heart of this world—this world's soul wrapped in a whorl of twisted bowel. What could possibly make those two friends?

I was still shaky and quiet about that as we parked and headed up to Uncle's office above a bank. Barc plunged into his work. His organizational skills astounded me. He knew precisely where he left off and exactly what he intended to accomplish at each study-interval. I spent my time playing with odds and ends, twirling keys, opening a few locked drawers and cabinets. Soon I was rummaging through Uncle's confidential files, seeing what was what. I made a point of appearing listless, for I, too, lacked neither savvy nor ambition.

Perhaps I'd come across an incriminating letter, a document pertaining to my existence, or a manifesto that had once been pinned to the inside of my jacket replete with my mother's prescriptions and a map of the future. Uncle Butter was too meticulous and too methodical to discard something that important. I was counting on his good, infuriating habits.

"What're you up to, Sparrow?" Barc's question was idle, and he seemed satisfied by my disinterested, mumbled response. His attention dropped back to his own work.

Uncle's clients were arranged alphabetically. Diving into the 'F's I flipped the pages in reverse. Fernall's daughter, the sexiest thing I'd seen. Ellerton's son was a prick. Absolutely nothing under Drinkwater. Flipping ... the next section of file was not C, but CH. CH? Within the paper folder lay a thin, mauve, ring-binder, which I removed from the cabinet and opened. Down one side of each page Uncle had handwritten a list of names, notated by a date in the corresponding column. At the far right shone a constellation of sticky coloured stars, of the sort that were awarded to children for perfect attendance or behaviour.

Many names on the list I recognized.

What had they done to deserve Uncle's starry approval?

Jogged by a conscience that said being a C.A. demanded scrupulous discretion, Barc checked up on me again. "What've you found there?"

"You tell me." I showed him the binder. "Why should it be filed under CH?"

Barclay's knowledge of the office had attained such a level of refinement that he didn't give the register a second glance. "That's the Cheaters' File." His pencil tapped a drumbeat on the desk as he observed me with unusual scrutiny. "Anytime Dad suspects somebody's been cheating on his taxes, he gives the government a jingle. You know him. Purge those who give money a bad name."

"You're kidding me."

"Think so? Remember the time he got tarred and feathered? That's why. The finks should've left him alone—he might have grown out of the habit by now." A hollowness had entered the timbre of his voice, as though his own memories had begun to resonate. "I think the tarring made him more conscientious, if that's possible. Bar none, Dad's the most fanatical bookkeeper in the northern hemisphere. Truly amazing, really. His greatest fear in life is that a cheater might prosper somewhere in his neighbourhood."

"Who merits stars? The biggest cheaters?"

"The stickers denote successful investigations and heavy fines."

A whistle sung out of me. Quite a number. No wonder Uncle had enemies. Amazing that he was still alive. Curious, I asked why the percentage of prosecutions early in his career looked more significant than recent times.

"Uncle used to inform on his own clients. When he did that, the government had them dead to rights. The word's out. Anybody who plans to cheat makes sure Dad never gets an eye on his books."

"I have to hand it to the old gus. Even if it costs him business, he sticks to his principles." Thinking I'd made a valid point, my curiosity was spurred by the slant of Barc's smile. "What?"

"Dad never does anything that costs him business."

"You said—"

"He turns everything to his own advantage. Let's say a local shopkeeper decides to dispense with his services. Dad goes into the store when the guy's busy with customers and publicly accuses him of being crooked. 'Only thieves use Jerk-off Jenkins.' That's one of his slogans. If he still doesn't get back the business, whether he thinks the guy is crooked or not he makes an anonymous call to Ottawa. People have it figured out. If they don't use Dad, their chances of being audited shoot up. He's no dummy."

"Gee." I felt both astonished and troubled.

"He's small-time, but he's tough. Nobody pushes him around. I told him to his face, 'Dad, that's extortion.' Which ruffled a few of the feathers on his ass. 'I'm the right arm of justice!' he tells me. He believes it, too. You know Dad. By the way, you shouldn't be scrounging around in those files."

"Just snooping."

Ditching the binder, I locked the file cabinet and noticed that Barc continued to have his eye on me. Circling around the office, I failed to travel beyond his range. "What's odd in here?" he wanted to know. "What's out of place? Pretend you're not familiar with this office, okay, that you just walked in off the street. What would you find peculiar?"

"Peculiar? You mean like weird?"

"What's curious? Not new, it's been in the office forever. But it's out of the ordinary. Something subtle."

The game had a certain attraction. I scoured the office from bow to lazarette and back again, then sighed, defeated.

"Nothing?" Barc probed.

"The usual boring stuff. The only thing I've always wondered about is why he has two safes. I can't figure out why he needs one safe, let alone a pair."

"Bingo! Good for you, Bird. I was betting against you. Dad needs the big vault for customers' documents," my house-brother divulged. "Temporary safe-keeping. Stocks and bonds, insurance contracts, other records, papers that have to be secure from fire and theft. But that doesn't explain the second safe, does it?"

Barclay pushed himself away from his desk. Where the strong-box squatted beneath the shelf supporting the water-cooler, he knelt down, balancing himself with an affectionate hand on the surface of the vault. He commenced telling a tale. Rarely have I heard him so gregarious, except for those occasions when he'd rant about business, money, or accounting procedure. I would realize soon enough that he was referring to all three.

"Never let Dad tell you differently. Don't believe him if he does. During the war he was a valet in the army. He didn't fight, he didn't march, he never came within earshot of the front. He pressed suits. Did it so well he became the personal attendant to a Lieutenant-Colonel. The man was accustomed to servants. In private life he was heir to a vast personal fortune. Old money. He'd gone to war for kicks. After they were discharged, Dad had his family to look after, he gave up on the idea of returning to school. But his former commanding officer didn't forget about him, they had forged some sort of alliance. Wartime comrade stuff. Dad calls it friendship, but I don't buy it. My guess is, they'd been through a war together that hadn't lived up to their expectations. Hanging out, they had learned they could be useful to each other. It's that simple. The Colonel did not invite Dad into the family business. Having one more corporation cog around the house was not his plan. Instead, he helped Dad set up his own business. The Colonel became the first, and he remains Dad's most important, client."

My interest had quickly begun to flag. Business chitchat did that to me.

"We're talking interesting dollars here, Sparrow. Dad doesn't draw much of the Colonel's accounting business. Strictly special assignments. Probably the dirty stuff, but I don't know that for sure. Whatever it is, it's so confidential that the man cannot allow his personal accountants or lawyers to know what's going on. He will only trust his wartime valet. I've never been able to see inside this little beauty." Affectionately, Barclay patted the top of the safe, stroking it as he might a sad, low-slung breast. Money was his lover. "Staff aren't allowed in the room when it's open. He sends them to the bathroom if he has to get inside. Anyway, long story short, what we're both expecting when I get my C.A. is that Dad's client will give me a huge chunk of his business. Dad says it's a lead-pipe cinch."

"Great." One more coup for Barclay Butter. One more boost up the tower of power. Living under a rainbow, pots overflowing with gold materialized under this boy's paperweights.

"Still don't get it, do you, chump?" He twirled the black dials on the stalwart safe like a gigolo tweaking nipples. "Hell, you're old enough to know for yourself. You have to swear not to tell Dad that I told you, or anyone. You have to keep this a secret."

"Sure. I swear."

"Believe you me, I'm not a violent person. But if you tell Dad I'll kick your balls in."

Coming from this gentle giant, the threat carried impact. I was pleased to hear that Barclay had ventured far enough into the world to learn at least a fraction of its vocabulary. I repeated with the appropriate solemn emphasis, "I swear."

"Sparrow, inside this minifortress of steel and secret codes, Dad keeps not only the record of his nefarious deeds in support of his ex-commanding officer, but, my guess is—because it's a part of that service to a valued client—inside is an account, probably in every detail, about your ancestry."

Struck dumb, I scarcely managed to utter, "What?" Perhaps the actual sound I made was a croak.

"Since when has Dad made a habit of adopting stray waifs off trains? You're the only one I know about. There has to be method to his madness. There always is." Barclay patted the safe again as if fondling a woman's derriere. "Is that what you wanted to find out with your snooping? Crack this safe, Sparrow-bird, and the meaning of life is in your hands."

At that instant the telephone rang, as if my own shock had instigated the trill. Too stunned to move, I was only vaguely aware of Barclay's responses. "Mom—. No, lis—. Slow down. Mom, stop! ... Get serious ... an *earthquake*? Mom ... Ma ... Okay, we'll leave the car—yes, we're heading home." He hung up.

"Mom says there's been an earthquake."

"Huh?" I was wrapped up in other news when a trolley in my brain derailed, triggered by possibility. "Where?"

"Here. In Park Ex. Around our house. Leave the car, she says. Part of the street's caved in. Gas lines and water mains burst. Sounds like she's flipped a lid."

"Oh shit," I exclaimed. "Oh no."

"Sparrow? She's just being batty. I'm sure there's a logical explanation."

I looked right at him, needing at that moment to assay a human connection. "Let's check it out." I headed for the door. "Something's gone wrong." A sick feeling twisted inside me, as though I had missed an earlier premonition. What precious signal had I flubbed?

At nineteen, Barclay was large and powerfully built. Offensively handsome, he was lean back then, six-three, dark-haired, broad-shouldered, square-jawed—the works. If he had had any balls he'd have been a tight end instead of being such a tight ass. Girls noticed him, but they did not swoon. A softness to his skin, and an absence of visible muscle, suggested even then that "pleasantly plump" was his attainable goal in life. Barclay was tailoring his body to fit large, imposing suits. Pin-striped. Double-breasted. Quality worsted. In a family where his father was wiry and diminutive, and his mother as chubby as a tea biscuit, this boy was freakish. His physique borrowed heavily from youth. His peers predicted portly prosperity and multiple chins. Perhaps we wished it on him, hexing him with our envy. Between the two of us, I was the superior athlete, and set the pace on our sprint home. As he sputtered, I chided his accountant's stamina and bookkeeper's stride.

The advantage was all mine. I was running on fear. Barclay had little more than curiosity to motivate him.

We gagged on our first portent of disaster, a whiff of natural gas. Small fires sent signals from a distance. Dipping into a ditch—a trench that had never been dug—automobiles resembled horses bending for a soothing drink. A bus had parked on the sidewalk. Two moving vans blocked the intersection. Right then—a flash, the air above our heads crackled and we were thumped by hollow, concussive sound. Orange flame ignited the air. An odd explosion. The fire disintegrated above the rooftops with an eerie *whooooossshh!* as if it was nothing more than a madcap wind. Sprinting again, enchanted, I lost track of my house-brother.

Flee or stay put? Evacuating their homes, spectators had no clue what to do. Had the worst occurred or was it yet to come? When sidewalks burn and the pavement sinks, when front lawns buckle, people swarm together, they gather under the evening sky, conscious of being alive.

Flames, burning uniformly, spurted fifteen feet high from a sewer. I could trace the pattern of the ground's collapse by rote. The ditch spanned Bloomfield, cut through yards, reappeared crossing d'Anvers. The tunnels had caved in, creating a fault line deking crazily about my neighbourhood. Water mains wrenched out of alignment showered the air above the corner of rue d'Anvers and Champagneur, the twin spouts of water and fire competing beside each other. My apprehension hardened, and grew brittle. I needed to know that Mr. Cherkova had not been buried. Where else would he be on Thanksgiving Day except underground? Right where I had left him.

I found Ludmilla outside her home inspecting the interesting new contours of her garden.

"Sparrow! Dank God!"

"Where's Mr. Cherkova? Is he safe?"

"Sure, safe. In basement."

"*Whew!* I was worried. Does he understand what's happened? He must be upset. What's he doing?"

"Vat you dink he doink? He diggink."

Entering the basement—tentatively, checking the arch of the doorway for structural damage first—I scooted through to the furnace room. Mr. Cherkova was not around, and the curtain which concealed the entrance to the tunnels had been pushed aside. I stepped through the portal. Listened. Then shouted his name. The echo of my voice a grim response. I hesitated. Part of the tunnels' attraction was the provocation of fear, the worry that the earth might shift, the walls crumble, that the mountain of world above would collapse upon all daring trespassers of this subversive realm. Nothing stimulates like fear. And yet, I hesitated, and tried unsuccessfully to evict myself from that place.

I had to go down again. Climb down the ladder, take a flashlight from the shelf, and flick it on. This time it was difficult. Perhaps for the first time I was understanding how foreign, how strange, this place had become. I began to move more quickly through the familiar dark. At the narrow gap, I squeezed through to the first main chamber, and found Mr. Cherkova. Shovelling furiously, he was working himself up to a heart attack.

This was the dementia dimension. He had created his own unique, whole, astonishing empire, and it had caved in. "Mr. Cherkova?" My voice was strained by sympathy and lament. He swirled and brandished his shovel like a baseball bat, my head the fast ball flying into his strike zone. "Mr. Cherkova. It's me. Sparrow."

Lights slung from the ceiling cast our dreary, decomposed shadows against the earthen walls. I anticipated the slugger's mighty wallop.

"Stand back!" he warned me. "Come no closer here! I knock off your block here!"

"Mr. Cherkova, hey, it's me, Sparrow. We're pals."

"Sparrow!"

"Yes. It's me."

"Dig!" he commanded, the most value that any friend might have. "Dig, Sparrow!"

"I forgot to bring my shovel."

He tossed me his, and in the same motion fell upon the blocked tunnel, ripping the earth away with his bare hands.

"Better yet, you take this, Mr. Cherkova. I'm not very good with tools."

Blindly, as though his hands operated independently of his mind, he accepted the return of the shovel. In his delirium he confided one word which trampled my perceptions. "Rescue."

"Someone's in the tunnels? Who's in there, Mr. Cherkova?"

"Escape," he said, which confounded me. Where was he? Beside me, digging to release a trapped victim, or excavating memory, forging the tunnel that had been vivid in his dreams, the one that had comforted his nights after hauling corpses from the gas chambers of Auschwitz.

I needed to find out if anybody was in the tunnels, and Mr. Cherkova was not a reliable source. Run, Sparrow!

Outside, Ludmilla didn't know.

Instinct was my guide. I raced down Champagneur to the senior citizens' communal gardening plot, arriving in the nick of time to spot a familiar figure walking spiritedly away. "Neil!" He didn't turn around. I chased after him, ran right up behind him and he never seemed to notice. Grabbing his shoulder, I spun him around to get his attention. "Neil!"

His face and clothes were smeared with dirt. His hands and knees blackened with muck. He'd been crawling through the tunnels. Neil acted stunned, an exaggeration of his usual habit. His wacky smile snubbed me.

"You been down there, Neil?"

Silence can be ominous speech, a devastating form of confession. Silence infers that the admission is so broad and injurious that it cannot be broached with words, nor can it be bound by mortal imagination.

"What's the matter?"

"I can't hear you!" he shouted back.

"Neil!" I was yelling. "What's wrong?"

"Speak up!" he screamed at me.

"Neil!" I made a quick diagnosis, and bellowed in his ear, "You're deaf!"

Proud of his affliction, Neil grinned at me again. He hollered, "Dynamite! Boom!"

"Neil," I said in a normal voice, neglecting to scream, "where did you get dynamite?" The question, no sooner spoken, provoked the logical response. Neil was older than me. He had spent the summer at work on his uncle's construction crew as a timekeeper, an experience that had toughened him up. Everything had been planned for years—stealing the explosive and the caps, learning how to trigger dynamite, luring Derek underground. "Is Derek in the tunnels, Neil? Is he down there?"

"I can't hear you! Speak up! I'm deaf!" And he strode away. Something in his gimpy walk—Neil could not swagger, he was incapable of developing the knack—warned me that he had just turned his back on his victims—on Derek, and on me as well. He was content to let us suffer.

Consider your options, was the advice of an insidious wee voice, the one which combated my desire to walk away from the situation. That I did not give my baser instincts currency ought to be credited to my account. I did think about contacting the police, but it was an alternative sure to sponsor humiliation. "Officer, honest, that was no earthquake, there are secret tunnels underground and a friend of mine just blew them up with a stick of dynamite he ripped off from his uncle's wrecking crew, he was settling a score." No use. They'd never believe me. This was one job I'd have to do myself. Hopping the fence into the seniors' garden plot, I jumped the harvested rows of earth and, behind the raspberry bushes, opened the secret hatch. Looking around first like Superman in a phone booth, I lowered myself down into the earth's anatomy.

The first section of tunnel had survived the blast, although the ceiling and walls had corroded. An accumulation of rocks and dirt impeded travel. A boulder that had once been a decorative wall-hanging supporting a light fixture had tumbled onto the path, crushing the lamp. Snakelike, I slithered over it, moved against the walls like a lover and kissed my life goodbye, unconvinced that I would manage to return.

Derek was clawing at the earth when I found him. He was battling his way through a wall of mud and dirt using a length of root as a pick. I said his name.

"Neil! You asshole!" He did not pause for a moment.

"It's not Neil. It's Sparrow."

This time he turned around. "Whad're you doin' here?"

"I live here. You?"

"You seen Neil?"

"He's above ground. Derek. I can show you the way out."

He resumed digging. Maybe I should have recommended him to Mr. Cherkova who, with equal fanaticism, ploughed the other end. Down here, it would take them six or seven years to link up.

"Can't!" Derek claimed.

"The walls'll cave in any second—I'll show you the way out!" Were we both equally hysterical? Insane? The caves, I did not doubt, especially after a dynamite blast, could easily derange a person. Even I had to push back the demons of panic and mania resident in this place.

"You go," Derek told me. That's what he said. I never had any use for the creep, and now he was saying, "Get the fuck outta here! Save your fuckin' skin, Sparrow. I gotta dig Patty out!"

"Patty? Patty Correlli is down here? How did she get down here?"

"That was the deal," Derek ranted, working his stick as a lever to dislodge an impressive stone. "Neil shows me the tunnels, I set him up wid pussy."

"Where is she?"

My question sounded nuts to Derek, for he did not know that I was the cartographer of this dimension. "Down here, shit-face. She's buried."

"No!" I grabbed hold of him. "Where exactly? Tell me where you were. Describe it to me. Look, I know my way around down here. Tell me where she is exactly, Derek. There are other ways in and out."

Panting from his exertion, he required a split second to switch gears. "We're in a long tunnel, okay? A straight long tunnel. We found this openin' at the end to sit? All we're doin' is talkin', see. Then Neil, he says he's goin' for a piss. We hang around wid'out him. Then I get smart, see." Derek pointed to his temple, indicating the origin of his brilliance. "I got it figured out. The motherfucker ditched us! We can't get back wid'out him. So me and Patty, we go after him. Fucking near caught the sommabitch too, and Pats is right behind me. She's right behind me? We caught him tappin' somethin' into a wall. He's workin' under this electric light? And what's he got in his hand looks like one helluva fuckin' motherfuckin' firecracker. I couldn't believe it. The sommabitch is gonna blow us up! Whad'I ever do to him, the little schmuck? So I shout to Patty—the bitch screams, she runs back the other way. I'm duckin' down this side-channel? I'm swearin' at him the sommabitch, I want him to know where he stands wid me. 'Fuck you, Neil! Fuck you, Neil!' Fuck me, he punches down this plunger-thing with both hands, the sommabitch. The *sommabitch!* I just cover my ears and the whole place blows. Me, I thought I was one dead dork. Last thing I see, Neil's takin' off, the shit-faced runt."

"Come on. There's another way in. It's Patty's only chance."

I was not convinced that Patty could be rescued, for I had seen something that Derek had not, the damage at street level. The long tunnel where Patty was located had caved in along most of its length. She might have been alive in some small aperture somewhere, or she might have retreated to the holding station before everything fell in behind her. What I was doing, essentially, was getting Derek out. I was amazed that he had been willing to risk his life down there, and do whatever it would take to rescue Patty, although I understood the emotion. I marvelled at myself too, for I could not let myself vacate the tunnels without saving Derek's skin as well.

Bravery must have something to do with refusing to think straight.

With all our human might we heaved to open the trapdoor. Neil had come back and was busy covering the hatch with rocks and branches, anything he could find to seal us in our grave. Seeing it begin to open, he sat right down on the door, and we had to throw his weight

off as well. Once we wedged ourselves in the crack between the earth
and sky, between death and breath, Neil scattered. He vaulted the
fence and escaped down the lane.

We ran through the debacle of the streets, dodging policemen
intent on evacuating the neighbourhood. Cops gave chase. Neophytes,
they expired nipping at our heels. I led Derek around by rue de l'Epée
and into the lane that segregated that street from Bloomfield. I didn't
stop running until I was under the oak tree behind the witch's house.

"Now what?"

"Up and over."

We scaled the wire fence next to the witch's high board one, clasped
a limb, worked our way onto the trunk of the oak, and dropped down
into the yard. One person had been unimpressed with the threat of gas
explosions. One person had declined to answer her doorbell to the
police. One person for blocks around had remained behind, refusing to
flee with the other refugees. Almost, I thought as my feet and hands
touched ground after my leap from the bark of the tree, as though she
had been waiting for us, as though she had anticipated this trespass.

The witch opened her door wielding her magic broom.

"Where's the hatch?" Derek wanted to know.

"It hasn't been dug yet."

"I don't get you."

Trimmed grass indicated a measure of organization and procedure in
the witch's itinerary. I flopped down on all fours. Like a destitute myopic
searching for a missing contact lens, I scrounged around on her lawn.

"What the fuck we lookin' for?" An eager supplicant, Derek also
fell to his knees beside me.

"An air-hole. It's an aluminum tube. Two of them should be stuck
in the ground." Provided my calculations were correct.

"Fuckin'-A! I seen them from the other end!"

The witch ventured down her steps, holding her broom and muttering spells. "We lost something!" I shouted at her, hoping to penetrate her craziness. "We have to find it." We had no time right at that
moment to be swatted by a lunatic. The last thing in the world that I
desired, under the circumstances, was an introduction.

And yet, a renewed sadness billowed inside me.

She walked over slowly, pointing her toes forward like a ballerina's,
then holding a pose behind me. As attentively as a man caressing his
lover's skin, my hands carved circular patterns through the grass. I
craved the touch of metal bone. The witch postulated, "You must be on

a vital mission. You are the first juvenile delinquents I have met who have not run away from me. Perhaps you are from outer space?"

"I'm from Bloomfield Street."

"That was my second choice."

Looking up over my shoulder, I could have scaled a ladder of my sadness at that moment, so stiff and formidable was my gloom. The witch was not my mother. My mother had been twenty-one years old when we had departed Lougain, and I had been six. Fifteen years between us. A decade after slipping from the train she'd be thirty-one—this witch had seen fifty. She was not my mother by a long shot, and having heard her speak in a calm, mocking voice, I now had to doubt that she was even a witch.

"Found it!" Derek hollered.

Like a grasshopper, I bounded across to the small circular hole, shouting, "Patty! Patty!"

"You two are nuttier than my nephews, and three of them have been incarcerated," the broom-toting woman observed.

"Ma'm," I said, "I don't have time to explain. I'm Gerald Boisvert's son."

"You can't fool me. You don't look at all like Barclay Boisvert."

She had reason to be sceptical.

"I'm his other son. Sparrow."

"Isn't that strange? He never mentioned fathering a bird."

The brain is capable of computing dreaded information and filing it away for later study. I scarcely flinched, citing, "I'm sort of adopted. I'm like a foster kid. Ma'm? I can't explain that now either. We need a shovel."

"Why do I feel queasy about your request?"

That she lowered her lethal broom did not escape my attention.

"Please," I begged. "It's really important."

"Important enough for you to give me your name, rank, and serial number. You are so very forthcoming, young man. I suppose this has something to do with the commotion in the streets?"

Her cooperation was vital. If she started swatting us, we wouldn't be able to dig. "Yes, Ma'm," I said. And added, "A life is at stake."

"Curiouser and curiouser, to quoth Alice. You'll find a gardening spade under the porch. A fifty percent share seems a fair disposition of all buried treasure, don't you think? Plus a twelve percent royalty if you strike gold, oil, or any other precious commodity. Agreed?"

Derek was promptly back with the shovel, and handed it to me. He knew how to delegate responsibility. Petty thieves learn early to let the other guy hold the weapon. "This is serious," I told the woman, censoring her flippancy.

"In my backyard, only an infestation of sow bugs or teenagers can be deemed serious."

Putting my foot to the back edge of the spade, I dug.

The woman uttered an expression of surprise, but not alarm, when I broke through to air. "What's this? Is the earth hollow? Don't tell me. You've found a shortcut to China. What's down there, Sparrow?"

I was about to scoop more earth when the soil beneath my feet slid away. An unbroken free-fall threw me onto my tail bone.

"Sparrow!"

Looking up, I viewed the daft faces of my two former antagonists, the bully and the witch.

"What ghosts have you unleashed from this vacant grave?"

"Stay there!" I shouted to both of them. "I'll find Patty!"

Dread, and a wealthy foreboding, accompanied me on my crawl back into the tunnels. I didn't call Patty's name, for I feared finding her, expecting a dead hand to emerge from the rubble, or a mangled face presented for my kiss. Somewhere I had lost my flashlight, and the lights of this section had been knocked out. I thought I heard a reciprocal scratching sound, like somebody's crawl, or was it an echo? Ssshhh. Listen. Whenever I stood still, so did the other presence. When Patty and I bumped heads, each of us screamed like a psychotic fugitive. She grabbed me so forcefully I choked. I had to kick and squeal and for a moment I feared that I had met, at last, one of my mother's frightful demons. Patty emerged from her delirium ahead of me, and I, the boy who penetrated the surface of the earth and awoke sleeping nymphs from their graves, staggered from the dark grotto into the centring light of the witch's gaze.

She seemed impressed by my powers.

"Have you more damsels in your dungeon's safekeeping, Sparrow? I would prefer that you release them from their misery right now."

I swore that Patty had been the only one.

The witch stretched down her broom and Patty latched onto it. Derek pulled her up, then lowered the broom for me.

Cut, scratched, and lathered with dirt, Patty was quietly hysterical. She rocked continuously, uttering wee cries, and the woman encircled her in her arms and guided her into the house. She nodded for Derek and me to follow. What was more difficult, entering the collapsed tunnel to search for Patty in the dark, or stepping across the portal into the witch's magic lair?

The witch wrapped Patty in a Hudson's Bay blanket, the one with four marks to indicate it's worth. Washing the girl's face, she sponged her off, dabbed the cuts, and applied bandages to the deepest ones. Her medicines appeared commonplace, not a witch's brew. Patty was amazing. She was tough, and she relaxed, panicking only when the woman suggested that her parents be summoned. She would rather be buried alive than have her family know what she had been doing. Although tempted, I had the good sense not to question her, and the witch demonstrated similar good will. She plied us with sandwiches and hot chocolate milk, and the only person she'd quiz was me.

"Young Sparrow, where are your wings? I quite understand someone endowed with your name fluttering out of the tree and poking about on my lawn. Other birds do it all the time. It is another matter, however, for you to squiggle through the earth like a worm. What sort of behaviour is that for one of your species? I feel compelled to add, at the risk of seeming quaint or out of fashion, that I find it quite extraordinary that you would emerge from the earth with a lovely girl on your sleeve, as though you were off to the senior prom."

In bits and pieces, I explained as little as I possibly could and still make sense. My reticence never fooled her. She knew I had much to hide.

"You're certain that you have no more lovely girls preserved under my lawn, Sparrow, alive, or otherwise indisposed?"

"I swear. Patty was the only one."

As she rubbed a knuckle along the bridge of her nose, I detected the premonition of a smile. "That is a moderately satisfactory response."

We departed by the back way. Outside, the woman picked up her broom and swept us off. Fronts and backsides, bellies and bums, from our toes to our necks her broom swished us clean. She twirled the dial of her combination lock which secured the stately rear door to her garden. Like the drawbridge to a castle, the great door creaked open, and we were dispatched again into the real world. I experienced the same sad longing I had known on the day my mother and me had been purged from the garden at Lougain.

As I was about to utter my final words of thanks and apology, the woman whispered in my ear, "Don't turn around, Sparrow. Don't look back. If God turned Lot's wife into a pillar of salt, what will He do to a wee bird like you?" I heard the door shut behind me. I said so long to Patty and Derek, and the three of us walked, then ran, in three different directions.

*

Quite a Thanksgiving. Walking home through deserted streets, I took a detour around the conflagration of emergency vehicles, and reflected upon the secret lives of people. On the surface, I had passed through the world as an ordinary kid, rambunctious with enthusiasms and grievances, spoiling my plans with impulse. Yet, how many "ordinary" kids preferred to romp underground? Mr. Cherkova presented an image of the lazy, layabout husband, one content to have his wife run the family business. In fact, he worked himself close to death carving a subterranean connection to a reputed witch in the ludicrous conviction that she would appreciate the favour. The crazy woman he was stalking from below had demonstrated that she was immeasurably sane. The Wicked Witch of Bloomfield Street turns out to be a Sister of Mercy, excellent at restoring traumatized girls. I never knew what to expect out of life. Neil the Wimp was a homicidal crackpot who not only would have buried his hated enemy alive, but a girl he had been yearning to know. Some first date. For good measure, he had attempted to get rid of his one good friend as well.

More difficult to accept was the good news. In a crisis, Derek the Despicable Delinquent had been transformed as heroic. In secret, Patty the Nun was a harlot in drag. Or had her true self, be there such a creature, been lost somewhere between the two extremes? Waiting on my porch for my family to receive permission to return home, I considered the day's most infamous news. Barclay Butter had squealed on his dad. He had intimated that his father was connected to nefarious business. According to Barc—that rising sun of the business world—his father, that noted mountebank hawking the twin remedies of Truth and Honesty, maintained a secret record in a separate safe of his shady deals. That wasn't all. Skinny Sparrow Drinkwater, that bird of a feather, lived in the shadow of those transactions, the shadiest deal of all.

I had been searching for my mother. In a sense I had found her. She had proven to be someone other than my hope of last resort. The closer I had dug with Mr. Cherkova to the odd woman's house, the more I had begun to fabricate a possibility. It all made sense. Uncle took care of my mother separately from me. I might find her. Now ... it didn't matter. The tunnels had collapsed and my mother was not the Wicked Witch of Bloomfield Street. Nor was she the woman in her guise as a Sister of Mercy. And yet, in observing the secret and contradictory lives of people, I had discovered a subterranean access to her. In the covert schizophrenia of the world I had been brought closer to the mother I remembered and loved. Okay, my mother had less control over her life than any of these others, did that not make her less mad than people who deliberately behaved so strangely? My mother could not be crazier than Derek, who hid his heroic heart behind a pariah's example. She could not be more mad than the demented dynamiter of Park Extension, Neil Abrahamson. Could she be crazier than the Witch, who was perfectly sane, and pretended otherwise? Or more twisted than Patty who could not decide between a life of whoredom or sainthood? I drew closer to my mother that day. In a private, oblique way, I located her. I discovered for the first time that she was not as isolated as societies attest, her illness was not the foreign ailment that people believed, she was not the alien being that I had imagined over the interval of our absence. Comprehending this, my faith burst with renewal, my heart erupted with a transcendant belief in a possibility, that somehow she had conquered her fall and had successfully endured the lapsed time and distance between us. My desire to see her again had regenerated itself.

Eight days after the "earthquake," Uncle sat me down in Barclay's tantrum-chair on a fact-finding expedition. Following the great events, many parents were growing inquisitive about the leisure activities of their children, although few had cause. The truth was becoming known, the press of the entire world was paying bemused attention, and every teenager in the district had been catalogued as a suspect. Our particular patch of soil sowed delinquents. Guilt was automatically assigned to teens until the evidence could be analyzed.

The nature of our crimes was a matter for speculation. Were the moles robbers who intended to drill into basements? Rapists who would squirrel away their victims in dungeons? Were they, as one tabloid suggested, an alien mutant species? A sociologist confidently proposed that our behaviour was induced by fear of the Atom Bomb, and that similar underground shelters formed a grid beneath every city in America, to believe otherwise was blissfully naive. The tunnels were a hint of my generation's future.

Work crews repairing the damage excavated the tunnels from above. On the day that one led them, by ladder, into Ludmilla Cherkova's basement, Uncle proposed serious, exploratory discussions.

Under siege, I confessed to knowing about the labyrinth.

Uncle placed his face in his left hand and sagged under melancholy burdens. "It's ssso crazy," he admitted to me at last. That's what bothered him the most. Not the audacity, the secrecy, the lack of common sense, the flirtation with danger—he was concerned about my genetic propensity toward madness. He said it. "It's insane."

As I look back, it's easy to see that I had been stowing a range of grievances. I expressed the one that he had chosen to exploit. "That's all you care about it, isn't it, Uncle? I used to wonder why my marks at school never bothered you. I don't do half as well as Barclay and you never care one bit."

"It's not a competition," he protested.

"For him it is. Barc against the rest of the world."

"He has a gift. He's very bright."

"What do I have, Uncle? Shit for brains? You think it's a big mystery? I'm not so stupid. I know why you never cared. School marks, success in life, they don't represent the big picture."

"That's a healthy attitude, Sssparrow."

"Yeah, healthy for me. Because what's important is whether or not I'm sane. Right? Anything else is gravy. You expect me to go nuts. Just like my mother. You're waiting for it to happen. Is this my vulnerable age? Is that what your research tells you? Now is about the time when my mother's crazy genes should be kicking in? I'll be bumping along just fine thank you very much and then one day, *pffffft!* I go over the edge."

"Ssssparrow, that's not true."

Why was I being so mean to him? "Face it, Uncle. Okay, so you take good care of me. But you have all these incredible ambitions for Barclay. For me, all you hope for is that I don't go crazy."

"Balderdash!" Denying the truth never erases it. The tone of his protest convinced me that I had socked him pretty good.

"You know what, Uncle? I am crazy. I'm crazy. I'd rather live underground than at street level. Every single night of my life, in the summers, I get up and I go outside and I piss in the garden. Why do you think I do that? Because I can't find the bathroom? No—because I'm crazy. Because I want to be crazy. Because my mother used to do it and look what happened to her. A raven was perched on the moon, it glided down to earth and I was born. I keep looking for that bird to return. Once I thought it was you. Remember? You looked like my father, that day you were tarred and feathered, that's when I decided maybe I could stay here awhile. When you fell asleep—remember? Aunt made us pluck your feathers. I wanted to leave you as you were, I *liked* the crow costume. I want to be crazy, Uncle. I'm scared to be sane. I want to go mad. Because if I'm crazy then I don't forget where I come from, I don't forget about my real mother, I don't forget that my real father was a giant black raven or a crow or a demon of some kind. Maybe a man in feathers. He looked like you did that day but he wasn't you. He was somebody else. Something else. Some crazy thing. I am crazy, Uncle. That's how you have to accept me because that's how I am. I'm crazy, I'm crazier, I'm craziest! Crazy crazy crazy."

I stopped ranting. I almost had him convinced. I did not reveal that I was onto him, that Barclay had spoken about a secret client and that I had knowledge of his second, private safe. I might need that information some day. I was not so out of control that I let anything other than petty gripes escape.

"Sssssparrow," he started. Momentarily, he realized that he had nothing further to add.

For awhile we were silent together.

"Ain't that the truth," I concluded.

Mr. Kershner was found dead in the tunnels.

We had assumed that he had become lost after the evacuation, that he had misinterpreted being evicted from his home by the police. In his old age he had grown confused, we told ourselves, thinking he was pursued by the Nazis. Too bad we hadn't been right.

Mr. Kershner was located by a city road crew, deep underground. He had been wandering among his terrible memories and was crushed. As a young man, he had stood beside his father when the Nazi's blew a whistle and the carnage had ceased for the day. The Germans resorted to manners and decorum. Insane that—hideous butchery, a whistle blows, courteous conduct is resumed. The terrible schizophrenia of the world. Less than a minute after his mother and sister had been gunned down, a whistle blew, and the Germans requested Mr. Kershner to assist the feeble, the frightened, and those who were suffocating. (He had told Neil and me another story which had happened to a friend's wife. She and her children were hiding under the bed while German soldiers ransacked their house, throwing anything of value out the window for collection. Anything they did not confiscate they smashed. Then, from the street, a whistle blew. One of the soldiers knocked quietly on the bedroom door. He had said, "Excuse me, madam, may I use your telephone?" Yes, that happened.) The kindly gentleman who would stare at me until his eyes wept, had survived the shootings and the concentration camps, but he had not endured Neil's revenge.

The world, I understood, with examples tucked in my hip pockets, was crazy. With madness so prevalent, how could I be sane?

two

1958–1961

DESPERADOS

6.

Lonely Hearts Drift

Contrary to rumours worming through my neighbourhood—an underground network as intricate as the tunnels—my first lover was not the Wicked Witch of Bloomfield Street. True, she and I would become fast friends. Drinking partners and confidants. That's all. I was young and she was old. She was a woman, I was male. For reasons no better than those sick minds attempted to subvert our fun. Nudges, smirks, smart-ass comments aside, for us to have been lovers was unthinkable.

People didn't get it. I can understand why. No one could guess my natural affinity for lonely, loopy older women, or believe that my attentions were benign.

After the collapse of the tunnels I had been a beggar for a hangout. My vocation as a paperboy behind me, the unexpected inheritance of idle time remained anxious to be invested. Like a moon lost in the cosmos seeking a sun's reflection (the void of the world seemed that large to me, my isolation that immense), I'd wander by the witch's house flirting with the pull of her gravitational field. On a dull day, a year or so after I'd dug up her lawn, she rapped on the inside of the front window to signal me safely into her orbit.

Why was I subject to that polar attraction?

Her home, and the high fence of the back yard, reminded me of Lougain. She was nutty enough to invoke images of my mother. Yet my interest and my disquiet were based on something else, on a glimmer. Through her I could sense—as if she really was a witch adept at gazing into crystal balls—a clairvoyant view of the future. Which was something, for all other paths seemed blocked.

The witch's name was Diedre Plant, but I would never be permitted to call her anything but Miss Plant. "A bright young boy like you, Sparrow, you must have figured it out by now. This sorry world is unfit for human habitation." In the afternoons we had tea, a nice substitute for similar events with Ludmilla Cherkova. After our tea, we'd sustain a nip of Scotch. Or three.

"People treat one another with such antipathy it's miraculous that anything works. Sparrow, the lubricant that makes our society function is greed. Perhaps you haven't made that connection yet. Don't misunderstand, greed's not such a bad thing. Greed channels wickedness, it grants our malicious souls purpose, aligns them with a proper bearing. As sins go, it is far more enlightened than gluttony or sloth. I prefer greedy men to murderers, don't you?" I would nod in silence, trying to follow the swerves of her logic. "Think of the social benefits that derive from greed. Without greed, we'd be berry-pickers, millions would starve, the world would be inundated with malevolence and injury and hideous, repulsive acts. Which is true anyway, of course, but the worst violence occurs where greed knows no expression. Greed is our salvation from the mire. It undermines wickedness with aspiration. It gives evil something to do. Without greed, we humans could never ascend from chaos, we'd be stuck in the mud of our bestiality forever."

The benefits and attractions of her company were manifold. She would force me to defend the world against her assault. "Pretty grim, Miss Plant. Sure, money motivates some people. But just as many are inspired by the search for something higher. I believe that." I was young at the time.

"The search for something higher," ruminated the cynical Miss Plant. She'd crunch a Social Tea biscuit as if biting down on my crispy logic. "The search for more extravagant bank accounts. Are you absolutely certain that one is not parading in the guise of the other?"

"What do you mean?"

"Do you go to church, Sparrow?"

"Aunt drags me along." We were successfully lowering the mark on a Johnny Walker Red.

"Which one?"

"Livingstone Presbyterian."

"Your father goes too?"

"Uncle," I stipulated. Since we were becoming friends, I could insist on the preferred appellation. "Sometimes he goes. Rarely."

"Gerald Boisvert is a French-Canadian Roman Catholic," Miss Plant pointed out. "His patron saint is Johnny Baptist. Pray tell, what is he doing carting you off to a transplanted Church of Scotland? Why did he forsake the fleur-de-lys for the thistle?"

Months earlier it happened that I had broached the question with Uncle myself, only to have him slough it off with obvious irritation. Since then I had not deigned to challenge him. "Does it matter?"

"He married a Scotswoman. Raised his son to speak English. Converted to a Protestant Church. Do you think he had a vision? Like Saul, alias Paul, on his merry way to Damascus to lash Christian backsides, was he blinded by the light? Do you believe he underwent a conversion from one form of worship to another?"

Religion, to Uncle, applied to the realm of civic duty. "I doubt it," I had to confess.

"Ah, but he *did* convert. Your Uncle saw which side of the bread business buttered. From there he figured out how to streamline his son's career. Before Barclay was born, your uncle reduced his impediments to advancement. He named his first born after a school—a big, bold English name. If he had known better or done his research, he would have called him 'Harvard'. He enrolled his son in the proper religion, and raised him to speak the language of the board room.

"The search for something higher," Miss Plant repeated, amused by my earlier turn of phrase. "You are a lopsided personality, Sparrow. For someone who has spent so much time burrowing underground, you do have a penchant for altitude."

"Derives from my name," I commented.

"That's one clue. The other—what is this urgent striving I sense in you? A gift to forge, or uncover, or rediscover, or perpetuate—what is it? I'm babbling. Is it the Scotch?" With two fingers, she caressed the blue-veined hollow of her temple. Her eyes, a soft, bluish chalcedony, could never be accusatory or mad or witchlike. Her look conveyed a furtive heart, at once placid in its hiding place, yet wary of intrusion. Contradictory eyes, both cunning, and vibrant with fright. Every time I visited her I would be shocked anew by both the whiteness and the vulnerability of her skin. Sunlight rarely touched her. Miss Plant looked as someone might who had purged and cleansed her life with such resolution that the faint blue of her eyes lingered as her life's pure essence. Children and adults alike should be more circumspect about whom we label witches. "What do I say about a young man who uproots damsels from the muck of my garden? What do I feel from you, young Sparrow? The need to rise higher, to float to the heavens, fly?"

My hesitation swung me around to a side of myself I was inclined to keep private, an area of my thinking I allowed little credence. "There's one thing," I intimated. Emotions sometimes seized me and hindered my logic, making me sound daft. That my lower lip took its cue to tremble, and that a tear trickled free, really did not measure the pathos of my condition. I cry easily as a rule, so the facile teariness should be given little heed. "I'd like to find my mother, that's all."

"Do you think she's alive?" Miss Plant asked me quietly.

I rubbed that idiotic tear away. "Sure. Why not? Sometimes I tell myself she can't be. Deep down I've never doubted that she is."

"Then that's what you must do!" the witch of Bloomfield Street proclaimed. "You're wasting your time trotting off to a university. How will you discriminate between ideas? How will you know whether you should get rich or become holy—or both! or neither!—unless you have satisfied the quest that broils inside you? First things first, Sparrow. We cannot even continue this conversation, that's how out of kilter you are. Go find your mother. Until then, you will not be fit to darken my doors again. Get out of my house!"

"Miss Plant."

Time to place the Scotch beyond her arm's reach.

Despite her admonition, I would continue to be admitted inside Diedre Plant's doors. Her friendship meant a great deal to me, especially now that Barclay was rocketing into the corporate world, and the Cherkovas' small basement, bereft of both tunnels and employment, had been declared off-limits. Miss Plant had illuminated my secret obsession. She encouraged me to pursue my quest, and enforced the reminder that it would never diminish on its own. Never did she allow me to stray from its clear principles. Miss Plant helped me to sort out my frail ambitions. She declared that the half-heartedness of my interest in engineering (my maths had not improved) stemmed from the unresolved crusade deeper inside me. With no pussy-footing around, I learned something from her that was far more troubling. Each time I encountered a woman I was really searching for aspects of my mother. She made a point of kicking me out whenever she sensed I might be casting her in the role. "What do you think I am, demented? I won't be your mother, Sparrow. I won't be a kook for you. Get out of my house this instant!"

In calmer mind, she would persuade me, "This will be a big, big issue for you, Sparrow. Girls don't appreciate being cast as surrogate moms. Find your real one, or you'll live without a wife as well."

Scary news.

The woman could be insightful and harsh. Like a rioter urging a mob to new feats of daring and defiance, she persistently roused me out of my lethargy. "Sparrow, sport, you've spent too much time underground. Live on the surface awhile. The experience won't do you much good, but if you decide to 'reach for higher things', or become just another rich man, you should chirp about at tree level—ground level at least—before you fly."

"I eat steak," I grumbled. "Not bird food. I have two good feet. No wings. I don't intend to fly, for chrissakes."

"You taught yourself to map interior worlds. That's impressive. You rescue girls trapped underground. How odd. Maybe it's diet. Do you eat worms regularly? No?"

"No."

"Centipedes? If Montreal has an earthquake we can use that talent. You can feed the masses."

"Knock it off."

"You're weird, Sparrow. Admit it. You grew up in a nest for half your life—a big cage in your Uncle's house. The other half was wasted in a tunnel. If you don't fly the coop soon, little bird, you'll forget why you have wings. You'll suffocate."

"You should talk."

"*I* do not suffer your delusions. *I* am not searching for a 'higher way'. I'm not even looking for my mother. Mine's dead. You should be so lucky."

Miss Plant irritated me so much. How could anybody take advice from a fruitcake? And yet, day by day, I kept going back for more, fortifying myself for what had to be a major conflagration ahead. The combatants—I didn't have to figure it out, she told me—would be fragments of myself.

*

One of the great tragedies of modern society is that countless nincompoops are armed with an unlicensed weapon, one as devastating as an Uzi. What can possibly be more lethal than superficial knowledge of Freudian thought? Not that Herr Sigmund was the first or, thankfully, the last; Oedipus had a problem long before Freud defined it, and minions have since embellished the theme.

Diedre Plant's remarks to me had included true and injurious comment. To argue that my fixation with my mother derived from unusual circumstances could grant me a reprieve, yet be brutally self-incriminating as well. A bind. The inherent difference between my situation and that pertaining to Mr. Oedipus was that I did not know my mother.

I had lost touch with the ability to conjure her appearance. Apart from customs that honoured a semblance of her memory—like peeing in the yard at night, or latching onto oddballs—her absence, not her influence, remained the resident, resonant voice articulate inside my head.

Her truancy was my singular point of reference in the real world.

Miss Plant had jangled sensitive nerves. Anytime I got close to a girl I was forced to wrestle angels. Before romance, before sport, the spectre of my missing parent needed to be pinned to the ground and made to cry uncle. As well, my inherent fascination with kooks undermined heated attractions to girls and women. We can't call it an accident that my first lovers mixed weird aberrations into the arcane pudding of lust, joy, and wonder.

Then why, if I give the boot to Oedipus and his ruddy complex, do my cheeks remain lathered with this blush? Could it have something to do with my first lover being double my age? Hard evidence, except that I hasten to make the point in this self-inflicted cross-examination that she was anything but motherly.

Thank Barclay for setting me up with her. A side-benefit to being quasi-related to that rising star of business accounting procedure was that the boy who used to kick his feet in our kitchen, the sniveller, the griper, the golf-course cheater and prodigy-of-the-ledger, had steadily been developing connections. I needed summer work. To keep Barclay content, three companies vied to hire me. Imagine that. I went to work in a camera importing firm under the Accounts Receivable Manager, a highly-strung Latvian woman with a history of emotional congestion.

"Be careful," the prescient Miss Plant forewarned. Old-fashioned, she distrusted women in business. "A woman like that, she can chew you up, a pretty young boy."

I scoffed. Both the idea and the adjective were ridiculous. "Boys are called handsome," I instructed my new friend. "Girls are pretty, not boys."

"I've offended you."

"Damn right. Apologize."

"I am in such shady despair. A baby-faced boy like you, considered pretty by a nasty old hag like me, how could I speak such heresy? Can you find it in your heart to forgive me, Sparrow?"

Whenever she made fun of me, I squirmed, unsure how to retaliate. "You think you know everything," was the meat of my criticism.

"Witches do."

"You're no witch. You're not a hag either." Why was I defending her? Wasn't I the one under attack?

"We'll see."

My Accounts Receivable Manager, Betty, wore sunglasses at work one day. She insisted that we put in overtime (that old, old saw) and summoned me to her office once we were alone. She kicked her shoes off. Literally. They arched through the air and tumbled end over end into the waste basket on the opposite side of the room. A neat trick. Betty sat in a swivel chair, dumped her feet in an open drawer, and nibbled the arm of her sunglasses between her teeth. Eyes I had not seen all day. Of greater importance, this was the first time that I discovered myself to be the recipient of such a look from a woman. My mischievous member rose to question her attention.

"Sit, Sparrow," she invited, which I did as she stood. "Would you recommend that Denise Lantrelle's typewriter be replaced? You're a boy, you must be mechanical. Would you mind examining the service record?"

She passed me a page. A blur. Standing, Betty came around the desk. She stood behind me, and leaned over my right shoulder. I could not be certain if the point of her left breast had found the nape of my neck, or if that touch could be explained by a soft shoulder or an incidental, padded elbow. Then she switched her contact to my left shoulder, and I glimpsed our reflection repeated in the window. Definitely! Her breast was resting on my neck! (The image galvanized a recollection. When Barc and I had been considering offers, he had cautioned that Betty "goes off the deep end every so often." Had that intimation of mental distress inspired me to take this job? Did I feel more comfortable, or more curious, around crazy people?)

"Is something wrong, Sparrow? Don't you have an opinion?"

I managed to mumble gibberish about overhauling the machine as an alternative to a new purchase. Certain that she was oblivious to our contact, and afflicted with the sort of chivalry that wanted to remedy her inadvertent immodesty, I tucked my torso in upon itself, bending lower.

The breast followed my neck down.

The pressure increased.

My head hovered inches off the desk, the fact-sheet too close to decipher.

"What seems to be the problem, Sparrow?" Betty shifted sides again, without breaking contact. Cigarette breath. "Are you weary? Had a long day?"

To mention that my head practically lay on the desk because she was unaware of the thrust of her bosom struck me as impolite. I said, gasped, "Not used to overtime."

"Overtime," she whispered, her equine voice unbridled in my ears riding roughshod across my senses, "is the best time of day. Put your head down on the desk, Sparrow."

"It's okay," I stammered. Yet I could not lift up, as though my neck had developed a permanent crick. To move against the breast clearly would be a violation of conduct. Would she not soon realize my difficulty and jump back, flustered and embarrassed?

"No," she contradicted. "Listen to your boss. Put your head on the desk, and close your eyes." The firm hand on my scalp forced me to oblige. I heard her moving behind me. "Have a nice little nap, you'll be as right as rain. Close your eyes now, dear. No peeking. You are such a pretty baby, Sparrow."

My eyes snapped open at that remark, cross-references snagging on humiliation and disbelief. Shutting them tight again, I gave myself fair warning to hold my imagination in check. Betty was merely unhinged, she had regressed to a fantasy of kindergarten, in her middle age she had lost touch with how to treat someone who was all of seventeen. Then I felt both at once. One on my shoulder. The other across my mouth. How could I account for an oversight this extreme? A breast might contact my flesh, my fascination with the female form might read into the event more than was intended. Yet how do I point out to a woman that she has absent-mindedly removed her jacket, blouse, and bra, and unaware of her state has unwittingly, without premeditation, pressed both bare breasts upon my hysterical skin?

What do I do except freeze?

While my body blazes.

Remaining the dutiful underling, I followed the various instructions that Betty had devised for my employment. Not wishing to offend, I removed my shirt on command. Took off my pants. As slowly as paint drying she slid down the zipper on her dress. Now, this was something new. She skimmed off her lavender panties, revealing herself in garter belt and nylons and as quickly as the Lone Ranger on Silver mounted me and galloped away. I reared up under her in the swivelling chair. *I was having sex! Yippee!*

Wow.

We sealed ourselves in the office when the night cleaners arrived, and later used the reception room sofa, the board room table, and the leather chairs in the partners' offices. Uncle, when I came home, was pleased with both my ravaged look and the late hour, complimenting my work ethic.

"It's an okay job," I told him.

Naturally, going into the office the next day, I prepared for a chilly welcome. Betty would either declare her remorse or profess no memory of our folly. I would do the honourable thing and not speak of it again. Submit my resignation, if asked. Once again, however, I had failed to divine the rules. During the morning coffee break I was blown—my semen milked at the last possible instant into a styrofoam cup—and during the lunch hour we shared our sandwiches, her orange, my apple, Aunt Butter's butter tarts, and at the conclusion of our feast Betty hoisted her skirts to reveal, while leaning across requisition forms No. B7Y-9648, a spankingly white bare bottom.

"What if somebody comes in?" I, the child, murmured. Could I get fired for this? Demoted? Arrested? We had a lock on the door, but how do you explain refusing to answer the boss's inquisitive knock?

"Nobody's around but us chickens. Hurry, Sparrow!"

I plundered her roost.

The absence of panties—that did it for me. I finally figured out that this woman was amenable to having sex with me. Women like her might exist in Bangkok, or in Munich, but I would be wise to make the most of this opportunity. Undoubtedly she was the only such creature in the entire city of Montreal.

My Latvian lover lasted through the long, hot summer before going crazy. Perhaps I was infected, that became my crucial worry. In some mysterious way, had I been contaminated from birth? Given my lineage, I could only assume that I was somehow responsible for driving her insane.

Intimations of Betty's impending demise should have been obvious. I lacked the experience, and was too flush with sex, to interpret the clues. First she wanted me to introduce her to my friends. Not totally without guile, I deduced that she was less interested in evaluating my influences than she was inclined to corrupt them. That issue, corruption, caused me some distress. I had scant interest in pimping for her. The day I told her as much she made a scene along Dorchester Boulevard that stopped traffic. Later, at her place, while she lolled about in the nude, she asked me to try on her nylons. I was out the door, she missed a week of work, when she showed up her face was bruised and harrowed by fatigue. Betty ranted at the Director of Services that she could not possibly be expected to drive to work each day, that her parking space—nobody could understand this one—was way too small, and that she absolutely required a limo and a driver at her disposal around the clock. (She might have been promoting me for the job.) Having been through similar scenes with her before, the D.S. knew which number to call. Attendants in white gowns arrived for her. Betty was curled between the water cooler and the wall, trying to chew off her bra strap in the way that trapped animals gnaw through limbs. My first lover was hauled away. Her eyes crossed mine as she was being dragged out, yet, sadly, they showed no glint of recognition.

Betty was somewhat older than my mother. I had to hope that she was considerably crazier than her too.

Fortune. Luck. Coincidence, let's call it, or fate?

Arriving home on the evening after Betty's demise I found Uncle summarily erect in the living room. The vestments of his business day had yet to be shed, which, coupled with his forthright posture and disposition, usually indicated that an important announcement was imminent. In his right hand, Uncle clutched an envelope as he might a serrated knife, which he used to methodically saw his closed left fist.

"A letter arrived for you today, Ssssparrow."

"For me?" I countered. "And you opened it?"

"It's from the Faculty of Engineering, McGill University. Your education is a family concern. I offer no apology for opening ssssuch correspondence. You, on the other hand, may be interested in formulating words of penance about the contents."

"How come?" My legs were rickety in the joints, mushy through the muscles. I contrived, to the last, to forge an alliance between confidence and humility.

"You have failed McGill. A sssson of mine, given the opportunity, given the privilege of higher education"—with each syllable his voice rose a decibel—"has ssssquandered his chances and flunked out!"

On the brighter side of this sad episode, I did not need to fake the appearance of a contrite heart. I had wanted to be an engineer. The facts attested to my weak commitment while shining light upon a bungler's brain. I will not pretend that my devotion had been exemplary or that my attention had been focused. Allow one faint whimper before I keep my peace. I had wanted to be an engineer. In reverie I constructed huge things. Not blessed with the right turn of mind I had failed, which hurt. Nothing could be more official, nor more heartless, than a verdict delivered in the mail. To complicate the ignominy, to drive home the humiliation, Uncle had opened the notice and read it out loud to the family.

I wept.

Crushed.

My tears were not a ruse. I had been stripped of my ambition. Aunt held me while I shook, Barclay consoled me with his silence, and I suspect that whatever fleet of insults Uncle had floated to counter my indifference wrecked on the shore of my obvious distress.

"How badly did I do?" My cracked voice quavered.

"It makes no difference. You fell below the line."

"By how much? Please, Uncle, I need to know."

He relented. After all, it was *my* letter. "In half your courses you were less than ssssatisfactory. In the others, you were in over your head."

The news made things worse. That I had had good reason to fear such a result did not mollify my dismay. I'd been found wanting. I had failed. The heel of the world's boot had stomped on me as though I'd been an ant, squishing my lofty ambitions into grease.

I was a stain on the landscape of the world.

Uncle sat down beside me. "This does not mean that you are ssssstupid. You wanted to try engineering, I did not sssstand in your way. Your aptitude lies elsewhere, that's been demonstrated now. Beginning tomorrow, Ssssparrow, you can get on with your life." I knew exactly what was coming. I could have quoted him verbatim in advance. "You will ask to be admitted to the Arts Faculty. Ssssomeday you will be a magnificent lawyer, Ssssparrow, and the pain of this moment will be vanquished." He wiggled his moustache to confirm the authenticity of that prophetic vision.

"Yes, Uncle." I needed time alone, aloft, and the attic beckoned.

"Sssparrow," Uncle put in as I climbed the ladder. "This means no more football."

"Uncle—"

"It's not an issue. McGill requires high grades from its athletes, you know that." True. After a fairly brilliant freshman year as a first-string flanker, I would be booted off the squad. The school newspaper would tell everybody why. "If you do very well," Uncle held out to me as a carrot, guessing that he had to assail my disinterest in law, "if you reverse this year's grades, we can discuss a return to football the fall after next."

Wings clipped, I crawled up to my nest.

Of course, I would want to speak to my counsellor about the chill winds of these events. "Fly south with the birdies," Diedre Plant advised. "Take at least one year off. You're not ready to enrol in anything new just yet."

"Uncle would never let me."

"Who's he to let or not let? Did he *let* you dig tunnels and rescue damsels from the clotted earth? Did he *let* you mess about with your boss-lady? Heck, I know about her. Witches know everything. It's in your eyes. It's also why you haven't been around much lately. Stop that blush, Sparrow, it doesn't become you. It makes you look pretty, which *apparently* you hate so much. Listen to me, if you possess half the natural talent to be argumentative as Gerald Boisvert suspects, strike a deal with him. Or, as he would say, sssssstrike a deal!"

"But," I began, still nicked by failure, by the idea of having failed. Where would I go, why would I go there, what was the point of bumming around? What if I failed at doing nothing?

"Sparrow," Miss Plant directed me, "pick up your bed and walk, trot, run. Fly. Sssssstrike a deal! Go hunting for your mother."

So I did.

Like Huckleberry Finn with shoes, Ulysses on his yacht, or Jason accompanied by the Toronto Argonauts, I was off to see the world, hounding and abounding after my quest. I kept my eyes peeled for the golden fleece of my mother's hair.

Surrogate manes, I'm afraid, flagged down my interest first. These were the brash, lucid days of my youth, the time in memory I enjoy most. A redhead was my tour guide in Georgia. Confounded and dismayed that Okefinokee had been turned into parkland boasting of canoe tours, paved roads, and boardwalks that accessed the swamp, my aggravation took solace in the company of this Georgian apricot. My long-limbed beauty moved at a gentle lope, we walked miles. She urged me to ride her long into warm subtropical nights, and again through days whenever whole gales sealed us indoors.

Investigation turned up a likely pick for my mother's old school. Spanish moss hung upon the walls like wet, matted hair. Doors had been removed from their hinges, which bequeathed a toothless smile to the face of the building. Stripped of refinement, stooped with age, the body of the school had been left to sag into a bog. Large portions of the roof had been confiscated to refit local shanties filled with dark-eyed Guatemalan refugees, and while that was a worthy use for the material, I took the school's lack of dignity to heart. I walked around that shambles, in awe, as though I owed my procreation to this enchanted realm.

When my Georgia-girl indicated that she was through with me (cold coffee and warm lemonade my first indicators), I crossed the State Line into Florida, where I sang ballads to the moon and slept wary of shadows floating above the loose, flat earth.

Where was my mother's fair head?

In New Orleans my acrobat-lover's hair was a lustrous brunette coif. She kept it shiny and stiff, sprayed into place to keep the cut from unravelling during trapeze twirls. We had met at a county fair. Rather than have me run away with the circus, she opted for time-off. Together we browsed through Louisiana then into the city. I walked the streets of Old Town, and along the banks of the Bonnet Carré Spillway. Drove relentlessly across the bridge over Lake Pontchartrain, my weather eye on guard for hurry-canes. Sex with my new companion was gymnastic, the contortions she manoeuvred both amazing and dangerous for any male without football experience. Net result, I could not find my mother in New Orleans, and no streets appeared similar to my distant memories.

The Rawlins' had moved on, or passed on, they were not in the book.

The Commission responsible for the waterways looked up Sturgess Rawlins in their records. They reported that he had died. A woman in the office vaguely recalled that he had drowned while out fishing on Lake Pontchartrain.

"Oystering," I corrected her. "Not fishing. He was out oystering."

"Not on Lake Pontchartrain, he wasn't."

"Yes he was."

Nothing, as I remembered it, had remained intact. How much had I fashioned from the gambit of my imagination? Nagged by the provocation that my past life had been untrue, that adventures had evolved differently than I had perceived them, I was often caught glum. Rarely was I much fun. Tired of her grouch, my contortionist rejoined the Fair. All for the best, I consoled myself, though I hated to see her go. My biggest worry had been that she might bind me into knots we could never untangle.

Where would I find my mother's curls?

In St. Louis I came close—which counts in love as well as in horseshoes. The girl I romanced had been blessed with my mother's hair, a glitter and scuff, the hex of beach sand. Freckles, formed into a shade tree's shape, frolicked up her back. I dallied through days kissing the russet autumn leaves (memories of home?), slipping my tongue along the ridges of her spiny trunk, feeling her sap run on my fingers. Cathy worked in the university library. Her odd earrings and occult broaches were intended to ward off evil spirits while attracting stranger ones. Like me. We'd love one another often amid the stacks of dusty books, and, afterward, mull through the tomes.

I did locate a record of my mother's disappearance from the train.

The newspaper account jibed with my own recollections. A bandit's body had been recovered from Missouri's Wataminga River, below the railway trestle. A week later the front page announced the arrest of the missing robber. Stretch was alive! He had made it! He had fallen from the bridge at the same moment as my mom—and survived. I was delirious with hope. The article went on to say that, as yet, no trace had been found of the woman passenger, Sheilagh Drinkwater, who had also belly-flopped into the swollen stream. The search party had disbanded. The tall robber—larger than his cell was long, he had had to sleep with his feet poking out between the bars—insisted that the last time he had seen the Drinkwater woman they had both been standing on the tracks. He never would have fallen had she not waltzed him off the bridge. That's what he said. He called my mother "the real criminal in this crazy business." He called her "a nutcase" and "a menace" and "a dancing fool."

He did!

Next, I located and visited the orphanage where I had served my purgatory prior to being admitted to the heaven of Uncle's attic. Records mentioned my temporary residence, also my official consignment to the guardianship of *Boisvert, Gerald*, of Montreal, Canada. Following a bleak morning in the cellar where the records were maintained on microfiche, I headed back to the university for lunch and encountered a fusty, bearded old coot of a professor seated in what had become my regular chair. He was ponderously flipping through the pages of a book anaemic with age and mildew. As I turned the corner of the low shelf, I virtually tripped over my sweetheart squatting at the man's feet and fiddling with his fly. Cathy, as always, was a vision. The mangy, goat-faced prof resembled a besotted frump—who can reconcile the blend?

Cathy had my mother's hair.

A glitter and scuff. The hex of beach sand.

That was as close as I got.

I said nothing.

Turned around and walked out.

Looked back in anger once.

Her face was in the professor's pants.

Which I took as a sign. The time had come to return home. Money earned in Betty's employ was almost gone, and I did have my arrangement with Uncle to consider. We had struck a deal which allowed me a year away from my studies. Not without acute embarrassment, I confess that I was among the first of my generation to have quipped, "I need some space. I have to find myself."

Uncle had not been amused. "Are you lost inside your own sssskin?"

Dreading that I might offend either Uncle or Aunt, I devised my arguments as I went along. To let slip that I intended to find my real mother might disavow their courteous custody of me. At the same time, Uncle knew more about my past than he had cared to reveal, and I assumed that both his silence and his complicity were intentional. In his company, I was obliged to be strategic.

Passionately, I argued to see something of the world while I was still young. After a year's sabbatical I would return to school, renewed, (I told him), invigorated, (I promised), more wise. At that time, I'd be prepared to devote myself to an undergraduate degree and to honour the expectation that I would pursue law. Uncle conceded. Why not? He got everything he wanted. I had negotiated nothing more than a time-delay.

My next act was to purchase and inscribe a series of art postcards, then arrange with travelling friends to have them mailed from the capitals of Europe. In this way, the true nature of my quest would remain concealed. In St. Louis, money ran out. Fun ended. No more stones remained to be turned on my mother's trail. My latest girl had lacked taste in both her accessories and her consorts. Clearly, the time had come to trudge home.

On that winding ride north (reminiscent of my first migration with Uncle, although I mostly hopped freights), I felt burdened by failure. A pattern had threatened to emerge. Sparrow Drinkwater had flunked out as an engineer, he had also botched his life's most intimate quest. Young women, the record showed, tired of him before he did them. The poor boy was doomed to study law and fulfil ambitions ascribed by a man whom, in Sparrow's most sour and ruthless moments, he condemned as little more than his benevolent kidnapper. Magnifying such grim prospects, he would have to muddle through the upcoming academic year without scoring a touchdown, without catching a pass, without slipping a single open-field tackle.

Not much wonder then, that in returning to Montreal and McGill University, I, Sparrow Drinkwater, would continue to seek solace in the company of women, and that I would choose to cruise the Beat and the off-beat, searching, I suppose, to sustain my connections to the waif I once had been.

Home again, I had a hard time explaining to Uncle why he continued to receive postcards written by me and mailed from Milan, or Belgrade, or Mikonos. "Hi!" my postcards gushed. "You won't believe this weather!"

"Where were you really?" he kept after me. "Downtown?"

*

We have flipped to the dog days of the Bohemian era. To its credit, the Beat Generation enjoyed a literary facade. To its detriment, it rarely produced good music of its own. That inherent dreariness, that failure to *sing*, worked through the scene as a slow poison. In 1961 little more than a sickly skin of the Beat days remained. As an embattled, waggish twenty-year old majoring in history, I drifted through the ruins in search of whatever could be salvaged or procured.

The upstairs loft in the Bleury Street building was huge. Fossilized imprints, like the corpses of shadows awaiting burial, identified where sewing machines had once whirred. Ghosts of the operators hummed the bittersweet tunes of their absent, broken-down Singers. Now artists occupied the space.

The stairs ascended as high as Jacob's ladder, lifting visitors into a room stoked hotter than a kiln. Panting like mountaineers, guests needed a moment to resuscitate their hearts at the door. As did I.

I had not arrived alone. True, I had set off for this place on my own, but along the way I had been accosted by a madman.

"I'M ON STRIKE!"

Wiped spittle from my cheeks, and prayed that it wasn't infected. On the street, the skin colour of the apparition was made sickly by the glow of late-night neon. "Buddy, I'm on your side right down the line. Go for it, man. Good luck." I shook my fist to affirm the mighty resolve of my support.

Crazies possessed an affinity for me. If a thousand people occupied a sidewalk, roving lunatics inevitably would single me out for their attention. Detecting my sympathy for their plight, they'd pounce.

"BUMS OF THE WORLD UNITE!"

This one was going to be trouble. Bad enough that he had conscripted me as one of his own, I noticed for the first time that the bum was dragging a placard behind him like Christ's cross. Hoisted aloft, it swung too far forward, nearly decapitating me, which not only grabbed my attention, it also forced me to stand in the middle of the sidewalk and read the inscription.

F.U.!
BUMS TOO!
ALL'S FAIR!
GIVE US OUR SHARE!

Quills of rusty spikes and eye-gouging splinters sprouted from the hefty timber. I expected the paint to be a lipstick scavenged from a purse-snatcher's discarded loot, although—the thought made me flinch—the ink could have been real blood. The sign's weight made it difficult to manoeuvre, and there was a running threat that a passerby might casually be impaled.

"PANHANDLERS PREFER CASH!"

His eyes, insanity's eyes, were glazed from too much starvation and insufficient drink. Splotches on his skin were physical evidence of the internal fracas between dementia and revelation. His teeth had been sharpened by decay. The ragged black edges and empty spaces were particularly menacing under the afterglow of street lamps. I had been a wide receiver, I'd shaken off defenders before. Fake to the right, cut back to the left. Geez. He had shifty feet. Where was the referee to blow the whistle on this guy?

"Sorry, buddy. Ordinarily I'd help you out. I'm not flush tonight."

The wrong thing to say.

"BUMS DEMAND HIGHER WAGES! Y'GOTTA GIVE ME SOMETHING! WE DON'T TAKE NO NO MORE!"

"Hey, I'm a student. I'm as poor as you. I don't have any dough. If I did, I'd give you what was leftover if I hadn't already spent it by now, except I would've spent it by now so I wouldn't have any leftover even if I did have some once, you get me?"

"GIVE ME YOUR WATCH!"

Circling around the Biblical apparition, the flow of pedestrians parted like the Red Sea for Moses. Now that I was negotiating with him, the bum let the top of the sign fall at his feet, which nearly lopped off the white pumps of a movie-goer. On the faces of my fellow citizens

I read evidence of their immeasurable relief that I, not they themselves, had been called to public account.

For the bum's edification, I displayed my bare wrists.

"Y'GOTTA GIVE ME SOMETHING! BUMS DEMAND HIGHER WAGES!"

I showed him the empty envelope of my wallet. Pulled the pockets of my jeans inside out. I stood in the middle of a downtown sidewalk, four white flaps waving from my pants like handkerchiefs beseeching surrender.

"CIGARETTES!"

"No can do." I'd been reduced to the vocabulary of the old American west, the language of the trapper conversing with Apaches. Five minutes earlier I had smoked my last cigarette, and I wasn't about to tell him that that had been a butt retrieved from an ashtray in the Students' Union. In one sense, I was better off saying, "I don't smoke."

Wrong answer.

"YOU STUPID FUCK! YOU HORSESHITTING MOTHER FUCK! WHO YOU SAVING YOURSELF FOR, JESUS? Y'THINK GOD WOULD'VE GIVEN US LUNGS IF HE DIDN'T WANT US SMOKING? YOU USELESS SACK OF SHIT AND MANURE! DON'T Y'KNOW NOTHING? GIVE ME YOUR SHOES!"

"They won't fit."

"I WOULDN'T WEAR YOUR FUCKING SHOES IF YOU FUCKING PAID ME YOU FUCKING STUDENT SHIT! DON'T Y'KNOW YOU KNOW Y'KNOW FUCKING NOTHING! GIVE ME YOUR SHOES! I'LL DONATE THEM TO THE POOR."

"My shoes," I told him, "stay on my feet."

Our haggling had reached an impasse. The bum responded by pulling the thick handle of the placard between his legs and abruptly skewering the battering ram between mine. My gender was subject to the proximity of a protruding nail. Shocked by this, I did not notice right away that my assailant had used his free arm to hug me in a grip no underfed bum should be strong enough to possess. Worse, the apparition had begun to breathe on me.

Think fast. Time was running out. Pollution flowed amok through my arteries. "Okay. I'll make you a deal. How would you like to come with me to a place where you can eat—"

"BUMS PREFER CASH!"

"—and drink! You can eat and drink, cheap wine and beer for hours. Nobody will bother you, nobody will even notice."

The rafter between my legs was withdrawn, the embrace eased to a lover's tender hold, and although the man was drooling on my chest, the violence of his rapid breathing diminished.

"Are you on the level?" For once, my companion was not screaming his head off.

"Scout's honour."

"I can drink beer for hours? Free?"

"Free and unmolested. Can you handle it?"

The bum dropped his placard in the gutter and tagged along behind me, revising his demands. "Are we going to like a frat party?" The insane are eternally curious about the guise of grace.

"Nothing that tame."

Our destination was only a few doors away, that's how close I had come to eluding this intercession. Together we climbed the steep narrow stairs into an atmosphere of smoke and music. Halfway up, the bum had to rest. He was holding his stomach and lungs which were struggling from the exertion of the ascent. My companion confessed, "It's the altitude. Guess I'm not used to heights." He said, "My name is Stuart Oliphant, what's yours?"

"I'm Sparrow. Like the bird. Sparrow Drinkwater."

"Hee! Heehee!" Out of proportion to the news, Stuart cranked up a tubercular laugh. "*That*," he delighted, "is one *ridiclelous* name."

Which was always a problem endemic to insanity's slaves. They could endear themselves to me in such nutty ways.

Allowing for his preference to remain inconspicuous, I led Stu along one wall. He was doing well, until flummoxed by an icy blonde measuring men's flaccid penises. Nothing especially erotic. The young woman planned to knit winter socks, custom-fit, having turned her hobby into a thriving cottage industry.

My own attention would be diverted by the excuse for this bohemian vernissage—the massive structure located in the centre of the gallery concealed by huge, mouldy tarpaulins. All that was known about the piece was its vogue title, *Catharsis*. Forty feet long, half that width, fifteen feet high. Inside a bellows heaved with deep gurgling sighs, a regulated intake and exhale of breath. Like a gigantic, disembodied lung, the form sadly toiled beneath its cover on the dark warm floor.

Modern art has consistently been called upon to answer a rhetorical question, one that's usually intended to ridicule—*what does it mean?* We are, everyone, participants in the adventure of art. Don't you just love it? In that Bohemian loft the premise had been taken to extremes. While a living breathing sighing groaning organism gasped for breath, the visitors ignored the struggle, guzzled a brew, and passed the canapés.

By the bar at the far end of the room, a racket of music blared from the fifties' poor excuse for a sound system. Occasional snippets of chat pierced the din, out of sequence, unrelated to anything recently spoken. Heads nodded in rhythm to the gibberish, some guests tried reading lips, most jammered on. Stu coped. He grabbed two beers from the tub and sat next to the speaker. The bum in his heaven wore the cacophonous noise as a bad odour, nobody could get close to him without suffering eardrum damage. I left him alone, my one very good deed for the decade accomplished.

A clannish party, one that would be difficult to penetrate, and I was the ultimate suspicious character—the loner desperate to mingle. My best bet was to command an observation post by the window, a strategic location where, sooner or later, everyone had to wander past for a gulp of air. Making myself comfortable on the broad sill, I put a foot up, took a swig of beer, and affected a disinterested pose while awaiting formal recognition.

Which came.

A voice shouted, "Aren't cha some kinda bird? Like a swallow?"

"Sparrow." Cut from a supple hide, the leggy woman in leather, chains, and black tights invited a leer. I was not convinced that she wore anything under her jacket. While it's true that I had come to this place hoping to score, this one had me worried. She was a marauder, while I preferred to survive the night. "Was I drunk when we met? I would've remembered you."

"You? Drunk? Naw, you was just scared." Measuring me with amusement, her look did not convey carnal attraction.

"I would've remembered."

Her laughter aroused me. I could caress her dusty tones, kiss the desert of her voice and never cry out to slake my thirst. Tugging the zipper of her jacket down a notch exposed a tantalizing curve of bare breast. She reached inside to retrieve a pack of Player's Plain. This rough woman stuck a cigarette in her mouth before thinking to pass the pack around. I was innocently reaching for my matches when she unzipped a pocket over her biceps and extracted a lighter. A torch. The blue flame leapt nine inches in the air. She lit both our cigarettes. As my shock continued to calcify my skin, she circled my face with the blaze.

"Mo!" I exclaimed, my voice parched.

"Been a long time, paperboy." Snuffing the flare before the fire department was alerted, she pocketed her lighter and drew a deep drag on her smoke. Despite the passage of years I felt safer with the flame extinguished. "Still got a route?" she needled.

"Not if you're back in town. You'd take my money and ignite my skin."

"Sounds like yer carrying some kinda grievance? Figure I owe you sumpin', paperboy? You gotta grudge?" To make herself heard, she'd lean forward and bellow in my ear.

I'd do the same. "Be cool, Mo. I'm kidding."

"Maybe I don't dig yer sense of humour."

"Who does? What are you up to these days?" Anything to get her off the subject. Mo never was someone I'd choose as an adversary.

"I'm an artist." Contempt structured her response. Not recognizing her as a tortured creative genius right off the bat diminished my validity as a human being. I had to jump to heal the rift.

"That much I figured. What discipline?" The words were no sooner out of my mouth than I willed them back. 'Discipline' was not a word to broach with a fire-eating dragon in leather and chains.

She played it straight. "Art-welding. Mostly with steel. Mostly with trash-objects I haul outta the city dump. Garbage art, mostly."

Someone turned the music down a few decibels to the applause of many. Conversation had become feasible.

"I'd like to see your stuff someday." The image of Mo with an oxy-acetylene torch burned through me.

"Stick around. The future might hit sooner than you think."

She terminated our discussion with a kiss seared on my skin like a brand. Mo's mouth contacted mine in the usual fashion, then she chewed my lower lip between her sharp incisors. She laughed at my consternation, and moved on, spinning into the arms of a trio of admirers.

To have seen someone from the old neighbourhood getting along in the world, you know, it made the heart glad.

"Welding trash. Now there's something the world's been waiting for."

Cynical words for our milieu. Had they drifted in through the window with the street noise? Or was this the voice of God and she really was female? I twisted on the sill to identify the source of this subversion, discovering on first inspection, from the knees down, the crossed legs of an unidentified interloper. One leg bobbed above the other. Comely, shapely calves. Bony ankles. Wee feet fit brilliant red loafers—a seditious gesture, for any attempt at colour was an obscenity in this room. Weaned on black and white television, coaxed along by dire predictions for the earth, and attracted to the mock solemnity of the proletariate, transients of the Beat Generation preferred sooty tones to express a funereal vision of the world.

"She must be making a statement," I said. When in doubt, recite gospel.

"Right. Statements by imbeciles—we've achieved Utopia. I ask you, for what more could anyone ask?"

Definitely, a more comprehensive look at this insurgent was required. Black pants hinted that the speaker was hip to the times, but while she had the dress code down pat (if we allow for the eccentricity of the crimson loafers), she did require coaching on her attitude. Standing, I curled my head around the cement column dividing us.

She returned a smirk. "You were expecting maybe a Playboy bunny?"

The girl with the mouth was barely twelve. Her costume was entirely black, with the exception of the riotous shoes and an equally vivid smear of paint across her lips. Lengthy earrings tugged at her lobes, cheap Caribbean baubles, and she had sewn a skull and crossbones—a statement—onto the bridge of her left shoulder.

"I can wait." Her face had been sweetly drawn. In that light, the rich lustre of her hair belied a straight, solemn style. Bangs drooped below her eyebrows. She'd developed the habit of dipping her eyes under them in order to look up. "Six, seven years from now, check the mirror. A bunny might be staring back at you."

"Ugh! Puke! I'll slash my wrists before I shake my cottontail. I'd rather bleed in the customers' drinks. Drip, drip, drip." Raising one hand, she indicated the falling drops with the other. "Every cocktail a Tequila Sunrise. Vodka on the rocks? Yes sir. Why is it red? Hey, it only looks like grenadine. It's our house mix. Try it, you'll like it."

Not your average twelve-year-old. "You have a sunny disposition. There's nothing morbid about you."

"What can I say? I liked Ike. Kennedy gives me a runny nose. I was born the day the Rosenbergs were arrested. I'm allergic to T.V."

"What happens if you watch T.V.?"

"I get a runny nose."

"So maybe it's not Kennedy that bothers you, but the set."

"It's Kennedy. When he's on the boob-tube both nostrils let go. It's a flood."

"Has anybody ever told you that you might be a little flaky?"

"Some have tried. Dullards. Loads of people think I'm crazy. Every-one of them assumes the world is sane, so you figure it out."

I had not gone to the vernissage to babysit young girls, and was feeling mildly impatient with myself for getting a kick out of her com-pany. Partly it was convenient—talking to her staved off the ignominy of being totally alone. Yet her mind was quick, her attitudes hostile—I liked her. I found myself intrigued.

"What are you doing here?" She was the only child in the place.

"Never mind me," she fired right back, "what are *you* doing here? I saw you bring that rummy through the door. Are you some kind of social worker? Or just another do-gooder schmuck?"

Sipping her beer, the girl gazed about the room with the eyes and cunning of a feline.

"You're too young to drink," I pointed out. I'd been twelve when I learned which Montreal taverns served children. But that had been me and that had been back then.

"So are you."

"I'm old enough to fight in a war."

"Who's stopping you?"

"There's a shortage of good wars right now."

"Start one." She held the bottle up to my nose. "Sniff."

So that was it. The child was chugalugging ginger ale out of a beer bottle. "I'm surprised. I'm shocked. You don't strike me as the type to do things for appearances."

"Beer's disgusting. The bottle's a survival technique. If I don't show a vice the weirdos try to convert me. Drink this, smoke that, pull down your pants, little girl, let's go in the back, little girl, we'll shoot smack, little girl." She'd rock her head and shoulders with the cadence of her words. "Generally speaking, people don't bug me so much if I act like a drunk. Life is a whole lot easier. I get away with murder because my family's friends figure I'm a lush. Nothing they have to worry about."

"Where's your family?" Nothing in her deportment indicated parental discretion, guidance, or influence.

"In there." Nodding with her chin.

The reference eluded me. "Where?"

"Somewhere in there." Under the canvas, within the breathing lung, lurked the mother and father of this candid, funky young girl. "Stick around for the unveiling, I'll introduce you."

Making a beer run, I checked on Stu, who had remained on top of things. He had refined a technique of holding up a beer bottle and shaking his wrist, which brought him another. Some of the visitors assumed that he was part of the exhibit, staring at him as they might a Picasso. *What does it mean?* Art lovers debated the symbolism.

Back at my windowsill, the young girl was siphoning ginger ale from a thermos into her bottle marked Molson Ex. "You at McGill?" she grilled me. "You look McGill. Like you study Chaucer in the afternoon, Blake at night. Thesis on Shakespeare?"

"History major. You know you're a smart ass? You know that, right?"

"History shmistory. You're an arts student. How extraordinarily typical."

"What will you study, wisenheimer?" Talking to her, it was easy to forget that she was a kid. A prodigy, perhaps, but a kid.

"Entomology."

"What's that, insects?"

"I prefer bugs to people. People bug me. Bugs people me."

"Bugs people you?"

"I'd rather pass the time of day with a cockroach than a human being, wouldn't you? You know there's more cockroaches in this room than people."

"That should make you happy."

"The exterminators were in last week, spread their poison-powder in every nook and cranny. After they left, I got out the Hoover and sucked it up."

The girl was well pleased with herself.

"Cockroaches will survive the A-bomb, you know. They'll outlive humanity. Thank God."

"You're full of joyful news."

"Nina usually is," commented a third, unknown voice.

The girl could be entertaining, I had grown confident of that. What I had not anticipated was her talent to help me pick up women. A bonus. The standard collegiate beauty who had just spoken was about my age, petite, scruffy, scented, dark-haired with a Mediterranean skin and an affluent complexion. A strong nose belied a striking, full-lipped mouth. She and my new friend kissed both cheeks in the Québécois style. Suddenly I was fair game for both of them.

"This is Hannah, Miss Cocktease, 1961," the younger of the pair began. "I'm her friend because nobody else will be. She's also my cousin. Don't marry the bitch, Sparrow-bird, or whatever your name is, but please, do us all a favour, take her to bed tonight. She's a pain in the butt when she hasn't had any. What's it been, three years now?"

"Nina."

"She lost her virginity in the front seat of an Impala and ever since then she's had this thing for gear shifts."

Having blushed, recovered, and turned a pink hue again, I spoke shyly to the new arrival. "Quite the matchmaker, your cousin."

"Nina's a pimp," the older girl volleyed.

"Hannah, dreariest," Nina purred, "allow me to introduce one of the planet's lesser fowl. This here's Sparrow. A history major, gag snort puke, so you can't have everything. But in your case, frustrated beggars don't get to choose."

"How's the training bra fit, Nina pet, comfy?"

"Sparrow sees bunny potential in me, drear." Nina promptly jerked Hannah's jacket open for me to make my own evaluation. "I hope you're a late bloomer, kiddo, or there won't be any stapled belly-buttons in *your* future."

I had to laugh out loud. "Do you two never quit?"

"I do," Hannah declared. "I'm adult. I'm mature. The child, well, we can always hope that she falls asleep. Where's Mommy and Daddy, Niny?"

Strangely proud of my secret knowledge, it was my turn to interject, "They're under the big top."

The choice of words gave Nina the giggles. "That's right! They've hired out as circus animals. Mom's a tiger, Dad's the elephant act."

Hannah studied me, then Nina, then the huge tarpaulin. "They're under the sheet?" she queried in a tone that conveyed worry rather than fascination. To me, "You know, we only humour this child. Truth is, she's a direct descendant of the lunatic fringe."

"You're just pissed because you're so middle class."

"Hannah, can I get you a beer?" I butted in.

"Candy's dandy but liquor's quicker," chanted Nina. "Sparrow, are you one of those guys who need their women falling down drunk before you plough them?"

"You've got a big mouth, you know that, Nina?"

"Sorry. Sheesh. Touchy little guy, ain't he?"

"Thanks, Sparrow, I could use a beer," Hannah accepted.

"Be careful, sweet blood-pump. I think he's a romantic, gag snort puke."

Stuey was having a great time entertaining the radicals by the beer tub when I went over. They were empowered by the knowledge that they had bumped into contact with an authentic replica of the earth's great unwashed. In those days, as now, there was nothing like a visit from one of the wretched of the earth to boost a politico's spirits.

"You're drinking too much," he yelled in my ear above the din. The intimacy of our communication, and the slight contact of our shoulders, elevated my stature in the minds of the Trotskyites. I accepted the envy of the smug left and walked away, selfishly leaving Stu to bask alone in their admiration.

My return to the company of Hannah and Nina coincided with showtime.

Lights dimmed. Slowly, dramatically, the massive tarp lifted to the ceiling revealing a gloomy superstructure of cast metals and wire struts, glass, mirrors, and twinkling coloured lights. The music booming against Stu's ear was switched off, a cue for the trash heap under the tarpaulin to crank itself up as a radio of hysterical, modern squawk. Progressive jazz beat a stick against Aaron Copeland. Gershwin got drowned out by sirens, horns, and flatulent trucks.

Initially, the organism was faintly lit. The room's heavy smoke seemed to have been emitted from the ash of its pyre, a skilful illusion. Details remained out of focus. A few flickering lights were repeated into infinity by starry mirrors, allowing for a sense of place—the burnt out cosmos—if not direction. We, the uninitiated, stood about as murky shadows and alluring silhouettes. I gathered that primordial swamps would have looked much like this had the earth begun with electricity, ochre lightbulbs, and discarded steel. The overheads were shut off entirely. The encased creature became an amoebae of the modern world, gasping for breath, flashing quick urgent signals of identity, defining itself as our eyes adjusted to this new, base dimension. Increasingly cacophonous, the noise grew strained, under stress. The beast's breathing intensified, and the interior symmetry of red, blue, and amber lights was augmented by a strobe. We glimpsed the grim details.

"Oh shit," my new twelve-year acquaintance muttered. "Okay. That's it. This time they've gone too far."

The pile of debris, a fetid, living organism, served not only as an artist's representation, it thrived also as a home to humans. Naked humans, as was soon revealed. The Adam and Eve of this reverse-Eden, of this futuristic garden of junk and filth where the primary industry is waste management, turned out to be Nina's mother and father. She had been conditioned to expect the avant-garde. Yet the public nudity of her parents presented a difficult adjustment.

"That's it. I want a divorce. Hannah, I'll be good. I swear it. Can I come live at your house?"

"Don't go freaky," the older cousin advised, her tone taking a sharp turn. Hannah reverted to being legitimately caring, treating Nina as a young girl upset by her circumstances, not as a tough crony with a lip. "People know what the human body looks like. It's no big deal."

With an exaggerated Neanderthalian lope, the forms moved through the superstructure. The man's knuckles scraped the floor, the woman covered her large white breasts and swung her head from side to side, fearing mechanical brontosaurs. These were the survivors of the race, and from time to time the torment of their ancestry bounded through their veins. They'd hurl themselves against the gates of their inherited hell, bodies deformed, faces contorted, their screams mute evocations of the macabre.

In many respects, the sculpture was reminiscent of the monkey-bars we had played upon as children. The two participants climbed amid the gnarled metal as if scavenging the wreckage of our civilization for food. Tunnels—evocative for me—were penetrated and wiggled through, and both the culverts and the monkey-climbs looked like fun. (If fun was permitted in this realm.) Really, I wasn't sure how to take the presentation. With amusement, instigated by the symbolic playpen? With solemnity, in reference to the prophetic carnage? Or should I be titillated by the naked, attractive forms? In the midst of my confusion, I noted that Nina was not at all puzzled. Somehow, I had been counting on her to deliver a succinct summary. "Know what this *work of fart* says to me? We are scavengers in the garbage pit of the world. Know what else it says? My parents are too lame-brained to wear hubcaps over their privates."

"They're trying to create an authentic experience," was my way of soothing her.

"That's true," Hannah chipped in. "Nina-pet, you know the score. Shock-value sells art. Your folks need that kind of attention, that's what they have to do to get the recognition they deserve. When you look at it, I mean when you look at the art and take your eyes off them, it's really a wild creation. Don't you think? Your Mom and Dad don't believe in dead art. They believe the piece has to be alive, that the viewer should participate as well as the artist. Admit it, they've captured everyone's interest."

No dunce, Nina objected to this line of logic. "Hell, even I'd draw a crowd if I stripped butt naked."

The approach to art chosen by Nina's parents, as articulated by Hannah, soon crystallized. Mo—Derek's old girlfriend with the flamethrower—who had not created the piece but who had, I would find out, contributed the welding, revealed why she had worn nothing beneath her leather jacket. At the end of the sculpture where the automobile fenders and twisted sheet metal formed an igloo-shaped entrance, Mo peeled off her leather, getting down to lace panties. A stunning erotic creature. My sex responded as she fell to all fours and crawled inside the sculpture. Men quickly followed. Soon the audience was lining up for admittance, the guys sniffing at the tail of Mo, the women crawling in after their men, the radicals stripping off their clothes to skip bare-assed through their brave new world, the junkies tentatively unbuttoning their shirts while keeping their needle marks covered.

In line with Hannah and Nina, I was rather unsteady about how to play this.

At the entrance, my mind was piqued by a vision of gas chambers and similar horrors of the Holocaust. The mob's clothing had been piled into a terrific mess ready for sorting. We had to hike over shoes and boots to reach the threshold. As works of art go, I must admit that this one had impact. Viewers had to weigh their personal values and discriminations. We had to decide whether to remove our clothes in public—and this was no sedate club of volleyball players, these people were strangers, and many of them were strange—and we had to be prepared to defend our choices. Those who stripped conformed to a certain level of peer pressure. Those who did not restricted themselves to the cultural habits of another epoch. Down on our knees, we crawled from the upbeat realm of 1961, with Kennedy in the White House, through the fatalism of nuclear destruction, into the post-civilization age of survival amid the smoky ruins. And we had to do it, if we wanted to do it right, with the clothes burned right off our skins. When put up came to shut up, I would shed shirt, shoes, and socks. Hannah kicked off her boots to go barefoot, and, to our dismay and against our protests, Nina peeled down to her skin.

What could we do to stop her? If her parents were intent on displaying the family flesh to the universe, she had been given license to make a statement of her own.

"What are you waiting for?—scoot!"

A cranky, urgent voice. Her body, nude, pubescent, bony, gawky and frail, was sadly vulnerable. Fit for extermination. I went in first, Hannah followed, and Nina moved through after us. By the time she made it she was trembling with embarrassment and fury. Hordes were coming in behind us, we could not return to our clothes, and Nina began to shiver.

I would have been a gentleman, except that I had already split the difference and left my shirt behind. Hannah had not removed her jacket, so she was able to cover the poor girl in the midst of a trembling jag. She rocked her young cousin in her arms, and soon the girl was herself again, bitter with comments, strident with keen invective.

"Look at the droopy testicles on that piece of flab," Nina said, revelling in her abuse. "I'll never be able to admire his paintings again."

The three of us had formed our own self-protective cell. Indeed, we behaved as a family unit, with Hannah nurturing our adopted child, while I busied myself with fortification and survival within this network. Each to his or her own. One couple, high above, splayed across the detached hood of a Buick, fornicated. Directly below them, Mo performed a sexy shuffle, kneading her breasts before jutting out the nipples, either encouraging someone's burning touch, or a match. Many of the politicos had formed their own union, discussing the contradictions of the class struggle, formulating a response to the nihilism of the new age. Here and there, nomads picked their way through the debris, commenting on artifacts, ruminating on how a particular item might look framed above their mantle—consumers throughout eternity.

Indeed, on another level, the breathing steel lung prospered as a form of heaven, the revealed afterlife, the participants hungrily reaping what they had sown. In devils' chambers the compulsively horny thrashed around, uttered nightmare fables. Blithe angels paraded their nubile innocence about the perimeter of the cage, amused and charmed by distortions, oblivious to the sordid. Harvested now as participants, many spectators unleashed a litany of lament, indulged their fantasies for theatrics, screeched, moaned, and beseeched sundry gods to show their faces and recognize their great hidden talents once again.

Women cried to be levitated above the crust of the earth.

Men sang to be consumed by women.

One fellow, fully dressed, copied down the phone number of the nude vixen he had just met (so that faith in some kind of future prevailed).

The three of us were wandering through the human wasteland in search of Nina's family. We found them playing cribbage across an antique wood-burning stove. Their ritual meant something, I presumed, a meaning that eluded me.

"Here, Mom. Put this on." In the throes of her performance, the mother did not acknowledge her daughter. Nina held out a lampshade that might fit over the woman's head, rest on her shoulders, and mute the glare of her bulbous breasts. "She's in her zombie-robot phase," Nina complained to us.

I took the shade and fit it over the woman's head myself. The wires needed to be bent out of line, the fabric tore along a seam, and the woman's arms ended up being pinned to her sides. Otherwise, the get-up suited her.

"Here, Daddy," Nina intimated. She had resorted to her original idea, and passed him a hubcap. Daddy was less somnambulant than his wife, he liked the idea, clamping the next-world's notion of a fig leaf over his privates. Then he took a recognizance check of his daughter.

"Nin, where are your clothes?"

"Clothes?" Jerking back her shoulders and arms, she shed Hannah's jacket in a jiff. "I prefer to remain in fashion, Pops."

"Nina!" waking from the dead her mother caterwauled. "Get dressed!"

"Momsy," Nina said, "you really have to do something about that streak of hypocrisy running down your spine. I'd see our family doctor."

"Don't back-talk me, young lady," she yelled at her, arms pinned. "You get dressed right now."

Picking up her jacket, Hannah covered the girl. "I'll take care of her, Mrs. Goldson."

The three of us wandered off to see what else we could find on this elusive side of the looking-glass.

A trick-mirror gave me a belly as jolly as Santa's. Another turned Hannah thinner than a pen. At one turn in the frame, we landed upon a guy making wiener schnitzel. We each received a bite lathered in hot mustard. Eventually we settled onto a bench salvaged from an old streetcar and talked about the mundane affairs of the real world. Somehow that was significant too, somehow that was symbolic.

Conversation was steaming along nicely when we were interrupted by a burst of applause. Everyone who had been in the room was now inside the lung, which apparently was a cause for celebration. I remained sceptical of the news, and searched the room's furthest shadows. Finally I called out, "Stu! Stuey! Hey! Stuart Oliphant!"

My mangy mooch emerged from his cranny.

Entreated to join us, he was being asked to surrender his independence and unlimited access to the beer tub. Although born to comfort, Stuart Oliphant had not enjoyed a morsel of the good life since the Second World War—some such story was etched on his skin. His fresh brew of benefactors and detractors were disposed to an artist's impression of a futuristic bleak terrain, while Stuart had inherited the whole of the present. He was alone in the present without us. He enjoyed the bounty of his actual domain. Stuart could not drink an artistic impression. He could not feed himself with futuristic vision, especially when he was currently living that prophecy. Alone among us, he was content to remain in the present. To say so, Stuey gave us all the finger, did a token jig, and sucked his beer with a vagrant's fury. I noticed that he had already peed his pants, probably several times. For that reason alone I was glad he didn't get sucked into our desolate perimeter. That he was capable of distinguishing between good fortune and absurdity (something that troubled the rest of us) delighted me as well. Stu drank, and danced, and pissed his pants, and scorned our affection for oblivion. Stu chose to live, symbolically and actually, and numbered the rest of us among the dead and the insane. Tickled that the inhabitants of the steel mesh were snubbed by Stuey, I was glad that his contempt for us was deeply felt. Of course we deserved it, in kind.

The volume of the music had begun to descend when something very scary occurred. The giant tarpaulin drifted down like a mushroom cloud, threatening to obliterate us once and for all. Claustrophobics panicked. The cave exit accommodated no more than a few people at a time, and then only in single-file. Many were scratched and stymied trying to escape through the side fences. If the creators of this living art had aspired to maniacal human emotions and fear, they had achieved that goal. Playing in the park of the future had been a game, being smothered within this tent of the insane was no sport. I grabbed both Nina and Hannah before they joined the crush to escape, nodded to them, and led them on an ascent while everyone who was above, fled below. I could not have entered such a maze without taking note of alternative forms of escape, tunnelling had done that to me. Our climb was a simple one. We mounted a spire of the superstructure, and the descent on the outer rim of the sculpture was easy for sure-footed, dexterous young people. We made it out seconds before the fall of the canopy, and, hearing the sounds of clamour and panic inside, scavenged the litter for our clothes.

People emerged furious. Art, they had assumed, even avant-garde, ludicrous art, had been created for their amusement. They were upset to have been churned into fodder for the creative contempt of artists. Statements were supposed to be made against the easy targets of imperialism and capitalism, not victimize the very community that engineered its support. For many, this excursion through the future had been no fun. They had not meant to be guided so close to the edge. Desolation, riot and imprisonment were less humorous than advertised, and a few spectator-participants clamped on their bras, zipped zippers, and took out their disillusionment on the artists' progeny.

"Nina. Tell your parents they can go fuck themselves."

"But Mrs. Greer, they do that all the time anyway." I hardly knew her, but I was proud of Nina. She harboured her own grievances, yet she defended her family against this outside invasion. When her parents emerged, dressed, from their creation, sharing the spotlight with Mo-the-Welder, Nina basked in the praise extended by the coterie appreciating their genius. Hectic, if scattered, applause. Wild shouts. And none clapped and whistled more loudly than he who had gained the most from this event—Stuey Oliphant. Rarely did the city's cultural elite sponsor a performance just for him.

"Guess I'll head out," I mentioned. "Ah, are either of you two going in my direction? Can I walk you home? I'd invite you out for a coffee, maybe a doughnut or something, but I'm flat broke tonight."

"I go west," Hannah said.

Naturally I made it my direction, although truthfully I still lived at home, with Uncle and Aunt, which was north.

Nina deferred. "Three's a crowd. You two should make it, so I'll stick around. Mom'll want to talk. A show gets her wired. She'll be a lot better off if somebody listens."

"But I'll see you again?" I was serious. She might have been twelve, but good friends should not have their imperfections levied against them.

"Come see me when I'm twenty. I'll save myself for you. We've been through the future together, Sparrow, who can split us up now?"

Hannah and I were sharing a laugh as we departed the loft when, right in front of us, Stu Oliphant fell down a dozen stairs. I heard bottles breaking in his pockets. Beer bled from his coat and pants. He picked himself up, made progress standing, then tumbled the rest of the long way down on his ass. His was the faster method. By the time Hannah and I made it onto the street, Stu was already going strong, accosting strangers, demanding deposits from the wealthy, promises from the poor.

"I DON'T WANT YOUR FUCKING SPARE CHANGE! I WANT YOUR MONEY!"

He hollered right in my face and never showed a glint of recognition. That's the problem when insanity gets drunk, it shows no gratitude. Hannah and I skidded out of his way, and this time he was too loaded to trace our steps. He picked on another couple without cottoning on that these were different people.

A chill had hit the streets. I tucked Hannah in beside myself and she wrapped an arm around my waist.

"What do you think?" I asked.

"About what?"

"Nina set us up. Should we trust her judgment?"

"In true life Nina's an angel. She only looks like a kid. I think we'd be tempting fate to mock her."

We had stopped on the curb, both symbolically and pragmatically waiting for a green light. Hannah and I were looking as deeply into one another's eyes as that frail exercise can allow. "Then you're willing to take me home with you?" I requested.

She made a face by tensing her neck, which told me that she was a little leery about these fast moves, but not put off.

"I don't think Nina would have it any other way," I pressed.

"She'd probably be shocked. But we don't have to tell her," Hannah laughed, lightly kissing my cheek. "You're a nice guy. I don't usually like nice guys."

The walk down rue Ste. Catherine in the sinking cold revamped and coalesced our spirits. We had about twenty blocks in which to get acquainted. I rejoiced in those twenty blocks, in the young turks emerging from bars, in an elderly couple coming out of a horror flick, flush with fright. We were still alive, the world had not yet been reduced to rubble. Best of all, we had found someone else with whom we'd not only be willing to march through a prefabricated hell, but with whom we had actually taken a symbolic stroll through the region. What more could there be to life than this?

*

In the middle of the wondrous night following the Bohemian vernissage I sat at a loft window, watching snow swirl. Montreal had escaped March with nothing more than flurries. The smooch of spring was in the air, when suddenly, rudely, midway through April, we were being abused by a freak blizzard. Barefoot Hannah crept up behind me. Wearing an unbuttoned man's shirt with long tails, she lay her head upon my shoulder. Reached around and with her lengthy nails gently touched the mat of hair on my bare chest.

"That feels good," I accepted, nuzzling her warmth.

"You feel good. What are you up to, Sparrow? Nocturnal? I'm used to my men conking out. This could be a serious slight to my reputation."

"You've had that many then?" Oh. Bite my tongue. Rip it out, stir-fry it with water chestnuts and soya sauce. Take those dumb stupid ridiculous words back. I didn't say them. Honest, it was my evil twin. God. Please. Don't let her hear me.

Catlike, Hannah stepped away and curled up in the corner of the black leather sofa, looking out over its high back at the storm's white fury. "Five months ago, no more than that, I lost, gave up, surrendered, bartered—what's the word? Five months ago I got laid for the first time. So there was that boy, then another, then one more, briefly, now you. Call me a loose woman. Call me a bitch, see if I care. Call me anything you like, Sparrow-bird, but call."

I had struggled into my Levis for this after-midnight ramble, and now kneeled beside her. Hannah lived in an artist's huge loft. Paintings shuffled shoulder to shoulder along each wall, while the furnishings were an uneasy marriage of collector's antiques and modern leather. For a co-ed to be enjoying such privilege surprised me. "I'm sorry. Usually I'm forced to plead and coax."

"You learned to bargain well."

"Meaning?"

"You're not inexperienced."

"No."

"Hey, I'm the one who's sorry. I was easy and you're a romantic, like Nina says, so you got cheated. Life's tough. I didn't want to be alone tonight, okay?" She brought her knees higher, and gave her lovely thigh a quick scratch. "Blame the sky. My bunions felt the storm coming. Some nights I get moody."

That she had been quick to indulge my advances was the least of my worries. Obviously, I was not expressing myself properly, and had to think fast to rescue this connection. Both of us had been on the timid side in bed, but privately, I was very happy. "The reason I'm walking around is, this time of night I usually go outside and piss on the flowerbeds."

"Pardon me?"

"Long story. Old habit."

"We have all night."

I smiled. Being with her was a pleasure. Talking was fun. "Okay. Condensed version. From spring to fall I go outside every night and piss on my Aunt's plants."

"What a thrill. Interior plumbing gives you the willies? You're afraid to flush?"

"Something like that. It's more than a habit really. I keep telling myself, if I don't do things to mark myself off as being different, I'll forget where I come from."

"Where do you come from?" Hannah asked the question with some trepidation, as though I might name one of the nether galaxies.

"A swamp. I was conceived in a swamp, my mother's still out there, in the wild world, somewhere. We got separated. Forgetting her, that would be hell, but remembering gets harder every year. Some days—. There are days when it hits me that I don't actually care if she's alive or not. You know? If she's alive she's just another person, one more nutty stranger. So I fight that. Pissing outdoors at night keeps me connected to her. Keeps me caring. She used to do it herself. That's how she stumbled upon the guy, or the phantom, whatever, who made her pregnant. She was out pissing and I'm the result. Repeating the ceremony, in a way, keeps me connected to myself. Keeps me in touch with my swampy past."

Hannah suggested, if it would make me feel any better, that I go downstairs and piss in the garage. "Dogs do. The janitor does. Nobody will know the difference."

I sat beside her, pulling her ankles across my lap. Caressed her calves and feet. "The blizzard helps. I'll make believe it's winter and use the flush toilet."

"Don't let me civilize you."

"Would that be such a terrible fate?"

"Mmmm." In reference to something I'd let slip earlier, during our skirmish of lovemaking, Hannah said, "I still can't see you as a lawyer."

When we first arrived at her place, clamped together, wedging ourselves through the door, we'd been getting acquainted at an accelerated pace. Flurry and flap. Flipping through our resumés as we doffed clothes. We mapped ambitions while bending to chew a nipple or tongue an inner thigh. Dumped on the bed, she and I settled into exploring the folklore of our histories while finding a mutually driving

rhythm. Both lovemaking and introductory remarks were interrupted
when I moved above her. Hannah squirmed free. She posed a question
germane to our activity. "Bring anything?"

"Huh?"

"You know." In the half-light of the bedroom, her eyes had conveyed what modesty would not permit being translated into words.

"Ah, no. Don't you have anything either?" This early in the
decade, the pill was not standard issue. "I could always pull out."

"Too risky."

With me at the throttle, that was undoubtedly true.

Would I be returned to the blowing snow in search of a pharmacy
that kept late hours, then hope that it carried condoms (in Catholic
Quebec in 1961 that could never be assumed)? Hannah's solution was a
most agreeable one. I was to discuss the meteoric rise of my house-
brother, Barclay Boisvert, whom I'd previously mentioned. He had
graduated with the starriest report card in the nation. Then the message had come through that his marks on the C.A. finals were the highest in Canadian history. Barc would be honoured by the Governor
General in a ceremony at the nation's capital while Uncle walked on
the billowy air of his pride. One year after commencing his professional
career, Barclay was made a junior partner in a prestigious firm, shatter-
ing, mocking, all previous ascents to the top. Even Hannah had heard
of him. Who hadn't? While she conveyed her amazement that I was
related, vaguely, to the surging young pinnacle of business acumen, I
ejaculated into the warmth of her artful fingers.

And in the sweet denouement, I was bent on explaining that I
remained only in first year arts because I had previously flunked out of
engineering, then taken a year to travel through Georgia, Mississippi
and New Orleans. When I mentioned St. Louis Hannah clamped her
legs together, trapping my hand between them, and hollered so loudly
she shook her cat from its lair and rattled the neighbour's windows.

(True. Revisionist theory today suggests that the windows trembled
from the first full volley of the storm.)

After mopping up, we slept. I awoke, having difficulty breathing.
Hannah's cat had returned to the scene of the commotion to lounge
across my face. Extricating an ear and my neck from the knitting claws, I
rose, dressed partially, went to the window to gaze at the storm, and wondered why, when I felt so lucky, I had also succumbed to melancholy.

Mother.

She's never there.

She's never where I want her to be.

"You don't look the lawyer-type," was Hannah's point.

How do I explain to her about the twists and forces prevalent in my life? "Personally, I'd rather be an engineer, but my brain's addled. I have the stuff to be a lawyer. Lawyers have a lousy reputation. Which I happen to think is deserved—"

"Thanks. My father's a lawyer," Hannah mentioned.

"Excuse me while I extricate this foot from my tonsils." I loved the way she laughed with her eyes, her affection for life evident in the wrinkles of her smile. "I have this uncle who takes a strong moral position about how the world should work. He's very up on ethics. For him it's the good guys against the sleazeballs. I've resisted his position, partly because he's a poor spokesman for his own cause, he's a Daffy Duck. But the thing is, at the heart of it, he's right. The more I see how screwed up and how ruthless the world is, the more I believe I can make a difference."

"As a lawyer?"

"As a sonofabitch who won't let the bastards get away with it."

"A legal Don Quixote jousting against corporate windmills." She had a knack to kid me while at the same time conferring praise.

"That's one thing Barclay's proven. There are no limits. He's a poor boy from Park Ex, the son of a small-time pencil-pusher. By the force of his brains he's blasted through the financial world. Barc will make a name for himself beyond this city, that's obvious. If he can do it, so can I."

"Good for you. You're very intense, Sparrow." Kidding me again. Praising me again.

Lifting her shirt, I slid a hand up her belly, captured a nipple in my fingertips. Her own hands opened the shirt to caress the opposite breast. This girl, with simple moves and gestures, was pushing me beyond the boundaries of my amateur status.

"How come you live so high off the hog? Daddy's that rich?"

"What hog? I'm not kosher, but I don't eat pork."

Legs curled around me. An ankle cupped the back of my neck, guiding my head downward. I had known that men did this, believed that I would do it myself one day, yet the threshold was both alluring and frightful. Prickly hair gave way to softer down, my tongue tasted the occult elixir of her quim. Mmmmm. Tasty musk. Each flick of the tongue and lip-nibble was encouraged by a corresponding quiver in her body. Hannah was so slippery and lithe. She cooed while I probed and experimented. "You bastard," she said. And repeated, "You bastard." I worried that I was doing something wrong. "In the morning, you bastard, you're going shopping." The thought made her cry out again, her hands pressed my lips upon her sex. I screamed too as the cat raced straight across my back, its nails slashing my skin for traction.

I love this sport.

Hannah required time to come down from her plateau. I rocked her gently, kissed her back to earth. Able to focus at last, she said, "Fair's fair." So I kicked off my jeans. "To answer your question, the place isn't mine. God, you have a sweet tush, Sparrow. It's my art teacher's. I love your penis when it's hard. He's on sabbatical in Paris. It's just the right size. Your penis. The loft is too big. I'm just renting it for a year, looking after it, really. Don't you adore this shade of purple? It's cheap."

"What?"

"The studio. The rent's cheap."

The trauma of her mouth on my cock, her moist tongue, the gentleness of fingers lightly stroking my testes, the wonder of her diligence—screech of brakes, crunch of metal, the collision and wreckage of my body. To this day I have yet to bellow again with such abandon and desolation. As I lay in her arms on the sofa, Hannah confided, "I never swallowed it before, Sparrow. I'm glad it was you for my first time."

It's this need to record firsts, to believe that a first is a measure of evaluation, of intimacy, a reward reserved for a special someone, that conflicts with more important wonders. Wrapped in a blanket, snug in one another's lives, we slept with joy, and really that should have been enough.

*

At the crack of dawn in Hannah's apartment-loft, my feet were in the starting blocks.

A simple plan. No sooner would the doors of the nearest pharmacy open than I'd be at the cash, acting cool and a trifle bored, paying for a box of prophylactics.

Back in time for scrambled sex with breakfast.

One hitch. A false-start. I was broke. First, I would have to borrow the money from Hannah. As well, I was in a quandary about the etiquette of box size. Did a package of three condoms send the wrong signal? Was thirty-six presumptuous? Did an even dozen knell too chickenshit a compromise?

The experience is not recommended. Young men, do not sleep with your heart's desire and the next day borrow money from her. Although

Hannah and I negotiated the ritual with a modicum of strain, she was worried. Her trust had been placed at risk. Twenty bucks would not fly me to Bermuda, yet the precedent had been established. The inference hung in the air that I was likely to ask for more. I had no visible means of support. Exactly what sort of loser had she bagged?

"What's this?" I asked.

"Twenty dollars."

"It's wrapped in cellophane." I examined the gift closely. "It looks starched."

"Sorry, I didn't notice." Hannah blushed with mild embarrassment. "You can unwrap it. My mother gave me that one. She does that sort of thing."

"What sort of thing?"

"Mom washes her money. Then she irons it. Then she covers it with Saran Wrap. She has a long-standing phobia about dirty cash. Unwashed bills might give her typhoid or skin cancer or Lou Gehrig's Disease."

Engendered by such a loopy lineage, how could I not like this girl?

Hannah carried on to deliberately test my money-management abilities, adding more items to the grocery list without further contribution to the coffers. I retaliated with a request of my own. "Slush-city. You don't suppose your absentee artist left behind a pair of rubber boots I could borrow?" I took exception to her sigh. "What? How could I predict that winter was coming back? There's two feet of snow on the ground. Look at it out there. Even the city's not clearing the streets. Their equipment's in warm storage."

"It's a trend. You don't seem prepared for anything."

"I'll pay you back the money. Scouts' honour. I just want to go shopping for rubbers wearing rubbers. How was I supposed to know I'd meet this knock-out chick and spend the night with her? I'm sorry, Hannah, I'm not accustomed to blessings of this magnitude."

Smiling, she kissed me, and foraged in the professor's closet where he had stored his private things. With the flourish of a magician holding up a rabbit by the ears, she pulled out a magical pair of overshoes. "He showed us these in class once, he's so proud of them. He bought them at L. L. Bean." Black, made of a thin and highly flexible rubber, the boots had no apparent form until they were pulled over a shoe. Mushed up, they could easily be transported in a pocket. The boots fit loosely over my sneakers. "What is this guy, seven feet?"

"Six-eight. He's huge."

The rubber soles flapped like clown's feet.

"I'll trip."

"Take it or leave it. At least your toes'll stay dry."

"Okay. I'm off."

"Hurry back."

Retreating from her loft I had a thought. Did Hannah add grocery items to the list so that I could not afford more than a three-pack of condoms? "Sparrow!" she called down the hall while I was waiting for the elevator to creep up. "We need toilet paper!" The message cast a smile on the old lady waiting beside me. I asked myself when, how, and why I had crossed into this frontier of chancy domestic bliss.

Wearing rubbers—on my feet, I mean—proved to be the wisest of my decisions in quite some time. Warm air had wafted up the St. Lawrence valley from the American south, and the rapidly melting snow streamed down the steep hill of rue Guy to spread in oceanic pools along Sherbrooke and de Maisonneuve. Avoiding the splash of cars was hopeless. I puddle-jumped my way to one of Montreal's underground minimalls, where everything could be purchased without venturing outside. I had first to figure out what things cost, then determine which items I could afford. The bacon, eggs, milk, and other groceries were easy. In the pharmacy, where the pretty cashier was far too "nice" to be compromised into selling sexual aids to strange young men, the decision was made for me. Decency demanded that I spare her the embarrassment. To account for my presence, I bought a four-pack of toilet paper. The prophylactics, a convenient dozen, were shoplifted.

Ascending the escalator to street level I carried one large sack, having topped up the groceries with the rolls of tissue. Undetected, I felt home-free, as well as sexually aroused by the nature of the theft. Ascribe my carelessness to a random horniness, for when I suddenly tripped and hit the floor, the stiffness of a certain appendage hampered swift recovery.

At the top of the escalator, my face lay smack on the floor.

Groceries had wildly scattered about the foyer.

I tried to stand but could not.

People coming up the escalator were stepping over and around me, sometimes on me, as the moving stairs kept spewing them out. I had to duck the stampede of trampling feet. What pinned me down? It's hard to judge the passage of time, but in a moment or two the nature of my predicament became apparent. The teeth of the escalator, where the stairs disappeared into the floor, had taken a bite out of the toe of my floppy boot. The jaws of the escalator now masticated the overshoe, and they were set on devouring my foot. Violently kicking to save my tootsies, I managed to slide the endangered limb free of the flimsy rubber boot. Then watched with substantial horror as the escalator swallowed the professor's magical, prized overshoe from L. L. Bean with a rude, noisy, uncouth *ssshhhlllluurrrrrp!*

I was, for a spell, traumatized. I don't know about other cities, but in Montreal machinery does not routinely attack shoppers. My plight had drawn an audience, everyone appalled and amused by the voracious appetite of the moving stairs.

The professor's boot!

How was I going to explain this one to Hannah?

Sorry, girl, it got eaten by the stairs.

Warily, I rose to my knees, in time to notice a youth skim my bacon off the floor and race for the exit. That's when I realized that few of my groceries remained. Looters had pilfered the bulk of the purchases, the eggs were cracked, and I'd been left with an empty sack.

"Hannah," I rehearsed to myself, "I lost one of the boots. Sorry. I got mugged by a building. The groceries? They're gone too. It's a conspiracy. Skyscrapers are stalking the streets. We always figured nature would fight back and reclaim the earth one day—we were wrong. Guess what? It's the products of our civilization that have come to life, they're taking revenge. It's unbelievable. Cars put themselves in gear, slam into prams. Walls toss bricks on pedestrians. Plexiglass windows explode from tall buildings. The roads are unravelling, potholes are ravishing Pontiacs." Could I placate Hannah, bring her around, salvage token respect? At least I could wave my package of condoms, the theft tucked away in my jacket pocket, at least I had done *something* right.

Back on my feet, I gathered what little remained of my supplies, not to mention dignity, and looked for an official with whom I could deposit my wrath. At the very least, I wanted the escalator torn apart and the boot returned. In this state of blind fury, I happened to be looking through a glass partition which divided the street from the entrance to the subterranean mall when I saw my rolls of toilet paper scurry by. I don't know how, I just knew that they were my rolls on the run, as if they had feet. I blasted through the doors and ricocheted down the street like a human bullet, prepared to explode on the brain of the thief. The other loose boot slipped off in the pursuit. I stopped, considered retrieving it, but one boot is a worthless prize. Continued running. The woman—who looked downtrodden, who looked like she didn't have much of a life and eked out an existence—noticed me on the warpath. Did she stop? No. Did she throw away her stolen merchandise? Hardly. She crossed the traffic on a red light, nearly getting herself killed, and splashed through the water that had flooded the sidewalk along de Maisonneuve. I chased after her. Sure, she was poor, and that tempered my rage, but I was poor too. I'd had enough. I had to return to a girl I'd just met and explain that her money had been spent as instructed, but that everything had been lost. At least I could recover the toilet paper. I risked my life in the traffic on Union, flew over puddles in reckless pursuit. The woman was too small and too frail to be a successful thief. I ran her down. Charged right up beside her and clamped a statutory hand on her shoulder. Yanked her to a stop. Ripped the rolls of toilet paper right out of her mitts.

"You goddamned thief!"

She trembled and shook, so I lowered my voice.

"I'm down, I'm on the floor, I could be injured for all you know, and you take advantage of my misfortune to steal my toilet paper? That's despicable! It's an outrage!"

"I saw thee stealing," was the woman's rationale.

Taking a second to catch my breath from the chase, I could not believe my ears. The woman was well-dressed for winter, wearing three moth-eaten sweaters, a scarf, warm socks, and a wool dress. The homeless and the crazies tend to be a season behind, wearing summer clothes well into autumn and winter duds through spring. Late storms find them prepared. The woman was not especially old. Her costume added ten years to her appearance, and the stress of hard living etched the torment of her years under her eyes and across her forehead. "What did you say?" I was beginning to dislike nuts for their knack of catching me off-guard.

"I see thee stealing. Down in the drugstore, I see thee put something in thy pocket. Thee didn't not pay for it." Great, another representative of insanity's foreign legion. I should introduce her to Stuart Oliphant. If they're not already acquainted, they'd make a great pair.

"What are you talking about, woman? You swiped my toilet paper and now I'm taking it back. There's nothing here to discuss."

"Don't hit me," she pleaded.

I despise the wiles of the pathetic. They keep trying to get you on their side by exposing their vulnerabilities. "I'm not going to hit you."

I noticed that our dispute had been awarded a few witnesses. Being healthy, young, and male, I had to watch my step. "Don't you ever steal from me again."

"I won't not."

"You better not."

"Can I have the crap paper back, Sparrow? I need it."

"I need it too. It's mine. You can't—." I stopped as if punched by an invisible heavyweight. Took another measure of her. I tried to remember where I might have bumped into her before. "How did you know my name?"

"I know it."

"How?"

The woman gazed up at a skyscraper reflecting the bright sun. An icicle melted on the overhead wire. She poked out her tongue to catch the drips. Looking back at me, as if I was the stupid one, she said, "I gave thee thy name."

Was it my deep longing, my endless searching, my despair at finding her that did not allow me to doubt it? Or did some nuance of recognition click, the size of her, the voice of her, the innate sense and scent of her, register in my brain as emphatically as a gun's retort? "You're my mother," I said, and my voice cracked, my chin trembled, my eyes misted with old tears. I was convinced. "You're my mother." And I drank in the ruination of her, the wretchedness of her clothing, the suffering explicit in her eyes, the havoc of her mental state. In an instant, I crumbled, fragments inside me exploding apart. "You're my mother. God. My mom."

"What did thee steal?" she asked me with a conspiratorial smile, as though this meeting was routine for her and not finagled by the gods. Either that or she could scarcely comprehend my presence.

Foreign sound rose out of me. I cannot duplicate or describe it. I was murmuring to God and blubbering, and the point is, between the two of us, I was the one deranged at that moment. The toilet paper had long ago fallen into the puddle in which we were both standing, and my mother reached down and retrieved the rolls. Holding them against her chest, she hugged them, and that is the moment I bound her with my eyes. That's the instant my delirium broke loose, and really I was the lunatic, the maniac escaped from an asylum, I was the one who lost control and uttered strange noises and felt a pain of grieving and love stagger through me to pinion my heart against the wall of the world. "You're my mother. I found you!"

I thought she said, "Please don't hit me." I swerved back again into myself, returning somewhat to the vicinity of my senses. Wisdom warned me to be careful with her, I understood the need to manage my own reactions.

"No," I said, "of course not. Don't worry."

But my mother had said, "Please don't hate me," and she repeated herself.

"I'm so glad to see you! I'm so glad to find you! How did you know it was me?" I was joyous. I didn't know what to say or ask. She appeared to me as someone scavenged from the dead, yet to her I was a threat. I didn't have the ability to dismiss her concerns. I said, "I love you, Momma. I love you."

The power of those words, rearing up out of the boy I once had been.

My mother dropped her larger fears and pulled herself more fully into this moment. Suddenly she was right there on the sidewalk. Not vacant, nor absent. Standing in a puddle above her ankles, she caressed my cheeks with one hand. "That's my Sparrow," she said, words like splinters in my heart. "That's my birdie," she said, and we held onto each other then. I grabbed her and held her tight. From both of us came a ration of noise, utterances of our pain and grief and longing.

Perhaps I was choking her.

I held her against me and I wanted to know so much. Held her, fearing that if I let go she would become someone else, or not recognize me, or that her mind would veer off on a slant. A crazy instinct—I feared she might become amorphous. Be awash in the puddle, as though the Wataminga River had deposited her in this cove. Or would she ascend into the sparkling sky, or jump down an alley? *How did you know it was me?!* I held her and I could not believe how mad and how lucid the world had become. Could not believe the overpowering love I felt for this ragtag apparition. Berserk with happiness, insane with grief, I was beset by incoherent rage.

In danger of hyperventilating, scared that I might crush her, I pulled away from my mother's embrace. Breathed heavily. Unwilling, after this spill of time, to let go completely, I gripped her upper arm.

What to do? What to do?

"Mom. Get out of the water. You're soaked."

She looked down at her sodden feet, and at mine, and gazed up at me with some consternation. "I am standing in the water," she confirmed. Her tone seemed to ask, did you expect me to be dry?

"You'll catch pneumonia." She jumped out of the puddle, mortified.

"Why?" she asked me. "What's that, new-mona? Why do I catch it? Help me, Sparrow."

"You're all right now," I told her gently, and held her hand. "You're out of the puddle."

"That's a bad puddle," she said.

I agreed. "A very bad puddle. Wet."

"Very wet."

Oh, God. What do I do now?

I could not bring her back to Uncle's, not right away, not like this, both of us baffled and crazed. Her presence in that house was bound to precipitate other emotions, in me and in everyone else, which she might not be able to bear. A more calm, more neutral environment was necessary. A place where we could sit and talk, and get acquainted. I couldn't leave her on the street. She was already dipping her toes into other puddles, tempting *new-mona* to catch her. She looked too weird for us to be comfortable in a restaurant, plus I didn't know how she behaved in public. Hannah's? What choice did I have? In lieu of the groceries and the overshoes, I'd bring Hannah my mother, and hope that my new girlfriend could accept the substitution.

I had found my mother. At last. I had nabbed her red-handed stealing my toilet paper.

*

I might have believed, at that hour, that my quest had finally been concluded. Borrowing heavily from the wisdom of retrospect, I must say instead that it had just begun.

Having located my mother on the streets of Montreal, I now had to find her. Truly find her. Who could have guessed that the danger in discovering Sheilagh Drinkwater, in comprehending her dilemma and supporting her recovery, lay in losing myself? What human could possibly have been that wise? Then why am I blamed, why do the minions cry for fresh pints of my blood, when clearly the consequences and choices were beyond anyone's cognition, especially my own? Why?

Or am I looking to pipe in a few excuses?

The treachery of the world is rampant, God knows. Finding Mom again would prove pivotal. The event thrust me into the world in ways that would not have occurred otherwise. How can that be denied? I'm not reciting excuses, but neither am I willing to kick against the frontiers of fate, against the many linked conspiracies turning on our moment like galaxies spinning in their silent eternities.

I had found my mother.

That was all.

Now I was obliged to find her.

7.

Eightball

Guiding my mother towards Hannah's loft became a battle of wills. She was wary of abduction, and frightened to leave the bounds of what, for her, was a safe perimeter. "Bad guy lives down there," she warned me, nodding to the alley where I had pitched our sodden toilet paper. "Very bad."

The ogre of her imagination could well be real—a compatriot street-person aggressively intolerant of anyone rummaging through his designated trash. As likely, the "bad guy" was a wraith of her own creation, a meld of fears and imagined shadows.

A lifetime ago, on the grounds of the Mississippi asylum, my mother had transformed pools of rainwater into miniature swamps. Now she was pestering the slush and puddles created by the melting snow. Mom drained lakes into sewers, and then, in no hurry, hung back to admire her handiwork.

I remained in a kind of suspended, euphoric shock. This creature was a marvel to me.

She plucked a cigarette butt from a snowbank black with debris.

"Hey, come on, throw that dirty thing away."

"Got any matches on thee, Sparrow?"

"Sorry."

"Go ask that nice man there. Bet he's got matches."

"You ask him."

Mom begged a light from the gentleman in a plush topcoat while I pretended that we shared no lineage.

All so strange. Like being in love. Clarity, and subtle graces, transformed the city. As I walked beside my mother, the covert textures of buildings revealed their pleasures to me. Surfaces of glass and concrete seemed radiant. I was conscious of sunlight slanting across my skin, the way the hair on my wrists lifted to the light. An unfamiliar traveller in

this state of enhanced perception, I was stunned by the clairvoyant
virtues of colours, startled by my eyes' keen focus.

In Hannah's huge loft, my mother was immediately comfortable.
She had space, and wandered through the street-fair of paintings introducing herself to surrealist portraits as though greeting celebrities. "Hi!
My name is Sheilagh!" Before the drawing of a nude whose breasts
hung heavily, whose thighs were gargantuan, she squinted, then squatted, preferring to gaze at the woman from a vantage low to the floor.
"Thou hast big knees," Mom surmised at last. "They sore?"

Leaving Mom to do her own introductions, I joined Hannah in the
kitchen alcove. My new girl was not in a great mood. "Sparrow, we had
a nice thing going. An okay beginning. Maybe the physical part got
above mediocre. In the heat of the moment, who knows, maybe I
blurted out a line or two worth regretting later. Absolutely, I do not
recall saying to you that I wanted to meet your mother."

"You're not seeing the full picture here. I just met her myself."

"Unhunh. You bumped into her on the street and said, 'Hey, Ma,
come meet the chick I laid last night.'"

"I told you, we got separated a long time ago. I didn't know she was
my mother—"

"You just found that out. Congratulations. She's what to you
exactly? Mother Earth? A mother substitute? A metaphor for mother?
Mother Hubbard without her cupboard? Mother Goose on the loose.
Motherfucker, what?"

Notes hastily rehearsed on the way over were failing me in the fury
of this skirmish. I got sidetracked. "It's hard to explain. What did you
mean, 'above mediocre'?"

"Who's the bag lady?"

I checked on her. Preoccupied with exploring the paintings and
sculptures, Mom seemed content. She didn't appear tutti-frutti at that
moment, although she did remark to a jumble of cubist shapes in the
form of a man, "Art thou off thy meds?"

"She's my birth mother, okay? Fourteen years ago we got separated,
when I was six. Then this morning I caught her stealing our toilet
paper—"

"I thought you were a nice guy, Sparrow."

"I am, I—"

"I thought you were a normal, down-to-earth, all right human
being. I sized you up wrong."

"Give me a break here, I—"

"You're some kind of fringe society, am I right? You're the President of your own nut club. Home is the mental ward."

Clutching Hannah's shoulders, I did my best to convey the urgency of the moment. (The feel of her remains crucial in memory. It's extraordinary how her body, against her wishes, snugged up into my palms.) "If I had some place else to bring her, we'd be there by now. Hannah, for God's sake. I'm sorry to spring her on you. We had nowhere to go."

"So where're the groceries?"

I released an expository gush of air and let go of her lovely shoulders.

"Sparrow, where's my money?"

"I used the money to buy the stuff, okay? When I fell down, the escalator swallowed the boot."

"What?"

"It was wild. Think about it, isn't it just like human nature, isn't it just like people to kick a man when he's down? I told you I'd trip. The groceries—"

"You lost my teacher's boots? Sparrow—"

"What a scene. Hannah. The groceries were scattered across the floor, and people—*homo sapiens!*—stole our food. My mother, what can I say, she came along and swiped the toilet paper. Lucky for me she was the one I caught. I didn't know she was my mother—"

"Why can't you simply say, 'You're out of my life, Hannah. You're dumped.' Why drag a bag lady into it? Last night you were cute—I saw you escorting that bum-person into the gallery. I said to myself, 'Hey, girl, there's something you haven't seen before. A cool-looking dude leading a degenerate to booze.' I got curious. It showed a certain sensitivity, you know? That's why I came over. I suppose now you're going to tell me he was your father. But this—" and she indicated my bedraggled mother, who was attempting to make sense of an abstract painting (with her particular adjunct of mind, she was probably succeeding)— "this is not cute. This is insulting. It's degrading to this poor woman and it's insulting to me. Obviously, you have a problem with derelicts. Fine. Get help. In the meantime, keep them out of my life, thank you very much."

"I'm sorry, Hannah." Wearing my most forlorn, most conciliatory voice, I spoke as though my larynx had been coated with shame and honey. "You're right about everything. Springing my mom on you—dirty pool. Where's my head? But—. As harebrained, as wacky as it sounds, what I said happens to be God's truth. I'll swear it on a stack of Bibles as high as you want to pile it up."

"Surprise, scuzzball." Apparently my syrupy voice had failed to persuade her. "I don't appreciate being taken in by penny-ante hustlers. I want my twenty dollars back."

"Hannah—"

"How many Sparrow Stinkwaters can there be? You have a distinctive name. Varsity football, am I right? Think I didn't know that?" Hands on hips was her favoured attitude of defiance. "My dad's a lawyer. He's friendly with the faculty. He'll track you down and make you pay. Through your left nostril."

As a final, desperate gesture to promote good will among the natives, I reached into my jeans jacket pocket and extracted the small, intimate box. "You should have these, at least, on account." Hannah bashed the condoms away, I don't know why. The box flew across the room and she stood in the kitchen fuming, the heat of her anger sufficient to power an oven. I was stuck. I didn't dare retrieve the box for future use. I was left trying to broach the one subject more difficult than sex—money. "I don't know how to put this."

"Please. Go. Now." Under her breath, she murmured, "Bastard."

"I'm going. Since I owe you, you know, twenty bucks anyway, I wonder if—she's my mother, Hannah—do you think maybe you could, you know, spring for cab fare? There's another place I can go, but it's far."

"Walk." Hands on hips, she flexed her elbows forward, a sign of her ultimate disapproval.

"Hannah, if it was just me. But my mother. I can't drag her across town." The level of personal humiliation had intensified. For my mother's sake I had reduced myself to begging, and could not blame Hannah for giving me the bum's rush. It's disappointing that she hadn't taken a shine to Mom, or given her much of a chance, but that expectation had been quixotic.

"I don't know what game you're playing, Sparrow Drinkwater, but stop it right now." Her eyes moistened. I accepted the flush on her cheeks to be a reasonably accurate barometer of her temper. Hannah was hurting, and at that moment nothing could ease her pain. She honestly believed that I was giving her the business.

"Hannah, one bus ticket. I have one of my own. It was going to get me home last night except I met you. Let me have one for her. For her, Hannah, whoever you think she is. For humanity's sake, spare a bag lady a ticket."

"I got me one a them."

The breathless, high-pitched voice, which so tugged on my heart-strings, jerked my head around. In the studio, my mother was foraging through the pockets of her ripped wool coat. She pulled out a bus fare. The ticket looked bleached, as though it had been rescued from a snowbank and dried on a sunny sill. I knew so little about her. She'd been listening to Hannah and me fight, comprehending our quarrel. What else did she know? How much did she understand?

"Okay," I petitioned Hannah, anxious for damage control. "I didn't know. She has a ticket. We're all set. I'll see you. Okay? Give me some slack here. Look, babe. She's my mother. Okay? Okay? She's my mother. I'll pay you back the twenty I owe—"

"Believe it," Hannah decreed. The girl was tough. "Add another twenty for the boots."

"Forty altogether. Disinfected and dry-cleaned."

"Slip it under the door. Don't ring. Don't knock. By Tuesday."

"Hannah—"

"Leave. Pardon me if I don't say please."

Wounded, I walked to the door, and guided my mother out. I tugged on her elbow, but Mom insisted on stopping to wave goodbye.

Hannah had been observing us. Was that sadness in her eyes, in back of her ire? When Mom donated a big smile my lover was obliged to return it, then she glowered across at me with unconditional fury, as if daring me to misrepresent the gesture.

If looks could maim.

Striking a compromise, I offered a friendly sort of motion with my hand, refusing to superimpose a smile. I wanted Hannah to suffer, to get an inkling of how miserable it felt to be kicked out of her place dragging my mother along on one arm.

*

Despite an accumulation of warnings, the change of lifestyle after an infant's birth rocks rookie parents as a revelation. I counselled myself that things were bound to be different, perhaps drastically affected, now that my mother had been resurrected into my life. Experiencing is believing. As we departed Hannah's loft and walked in the sunshine, the true dimension of that disruption began to dawn on me.

"Nice picture-paintings that place," Mom offered. "Can we go see more them? They got picture-paintings in a museum but I seen those."

She was mentally unhinged and a bag lady, was she an art critic too?

"Do you go to the museum often?"

"Alla time."

"We won't be visiting museums," I told her. "Another day, perhaps."

"Toooo bad. Soooo sad. Sparrow?"

"Yes?"

"Doesn't thou got smokes?"

"Sorry, no. And please, no more butts from the gutter."

What'd I say? Why was she sticking her tongue out at me? Why was she looking at me cross-eyed?

"Enough. Enough. Will you make your eyes straight again, please? Thank you."

Judging by her familiarity with the procedures, my mother had travelled on buses before, perhaps frequently. She dropped her own fare in the box, stuck out her hand for a transfer, and chose a seat without depending on me. Tucked against the window, she did not appear particularly slovenly or especially downtrodden. No one mistook her for a socialite, yet she wasn't overtly crazy either. On the No. 80 bus heading north along Park Avenue, Sheilagh Drinkwater could pass at a glance for a needle-trade worker, or a mother of eight, an encouraging sign. Then I remembered—once upon a time she had attracted men in abundant supply. Soldiers, demons and cowboys had freely imposed themselves on her, rubbing up against her odd beauty. Hard to imagine that they did so now. Mom had grown frumpy. Her hairdo a suitable home for field mice. Etched with faint lines, the pallor of her skin had the parched, cracked patina of weathered wood. Only besotted, crazed derelicts would be aroused to her attractions, yet she was merely thirty-six years old. Struck by how aged she looked, tears blistered in my eyes.

I had to knot myself together again.

Once I started, my questions tapped a wellspring.

Where had she been? How had she arrived in Montreal? Where is she living now? How is she getting by? *How did you know it was me?!*

"I got thy picture."

"Where?"

"On my wall."

"What picture?" Or should I have asked, what wall?

"My friend cut it outta the newspapers. Thou was in the news. Lots of times I seen thee, Sparrow. Thou hast never seen me."

"Where did you see me?"

"Thou goes to McGill school. I watch thee coming through the gate. I watch thee in the mornings coming through the gate. Then I beat it. I scram away."

During my brief, almost-sensational football career, action shots of my catches twice appeared in the local newspapers, and several times in the student news. For being the only freshman in six years to make the conference all-star team my portrait had been published in both the *Montreal Star* and *The Gazette*. Suit and tie. Hair groomed. "If you saw me before, why didn't you say hello?" Why did she wait? How did she know it was really me? Why did you steal my toilet paper?!

"I needed crap paper."

"So you stole mine."

"Maybe thou would chase me."

What? She had deliberately tried to get my attention? It had been a ruse? She had planned for me to follow her, and catch her? Why didn't she just help me pick up the groceries? *Why didn't you just say hello?!*

"Not allowed that."

"What's not allowed?"

"Hello. Thou knows. Me, I'm not allowed to talk hello to thee."

What? Who told her not to speak to me? Who made up the rules for her? How long had she known that I lived in Montreal? How many times had she seen me on the street? *Have you followed me before?!*

"Look at them children, Sparrow."

Taking advantage of the freak overnight fall, families had gathered on Mount Royal for one last toboggan run. I watched my mother's eyes. She seemed to be riding with the kids herself, zipping down the hillside, flying off bumps with abandon, merrily tumbling. The remote pleasure of her gaze was discombobulating.

"That's how I remember thee," she said.

That's crazy. We had never seen snow together.

"Mom, it's me, Sparrow, your son. I'm here. Right here. I've been looking for you all my life, since I was six. Don't you remember? We were separated. Whatever happened to you? Where've you been all these years? You fell off the bridge—"

"Not exactly," she pointed out. The precision—the clarity—of this remark, shook me like wind.

"What?" I was so confounded by her.

"Not exactly."

"That's true. That's right. You were pulled off, or you flew off, and then what happened to you?"

"I fell down a hole in the sky, now I popped up on thee!" She burst into a smile as large as the mountain, as bright as the snow.

"Yes! You popped up. Just like that. This is amazing. Don't you think this is amazing? Last year I went looking for you. I travelled all over the southeast, to Florida, and to New Orleans, to Mississippi. I went to Okefinokee Swamp. Do you remember that place? Do you remember your old school? You used to tell me about it."

"Thou went looking for me?" She asked this question shyly, head down.

"Yes."

"Did thee find me, Sparrow?" Mom raised her chin a notch.

"Ah, no, Mom."

"Me, I was not there anywhere." She was gazing out the window at the children on the slope.

"No. You were—. Where were you last year?"

"I was here. Thou was on the mountain."

What? "What do you mean I was on the mountain?"

"I saw thee on the mountain."

"You did? Why didn't you say something?"

"People chase thee on the mountain. Strike thee. Too many people. I tried to hit thee too. Thou's in a cage and people hit thee and spank thy bottom."

Oh dear. We had been going great guns, now this snag. A work stoppage in the brain. "I was in a cage," I repeated. Vision or dream, whatever the nature of her account, common sense was to be excluded, genuine contact denied.

"Isn't that funny?" Her voice carried a light, shy giggle, as though she tried to prevent her laughter from escaping, as though she had been taught to keep still. "A birdie-boy like my Sparrow—in a cage!"

"On the mountain," I repeated, sadly.

"On the mountain," my mother insisted, with a perplexing degree of happiness and fervour. "In a valley on the mountain. With big shoulders. In a cage."

As though time had been suspended, dead chickens hung in the windows of Park Avenue poultry markets. They could have been the same dead chickens that had greeted my arrival in Montreal when I had voyaged down this street with Uncle Butter. What had escaped my understanding then eludes me still. The street, grubby, dense, a bewildering mix of Hasidic Jews, robust Greeks and lanky Haitians, struck me as covert, coded with intrigue and plot, its secrets revealed only to the prescient. In each sequence, with Mom, with Uncle Butter, I'm left curious about life's glitches, at a loss to know what is accident, and how much has been purloined by design.

My impulses had to be reconnoitred. Hug her. Kiss her. Shout. Dance in the aisle of the bus. My joy would not be stalled by inhibition, although I was often surprised and frequently dismayed. I feared how Mom would react to any outburst of mine. What were her parameters? What did she comprehend, believe? How could I identify her threshold? By the time the bus bumped along Champagneur in Park Extension, approaching the end of its line, I held my mother's hand in my lap, aware that the last time we had travelled together I had slept in her's.

Holding hands was the limit of my expression. The most that I would dare.

Her hand.

It felt so light, distant, rough.

Chafed, worn skin, reddened and denuded as on a child's nursing thumb.

"I feel so happy," I told her.

Mom thought about this. "I'm real sad," she said.

After a minute, I managed, "Knowing that you're unhappy makes me sad."

Immediately she smiled again. "I'm happy, boy!"

What?

At d'Anvers we disembarked, passing precariously close to Uncle's house.

As a boy I had played under the surfaces of these sidewalks and yards, and prowled through tunnels beneath our very steps. My unsteadiness could be attributed to memories of that upheaval. I feared being ambushed by geysers of flaming gas and hosed down by burst watermains. To have suddenly recovered my mother made all improbabilities possible, natural disasters were now more likely, the supernatural had become both commonplace and incidental. Walking, I half-expected the earth to quake, this time for real.

I led my mother up Bloomfield Street, for whom could I entrust with her care and safekeeping except our neighbourhood's virtuous witch, Diedre Plant?

We crossed over.

"Miss Plant, this is Sheilagh Drinkwater. My mom."

My mother piped up, "This a nice little house! I never been inside a nice little house before! Can I sit in it?"

"Go ahead," I directed. She bounded through to the small living room where primly, properly—sanely—she seated herself on the sofa. In this setting she looked like a normal person, discreetly shabby, as if she had recently survived a flood and now patiently awaited government relief.

"Sparrow! You found her?" Miss Plant was reacting strangely. Rather than exultant, or at least happy for me, she seemed distressed.

"She found me, actually. Can you believe it?"

"Seek, and you will be found. Didn't I always tell you that?"

"I don't remember that one—"

"No?" Miss Plant sagged back against the arch of her small foyer, and I must say that her response to my mother's arrival seemed sadly, and inappropriately, subdued.

"To seek is to become, that's one of your favourites. I guess seek-to-be-found is a variation on the theme. Not that I ever figured out exactly what you meant by any of that, but—"

"I suppose you want her to stay here. I expect she's moving in."

Her tone was both disconcerting and a puzzle. "Is that okay with you? It's a lot to ask. Jesus. I have no idea how Aunt will react to this news. Heck, I don't know how *I'm* reacting to this news. I'm all over the map. Should I ease Aunt into it? Do you think? And Uncle? I have to tell Uncle. But with him I have to find some things out first."

"I'll pack my bags."

"Pardon?"

Diedre Plant was perfectly serious. Leaving me to stand confused in the hall, she disappeared into the privacy of her bedroom, emerging a moment later. At first she didn't seem to know where she was going or what she was doing, but she soon strode to the closet and asked that I fetch her suitcase down from the top shelf.

"I don't get this. What are you up to?"

"I'm sitting here!" Mom let us know.

"Pass me down my bag, please, Sparrow."

I obeyed her request, then, somewhat boldly for me, followed her into the bedroom where she ransacked her drawers. "What are you doing?"

"Packing. You don't honestly expect me to stay here with your mother in the house. What will be my job? Maid? Cook? Nurse? Chief bottle-washer?"

"Miss Plant?" She was busily harvesting the contents of her dresser. "Miss Plant, stop packing!" I sprang forward and with both hands held down the clothes she was about to unload and compress into her suitcase.

"The furniture is mine!" she bellyached. "Mine! I'll send a truck. Sparrow, I'm so disappointed in you. Where's your decency? How dare you turf me into the street? With no time to find another place, that's cruel. Oh God, if it snows once more I'll die. I'll die anyway. I'll catch my death. Sparrow, don't you know? Didn't I ever tell you? I go crazy out-of-doors."

"Hold it. Hold everything. Stop the clock. Time out here." I always relied upon my friend to be sly and eccentric, but never deranged.

"I don't think—"

"Sit down, Miss Plant. Let's get to the bottom of this. I did not mean to upset you. I'm sorry. I certainly did not intend to kick you out of here. Good grief. I need a place to put up my mom, that's all. I thought of you. You're my friend. I figured you could use the company. You're a sane, level-headed person—"

"Don't throw that in my face!" She jumped off the bed to hurl her petition at me. "I can be as nutty as any of them!"

"So I'm finding out. Have you been drinking?" Complicating my difficulty with her, I was attempting to conduct this argument in whispers to spare my mother any upset. I had never encountered Miss Plant this animated, or out of control.

"I need a place to live too! I got my rights! You can't throw me out in the street because I'm not as crazy as her!" Tears glistened in her eyes. "That's what they always say. I'm not crazy enough. Well, I am! I am, too!"

My world wobbled in its orbit. My mother's return had precipitated a shift in life's polar axis.

"Will you get a grip, Miss Plant? Geez. I'm not kicking you out of your own house."

"What did you say?" From the bed, hands crossed on her lap, she gazed at me with an inquisitive fright thoroughly out of whack with her customary intelligence and forthright deportment.

"I am not kicking you out."

"After that."

"Pardon me?"

"What did you say after that?"

"I'm not kicking you out—out of your own house."

That oblique point seemed to calm her down. Her breathing relaxed, and she found a Kleenex up her sleeve she used to dab her eyes and nose. Miss Plant came to her feet. One of her soft hands, which possessed the fragility and delicacy common to elderly fingers, grazed my cheek. "Are we still so innocent?" she asked me.

"Miss Plant?"

"Ignorant. I meant to say ignorant. Do you remain so terribly ignorant, you woe-begotten waif?" A frail hint of a smile both softened her features, and sharpened the blade of her guile. "Do you live in the dark, poor Sparrow? Are you still buried underground?"

"Don't start with me. Tell me what's going on." As a youngster I had feared this house. I had imagined a variety of local terrors. In the recent past I'd grown accustomed to its atmosphere. This sudden emergence of dementia had me baffled.

"When push comes to shove, Sparrow, this is your mother's house. It could be argued that it's your house, too, really."

"I don't get it." How could I? I felt like a smashed heavenly body, a moon without it's planet, a comet with its tail hacked off.

"Years and years ago, Gerald Boisvert let me stay here instead of your mother. The rent's affordable. If she's moving in, doesn't that mean that I'm obliged to move out?"

My turn to slump down onto the bed. Hankering for release, adrenalin swam through my bloodstream. I was not accustomed to the impulse, but I wanted to smack someone, I was yearning for the crunch of a bony nose under my knuckles. But whose face? Whose shnoz? Name the demon who deserved to have his lights punched out. *Uncle.*

"You helped me," I snapped back at Miss Plant. "You encouraged me to find my mother."

"To seek is to become." She fluffed the hair around her temples as she spoke, signalling the return of her superior airs and arts in full measure. "Who knows? Maybe I did overextend my bounds. It occurred to me that if you went looking for your mother, you might become the man she'd want you to be. Naturally, I knew you would never find her in the south."

"How did you know that?" Suspicion welled. "How could you have been so sure?"

Tentatively, Miss Plant took the first of her things from the suitcase to replenish her dresser again. "Sparrow, I'm a witch. Witches know things."

"You're not a goddamned witch. What do you know?" On my feet again to press this assault. My rage created stress along her spine, a lengthy fault line, and Miss Plant made circles with her head and rubbed the back of her neck. The next time she spoke her voice was too quiet to hear. "Excuse me?"

She confessed, "I knew you'd never find your mother in the south because I had it on reliable information that she lived downtown."

We each have our natural limits. We achieve our thresholds, of pain, of learning, of love, of hatred. We go so far and then we stop. I actually stomped out of the room, deliberately pounding my feet on the floor. I did not have the stomach to hear more. Were it not for spotting my mother waiting in earnest on the couch, I might have barged out the door and left the entire mess to people who obviously knew more about the circumstances of my life than I did. But I saw her in plain view, my wretched, dowdy, blessed mother, and she smiled. I worried that she might be upset by some of the things she'd heard, but Mom said, "I'm sitting in this nice little house. Nobody bothers me in it." Such a rage captured me, such sorrow, that I spun on the area rug and stormed straight back into Miss Plant's bedroom. Bloomfield's witch had had more confidence in me than I had had in myself, for she had not budged. Nor was I obliged to ask the obvious question—Miss Plant had known that I'd be returning for the answer.

"It's not what you think. Oh Sparrow, tuck away that frown, it makes you look so un-pretty. I was never in on this from the start. How is it possible for me to be a conspirator? Use your head. I don't get out much, and evil conspirators rarely peddle their wares at my door."

"Tell me what you know." The anger in my voice a surprise even to me. I sounded lethal.

Standing, Miss Plant continued to restock her dresser. "Sparrow, sweet, I'll tell you exactly what I know. The truth is, I never had an inkling that you existed until you introduced yourself to me digging up my backyard. Your father—sorry, uncle, you call him—Gerald Boisvert often spoke to me about Barclay. He was careful never to mention you. Obviously he had a reason for that omission, but you must understand, I never guessed that he had been perpetuating an omission."

Inwardly, a glum note resounded. I contradicted anyone who referred to me as Gerald Boisvert's son, although I did feel perturbed that he had himself declined to market the designation.

"A new roof was going up over my head. Gerald dropped by to check on the progress—and, as he's wont to do, drive the roofers batty criticizing their workmanship. Luckily they didn't nail him to the beams. When I had occasion to speak with him, I asked about you. Simple arithmetic, Sparrow. This house had been prepared for a woman who was crazy. It became available to me because the other woman was sent to a group home instead. We traded places. For that reason, I was curious about her."

In putting away her nylons, Miss Plant looked closely at a pair in its bag, removed them, and pulled one stocking over her arm to closely examine the weave. I was embarrassed by this, by a woman checking her nylons for a run, and averted my glance.

At that moment Mom chose to make a minor fuss in the front room, and I slipped out to calm her down.

"I been sitting in this nice little house a real long time," she let me know. "Nobody throws me out of it. Nobody bothers me at all."

Revelation kicked in. My mother could say one thing and mean something else. She was actually complaining about our lack of attention toward her. I gave her a little kiss, which apparently sufficed, and asked that she sit still awhile longer.

Back in the bedroom, I demanded of Miss Plant, "Tell me more."

"A relation of mine arranged, through your uncle, for me to live here. As a favour. In exchange, I was obliged to relinquish my residency in the group home. The staff said I wasn't crazy enough to stay there, even if I wanted to, because there's nothing wrong with me except that I refuse to go out-of-doors. They even hold it against me that I am willing to venture as far as my own backyard."

"I don't believe this. Any of it. I don't believe this *day*."

"You'll have to go shopping for me, Sparrow."

Quickly, I recovered my wits. "Not for ladies' nylons, I won't."

"If I'm to take care of your mother ..." Above her dresser was a thin lip of a shelf on which were lined miniature coloured bottles. Each was stopped by a tiny cork, as if sealing genies inside. "Listen. The game worked this way. In return for giving up my spot in the group home, however reluctantly, the privilege of living in this house was inflicted upon me. Even I had to admit that it was more comfortable than the sidewalk. After you dug up my garden, I prodded Gerald to tell me about you. He said he took you into his home because your mother was mad. He admitted that he had kept silent about you, though he didn't say why. Probably he was just being discreet. When you told me the story of your missing mother, I guessed which parts of each tale fit. I figured out who she was. At least, I figured out where she lived."

"You told me nothing about this," was the accusation that had to be levelled. Worse than feeling betrayed, I felt abandoned and alone. Virtually adrift again, a floating heart in swamp water.

"Poppycock. How do I decide what's best? Who am I to know if you're ready? You wanted to search the wide world over for your mother—"

"No. You put me up to it."

"Fine. I encouraged you. The fact that an endeavour is ill-conceived does not make it unworthy."

"What a crock!" I bellowed. Then lowered my voice for my mother's sake. "Your high-minded philosophy let you stay in this house. You were looking out for yourself!"

I thought I had her with that thrust, but Miss Plant, as she was adept at doing, caught me by surprise. "To protect my frail existence, yes, I'd do much worse. I'm an animal like the rest. You're the one searching for a higher way, Sparrow, not me. I've never been guilty of that nonsense. As a matter of fact, I checked on your mother after I met you. I talked to her over the phone."

"You didn't."

"Did too. Found her fairly easily. Mind, I didn't have to veer past New Orleans. I knew where to look."

Though I wanted desperately to complain, to make some justifiable wail that would shake the rafters of heaven, I was so pent-up I was speechless.

"Your mother's a ding-a-ling, Sparrow."

"Don't say that."

"A sweet, feisty ding-a-ling. I discovered in our little chat a woman unfit to care for herself. You, child, were not ready to assume the duty. Half your life had been spent underground, the other half excavating young girls from witch's gardens. Besides, you had your schooling to occupy you."

"Hold it right there. You did your best to keep me *out* of university." She had an answer for everything, yet I kept feeling that each reply masked a different truth.

"I was waiting for you to grow up, nothing more. You have a discriminating memory, Sparrow."

Blowing smoke from my ears, I stalked the room. By craning her neck my mother was able to spot me, and she called through, "Nobody bothered me yet! I'm very happy in here! I'm still sitting in this nice little house!"

"Many people," Miss Plant continued, "more than you know, have been waiting to see how you turn out. Perhaps I did not make the right decision. Perhaps, as you have so carelessly implied, my choices were tainted by self-interest. Is that a crime? Never let it be said that I am a woman who messes in the muck of other people's lives. I don't keep to myself because I suffer from halitosis. I keep to myself by preference. If you were meant to find your mother, you would find her, a reunion blessed, no doubt, by the music of the spheres. It wasn't up to me to hand her over on a silver platter. What would be the good of that? It's not my business to sit down at some celestial organ and pipe music for besotted gods. Hell no!"

"We were supposed to be friends," feebly, I protested.

"We most certainly are friends. And friends we shall remain— unless you boot me into the streets. Then all bets are off. What reason more appropriate than friendship did I need to weigh the consequences of my actions? Would you like a cup of tea, pal?"

I lingered over one of many prolonged sighs. All the world was weighted with allegiances and alliances I could neither penetrate nor decode. "Don't talk to me about a goddamned cup of tea."

"What about your mother? You have to think about that sort of thing now. Your responsibilities have changed. Has your mother eaten today?"

Damn her, Diedre Plant was right. If my mother was to rely upon me for her care and nourishment, I'd have to forsake the luxury of my own rage and petulance once in awhile.

"Mom! How're you doing?"

"This a nice little house. I'm still in it."

Yes, my mother wanted a cup of tea.

No, she had not eaten since breakfast.

Yes, she was hungry.

No, she didn't want a sandwich. She hated sandwiches. "Got any soup?"

Miss Plant's pantry was a cornucopia of Campbell's cans. My mother's eyes grinned widest at the mention of Chicken Gumbo.

"That's one my favourites."

Yet another revelation. I had much to learn about the strategies and forces that manipulated both our lives. I was also obliged to fathom the details, the simple likes and dislikes, the easy comforts and discreet terrors that adjudicated her daily existence. I knew precious little about her, a profound ignorance. While she ate, she didn't talk much and exercised crude manners, hovering over her bowl as though it might vanish before she was finished. The three of us savoured the soup, the flavour enhancing our communion.

A measure of my extreme anxiety was dispelled by the warmth of our luncheon. "Thanks for lunch, Miss Plant."

"You're very welcome, Sparrow."

"Thanks for the good eats, Miss Plants!"

"You're most welcome too, Sheilagh."

"I never been eating inside a nice little house before."

"I'm glad you've had the chance, Sheilagh."

"Can I pee in it?"

Our hostess didn't skip a beat. "Sparrow will show you where."

Emerging again from the washroom, my mother yawned, stretched, and wandered back to the living room. She said, "I never had a nap in a nice little house before." I invited her to go ahead, and returned to the kitchen where Miss Plant was doing up the dishes.

"Now. Please. Tell me more. Tell me everything you know."

Centred in the room was a small, arborite, circular table, the only feeding station in the house. The four skinny legs did not adjust to offset the wobbles in the floor. Whenever an elbow was lifted or a forearm returned to rest, the table rocked. "Not today," Miss Plant told me.

"What's that supposed to mean, not today?"

"I believe it's plain English, Sparrow, even to a Park Extension illiterate like yourself."

"Don't kid around."

"Why would I? What's your mother doing?"

"Don't change the subject."

"Shouldn't you check on her?"

Head and shoulders under the coffee table, legs beneath the sofa, Mom lay in a curl on the living room floor. Why she had declined to take her nap on the sofa mystified me, although she had had the presence of mind to pull down a cushion for her pillow. After covering her with the throw-blanket Miss Plant kept handy for her own afternoon kips, I returned to the kitchen.

"Understand this much, Sparrow. Many doors must be unlocked. I shall decline to confuse you with false information, or partial information, or knowledge you clearly don't deserve."

"What are you blathering about? Miss Plant, are you going dippy on me again?" Now I knew why children hovered in the oak tree to fling acorns at her door.

"Dippy?" She took offense. "I am about to saddle you with the most important truth to have come within the bounds of your trust, and you have the effrontery to call me dippy?"

"Sorry. I was out of line. What truth?"

Her's was a glossy white kitchen, with bright red trim and cupboards. Within the stark quarters, words would resonate, abetted by the noisy plumbing and the rumble of the fridge motor. "You must unlock many doors in life, Sparrow Drinkwater. Each answer will be both a revelation and a preparation for the next test. Each revelation will both bewilder you and bless you with greater strength. Strength derives from knowledge of what is true."

Often I was the one, in those days, who sallied forth with a broom against the hurlers of acorns and snowballs, convincing Park Extension youth that I was a legitimate ogre in my own right. Never again, I vowed. Not me. Let acorns hail against her door, I was not answering the knock. "Sorry," I told her. "You sound like a dipstick to me."

"Smarten up. You have spent your entire life searching and digging for the key. Out of the blue, the key has found you. It's up to you to use it."

"Mumble jumble, Miss Plant."

"Oh really? Fine. I won't say another word. From this moment forward your time of testing begins—without my counsel." Furiously, she slapped the arms of her chair.

"No wonder you suggested lunch. You're out to lunch yourself, permanently, did you know that?"

Miss Plant fastened an invisible zipper across her lips.

"My mother's the key? So where are these locks? Okay, where are these doors?"

In clamping her mouth shut in an exaggerated style, she resembled an aged, cranky toad.

"Suit yourself. My mom's the key. Whoop-de-doo. The one door I'm going to open is the one out of here. I'm not so sure I'll be back. Thanks for lunch, but mostly, thanks for nothing."

"You're not going anywhere, Sparrow."

"Ah, the mummy speaks. Watch me, Miss Plant. I'm up. I'm moving towards the door. I'm on my way."

"Your mother's sleeping."

Again, she had called me back to the rudimentary realities of my fresh existence. Diedre Plant forced me sit down and sip more tea. We scowled at each other. She refused to break out the scotch. Bored, I made numerous trips to pee, each time checking on my mother like a doting parent, and perhaps it was the continuous exercise of my bladder that calmed me down, for my spleen relieved itself of a good measure of its venom. Mom appeared so feeble to me, so peaceful. Rich with calamity. Returning to the washroom yet again, I searched the mirror and erupted into tears on the spot. My red eyes wouldn't escape Miss Plant's attention. Damn her knowing look.

"So. My mother's the key."

"To unlock more knowledge than you can yet imagine."

"I'm supposed to thank you for this secret?"

She nodded, and showed the faint, furtive smile earned at my expense. "Either that or strangle me. Should you choose to annihilate my existence, be gentle, Sparrow."

"What am I supposed to do with her? Can't she stay here?"

"Take her home."

"I'm not ready for that yet. Aunt will have a bird."

"I mean to *her* home. She doesn't live in a dumpster, you know."

The thought gave me pause. "Where does she live?"

"You see?" Miss Plant sipped her tea, then blew steam from the surface of her drink. "Here you are badgering me for more information and you don't even know the basics."

"I asked her. She didn't answer."

"When she's ready to go home, she'll answer. This is a big day for her. She has finally made contact with her son." God help me, Miss Plant was making sense. "If she told you immediately, you might have dropped her off on the spot. And don't forget, she thinks talking to you is against regulations. She expects to get into trouble."

Taking a moment to fathom this twist, this possibility that my mother withheld information in order to manipulate me and other forces, I leaned over the table to comfort my chin in my hands. "She hasn't shown much emotion."

"Either she can't, because she's medicated, or she knows it will be too much for her. That's my guess. Give her some credit." Oh, how Miss Plant enjoyed all this, especially being superior.

"How come you know so much?" I asked her.

"How come you know so little?"

"I've been kept in the dark by people like you."

A nod of her head represented a mild concession. "Until now. From this point forward, Sparrow, you have a lamp to guide you."

"My mother's a lamp? First she's a key, now she's a lamp? Or are you the lamp?"

"You'll see."

"Listen, Miss Plant—"

"Don't apologize yet, Sparrow."

"I don't plan to. You got your nerve. You should be the one apologizing to me. I was wondering though. Could I borrow some money?
I ran up a few debts today. Wherever I'm taking her, I'd prefer to go
by cab."

"You'll find a hundred-and-eighteen dollars in the cookie jar in
small unmarked bills. Spare me a few."

"That's great." My mother was stirring in the front room. I shot a
glance at Diedre Plant, into her sagacious, blue, charmed eyes which I
had so assiduously been trying to avoid. Grudgingly, I murmured,
"Thanks."

"For what?"

I had to admit, that was a good question. I didn't have that answer
either.

                                    *

Pool halls in Park Extension were never any great shakes, and I had
wasted too much of my youth underground to have honed the proper
skills. Park Exers lost their innocence early travelling to downtown par-
lours where they routinely had their clocks cleaned by rich kids. That's
rarely noted in the mythology of pool, that the sharks are the guys who
grew up with a table in the basement of Daddy's mansion. Night and
day, the silver-spooned practised for free while learning the best games,
such as snooker. Us poor slobs were restricted to eightball for small
stakes on sloped, gouged tables with crooked cues, which is why my
neighbourhood never produced a single prodigy in the sport.

In the side pocket.

In your ear.

Up your ass.

Shove this!

Fuck you!

Congenial contests, pleasant Saturday afternoons. The game prepared me to accept defeat when necessary, to scrap when provoked, and
never to get too cocky when the coloured balls skipped off a tear in the
cloth to roll my way. These were the exact skills necessary to play pool
with my mother. She was the eightball that I needed to sink in society's
side pocket.

What to do with her now that she had been found?

Miss Plant was on the money about one thing, my mother knew perfectly well where she lived. She also knew how to get there. Deciding

that she was ready for home, Mom slipped me the address on a scrap of paper.

In effect, my mother, the bag lady, carried business cards.

"And you want to go back to this place? You don't mind?"

"Need my meds. Thou can't see me without my meds. Me I'm getting thin."

This scared me. She was speaking rapidly after her nap, staring straight ahead, her voice undercut by anxiety and threat. Although Miss Plant looked over at me, she didn't say a word. She didn't rub it in. How foolish of me to think that I was in any way prepared to care for my mother.

A large part of me remained elated, but I had been worn down by the day's emotional scuffles. My jousts with Miss Plant had left me frazzled. In the cab downtown, I rested my head, my mind in a maze, my bones stone weary.

"This here's my Sparrow-bird boy," Mother reported to the driver.

Immediately cognizant that he was dealing with an air-head, the cabby assumed a cordial, condescending manner. "Good-looking kid," he said.

Who asked you?

"He's much bigger now," Mom assured him. Between us sat the brown shopping bag stuffed with her ragged sweaters. Miss Plant had donated a couple of her own to the cause. Combined with a cautious brushing of her wild tangle of hair, and a few strategic bobby pins, the new clothes remarkably improved her appearance. "When Sparrow was a boy he was a lot more smaller."

"Is that a fact? Do wonders never cease?" The driver parked his mouth on automatic. "You wonder where the time goes. You turn yourself around, the kids have all growed up."

Mom jostled me awake to ask, "Thou got money now?"

"I borrowed a few bucks from Miss Plant."

"Pull over!" she suddenly screamed at the driver, and pummelled his shoulders and head. "Pull over! Pull over!"

"Mom! What's the matter? Stop hitting him." I grabbed her arms. She was stronger than anyone might imagine.

"Cigarettes!" she yelled at me. Her manifesto. "Cigarettes!"

"Okay! We'll stop."

"Hit the man, Sparrow! Bite him! Bite his face!"

"Mom, you could've asked him nicely to stop. You didn't have to hit him."

"Need my meds. Me I'm getting thin. Me!"

In the meantime, her smokes would have to do.

The driver had had enough, so we hailed a second cab. Heading downtown, Mom puffed like a chimney in winter.

"Streetcars buffalo sidewalk bridge," she muttered.

"Pardon me?"

"Streetcars buffalo sidewalk bridge." A defiant chant this time.

"I don't understand."

"Telephone cougar train-tracks church." Louder still.

I moved closer to her side. Wrapped an arm around her shoulders and snugged her in tight. "Easy, Mom. You're getting thin." Whatever that meant to her. I did my best to check my own rising fright.

"Oh, Sparrow, where my fucking angels? Alla time they're so fucking late."

"Easy, now, Mom, I've got you. I'm right here. We'll get you home. We'll get your medication."

"Too strong a dose! Too strong a dose! I get so fucking heavy! It knocks me so fucking out!" She clamped a hand over her mouth as though she'd said something taboo.

Getting nervous, the driver repeatedly turned around to glance at my mother. I did my best to reassure him. "If you want to step on it a little," I let him know in French, "that's okay too."

We gambolled through traffic.

"Tell him to hurry up, Sparrow. Tell him to hurry real fast."

"I did, Mom, I—"

"Oh, get this. Check it out. This real swell. Demons catching up. *Bite thy face, demon! Bite thy face!* Catching up. Oh shit me. Where my angels, Sparrow? Where my angels gone today?"

She was moving now, squiggling in her seat within my grasp.

"Oh, fuck off!" she yelled at an invisible rider in the front seat. "What the fuck thee looking at?"

"Easy, Mom. Take a drag on your cigarette. There. That's it." She inhaled down to her toes.

"Oh, fuck thee me! What're thou? Thou ain't no fucking demon-fucker! Shit, Sparrow, look the fucking squirrel. Thou art just a fucking squirrel! Fucking squirrel thinks he's a demon-fucker! Thou don't scare me. Piss off! Fuck thee! Fuck thy children! Fuck thee too! Get the fuck out of here!"

"Take another drag, Mom. We're almost there. We'll get your meds."

Her voice was different now, edgy and driven. "Oh, right!" she yelled, looking out the window and up. "That's thee bitches! Thanks a lot! Look that, Sparrow, look those assholes. My angels sitting on the rooftops. *A lot of good thou art doing up there! OH SHIT!*" She began thrashing and flailing, nearly burning me with the cigarette. It took all my strength to hold her. "Demons all over the place in here. Coming through the roof." She rolled down the window, shouting out, "Thee thou thy! Thee thou thy! Streetcars buffalo sidewalk bridge! Telephone cougar train-tracks church!"

"Mom! Smoke! Smoke, Mom." Each drag helped her for a few moments.

"Oh, great! Great!" she complained sarcastically, and I hadn't heard this sophistication in her tone when she was more normal. "They're down to the balconies. *A lot of good thou art doing me up there!* Angels don't like my language. *Thee thou thy!* They like that. Don't like me bad-talking my demons." But she shook her fist at one. "Thee get lost thou fucking squirrel thee ain't no fucking demon-fucker thou don't scare me!"

"Where is he, Mom? Over here?" I took a wild swipe at our imaginary rodent, but Mom got mad at me, frantically grabbing my arm out of harm's way.

"Look out, Sparrow! Shit! He bite your arm off. He got big teeth."

"I'm okay."

"Thee thou thy. *Thythy theetheetheethee thouthouthou!* Angel-talk. Gotta talk angel-talk. Get down here thee bitching angels! *Thee thy thou!* Streetcar buffalo sidewalk bridge. Telephone cougar train-tracks church." She started punching an invisible foe. "Fuck you, demon! Fuck you, too! My angels are so coming. They are so!" Out the window, she demanded that the angels, "Shake thy fucking ass!"

Male and female pedestrians were not amused.

"Take a drag, Mom, take another deep drag."

"Monsieur—"

"Drive, buddy. Step on it."

"Mistletoe rosehip grizzly-bear winter sweden fucking-frequency, fucking-frequency, cantaloupe bridge sophomore frenchie tomato onion quarterback broccoli face friday servant egg army rollercoaster shampoo street sandwich buffalo train-tracks bus *cougaaaaar!* window thee thou thy telephone enemy wichita caboose—"

"Mom Mom Mom," I'm babbling as well. "Stop it!" I wrestled her hand with the cigarette up to her mouth. "Smoke!"

She took another long draw. "Red yellow buzz beard plane—*where my angels?* Where my angels? Thou fucking demons!"

"Hang on, Mom. We're almost there."

"Why'd thee never call me? How come thee never sent me any Christmas cards?"

"Oh, Mom. Mom. Are you talking to me? I never knew where you were. I never knew you were alive. I couldn't find you anywhere."

We turned onto a narrow street, and my mother dropped into a different orientation. She was looking around the taxi as if confused by her environment and company.

"Are you all right?"

Head hung low, Mom failed to answer.

"She okay?" the cabby asked. He'd been a good sport.

My mother's gaze lifted from the floor. "Where my angels gone today, Sparrow?"

Looking at me, she never blinked or took her eyes off me. She seemed to be expecting an answer. So I pointed. Up.

Mom climbed out of the cab with her bag of sweaters and scanned the rooftops. "Fucking assholes," was her final proclamation. She slammed the door on her demons. I paid the fare while Mom hurried away.

We had been deposited on a nondescript block, a downtown side-street little more than a broad alley called Alexander. I had not taken notice of the street before, despite passing its busy corner at rue Ste. Catherine a thousand times. Mother knew where to go. This was her turf. She ran up the steps of a dilapidated mansion, and at the top, she twirled around and called back at me.

"This my house, Sparrow! Thou can't come in here! Only crazy persons crazy in the head come in this house! That must stay away!" With that, she opened the door and disappeared inside.

I was frozen where I stood momentarily, stunned by her outburst in the cab, and now by her edict from the steps. My mother was ashamed to live in a halfway house for the mentally estranged, that was her real motive in denying me entry. She was ashamed of the life she lived, ashamed of herself. All these matters would become apparent in time. Instinctively, for the moment, I had recognized that her speech on the stairs had implied more than an immediate restriction to her home. In her state, she had wanted to deny me admittance into the more demented aspects of her life.

Of course, my mother was out of kilter, so I did not follow her command. I knew, even if she did not, that there was no turning back. I climbed the stairs slowly, stood on the threshold of her home, and knocked for entry into her mind and heart. Then, I turned the knob, and I stepped inside.

8.

The Heist

The next morning I was busy psyching myself up when my guardian's cunning psyched me out. As I dressed, I rehearsed what needed to be said, adding generous drops of distilled venom to the tips of my barbs.

An opening might be, "My *dear benevolent, loathsome Uncle Butter*—"

"Don't call me that, Ssssparrow. You're not a child anymore. My name is Boisvert. Bois-vert!"

So I'd start again. "*Dear Uncle Weasel, a leg-hold trap is a kindness you do not deserve.*"

The harmony and violence of my reverie would be interrupted by his shouts. I put an ear to the attic vent. He was hollering for me to come down and meet him on the curb. "Should I bring my boxing gloves?" I yelled back.

"What?"

Fine. Bare knuckles it is.

Stepping into the sunlight, I believed that I had been bequeathed the perfect time and place to do battle. My obscenities would be modified in the open air. I was less likely to do him physical damage in public. And yet, in drumming up the guts to accuse Uncle of kidnapping my mother and me, of holding us hostage these many years, I was betrayed by my own reticence. Be cold, Sparrow. Be swift. As heartless as a blade. Be cruel. Force the bugger to incriminate himself. Then make him beg. Make him suffer. Do it. Now.

I gagged on enmity.

Uncle, as things turned out, was pumped up about something. He had more important affairs on his mind, and my untimely hesitation allowed him to establish his own priorities.

"Take a look, Ssssparrow."

I looked. "Gee. What a shame."

Overnight, someone had pilfered the driver's side hubcaps off his car.

Caught with my defenses down and my courage flagging, I was trapped into commiserating with him, and having been given an inch, the wily conniver swiped a country mile. Uncle shanghaied me into finding both the culprit and the missing loot.

"Unc, it's a big city," I pleaded, beaten back by my cowardice. "Take a minute. Add up how many cars putt around a big city. You're the bookkeeper here, you can do this. To figure out the number of hubcaps, multiply by four."

"This town's not big enough for me and that thief both. I'm ssssurprised you don't know that by now. That's the trouble with the criminal element—it hasn't figured out who it's dealing with. Let me tell you ssssomething, Ssssparrow, ssssssomething you can ssssay to the world. Gerald Boisvert's nobody's patsy."

Uncle lived realities elusive to the common mortal.

As he explained, the hubcaps were not generic, they suited only his model of Chevy. Four blocks along and one street over we located them after twenty minutes of reconnaissance, max.

"What did I tell you? Local punks. Teenagers."

As a recent graduate of that lesser echelon of humanity myself, I smarted from the automatic rebuke.

True enough, a parked car sported two hubcaps with a shine worthy of Uncle's vehicle. The other two caps were tarnished. Uncle Butter knocked on a friend's door and called the cops. They arrived in short order and Uncle kindly guided them through their investigation, plucking a pink bristle from one of the shiny caps, then showing the officers the soft pink broom lying in his trunk. Over the winter he had used the broom to sweep snow from his hood and rooftop without scratching the paint. He took pains to explain that it was a special broom. An expensive broom. Few people owned one. Impressed, the officers were also conscious of what stands up in court, and of what remains seated in the room of circumstantial evidence.

Our event had attracted a crowd, including the driver of the vehicle in question. Knock me down with a soft pink bristle, if it wasn't my adversary and subterranean adventurer from former days, Derek Mahoney.

"This your car?" I asked him.

"You got a problem wid 'at?" Since I had last seen him, Derek had pumped iron in a big way. He had bulked-up.

"You do," I forewarned.

In consultation with the police, Derek was not so sure.

Uncle asked us to consider his second tidbit of evidence. He described a dent on one of the hubcaps as looking like the Star of David. "Get up close to it. Ssssquint your eyes." After a period of analysis, with first the cops and then the spectators dropping to their knees to squint, the hubcap's cosmology was dutifully confirmed.

"Know what 'at proves, fuck?" Derek was playing to the jury of curiosity-seekers. "Nuts all. He checked things out 'fore we showed up. How many youse can identify a dent on a fuckin' hubcap? One youse gotta squint to see? The guy's jerking me around, fuck. Just 'cause I don't inspect my hubcaps night and day like on a regular basis, dat don't mean diddly-squat."

"One pair is shiny, the other pair's old. How come is that?" the senior officer quizzed. Holmesian deduction was not required to discern the obvious, that Uncle was a kook and that Derek was probably guilty. If the youth hadn't stolen the hubcaps from Uncle, he had lifted them from someone else. Alternatively, he had purchased the hubcaps and snatched the Chevy. The officer knew these things. He also knew that proof is usually an apocryphal commodity.

As a badge of his experience, the cop wore a regulation moustache, remarkably similar to Uncle's. The two men also shared language as a common link, although Uncle customarily disavowed his heritage, preferring to speak English. As politics might work in his favour here, he asserted himself in his riled, victimized-by-the-English, French.

"I bought a new pair, geez," Derek protested in his culprit-English. "Mine got ripped off. That's the diff', him and me. I pay my own way, fuck. He steals from me 'cause he got robbed, geez, the old crock."

"Punk," Uncle spat out in English.

"Geek."

"Bum."

"Old fart!"

"Uncle," I warned quietly, and managed to catch his eye. He might be able to win the war, but should things escalate he'd be outgunned in any name-calling battle. Derek sheltered the greater arsenal. As yet he hadn't deployed even his light artillery. Catching my drift, Uncle shut up.

While it was true that Uncle Butter, a community pillar, a bookkeeper renowned for his personal integrity, packed more credibility in his pinkie than did Derek in his impressive pectorals, what counted in these matters was hard evidence, not reputation. Derek-the-Dink benefited from an insider's knowledge about the law. He knew how wonderfully crooks were protected. With apology, the policemen dismissed Uncle's case, and the street-jury was discharged.

"Understand something, Mahoney."

"What?"

"My uncle, he's not like other men. He's ... eccentric, let's say."

"I'm shakin' in my boots." Derek performed a pantomime of a spastic. "Maybe you should be."

I had given him half-a-chance. I had offered him an opportunity to repent. Derek would not be defrayed from his swagger and boast. His grin, so seductive with the girls, magnified as the cops crossed the street to their patrol car. Uncle allowed them to reach it, the whole of the time staring into the teeth of the young punk's smirk.

"Officers? Come back here one minute, will you?" he asked in French. Less than pleased to be recalled, the men returned, thumbs in their gunbelts, their postures sullen and threatening. They were not on the verge of running him in, but Uncle was flirting with public censure. "Sssssir," he said, switching to English so that Derek would catch his nuance, "be ssso kind to ask this fine young ssspecimen of Canadian manhood what we can expect to find *inside* the hubcaps."

"Sssspace-man?" Derek asked the throng. "I'm a sssspace-man?" Then he charged, "It's a plant. Whatever the fuck it is. Who spends their life checkin' inside their hubcaps? I got better things to do me, geez."

The perfect straight-man for his routine, the kid cop asked Uncle, "What'll we find, sir?"

"It's a plant, fuck," Derek repeated again. "Dropped it down one of them fuckin' holes when nobody's lookin'."

"*Etched*," Uncle told the policemen, and told us all, "inside both hubcaps, you will find my name—G. Boisvert—and phone number."

A murmur went through the courtroom of the street. You could almost hear the judge's gavel, the jurist's gravelly voice demanding order.

"Bad luck, Mahoney." I took pity on my ancient enemy while the cops eagerly removed the hubs.

"Fuckin' geez," he lamented. "He writes his name on hubcaps?"

"Hubcaps. His shoes. Shorts. Electric razor. His telephone. He carves his initials on pencils. The thing to keep in mind about my uncle is, never bet against him."

That was the moment, the precise instant, when knowledge alighted upon my brow. *Damn!* Uncle knew. He knew about yesterday. He knew I had found my mother.

A ludicrous assumption, really, to believe that I had located her without word getting back to him. Suddenly, my ability to draw a simple breath had been placed in jeopardy.

Ungracious in victory, Uncle would insist upon the crook's arrest. When the cops wavered, the crime being a puny one, he bargained instead for the public humiliation of his foe. To avoid an incident which might run him afoul his parole board, Derek consented to install Uncle's hubs, change his oil and filter, and thoroughly clean the Chevy inside and out under the dedicated supervision of Uncle Butter. The work took four hours before passing muster. Four hours that I sweated through myself waiting to catch Uncle alone again. Four hours that Uncle purposefully stretched out to avoid talking to me.

After Derek had been dismissed, Uncle stayed on the street. This time I was determined to confront him. The man was gloating as I approached.

"Loved it! Every minute! I made the sssscum put the caps on right. Did you sssssee his face?"

I piped up, "You know about my mother, don't you, Uncle?"

Derek's humilation had been one of the great triumphs of Uncle's life, paying homage to decades of meticulous habits. My question had immediately spoiled his fun. Uncle never actually confessed, preferring to negotiate. "Don't jump to conclusions, Ssssssparrow. Don't tell Auntie, okay? It'll break her heart if ssshe finds out."

"What?"

"Auntie. Her heart."

Auntie's heart. Apparently Uncle and I needed to discuss Auntie's heart. For me to announce that my real mother had been located would tear Auntie's heart into shreds. So he inferred. I'd wear the consequences across my shoulders forever like sackcloth and ashes.

Grievances and questions, accusations and recriminations, aspirations and ideas for the future, everything had to be repressed, concealed for the sake of Aunt Butter's fragile internal pump. Her love for me would be brutalized by the mere mention of my real mother's name. Unable to split the difference and share my affections, Auntie was certain to wreck on the trauma.

"How do you know that? How can you be so sure?"

"I know my own wife, Ssssparrow."

What was it about Auntie that I had neither known nor appreciated?

"I just don't get it. You *knew*. All along you knew. You never told me my mother lived downtown as a bag lady."

"Sssshe's not a bag lady, Ssssparrow. How can you ssssay that about your own mother? I have sssseen to it that her needs are met. You've been to her halfway house. Ssshe's housed. Ssshe receives her medication. Ssshe's fed. Ssshe's clothed."

"In rags!"

"Ssshe prefers the clothes ssshe picks out of Sssssalvation Army bins to what we purchase for her. We don't know why. It's one of her things."

A sharp pang of joy. My mother was proud! Too proud to take handouts from her keepers, from those who contrived to lie to her and cheat her out of her own child. She chose instead the honourable tokens offered to her community of derelicts.

Either that, or she subscribed to a different fashion sense.

"All this time, you knew. You lied to me. You lied to her."

"Sssparrow, remember Auntie. I've never told you this before, ssshe's not that well. Believe me, keeping your mother a ssssecret was for the best. Haven't we given you a good home? Do you really think your mother could have provided for you? Brought you up? Given you an education? Think of poor Auntie. Ssssshe loves you as much as any mother can. Please, Sssssparrow, think of her."

We were talking over the hood of the Chevy sparkling with cleanliness in the sun. Uncle used his vehicle as a buffer between us. I wondered what was going on here. Admirably, Uncle Butter appeared solicitous towards his wife's well-being, how could I be opposed to that? He emphasized that she would be mortified to learn that I had located my real mother, that the pain might kill her.

"Ssshe'll feel ssshunted aside, cast off like a, like an old mop or ssssomething."

I thought long and hard about Aunt, about the confused emotions she would be expected to endure upon learning of my mother's return. Pitch-poling in the swells of my strife, I might have drowned in that emotional quandary had I not been rescued by inspiration. "Hey. I get it. It's coming clear to me now. You don't care one whit about Auntie. You're worried she'll box your ears!"

"What are you ssssssssaying?"

I listened to myself, and to the tone of his response. Suddenly it was all so rich and true that I practically leapt in the air to test my theory.

"Ssssssparrow—" Uncle wailed across the lawn.

I shouted from the stoop, "She'll tan your hide! That's what you're afraid of! You never gave her a choice. She thought she had to raise me or throw me out with the trash. You lied to her, too."

"Ssssparrow, that's not true." A weak protest. Uncle strained to keep his voice down, hoping to entice me to lower mine. The neighbours weren't his only concern, although decorum remained one of Uncle's fixed tenets. He was valiantly trying to deflect the truth.

"Bullshit! This has nothing to do with breaking her heart. You're out to protect your own skin!"

"Ssssspare your Auntie heartache, Sssssparrow! If ssshe has to sssshare you—. If ssshe's not your only mother—." His arguments didn't make sense to him anymore. He couldn't complete a thought. "I don't know what ssshe'll do."

"Liar! Liar! Pants on fire!" One of Barclay's old chants had spurted loose. It seemed appropriate at the time. "I know what she'll do. So do you!"

Cruel and resolute, I charged through to the kitchen where Aunt, swathed in her apron, kneaded dough. No time to pull punches. "My real mother lives downtown in a home for crazy people," I blurted out. "Uncle knew about it all along. He put her there! He lied to both of us."

There was that silence. Interminably rising like one of Auntie's breads. I had to endure that silence. I anticipated her heartbreak, suddenly fearful that I was in the wrong, that I had become the wanton destroyer of this gentle and delicate, simple and loving person. When she did manage to respond, recovering from the shock of my ballistic delivery to assimilate and comprehend the news, Uncle was proven correct about one detail. Aunt Butter did indeed reply from the heart. Credit the storm in her heart for lifting the dough in her hands. Uncle scattered. Usually he was speedier, but the tornado of Aunt's scorn caught him before he made it to the door.

Dough flew through the air.

The first act of violence witnessed in that peaceful home.

In the living room, Uncle resembled an uprooted elm. His limbs lay loose about him. Akimbo on the floor between the sofa and the turned-over coffee table, he appeared discombobulated, ransacked by a twister. Toppled by flying pastry. Amid the silent, unseen winds of her fury, Aunt stood above him. Mercilessly, she glared down upon him through a hurricane's eye.

The inner wrath of her life remained too rampant for speech.

Silently, I climbed into my loft for the last time. Packed my things. Much of what I owned could now be discarded—teenager stuff, the dregs of my past existence here—and I compressed what could be of use into a solitary, lone-soldier of a duffle. At the last moment, I included one book. Between its pages were the dried flowers, the floating hearts, from my mother's youth. Confident that my true life was about to begin, or at least emerge, I journeyed down the rungs of the ladder.

Having retrieved the dough from Uncle's brow, Aunt had returned to her marble slab, where she kneaded the violence out of her system. I said goodbye. She confessed her love for me, and I assured her that I understood.

She loved me. I knew that. Knew also that her years of dutiful service to my upbringing had been accomplished out of a moral sense of what was right. Of what had been necessary. Uncle had schemed to make me necessary. He had cheated her. He had played her for a fool. He had wanted me in his home for reasons privy to neither her nor me, and while she was restricted to mustering her anger and pummelling him with pie crust, I was free to do something more constructive. I was free to find out why. I was free to reclaim my past, if not my future. I was, at long last, free to act.

Uncle had stolen me from my mom.

Auntie's heart, as well as my own, convicted him of the crime.

At the doorway to the back garden, where I had peed as a sign of my dislocation, as a gesture subversive to my exile, I paused. One more word needed to be spoken. "Auntie," I began. We both looked at one another through the sparkle of our tears. Sunlight basted the pastry-flesh of her cheeks. "Thanks."

That said, Sparrow Drinkwater decamped.

*

I was searching for a description of myself. I had set my course. I was transmogrifying into my true nature again, that's what it felt like. I had returned to my true heritage, in flight from a swamp. Hijacked, kidnapped from my true life and forced to grow up, become schooled, be principled, adapt, be clever and wise, I had emerged as someone other than myself. Someone shaped to a foreign mould. That's what it felt like.

I would break into Uncle's office and plunder the secrets of his alternate safe, rescuing my history from a maze of deception. My true calling was to seek out and confront the manipulators of my existence, the invisible beings who had discarded my mother to an asylum, then contrived to boot her out. They had booked our passage across America and—*whoops!*—lost one of us off a bridge. Whose grand design had that pilgrimage been? God's, or some equally fuzzy imitator's?

My mother and I were travellers in the puzzle of this world together, it was our natural habitat. Evicted from one home we had been consigned to another, yet its destination had been concealed from us, our options removed. Vigorous new zeal swelled in my chest—my old life returning. A shin-kicker and wrist-biter again (no wonder I had been a natural at football), I had reclaimed my destiny as Mom's protector in the wicked realm. Things were coming full circle, and me, and she, the two of us, reunited, were about to occupy our true lives and enjoy our true adventures—not the false ones created for us—at long last.

From Diedre Plant's kitchen, I called through to the living room where my mother was learning the game of checkers. Sheilagh kept jumping indiscriminately, always to her own advantage. "Play nicely, Mom."

"I'm winning, Sparrow!" she shouted back.

"Your mother is cheating, Sparrow," Miss Plant qualified.

"Am not cheating! Why cheating? Thou cheats! Bite her face, Sparrow!"

"Yes, Sparrow. Come in here and bite my face," Miss Plant insisted. "I double-dare you."

"She double-dares thee, Sparrow!"

"I triple-dare you."

"Sparrow! Hear that? *Miss Plant triple-dares thee!*"

This was what I believed—a man with a mission is a free man. I was a free man. A desperate man, if we can forgive my youthful ardour and allow the portrait to be enhanced by an infatuation with my status. A free, desperate man, and the best word devised for that is *desperado*.

I liked the term. Appreciated the high office. I had been looking around for others of the same ilk to form a merry band of plunderers—safe-crackers in the dead of night.

We were after a loot more precious than jewels or cash, more alluring than art or commodities. Four of us, four *desperados*, were poised to swipe secrets, the signposts to my existence. I was after clues to guide me through the mythology and mystery at the centre of my life, that muck and mire. Barclay, the accountant, the financial whiz-kid, the hotshot junior partner, also wanted secrets divulged. "Your past is in the safe, Bird," he had confirmed once again, "and my future." He was hoping to discover keys to unlock a monetary kingdom. Which made me think. Ponder a few things. A weird situation, as though I stood at the Gates of Heaven demanding entry, challenging the scoundrels and sentries who had presumed to kick my mother and me out. Barclay braced himself at the outer enclosure to different premises, a palace of brimstone and ash and scorching heat, insisting on entry to the vaults.

I wanted answers and understanding, I wanted access to the truth. I wanted to rescue my mother from her miseries. Barclay desired connections, leverage, a hand-hold on fortune. Who was right, who was wrong in this affair? Gutter-life was stressful for this sensitive soul. I was looking for a chance, an edge, another dimension or some glimmer of knowledge, some revealed secret to free me from the constraints, the sadnesses, the tragedies and collapsed tunnels of this realm. As asinine and as heroic as it sounds, I wanted my mother to find some way out of her mental illness. Barclay's scramble was for the old standbys of power and fame and possessions, and I could appreciate the directness and single-mindedness and even the achievable possibility of that pursuit. We might both have been crazy, that was a given. Otherwise, one of us was definitely nuts. We couldn't both be strollers on the true path. I gathered that I was the most likely candidate to be off the wall, and yet, considering my family history, that was okay with me.

I did not pursue my meditation or fully articulate the premise to myself. I was responding instead to an inner urge and momentum. What is theoretical now was instinctive then. I hoped that whatever we gained from the secret safe would confirm that life was a search for heaven—I wanted my mother redeemed, made whole. I wanted myself made strong enough and bright enough and able enough to care for her—I was in hot pursuit of the miraculous. I wanted salvation to be our pedigree. And I wanted Barclay debased for his greed and wanton search for wealth. The opposite would be more plausible. His bias was likely to be exalted while my flighty aspirations were subject to ridicule. I wanted, somehow, hoping against hope, for Uncle's safe to spill the pertinent secrets to existence.

Didn't I desire to clutch, and treasure, the clues to life itself?

Don't we all want that? Was it too much to ask?

Was it? Is it?

All in all, I was plotting no ordinary crime.

From the other room, for the umpteenth time, Mom sang out, "King me!"

"Well, no, Sheilagh, I can't do that," Miss Plant told her.

"Why the fuck not?"

"Sheilagh! I'm not going to play if you talk that way."

"I'm sorry, Miss Plants. King me anyways."

Lumbering apelike down Miss Plant's hall, I grunted like a gorilla. I jumped on Diedre Plant and pretended to bite her face off, while my mother squealed with delight. The checkerboard went flying, the black and red pieces scattering for cover. Pinning the kicking Miss Plant against the sofa, I asked my mother, "Should I bite her nose off first?"

"Yes! Yes!" She clapped her hands as I put that little nose in my mouth, then masticated voraciously. Mom loved it whenever I acted as her staunch defender. "Is it good, Sparrow? Is it good?"

"Mmmm, yum yum. Like a bite?"

"No! Not her!" Miss Plant objected. "She'll cheat. She'll eat me for real."

"Isn't that what good people do to witches?"

"I'm not hungry," Mom said, and suddenly she seemed less interested. Apparently she found witches unappetizing.

"Are you sure? Not even a nibble of ear? Remember, she triple-dared me."

"Okay, I guess. Maybe a little piece."

"Cooked or raw, Mom?"

"You'll both be cooked if you don't cut this out!" sang Miss Plant, but she was having the most fun of all.

Mom was busy thinking about my question, staring at the ceiling. When she came to a decision, she celebrated by clapping her hands together and declared, "I know what! I know what!"

"What?"

"Let's have some hot ear stew!"

Her eyes were wide and famished.

I looked at her. She was my cause, my position. More than any other reason, I needed to break into Uncle Butter's office for my mother's sake.

Diedre Plant, who was prone to her own assortment of delusions, believed that her house was my house. She had granted me provisional residence upon her living room sofa. In return, I had promised that on the day I chose to kick her out I would have the common courtesy to honour her with eight hours notice.

"Sounds fair to me," I agreed.

"You are potentially, Sparrow, a gentleman. I have perceived that in you from the start."

Living with me under the same roof gave her cause to revise that standard. Not that I approached being slovenly or inconsiderate. I took pains to be an agreeable ghost. Yet she discovered, in being privy to my life and indiscretions, that close scrutiny found me wanting. Squealing and scratching, I was subject to her influence.

"What are you talking about, you fool? My mother hates doctors. With a passion. Once in a blue moon they drag her to see a doctor at the residence. It becomes necessary to wrestle her through the door."

"Sparrow, you are so naive you're delicious. Why do you insist on thinking the best of people?"

"You think the worst of people in every situation, it's automatic, I've found that out."

"Now we straddle the difference between wisdom and foolishness." The supercilious lift to her head made me furious, undermining my ability to counterattack.

"You're the foolish one. Guaranteed."

"You're willing to wager your mother's life on that?" She'd touch two fingers to her lips whenever she thought she was winning.

My fondness for her never prevented me from becoming royally agitated in these debates. "How exactly am I risking my mother's life?"

"Your mother dwells among destitute people."

"Who happen to be her friends."

"She lives in a run-down neighbourhood."

"I could say the same thing about you. Shall I make a doctor's appointment for you, too? At least my mother has the moxie to step outside."

Earlier in the morning, in fact, my mother had romped in the backyard practising croquet strokes. I had revived the game we had played together in Lougain, and Mom had taken to the sport with savvy fascination. The last time I had checked on her she had departed the yard for the lane, hooking up with a bevy of young teenage girls who had been hanging out.

"Her so-called home is a dilapidated facility," my hostess interjected.

"It's not that bad, Miss Plant. The staff treat her well."

"Then you are convinced beyond the shadow of a doubt that the finest physicians in the city compete with one another, scramble and bicker with one another, to make housecalls to her residence?"

"I said no such thing. If you insist on putting words into my mouth, at least make sense. Of course it's not a competition." Miss Plant could, at times, be ridiculous. In these arguments I tended to be suspicious of her motives, never forgetting that she was the one who had encouraged my continental, maternal search while knowing full well my mother lived downtown.

She hammered away at her idiotic theme. "For whatever misguided premise you wish to hold dear, Sparrow, you believe that your mother is treated by the finest physicians, the most celebrated psychiatrists, in all the land."

"Why do you keep harping on this?" I protested. "When did I say any such thing? Are you going senile on me or what?"

"But Sparrow, why should I concern myself with what you say? I judge you by your actions. You believe that your mother receives the finest care possible. That's obvious." I had not previously noticed the rise of her left eyebrow, a miniature Arc de Triomphe. Under the broad sweep of its vision marched the conquering army of her debate.

"I don't get you."

"What's not to get? Your mother is treated by physicians who handle one of the most odious jobs in the city—visiting lunatics in their wretched hovels. What doctor in great demand does such a thing? How many Albert Schweitzers do we have? Her doctors must be saints. If they're not, then they're students, quacks, or incompetents, and I'm positive that you would not allow one of those near your own mother. So they must be saints. They must be physicians of great renown."

She had a point.

"What should I do, Miss Plant? And please, cut the crap."

"Do this. Find out who are the city's most celebrated doctors in the treatment of schizophrenia. Set up an appointment. Use Barclay Boisvert's connections if you have to. He must be on a hospital board or a fund-raising committee by now, he must know people who can yank the necessary strings. Get off your butt, Sparrow. Do something."

My mother had last been sighted playing hopscotch in the lane with teenagers. I returned to check on her, and learned that the party had moved on. Mom was gone. Once again, as if this was my life's proverbial quest, I set off in search of her. Younger kids gave me directions, and older boys also knew where the girls had gone. I found her running loose on Jarry in the company of her pals. Somewhat retiring in their company, Mom looked bewildered by the girls' commotion and nuttiness. She happily giggled in unison with the others, and covered her mouth to mask frequent embarrassment. Learning things. Each of the girls, thirteen- and fourteen-year-olds, smoked a cigarette, and a few lugged cases of beer, which explained why my crazy old hag of a mother had been admitted into their exclusive circle.

"Mom, you can't go around buying beer for young girls. It's against the law."

"It's okay, Sparrow. They give me money for it."

"That's not the point. Young girls are not allowed to drink beer. They're underage. They can't buy it themselves. They're using you to buy it for them. It's wrong and they know it."

"Those girls my friends, Sparrow." We were walking arm in arm, and it was apparent that my mother was suffering from her son's rebuke.

"Fine. Just don't buy them beer or cigarettes."

"What's wrong cigarettes? Thou is mean, Sparrow. Thou won't let me on the street. Thou won't let me play with my friends. Why art thou so mean to me? Mean mean mean. Thou don't like my friends, thou can go fish!"

"Mom—" Arrggghhh! I never knew what to say.

The easiest part in following Miss Plant's advice was to find a pre-eminent psychiatrist who would agree to see us. Barclay helped, and did so with elan, delighted to demonstrate the magical powers of his position. A far more difficult hurdle was convincing Mom to submit to yet another demeaning, insensitive probe by medical staff. Doctors were the enemy. Hospitals were medieval dungeons where hideous rituals were concocted and performed. Mom believed that I had betrayed her.

"Why art thou being mean to me? Thou's a bad boy, Sparrow. Bad boy."

"I wouldn't do anything to hurt you, you must know that. I won't let anybody else hurt you either. This is for your own good."

"They hurt me, doctors. That's all they do. They have fun hurting me. They get their kicks."

"Mom, we have to find out what's wrong. Maybe they can help. Every day doctors make new discoveries, they have new methods and drugs—"

"I take my meds! I'm honest. Thou is bad, Sparrow! Bad. Mean and bad and not nice!"

Although I had encountered her obstinacy before, and considered her stubbornness to be necessary for her day-to-day survival, she could get under my skin. "The examination is for your own good. This doctor, he's one of the best."

"Give me a cigarette."

"I bought you a pack an hour ago. What did you do with it?"

"Don't want those!" Usually when we fought, her logic would dissipate into nonsense.

"What's wrong with them?"

"They're my cigarettes. Thou canst have them."

"I don't want them. I don't smoke. Much."

"Give me a cigarette!"

Her little tests were deployed to determine the limits of my allegiance. I said nothing until we reached the corner, then went into a
deli and purchased another pack. Outside, I lit one for her.

She inhaled as though it was her last breath, and we continued our
walk up Bloomfield.

"I promise. You'll like this hospital, Mom. It's nicer than your usual
one. We'll get you a room with a view, and of course a television set."

What the heck happened? She was right beside me a second ago. I
spun around, looked back, and discovered that she was staring at me,
paralysed on the sidewalk, the smoke between her lips.

"Mom? What's wrong?"

She was incredulous. "Thou art putting me in a hospital?"

She had been through so much over the years. Mom had learned
to expect little from people and rarely did she receive more than
that. Yet she had harboured one ideal, one persistent and desperate
longing—that she would find her son. She had assumed that my
arrival heralded a new cosmic order, a revised planetary alignment.
She placed upon our reunion expectations that others may hold for
the Second Coming. Mom expected her miseries to end, not to be
regenerated all over again. As an absolute minimum, my appearance
was supposed to signal the banishment of doctors to ice-floes and the
dynamiting of hospitals. Clinics were marked for the wrecker's ball.
Her disillusionment at that moment, with me, with her prospects for
the future, with life, was colossal. Here was an adult felled by the
kind of apocalyptic pain that only children know. To mollify her I
did what I usually tried to avoid, I escorted her into a coffee shop,
one of her favourite treats.

In the old days, before my return, she'd be kicked out of coffee
shops before she had a chance to sit down or warm up. She loved her
current status as a legitimate patron.

Once again I coughed up the reasons why entering the hospital was
important and beneficial and why I wasn't a bad son for saying so but
really I was a good son, the best that I could be. She had the knack to get
me talking in that vein, arguing my worth, I suppose because the issue
counted with her. Mom fought back. She regurgitated everything that
she hated about the idea, a considerable effluence. Many of her objections were common to everyone, and most of these could be softened. "I

promise. I swear. You won't have to wear those silly nightgowns that tie in the back. I'll buy you a nightgown of your own." (Where was I going to find the money for that? Hmm, Hannah was about her size. I had returned her forty dollars, crisply ironed and shrink-wrapped. We were getting along again, although she was insisting that we go slow. Now, if I could figure out a way to broach the subject of a nightgown with Han without convincing her that I was thoroughly off my rocker myself ...) "I'll bring you candy and fruit, your favourites—and cigarettes, of course—to go along with the food. But you'll have to eat what's on your plate first."

Her two major objections were crushers, and I was dutiful in my vows to eradicate them. No matter what, I swore left, right and sideways, I would visit her.

"And bring me some flowers one time?"

"Your room will look like a garden."

Later she decried the cruelty of doctors, "They don't never tell me nothing."

Solemnly, before a cloud of angels, I vowed that everything they revealed to me would be passed on to her. If possible, I'd make them tell her directly. "Can we shake on this, Mom?"

My childhood disputes with Barclay had had to be settled with a handshake, and my mother also hated being obliged to make up her battles at the halfway house with an enforced joining of the palms. Yet we both respected the tradition, and she was willing to honour our pacts with her conduct. Getting her to shake hands was obligatory.

First, Mom considered the matter from all sides by picking up the salt shaker and sprinkling a mound onto the tabletop. (I looked away for this ritual, pretending I was not a witness, certainly not one who was related.) Wetting her forefinger, she used it to scoop salt onto the tip of her tongue. Tasty. At the conclusion of this process, she dusted the residue onto the floor, wiped her hand on her pants, and held it out for a shake. I counted myself lucky that she didn't spit. Mom was willing to be admitted, so long as I supported my end of the bargain.

And yet, it was obvious that she was sad. Doubts troubled her. Only her trust in me allowed her to take this step, and the burden of that trust cost me sleep. I'd wake up in the mornings edgy and grim. I had undertaken to submit my mother to her worst ordeal, with neither guarantee nor much hope that the trouble could be explained to her, let alone that treatment might be improved.

Resolutely faithful to my promises, I stuffed my mother with candy long after the nurses said stop, and never missed a visit. Let the truth come out—due to my attentions, she actually, profoundly, enjoyed her stay in hospital. To be visited during the prescribed hours was a phenomenal luxury for Sheilagh, she was accustomed to being alone while everyone around her received guests. When I arrived, she'd beam, as if showing me off to the other patients. She'd make me wheel her up and down the corridors so that staff, patients, and visitors could see that she, too, had a guest. An actual son. I brought flowers. And made sure that Barclay, Miss Plant, Hannah, and friends from the halfway house sent contributions as well. Her room became a hothouse and her delight was epic. I do believe that my daily appearances helped to rub out the memory of lonely trials in the past.

The day the doctor summoned me, I arranged for Mom to join us.

We both liked him very much. I believe his name was Larkin, or Lankin, or Laskin. He subsequently left the city, part of the exodus of the English with the rise of Québécois nationalism. A man in his mid-fifties, he divided his practice between hospital care and university research into schizophrenia. Not everybody would want such a man as their physician, but I appreciated the fact that he looked upon his patients as case-studies, that he was battling the disease with his mind, searching for fresh answers and new solutions, free from the determinations of the past.

"Unlike diseases that affect the organs or the nervous system, schizophrenia's course is effectively unique for each patient. This entails a certain amount of guesswork, I'm sorry to say, and a certain amount of experimentation."

"My mother's been used as a guinea pig before," I objected. "I've made a promise to her—no more messing around." A rainy day. Out the window behind the doctor's head dark clouds were gathering atop Mount Royal. I attached no significance to the weather, and would have been gloomy in any climate, but the clouds did reflect my mood.

Nodding, Dr. La-kin shuffled papers on his desk. I detected in his facial expression a measure of distaste, even disgust, for the actions of his predecessors. "I've examined her file. It would seem to be thorough." He looked directly at me. I admit to drawing confidence from his beard. His skin was tanned from a recent southern holiday, and that image of health and the intellectual countenance of this man provided a sense of assurance. "There is a significant difference in experiments done for the benefit of testing an anti-psychotic drug, let's say, and experiments performed to determine the tolerance of the individual patient."

"That sounds like an understatement to me."

"Noted." He leaned back in his chair and gave his beard a thoughtful scratch. "Always the problem with schizophrenia is the variables, the term, the form, the intensity. For someone in your mother's circumstances, there has been, up until now, a medical consensus to apply drugs and apply them heavily, and solve the problem by numbing her. It's an across-the-board solution to an illness that won't cooperate with standardized treatments."

"Too strong a dose!" my mother shouted out. Her common complaint, one voiced to every physician she had ever encountered, repeated in this room from force of habit.

"Yes, Miss Drinkwater, for you, it is too strong a dose. That is my conviction."

Mom's head snapped up. Her neck appeared to elongate. Patting her hand, I gave her a supportive smile. She had finally had her opinion validated!

"In about forty per cent of cases, patients are manic-depressives. They can be a threat to themselves and to others. For these, the argument can be made, in particular instances, for a mega-dose of tranquillizer and anti-psychotic drug. Your mother has been treated as though she is one of these when clearly she is not. She is subject to a distortion of perception, not seeing things for what they are, not understanding the meaning of particular concepts. She is subject to auditory and visual hallucinations, although we suspect her form to be mild."

"What's that mean?" The stay in hospital and diet of chocolate had improved my mother's appearance. A nurse's aid had given her a permanent, and Hannah's housecoat continued a matronly motif.

"You see things, Mom, that aren't really there." She was interested in the proceedings, watching Dr. La-kin's lips move, and checking my reactions to what had been said. Mom felt privileged to be in the room while she was being discussed.

"Figments of my imagination," she stated.

"That's right." Patting encouragement into her hand again.

"That's right," she agreed.

"In recent years, your mother has been taking Thioridazine."

"Mellaril!" my mom shouted out. She was on a first name basis with her pharmaceutical companions. "Mellaril! Too strong a dose!"

The doctor laughed, really quite merrily, rocking in his chair. He seemed to have developed a genuine affection for her. "Yes, Mellaril, and too much of it." To me he explained, "Mellaril is a brand name for Thioridazine."

"I see."

"It can have side-effects."

"Like what?"

"If taken in overdose, which, you understand, is always a possible accident, there can be severe cardiac effects."

"What's he saying?" Mom interjected again. I was not anxious to interpret the phrase—heart-attack. Instead I paraphrased Dr. La-kin by telling her, "It can make you sick."

"I know that. I told everybody that. Nobody ever believes me."

"Any other effects, Doctor?" I realized something, seeing his eyes flick from my mother to me, and back to her. He had called me here, and allowed my mother to be present, because he was sizing me up. Dr. La-kin was making an evaluation about my mom, me, and our relationship.

"In high dosages of Thioridazine, damage to the lens and retina may occur. I've had your mother examined by a specialist. Some deterioration has begun."

"What's that mean?" Mom was paying attention.

This time I addressed the doctor first. "I might as well tell her. I've noticed that my mother takes bad news rather well, it's one of her things."

"What bad news?" Mom nagged.

"Go ahead," the doctor concurred. "Try it."

"Your eyes are getting worse, Mom."

"That's okay." Mom composed an elaborate shrug, lifting her palms to heaven. "What can I look at anyhow? If I go blind maybe I won't see things, figments of my imagination, maybe I won't need no more Mellaril."

This time when he laughed, Dr. La-kin slapped his crossed leg, then adjusted his tie. "She's priceless."

"So what's the next step," I asked him, deliberately posing the question while I had him in a good mood.

"I think Trilafon, we'll try that first."

"Trilafon!" Mom ignited. "Too strong a dose! Make me shaky, shaky."

· "Have you had Trilafon before, Miss Drinkwater? That wasn't mentioned in your chart."

"Makes me shaky. Too strong a dose! My tits go leaky."

She seemed to be panicking.

"Mom, what is it? What are you saying?"

Dr. La-kin interpreted for me. "She's had discharge from her breasts, a side-effect for some women. Okay. I'm sorry, Miss Drinkwater, I didn't know that you had tried Trilafon. Have you tried Haldol?"

"Too strong a dose!"

"No doubt. What we'll do, we'll start you out with a weaker dose of Haldol than you've been getting of Mellaril, and then, this is the good part, we'll keep making it weaker until we find the level that suits you. How does that sound?"

"Thou wilt make my medication weaker?" Suddenly she was apprehensive.

"We'll try it," was the doctor's good news.

Mom was alarmed. "Maybe I go crazy."

Which led me to my most crucial question. "Doctor, as near as you can figure, I mean, bearing in mind that there's a lot of guesswork involved, what's her prognosis?"

Before answering, he again proceeded to give himself an elaborate scratch under his chin. "On average, schizophrenia runs a five-year course in women, where the patient's symptoms worsen. Your mother would have had her five years of deterioration during adolescence. About a quarter of patients will recover completely, and live normal lives. Obviously, your mother was not one of these. One in ten remain psychotic, severely so, and their lives are totally incapacitated. Most of these are better off institutionalized. Your mother doesn't fall into this group either. Given her circumstances, she has fared remarkably well. She falls into a broader category. I anticipate periods of recovery, Mr. Drinkwater, with intermittent lapses. With any luck we can handle the bad times with appropriate medication. The good news is, and this is something that we're only just now discovering, or admitting to, is that after the initial onslaught of the disease, after the five years I mentioned, schizophrenics tend to improve with time. They don't get worse. We don't know why this is so yet, but as the patient matures, it appears that the disease yields its influence. This happens even in the chronic patients, which, at least for now, is what we'll have to call your mother."

This was good news! Improved treatment, a weakening of the illness, a doctor who was both caring and savvy. Unknowingly, I had prepared myself for the worst, all this good stuff was making me crazy!

"I've spoken generally, of course. Specifically, there are good and bad clues to your mother's recovery. We have little early history. What we have pieced together suggests that the illness hit her quickly when she was young. A sudden entry into the disease means we can be optimistic about her recovery. Gradual entries point to slow recoveries. Also, when she has psychotic episodes, they seem to be brief. She's in them, she emerges from them very confused and disoriented, but the episode itself was brief, which also indicates a good chance of recovery."

This was wonderful! I was no longer confident that I could make it out of the office without weeping.

"You have already told me, Mr. Drinkwater, that you know little of her life circumstances in her formative years. What we do know indicates that those circumstances may have precipitated the disease. If that is the case, it's one more indicator that she can recover well."

Now I was the one delirious. I fully expected to hallucinate. Staggering good news!

"Also, her episodes can be intensely emotional. For example, her biggest social problem at the halfway house has been her excitable nature and—I trust I can say this to you—her rather high level of sexual interest. Once again, if she were demonstrating an emotionally flat plane, there would be cause for pessimism. Many schizophrenics suffer from what we call anhedonia, which refers to the loss of pleasure. Your mother has fun, she laughs, she makes strong bonds of affection with others, she feels desire. She gets into fist-fights. I can't emphasize how important that is. Her emotional level, particularly during her episodes, is the most positive sign we have that she can travel a long, long way toward recovery."

Glorious news! It kept getting better. "I'm, I'm just stunned. This is fantastic!" Tears came. Through my blurry vision, I noticed Dr. La-kin raise a hand to temper my euphoria.

"There are problems with her profile. Problems that are very real and serious."

Wiping my eyes, I smiled at my mother who seemed riveted on my excitement, especially my tears. "What are they?"

"She has friends, and enemies, at her home, and that's good. Yet, for the most part, she's been socially isolated. She's accustomed to spending her days walking the streets alone, and that's not a pattern conducive to mental health. You and I might benefit from a long walk, but your mother uses the time to regress. She needs to feel good about herself and not believe that she is a pariah. Being married would be better than being alone. Living in a family situation, as long as she also has plenty of friends, would be better than living in an institution. Her past history is not great. What we call the psycho-sexual adjustment factor has been poor, her past environments have been a disgrace, her history of behavioural disorders, especially her night traumas and her propensity for tantrums—these are links to the past which give us clues to the future.

"Now, just as you were sky-high a minute ago, Mr. Drinkwater, I don't want you to start getting depressed. The prognosis is promising. I'm almost at the point of saying it's excellent. But she does have some things to overcome which, the record shows, have been difficult for schizophrenics to handle. I just want you to be both optimistic and realistic. Things may work out well, it just won't be easy."

"I understand." I think.

"The key here, in my opinion, is that you have arrived in your mother's life. If you are willing to be a force in her life, provide her with the emotional stability and the support she requires—"

"Of course!"

"Then we've got a shot, Mr. Drinkwater. We might win this one."

"What's he saying?" Mom wanted me to translate.

Just as she could be light and flippant with bad news, Mom tended to receive good news with concern. It was one of the reasons people diagnosed her as crazy. Triggers misfired. It was frustrating. On to her, I had once considered telling her something dreadful as a means of cheering her up. I hadn't brought myself to do that, although I had frequently experienced the agony of listening to her turn good cheer into the blues.

One day, I had tried explaining the phenomena of shadows to her. Which meant tackling her perceptual screwiness in an attempt to switch her onto a logical track. A Sunday afternoon stroll was devoted to a lecture on the relationship between shadows and light. She caught on, although when I tried to argue that her own shadow had not flown away, that it had been an airplane's shadow that had skimmed across the schoolyard, she seriously questioned my sanity. In the end I did win, however, I did drive home a concept of shadows as non-beings that she was able to adopt.

I just wasn't prepared for her solemnity in the face of good news.

"So you understand? You did not lose your shadow. It did not fly away to Florida."

"I did not lose my shadow?" she wanted verified one more time.

"That's right."

"Then it must've been my soul."

And I was back to square one.

How could I interpret for her the doctor's words? How could I make her feel happy and hopeful about the possibility of improved health? Aware of my predicament, Dr. La-kin watched to see how I'd do. I suspected that his personal prognosis for my mother's recovery hinged on my performance.

Had I said, "The doctor tells us you're going to die," she might have jumped for joy, yet we'd be no further ahead. I had to take my chances with the truth.

"We're going to try some things to make you better, Mom. We're going to change your medication, you'll like that, and we'll watch you carefully so you don't have to worry about going crazy or anything. I'm also going to see to it that your life gets better, because that will make you feel good. I'll be around a lot. All the time. The doctor says there's a good chance that you might become well. If you don't become completely well, at least you have a good chance to feel much better."

Her head bowed forward. Her chin tucked itself down. In a moment the telltale signs of a crying jag were noted. Her hunched body shook, and she had the sniffles. Both the doctor and myself waited to see what misery she had concocted out of this good news—*this superb, wonderful news*—and I was determined about one thing. No matter what her perspective proved to be, I wouldn't let it get me down. She was ill, and whatever she had to say would be an effect of the illness, nothing to get mad about, merely the guise of an enemy we had yet to defeat.

"Mom? Do you understand? The doctor can make you much better."

And she managed to look up at me, vigorously staring through her tears. Yes, she understood exactly the message that the doctor had hoped to convey. She was not weeping with joy or with expectation. She understood more than we knew. Her tears expressed a profound distress.

My mother whispered her despair to us, and my heart palpitated with the calm lonely sadness of that lament.

The physician lowered his head.

Her illness might be subverting the moment, changing great news into sorrow, yet my mother had spoken from her heart and what she had said was true. Despite my promise to myself, I was moved, dejected, and demoralized by her remark.

What my mother said in the quiet enclosure of the doctor's office, in a trembling voice with a heart full of sorrows, was, simply, "One time—. Sparrow, one time—. One time I could been young. Me. Just me. Now I won't never be young no more."

You know. She broke my heart.

What further motivation would I need to put together my team of desperados and exact revenge? My reprisal was aimed at both Uncle Butter and at his secret alliance with a person or persons unknown—the villains who had wrecked my mother's life with their savage neglect.

*

Four desperados huddled in a Chevy. The Good, the Bad, the Ugly, and me. A sickle-shaped moon hung suspended above our necks.

I enjoyed our alley, its gamy smells, the grimy canvas of refuse, dirt, and oil stains. Hard edges of brick and concrete glowed in the dark, reflecting upon softer surfaces of scar tissue. Breathe deeply, catch a good whiff. The stink of plunder and dog piss. A faint hint of hasty, adolescent sex. Me and my gang, we kept the peace. Held our noses and kept our mouths shut too. We listened real hard.

Sssshhhh. A distant percussion.

The battered echoes of fist-fights and gang-bangs.

Home turf. You know, I loved it.

Drawn into the shadows, I found myself sequestered by the murk and intrigue. Mangled ghosts brayed at the moon. Us desperados, we reviewed the plan and, what the hell, synchronized watches. In time with the seconds, my heart beat more quickly, yet more steadily, alive. Somehow alive. What did this portend? What was to be learned here? In pursuit of knowledge, I was discovering things beyond the specifics of my quest, amazed by the rush brought on by fiendish, nocturnal deeds.

Who would have guessed it? Sparrow Drinkwater, a natural-born felon. Like red petals of floating heart, swamp-heritage rose to the surface. How astute of Hannah to have called me "Stinkwater."

With our action imminent, my anticipation of the crime was being eclipsed by the satisfaction of a job well done. The most difficult task in that operation had been to put together a crack team of desperados. In that regard, I had done well. Had I not tricked the "Good" into joining my gang? Had I not kept close rein on the "Bad"? Rode herd over the "Ugly"?

"A bank?" Derek Mahoney protested. "Youse never said nothin' about no bank. Fuckin' geez! I'm on parole. I can't knock over a bank wid no bunch a ama-toors!"

Sitting beside him in the front seat, Barclay explained in his best pompous-ass impersonation, a tone he was close to perfecting, "Mr. Mahoney, sir, we do the bank—or, 'knock it over', as you so aptly suggest—if we have both the time and the inclination. It is not our primary objective."

"Fuck that shit!"

I broke in before he had a fit and scotched the mission. "Wise up, Derek. Uncle's office is above the bank, okay? Barclay's pulling your leg."

"Fuckin' geez." At least he could laugh about it. Supposedly the experienced crook among us, no one was more nervous than him. Either Derek was agitated because he knew how easily things could go wrong, or his excitability explained why he got caught so often. I wasn't worried. I could not forget that Derek had stayed behind to dig a friend from a collapsed tunnel. That innate loyalty and instinct was worth having on our side.

Derek was motivated. When I had first broached the subject of becoming our getaway driver, he saw no reason to participate. "No money in it for me, fuck, no glory, just wha' cha call a high degree of risk. You demented or just nuts?" I persuaded him to join our team by tipping him off on the identity of one of his partners-in-crime, which perked a certain interest, and finally by revealing the name of the victim. "Why the fuck didn' you say so?" Oh yes, Derek, the Ugly among us, was more than willing to be my getaway driver for a chance to get back at Gerald Boisvert, my infamous Uncle Butter, the "creep with the hubcaps, fuck."

"Yeah, Derek," Mo told him, our fourth desperado, "wise up."

Three-thirty a.m. The street was deserted.

According to plan, Barclay unlocked the outside door to Uncle's office-building and stepped inside. He carried his leather satchel. I kept watch from the familiar comfort of the shadows, adoring the tentative, squawky silence and the gloom cast by street lamps. Derek's Chevy waited further down the block. A few remaining patches of winter's worn, compacted ice melted in the lane behind me as I listened to the sounds of drip and trickle, and felt the cool spring air touch the moisture on my brow.

Sweating.

In a minute a match flared—Barclay's signal. He had checked out the premises and everything was secure. I responded in kind. Lit a cigarette and made it look convincing, like one of Bogey's characters, then snuffed the weed under my sneaker. On cue, Derek started the car. He proceeded slowly, sticking close to the curb and stopping outside the door. The motor muttered quiet. Mo climbed out. She unlocked the trunk, then came back to the driver's side to return Derek's keys. I'm in motion by this time, crossing the street to meet Mo at the yawning trunk. Clockwork. We were moving with alacrity, precision, and a ghostly, eerie grace, in step with the rhythms of our master plan. Tick, tock. Tick. As practised, Mo lifted the upper end of the oxyacetylene tank, being careful with the valves, and I hoisted the base. As we traversed the sidewalk, we

passed Barclay returning to the trunk for Mo's torch and assorted paraphernalia. A diligent welder, Mo adored her tools the way a soldier wor-
ships weaponry.

Inside, she and I ascended the stairs. At the top we shuffled down
the corridor, burdened by our load now, and stopped at Uncle's office.
Barclay caught up. Used his keys to open the door.

"You locked the door downstairs?" My own voice sounded hushed
and urgent to me.

"Nah. Sorry. I chose to leave it flapping in the breeze."

Mo uttered a sound, a kind of cackle.

"Just checking, for chrissakes." I struggled to lug the tank around
the corner of a desk. Then Mo and I set it on the floor by the safe and
heaved it upright. A gung-ho recruit, the tank snapped to attention,
our fifth conspirator.

My first job was to investigate the street. All was quiet out front.
Derek drove off as planned. We didn't want the car attracting attention
in a No Overnight Parking zone, nor did we see virtue in having an ex-
con loitering outside a bank with his motor running in the deadfall of
night. Derek would be back.

"You really know how to use this thing?" Barclay asked Mo. He was
flirting with her! "That's remarkable."

"Let her work in peace, Barc."

"By all means." To defend against my censure, my former house-
brother raised his hands, palms out, in a motion of surrender. He took a
seat—his father's reclining swivel chair—arrogantly propping his feet
up on the desk. The most reluctant of our desperados, he was proving
to be cooler than any of us, outwardly the most calm. Given that he
had much to lose, I was impressed by that aloof indifference.

More thrills per minute than an audit, I guess.

Recruiting Barclay-the-Good had not been a matter of subterfuge.
No tricks. I simply appealed to his more excellent virtues, in particular
his appetite for knowledge.

"Barc, I need your help to crack open Uncle's safe."

"Get serious."

"You have the keys to his office. I'll take care of the rest."

"Visit me some day. You may find the keys lying around. You're the
thief. Snitch them with my blessing."

"Uncle has a white knight. You told me so. He keeps a safe exclu-
sively for the papers of one client."

"Do I detect an inference here, lurking in the shadows?"

"I'm asking. Did Uncle's knight come through for you? Did he give you the bulk of his business like you expected?"

Barclay had been silent awhile, mulling things over. I suppose he confided in me because I was his closest facsimile to a brother. "A white knight has not revealed himself, no. People are amazed, though, by the clients sliding my way. American branch plants call up. Or Canadian firms ring out of the blue. One common denominator. The firms do considerable business south of the border."

"There could be another explanation. You have a reputation for brilliance, there's your academic laurels—"

"Business is a boys' club. That's no secret. Someone, somewhere, in New York is my best guess, keeps sending me a stream of clients."

"I want him identified."

"Pop the safe, Sparrow, let me know what you find."

As I leaned forward, I was careful to weigh my tone with conspiracy. "To crack Uncle's safe, I'll need a little help from my friends."

"File that memo in the trash, kiddo. I'm an accountant, not a thief. Gracious, man, I'm a junior partner."

"Barc, if you want one shred of information out of that safe, one morsel, one crumb, you will have to participate. You can't use me, bro'. Are you in or are you out?"

A prolonged, profound silence wavered from his end of the sofa. Barclay Boisvert wanted something out of that safe, and he wanted it badly. Was he willing to place his reputation at risk? Would he lay his glorious career and bountiful future on the line? Identifying forces that manipulated our lives was important to me, was it equally imperative to him?

"Certainly," he conceded at last. "I will escort you through the door and deliver you safely back to the street. Nothing more. Cracking the safe, as you so quaintly put it in your racketeer's jargon, is strictly your responsibility."

"A friend of mine's cousin's friend is an expert with a blowtorch."

"Keep the details to yourself, Sparrow. Tell me no one's name. I'm sorry I know yours. Categorically, tell nobody mine."

Fair enough.

Uncle's office had a different feel to it at three-thirty a.m. Peaceful, almost rapt. The glow of the streetlamps and the bank's blue neon cast the desks as pewter rockface, the cabinets and machines as bronze. The floor had a metallic burnish, while the steel of the safe mimicked the character of stone, as though it was an enormous boulder rolled here to block the entrance to a crypt.

In the dark of the room, Mo adjusted her goggles over her eyes. Flicking a sparking device, her torch ignited.

It burned. A sound like the voice of wind.

As with the sun, or with the face of God, the mercurial white light of a blowtorch must not be observed by the naked eye. I turned away, yet continued to view after-images of that light searing the metal, melting locks and bolts, unhinging the steel door to my past.

"How's Mo doing?" From his privileged position behind Uncle's desk, Barclay adopted the pose of an upper-management luminary, his nose in everyone's business, his ambition in everyone's craw.

"She's coming along fine. Mo's an expert."

"Mo's amazing," Barc concurred. "Her diligence is wonderful, her excellent work habits are truly inspiring. In whatever endeavour she chooses Mo will find success. More than I can say for you, Bird."

Get a load of this guy.

"Mo's an artist," I revealed. "A sculptor."

"Why does that not surprise me? I'd love to see her work. I'm not so busy that I couldn't use a dose of culture in my life. Art soothes the soul, Sparrow. Art reminds us of our higher ideals. I could line up a commission for her. A couple of my clients are big-league collectors."

Poor Barclay, this was his way of indicating that he'd like to take her to bed. I had never known him to be in love before. Past dates suggested that his taste in women leaned toward neuters. Mo's extreme bearing had shaken him up.

Her goggled eyes remain fixed on the industry of her blowtorch. She gave no indication that she had overheard Barc's remarks, or placed either value or interpretation on them.

From the outset I had assumed that Mo the Torch would be the most difficult gang member to conscript, and also the most necessary. Not on a first-name basis with many welders, I knew none fitting my description of a desperado. Her expertise was crucial.

"Let me get this crystal-clear," Hannah had demanded. "You're asking me to give you Maureen's telephone number?"

"If you wouldn't mind."

"Tall. Leggy. An artist, so-called. Chains, black leather, boobs. The nice girl's nightmare."

"That's the one."

"Silly me. I've been living under a misconception. I thought I was the one who was being courted here. I never clued in that it was my job to set you up with other women."

"You don't understand."

"Funny how often you say that around me, Sparrow."

"It's not what you think. I need her for a job. A commission."

"Sparrow Drinkwater has money to spend on art? What am I, the Public Works Commission? I have paintings for sale."

"What I need is someone who can handle a blowtorch. Mo and me, we grew up on the same streets. I got a job in the old neighbourhood she might do for me free."

"You're a weird duck, Bird."

"What is it about you and me, Hannah? We slip into these oddball conversations."

"We're not making progress."

Meaning, in our relationship. I was still knocking on the door, and Hannah continued to answer. She had come into my life during a time of upheaval—in short order I had met my mother, left home, quit school, and embarked upon criminal activity. In those circumstances, I could not prosper as the level-headed, even-keeled, down-to-earth love of her life. My behaviour ripened her suspicions. The apple of my affections seemed green to her, perhaps lacking in ardour. Her expectations for me, for us, lay upon the ground like bruised fruit.

"I've been kind of distracted. Hannah, do you think you could do me this favour and I could explain later?"

She consented to talk to Nina for me. Her young cousin would know how to get in touch with Mo.

"He's got a thing for that bitch," Hannah prefaced for the younger girl. "I'm not allowed to ask questions."

"Could be worse, cuz," Nina pointed out. "He could have a thing for someone who's human."

To my amazement, once I called her, Mo would require little coaxing. What I had to offer no man had conferred upon her before—respect for her skills, and an unequivocal admission that she alone could do the job. Mo responded to appreciation, she had a hankering for nefarious adventure, and quickly she was aboard the team.

She fitted in well. Barclay's express wish, oft repeated, was that no conspirator should know his name, nor did he seek to be introduced to any of his fellow thieves. Setting his eyes upon Mo, spotting her in a black leather jacket and tight jeans and wielding a blowtorch, he promptly forgot himself and extended his hand. "How do you do?" he said. "I'm Barclay."

Beside her, Derek grunted, and our team was complete, our gang of desperados born.

"Derek back?" Barc wondered aloud.

"Nowhere in sight. He's got plenty of time."

"I grant you, the man has muscles. Is he trustworthy?"

"Time will tell." Electing to rattle Barclay's complacency, I struck fear into his conceited chest. "I hired Derek for his car. He's never had a reputation for reliability. Maybe that's why he gets caught so often."

"Caught? Caught? Derek's a real criminal?"

"Let's put it this way. Don't solicit him for your client base."

In a moment, I had no need to string Barc along. With the fury of a thunderclap the fear of God—and of the police—bound us all.

Kkkkkaaa-rrrunk!—the safe door crashed to the floor. Releasing a yelp, Mo jumped clear, and knocked over the oxyacetylene tank. As if in slow motion, I watched that Douglas fir topple. *Timmmmbbbberrrrr!* Shaking the floor. A mighty alarm—a sharp ringing bell—resounded in our ears like an air raid siren. Passers-by might have assumed that the arsenals of the world were in flight, every missile aimed at this target. The safe door and the tank battering the ceiling of the Laurentian Bank had annoyed a vibration alarm, and while in those early seconds a jeremiad of police sirens could not be heard, it was not difficult to imagine an imminent response.

"Scram!" I hollered above our terror and the alarm's choler.

"My stuff!" Mo shouted before her two brave confederates hightailed it out the door. She was calm, this artist, collected and professional. Switching off the valves on the tank, Mo was in control of her emotions, if not her destiny.

"Leave it!" Barclay ordered.

She got mad, flaring like the flame of her blowtorch. "Hey! This is my stuff!"

"I'll replace it for you free." In the blaze of the moment, Barclay was feeling unusually philanthropic.

"My name's on my equipment."

Fitting, I suppose, that Mo was as meticulous in her habits as was Uncle in his. My house-brother and I shared a quick glance, concluding that we would not trust our cohort to a phalanx of horny police inquisitors.

"Grab an end!" was my command.

"Hold it!" Mo wasn't ready yet. Now she had to unfasten the hoses. She insisted on pampering her equipment in the proper fashion. Everything had to be done religiously and by the book. I, for one, was prepared to slit the throat of whoever had written her maintenance bible.

The bells of the bank instigated Park Extension mutts to commence a nocturnal chorus.

Since we were obliged to wait anyway, Barclay, shocked into sum-
moning his wits by Mo's cool demeanour, grabbed his satchel and
stuffed it with the contents of the safe.

"Barc! Move it!"

"We didn't come here for nothing."

We were ready. Quick now, did anyone need to use the washroom,
make a phone call, file a grievance? Speak now or run. Barc thrust the
briefcase into my chest, spun, and hauled the tank onto his back. He used
his size and innate strength to advantage, something he never got to do
as an accountant. Mo collected the rest of her gear and together we beat
it. I was just about out the door, thinking safety was at hand, when Barclay, who thought fast and always thought ahead, called my name.

"*What? What?* Can I shine your shoes? Get you a cup of coffee?
What?"

"Smash the window. Don't close the door."

"Smash the window?" A tactic that confounded me. I assumed he
meant the window on the office door, but what good would that do?

"Use a chair. Do it!" And he lumbered awkwardly down the stairs
beneath the stress of his burden.

This was my operation, and I was not pleased to be taking orders as
I picked up a chair and nearly smashed the glass with the force of my
anger. My swing was in motion as if I was a batter jumping on a hanging curve when abruptly, and deliberately, I fouled off the pitch, redi-
recting my attack against the doorframe. Ah. I got it. Smashing the
window obfuscated the robbers' means of entry. Who would suspect
that we had had a key after taking the trouble to muscle our way in?
Which put Barclay, the guy with the keys, in the clear. Perhaps, who
knows, quietly shifting suspicion onto someone like the prodigal who
was no longer his adopted father's son.

I closed the door quietly, making sure that it was locked. I had my
reasons. Police first on the scene would not suspect a burglary if we left
no obvious signs, giving my gang extra time to escape. But I also knew
that closing the door implicated Barclay, and I was not entirely certain
why I was doing that.

One thing I did know—I was not being a good sport here.

I did it, then walked away.

Then ran, like an antelope, down the stairs, clutching the briefcase with its wealth of indiscriminate secrets. Below, Barclay had used

Mo's tank to smash exterior glass, vaporizing my wish to avoid early signs of a heist.

On the sidewalk, the noise was unbelievable. Fifty times louder to thieves than to anyone else. Lights down the block were being flicked on by men and women disturbed from their sleep. Hunters were reaching into their closets for deer rifles and shotguns, stretching high for ammunition on the top shelves. Like prey, hunters sleep wide awake.

At least eight dogs reviled the alarm.

"Where's Derek?" I canvassed above the racket.

"*You* hired him," Barclay attacked.

Failure was the heaviest of my burdens. Fingers pointing blame at me were cocked and aimed.

Mo believed. "He'll be here."

Tentative about contradicting her at the same time that he was trying to make a move on her, Barclay muttered, "I'm not so sure."

"I'm here," she pointed out. Meaning that she was a worthy prize. Was this the time to remind her that she had once ripped Derek off, stealing collections from his paper route while he was relaxing in reform school? Did Derek bear that grudge? Were the present circumstances opportune to address the suspicion that Derek might be gay, a jailhouse convert? Should I mention that detail? Oh God, had Derek signed on specifically to betray us all? Both Barc and I studied Mo's form once again, hoping that it was enough to attract our driver back.

Tick tock. Tick tock. Tick.

The three of us, under the tyranny of that scurrilous bell, hung on as the seconds mounted, scanning the street for our saviour in his getaway coach.

"If he doesn't show," Mo threatened, her tone finally indicating that she, too, had lost confidence in him, "I'll solder his nuts to his bolt."

Both Barc and me gave her a look.

In that strange light, vexed by the bell's long-suffering, virtuous peal, I noticed the corners of Barclay's lips curl slightly into a grin. Ain't no doubt about it, the man was in love.

Opposites attract. If Barclay was the Good within our crew, Mo was the Bad. The seriousness of her intent was not to be dismissed. For his sake, I did hope Derek showed.

Possessed, the ringing alarm became increasingly impatient and more shrill, somehow less loud yet more frantic, as if the mania of its rage had been depleted by exertion.

A car cut the corner, vaulted forward, then slowed down to inspect our situation. We acted nonchalant. A ringing alarm was a common nuisance, and the inebriated driver bought our act, or pretended to, carrying on home. He would want to park and get indoors before bothering to call the cops, a conviction for drunk-driving being beyond his civic duty.

"I'm counting to twenty," Barclay judicially announced, "at which moment I shall declare these proceedings null and void. I propose that we seek an alternate form of transportation. One, two ..."

"What about my stuff?" Our willingness to abandon her precious tools made Mo livid.

"We'll take it with us," I promised, "or ditch it in an alley for now." I joined Barclay in the countdown. "Seven, eight ..."

"Nine," Mo chipped in, "ten ..."

Derek flashed his headlights as his tires squealed turning the corner off de l'Epée onto Jarry. He picked up speed as if he planned to scoot on by, taunting us, and my right hand came up to give him the finger just as he braked hard against the curb.

God, I loved it. The symphony of squealing tires under the bray of a bank alarm, our lives at risk, could life get any better than this?

What a team. Acrobats ought to be so lithe. I whipped open the back door and Barclay and Mo shoved the oxyacetylene canister across the rear seat as if ramming a torpedo into its firing chamber. "Get in!" Barc shouted, and what happened next was too quick for the eye, almost too quick for memory to decipher. I was prepared to jump into the front seat beside Derek. That's how we had lined up, and Mo was already piling into the back to sit forward of the tank. I assumed my house-brother would wedge in beside her, that that was an opportunity he wouldn't want to miss. But no. He was accustomed to a higher level of comfort. Holding the back door open with one hand and the briefcase with the other, I suddenly lost the attaché to Barclay's nimble fingers. He was behind me, as swift as a cat, pushing me aside and dumping himself into the front.

No time to argue. Wary of the tank which looked and felt like a bomb, I scrunched into the car, thrown back roughly as Derek stepped on the gas and the Chevy peeled away.

"Youse hit the bank, fuck!" Derek screamed, driving off like a madman who had lost his glasses, careening up rue Outremont. "Bastards! Youse lied to me!" Endlessly, he repeated himself, before finally getting around to the crux of his disenchantment, "I want my cut!"

We were laughing our heads off, delirious with relief, fright, and adrenalin.

"Derek, we didn't knock over the bank."

"Don't fuck me around! I heard the alarm. Cheat me, you bastards, you die. I want my cut!"

Beside him in the front seat, Barclay displayed the contents of the briefcase. "Documents, friend. Welcome to the cashless society."

"The safe door crashed on the floor," Mo told him, which really was her way of apologizing to us. "I couldn't believe it. I didn't think I'd cut through already. Bam! Smash! Derek, it set off the alarm. We had to beat it fast. Where the hell have you been?"

"I'm on time," he argued, and I must concede that he was right. "Youse came out early."

"We did feel a certain urgency to be running along," Barclay commented. He was rifling through the loot of papers to evaluate what we'd earned. "Mo suggested staying behind for a nightcap—but Sparrow and me didn't take to the ambience. Slow down, Derek. Don't attract attention."

"I wish," was Mo's regret, "we could've kept that safe door. I could make it work in a sculpture I'm into."

"Just a wee bit incriminating, no?"

"Art at its best," she lectured, she was one of those, "takes risks." In a wink Mo became enormously excited, thrumming the back of Derek's seat with her fists, indulging the rush of an adrenalin rebound. "We did it! What a gas!"

"Take it easy," Derek begged. "Whad're you hittin' me for?"

Leaving her to this whirl of ecstasy, I peered over Barclay's shoulder. "What'd we get, bro'?"

"Too early to tell. This is interesting."

"Show me."

Barclay passed a letter back to me and there it was, a few pages in— instruction for Sally and Sturgess Rawlins in New Orleans. This was my letter! Strangely, I snapped it tight to my chest rather than read another word. Holding it there. This had been my duty as a boy, to protect the documents pinned to the inside of my jacket. The reflex was instinctive, proud, necessary.

We reached the boundary of Park Extension, heading south toward downtown. "Derek," I told him, "pull over. I'm getting out here."

Barclay twisted around in his seat to grill me. "I thought you vacated the family homestead?"

"I did. Moved in with a friend. But I still live in Park Ex."

"What friend?" Curious gus.

"None of your bee's wax."

"Little Sparrow's shacked up?"

"Try it yourself sometime."

"Maybe I will. What do you say, Mo? Do you think I can inveigle you into playing house?"

"In-veigle? Sounds kinky."

Derek staked a claim. "She's my girl."

"Sez who?" Maureen's challenge had an edge that shut Derek up and further piqued Barclay's interest.

Climbing out, I slammed the door shut, and signalled to my house-brother to roll down his window. "What about our bag of goodies?"

"I'll keep the documents safe. Give me some time to sort things out."

"I worked hard for those, Barc."

"Most of the documents are financial. I can get a better handle on what's important."

"Barclay"

"Sparrow, Park Ex is going to be crawling with police officers any minute. You can't walk these streets at this time of night with a bagful of stolen loot under your arm. I'll take care of it. Don't worry."

"Okay," I said, but I didn't like this. "Thanks."

"For what?"

"For getting us in."

"I didn't get you in. What did I get you in? Did I get you in something?" He put the question to our loyal confederates.

Said Mo, "He didn't get me in no place. What was I supposed to be in?"

"Yeah, Sparrow," Derek asked, "in where?"

"I get the message. Thanks anyway. So long."

The last thing I heard Barclay say was, "Driver! Downtown, please."

"Yes,"—and I'm not sure, I'm not convinced, but I believe that Derek said, or was on the verge of saying—"sir."

The car rumbled off to disperse that rough tribe.

*

Entrusted with my own key into Miss Plant's house, I entered quietly in the deadfall of night. Soon it would be dawn. The house, protected by evergreens and heavy curtains, dwelled in a subordinate darkness, one I stumbled through in blind search of the lamp switch next to the sofa where I slept. There I read the notorious letter, its pages brittle and made yellow by age. My childhood map. The hoops my mother and me had been invited to jump through! Amazing convolutions. What idiot had believed that we could succeed?

The experience of reading the letter unnerved me, I was beset by a garden variety of emotions. Shooting off on different tangents, I found it hard to concentrate. I washed up, and returned to the living room where my bed on the sofa had already been made. Naked, I crawled under the covers to read the document again.

I thought back to my mother and me, standing hand in hand, disembarking in New Orleans. Or boarding a train for St. Louis. Those events had been frightful for me as a child, imagining them from the perspective of an adult, they were terrifying. I asked questions about Uncle and his participation—his distance, his proximity. I read again about the myriad tests and obstacles we would have had to overcome. My mother. And me. Visiting bank managers. Arranging for tickets. Catching trains on time. Finding stopover accommodation. What would happen if a train arrived late, and we had to make new arrangements for ongoing travel? How could we have coped? I wouldn't bet on my chances today, let alone when I was six years old. Would Uncle have intervened? And the practical problems of feeding ourselves and seeing to ordinary hygiene and figuring out timetables and daring to ask people for directions and prevailing upon the courtesy of strangers and what person in his or her right mind ever could have assumed that we might accomplish such a trip successfully?

My rage simmered.

The lights were out, yet this would be a night without sleep. In the dark I make myself comfortable, and closed my eyes. My mind stayed awake with both the energy of our heist and the startling return of the letter. It was mine now, for keeps. Nobody would confiscate the missive again. I considered Uncle, his complicity. Laboured over my hatred for that little man.

Thoughts would mutate. Become snarled. I yanked the chain on the bedside lamp, and read sections of the letter again.

Sat up straight.

Had this not been a day for revelation? And intrigue? Insight cracked through the debris of my mood. Nobody—*in their right mind*—could have assumed that my mother and me would have achieved that journey without incident. Even Uncle, who had been warned to keep a distance, had complained about the enormity and impossibility of his job. Nobody could have foreseen that my mother would fall from a great height, but somebody—the author of this letter—had calculated that the mother and child inevitably would separate along the length of our complex odyssey. Whoever had written the letter *planned that my mother and I be separated.* Whoever had written the letter deduced that, given a choice between following the mother and tracing the child, Uncle would retrieve the child. Who would not do otherwise? Whoever wrote the letter intended that my mother be permanently lost. He or she or they expected to get rid of her. They were even willing to risk that I might be numbered among the missing as well. Perhaps this person, or persons unknown, guessed also that Uncle, morose for having lost the woman put under his charge, would suggest as his penance that he become responsible for the child's upbringing.

Uncle had been suckered.

What do you know. He had foiled the scheme by finding my mother and bringing her back, and it was then that my mother's history of walking off bridges was held against her. Uncle inadvertently fell prey to the conspiracy. He was used. My mother had not disappeared as had been wished and plotted, now she had to be cared for, and wouldn't it be best if she was kept apart from her son? Obviously, she could not raise him. She might throw him from a rooftop, if not herself. So Uncle was manipulated into proposing the only viable solution, that he be the one to raise me, and that Sheilagh Drinkwater be admitted to inexpensive, low-grade professional care.

And this was done.

All this came to pass.

Uncle believed he was being noble. He was played for a fool. Under the stark light of that room, I was sorry to have been unkind to him. I appreciated the sharp ridge of his sacrifice, the whittled innocence of his gesture.

Again I pulled the chain and snuggled down into darkness.

The turmoil of my perceptions worked through me. Continuing with my conspiratorial cast of mind on this day, I suddenly realized that Barclay had done it again. Like the time he had copped a dollar for a golf ball and decided that my share should be a dime, that night he confiscated the bulk of the material from Uncle's safe and tipped me with a letter that was already mine.

I bolted upright. Snapped on the light again. I'd been had. Immediately I felt less guilty about closing the office door without smashing the window. In my own small way, I had incriminated him.

Got the light again. Vexed by these recurrences of mutual betrayal and deceit, I returned to the darkness of the room, hiding out under the covers. Barclay was mixing himself up with rough company. He ought to be warned at how cleverly the letter's author had manipulated my life and my mother's, and Uncle's as well. First thing in the morning, I should let him know.

And yet, a persistent radical notion took hold. Perhaps my fellow desperado deserved the company he wished to pursue. Minding my peace might be the best thing to do, watching from afar, determining how he fared amid the conspirators who had danced the strings of his puppet dad.

I would make my peace with Uncle.

With Barclay, I would wait and see.

If things were to evolve as I then anticipated, I should be able to follow the trail of his success—or his ruin—to the person or people who had plotted to discard my mother's life while committing mine to a marginal existence. I was not expecting that he, she, or they cared enough for me that I could present myself as bait, but Barclay, that whiz-kid, the financial genius who could not miss unless he stumbled across his own ambition, he could exhibit himself as a tasty worm wiggling on the hook of opportunity. And I would be free to reel in that line.

As for my next move, it occurred to me that a law degree might come in handy after all. At the very least, it would make for a good disguise.

Life, as Miss Plant was so fond of saying, favoured the wicked.

Did it?

We would see.

That was one more secret to be revealed.

three

1968–1991

THE PALACE OF DECEPTION

9.

Across The Great Divide

In the middle of a night, in the bleak midwinter, I am watching gargantuan fluffy snowflakes alight upon panes of old, run glass, melting on contact. Is existence really this ephemeral? Inside, a lucky seven floors above the parking lot, life has been reduced to the touch of snow on warm glass and the sound of a persistent, amplified heartbeat—a mother's pulse thumping down corridors and through small alcoves. Each room has been kept dark to underscore the notion that we have entered the womb again where light is muted by the membrane of skin, where the singular, governing dimension is the sound of blood throbbing in the arteries and across the gentle waves of fluid washing upon the womb's safe shore. My second child is waiting to be born. He is being invited into a world of soft lights and stereo heartbeat, where it's desirable, I've been persuaded, to lull the newborn into believing that nothing much will change, that nothing out of the ordinary will actually take place, that this realm will be familiar and, should fortune shine, liveable.

Welcome, kid, to the Palace of Deception.

I hang about an anteroom, driven batty by the concussive thump of heartbeat. It's enough to make a foetus rush into the world to shut the damn thing off. I had thought, we had all believed, that the drastic attention-grabbing artistic experiments of the Bohemian era had vanished—good news, kid, you won't miss out, the kooks have invaded the world of popular psychology. My unsuspecting child is being born into an avant-garde vernissage.

It's been an hour and forty minutes since my wife was wheeled into the room, with no news since. Coaxed into madness by the sound system, I phoned home, letting Mom know that we had departed the house. She announced that she was coming down to the hospital too, that at one-thirty a.m. she would find a babysitter for Zack, our first, lickety-split, no problem.

Futile, arguing with her. I resigned myself to the rebuke of neighbours who were about to be awakened by my mad mother in the deadfall of night. That she would be successful at finding a victim never crossed my mind. Thirty-odd minutes later, that's my mother striding through the door, arm in arm with the intern from Emergency conscripted to be her guide.

"Mom, really," I say, and sigh, defeated before I begin, "there's no point being here. Everything's under control." She appears remarkably well-dressed for this hour of the night. I'm impressed by that.

"Where's Hannah?" is her first demand. Then, "What's that racket?"

"Hannah's heart. One that sounds like it anyway. It's supposed to soothe our new baby, or fool our new baby when it drops into the world."

"He won't hear his self think!" She routs around for trouble as she is wont to do sometimes. I don't know what she's after as Mom noses under cushions and it's only when she comes up with a dime and a penny do I see that this is an old habit, hospital routine, a profitable habit, in fact. "He won't see nothing. Or *she* won't if she's a she. He won't be able to see if she's a she or if he's a he. Why's it so dark in here?" At least we are in concert on these matters and I'm feeling glad of her company. "Where's Hannah, Sparrow?"

"You can't go in." Disoriented by the booming heartbeat, I am not entirely sure where Hannah's been taken, although that is not the issue.

"I'm her mother, me," Mother states. She's defiant.

"-in-law," I hasten to point out.

"Why does thou always gotta split hairs with me, Sparrow? I got a right. Thou got a right to be with her too."

"I'd faint."

"Thou big baby!" she rebukes me.

A physician, not our regular guy, passes through on his way out for a smoke. Mom grills him and he stalls, he won't answer a straight question while reporting that Hannah has a long way to go.

"What does thou mean, got a long way to go? Isn't she here?"

"She's doing fine," says he.

Mom presses her claim to be at her daughter-in-law's side, to witness the birth of her next grandchild. "I got a right."

"Sorry. We only allow husbands in the birthing room."

"Him? He'd faint. Better I go do the job. Hannah should have somebody with her."

"We're getting along just fine," the doc tries to assure us, backing off in the way that people often do around Mom. It's sad to see that happen. With effort, she can be made to listen to reason.

Of course, she doesn't help herself when she hurls after him, "I know all about fucking doctors! Thou art a snotty-nosed kid! Brat! Fucking doctor! Stick it up thy ass! Wring it out thy ear!"

"Mom. Easy."

Later, maybe twenty minutes later, our own obstetrician emerges, wondering if I wouldn't like to join my wife. We've discussed this for months, with me begging off. Hannah's exhausted already, he tells me, she could use the boost.

"Let me go in," Mom suggests. "Sparrow's a big baby, him. He'll faint on thee. Maybe fall down dead on the floor."

The doctor, the nit responsible for the mood lighting and the heart pump symphony, immediately concurs. I can't allow it, at least I cannot allow Mom in there on her own, and I hear myself announcing before I've thought things through, "I'm coming too."

Only to be waylaid at the door. "You'll have to sign a waiver," the doctor informs me.

"How come? My mother didn't sign a waiver."

"That's different. You're a man." Seeing that I have taken offense, that I am about to erupt, he modifies the insult in the nick of time. "You're a husband. It's different for you."

"Maybe. But here's a word to the wise, Doc. My mother's schizophrenic. Her rehabilitation is far from complete. At the best of times her behaviour can be erratic. You just set a fruitcake loose in your delivery room." For some reason, our worthy, avant-garde, holistic doctor seems rather perturbed by this news. Squeezing past him while he holds open the door, I add, "Have fun, sport."

*

Like I say, kid, welcome to the Palace of Deception.

The world grinds along on the wheels of conspiracy. Your Daddy-to-be should know. I had confiscated the very secrets to my existence, then promptly lost them to the wrong hands. Your Uncle Barclay never permitted me to get my sticky fingers on the contents of that safe. I tried to shake him down—he wouldn't flutter. I threatened him—he scoffed. I ransacked his apartment and he sent me the bill. I fought him, and he sat on me, just as he had done the day we met. He sat on me and demanded that I cry uncle.

"Barclay," I implored him after an hour of his crushing weight, refusing to give in, "tell me what was in that safe."

"Nothing that concerns you, Bird. I gave you the only item with your name on it—the letter. Everything else was business and finance, the personal affairs of strangers. All beyond your rather limited intellectual capacity to comprehend. Sparrow, why don't you go outside and play football somewhere? Muddy your knees. Scrape your elbows. You could use a good concussion."

"Show me the papers. What's the big deal? Convince me you're telling the truth." I was on my stomach, bound to the floor by his significant weight.

"Birdie, as I have repeated *ad nauseam*, I had no interest in possessing stolen goods. I shredded the lot."

"Liar!"

Barclay faced aft. He controlled one leg to keep me tame, twisting the ankle on a whim or whenever he wanted to hear me holler.

"Say, Uncle!"

"Eat another doughnut!" For that impropriety I received another twist, and yelped.

I never said Uncle, never would say Uncle, and long after darkness fell Barclay announced that we were up past his bedtime and that he was no longer amused. "All right. Let us negotiate. You need not say Uncle. Promise me that you will walk out of here and cause no further fuss."

"Get off me, lard-ass!"

"Cross your heart and promise, Sparrow."

"I'll promise you this. Within the next five minutes I'm going to piss on your carpet. I can't hold it in any longer."

"Then you leave me no alternative. I shall break your legs."

Under him, I considered my options. Barclay had celebrated each stage of his success by gaining more weight. He had finished first in the nation on his accountant's exams. That was worth ten pounds. Then the news arrived that he had scored the highest marks in Canadian history. Six pounds, five ounces. Prestigious firms vied for his services. Fourteen pounds. Within a year he had landed a junior partnership, with the promise of a fast-track ascendency. Twenty-two more blubbery pounds.

The tonnage exasperated me, but it wasn't only that. I felt the weight of the world's conspiracies compressing my bladder. I had no sooner stolen secrets from the father than I had lost them to the son. The world was treacherous, and I was frequently foiled.

Confrontation was getting me nowhere. Whatever Barclay had found in that safe was too important, too valuable for him to risk sharing with me. I had finally to make up my mind, and affirm my resolve. If I was to uncover the conspiracies and alliances that had burdened my life and my mother's, if I was to exact any form of credible revenge, I had to embark upon a scheme of my own. I had to hide myself, and conceal my motives, and move through the world with slippery guile. I had to concoct plans, and behave as someone I was not. To infiltrate those empires where conspiracies were designed, it was necessary to get close to those who knew exactly how alliances were born and perpetrated, and also why, and more importantly, by whom. I would feign to be one sort of man while secretly delving into the mysteries of my life, sustaining my search.

Barclay would not deposit his information with me because I could not be respected as one of his own. With patience and cunning, I had to hoodwink him into thinking differently about me. Foremost, I had to embark upon my new life by winning this initial negotiation.

"Tell you what. Let me up. Allow me the privilege of pissing in your toilet, then I'll leave quietly."

Barclay consented. The agreement kept his carpet dry, while I gained my freedom. A trade-off, on the surface. Little did he know that I had snared the greater prize. Under the humiliation of his bulk, I had gleaned my strategy for living in this world.

Had Barclay really tapped an important source of information? Or had he shredded papers of no consequence? I submit that the proof of my suspicion would be exposed by his conduct. Barclay was not the same man after cracking Uncle's safe. His lifestyle became subject to reproach. He drank excessively. He hung out with women such as Mo who carried kit-bags to his apartment. Mo's leather and chains appealed. In the public eye, Barclay's accelerated bee-line to the upper reaches of high finance swerved. He was seen in the company of shady entrepreneurs, and occasionally he was spotted boozing in the wee hours. At strip clubs. With unidentified Americans. Military-industrial-complex types. Mafia honchos, some said. Not an accountant's designated lifestyle. Barc seemed to flaunt his indiscretions, as though he no longer cared that a senior partnership might slip away.

Something in those papers had turned him around. Theft thrilled him, he had learned that much about himself. But something in those papers had damaged the boy.

No one could understand how the preeminent model of propriety could change so abruptly. Though I could, and I did, understand. When an innocent munches on the apple of knowledge, what else should we expect? Barclay had swallowed the fruit whole, core and all. The dark secrets of this world had been revealed to him, and the boy stumbled from grace.

He stumbled, and the combined bulk of his girth and the weighty principles upon his shoulders collapsed as profoundly as Adam. Barclay Boisvert plummeted from his high and mighty station into the true muck of this mire we call the world.—This dried up swamp.

Heaven noticed, I suppose. Though heaven showed no surprise.

What irritated me most, what bore down upon me, was if Barclay was selling his soul to a devil, then that was *my* Mephistopheles, that was *my* contact he exploited. He was selling out so cheaply too, for what bargain had been struck if not for more money, more women with whips, more power? But I, I would be patient, remain at close quarters, conspire to burn myself into those same inner sanctums to find the demons, my mother's demons, who had orchestrated the terms of our existence while denuding her life. Once these dungeon-dwellers were located, I would not merely sign a pact with them, as Barclay obviously had done, but I would visit their lies with truth.

So, kid, I made plans.

I studied law.

I accepted a full-time job.

I bided my time.

Also, I panted after your mom.

From the beginning I was comfortable with Hannah. Which meant, in part, that I could talk about Sheilagh to her and receive a cogent response. In the company of other girls it was easy to detect certain worries setting in. The fear that I might also be slightly touched. The suspicion that my attachment to her was unnatural. Is there a greater turn-off for a woman than a man who discusses his mom? (Dirt under the fingernails, apparently, is a close second.) With Hannah, there was no pretence, and no need to plead that my case was singular. She understood, without my having to make the point, that in many respects I was the parent in my relationship with my mother, and Mom the child. She also did not propose a quick-fix. One of my dates suggested solving Mom's problems with a hit of acid.

Another diagnosed her condition as "groovy." Contrary to such as these Hannah would criticize my mistakes, assail my laziness, applaud my efforts, and comfort my weary heart whenever I became subdued. She buoyed me up when hopes flagged. Hannah generously did so much, yet she declined to let me stay the night.

The lady had her reasons. The main one I could not refute. She was not in the market for a drop-by lover. Being slotted on a tight schedule turned her off. I had a law degree to chase, a job to do, and a mother in need of care.

As things turned out, Mom helped me with Hannah. She trained me well. After long hikes with her, I could walk for miles and scrutinise a vast array of details along the path. Mom taught me both stamina and observation techniques. One night I kept Hannah walking, and I kept talking, wearing down her resistance. On the mountain, under the stars, in the woods of the park where kids were dropping acid as well as their pants, we made love for the first time since the night we'd met. Something about the welcoming angelic wingspan of her tawny thighs ignited me more than sex with other girls. It wasn't comfortable love-making or safe or especially sexy or romantic. She liked to wrap her long legs around me and the eroticism of the moment quickened and astounded me in surprising ways. Loving Hannah, in the speech of the era, was primal, in the sense that I experienced the sweat and smell of the swamp and the mosquitoes of Mount Royal settled upon our damp skins in the fetid air. The nub of my horns grew. The parchment of my flesh glowed red. I felt hungry for her and bestial, yet she aroused both a fury and an incompatible tenderness in me—I became all of myself and more and she instigated both extraordinary fears and rambunctious strengths. For all my denials, for all our problems together, I loved the loveliness of her and her darknesses, how the moon-shadows of leaves caressed her thighs, the humour of her heart, the way she bent herself across a fallen limb for my astonishing access. I loved the piercing grimace of her love and her sighs and the tender way she put me straight and laughed at me and cuddled next to me and stroked my skin. Her delicate hand shy on my penis. I craved her large, so soft, dark nipples on chaste moonlit breasts. Eye to eye in the devious light, fastened together, locomotive and caboose, whistling through the night land, berserk and feeble, I really did love the girl and why was I denying it? I knew that she was feeling boisterous about me too.

So I asked Hannah to marry me.

"Actually," I warned her, "there's a catch."

She kissed my fingertips, once each, nibbling tenderly. "Don't worry, Sparrow. I know you're part of a package deal. We'll take care of Sheilagh too." Her way of saying yes.

We had a child. I plugged on through law school. Devised plans for a business. Moved through the world. I was biding my time.

Being married, becoming a parent, and caring for my mother would constitute a large side of my life during the sixties. Business, and my plot to penetrate the circles of infamy, lay claim to the rest. All fun, in the early days. Barclay had set me up with a summer job managing a small firm in distress while he shopped for a buyer. I finagled the means to take over the company myself, and the irony of that move was that it engendered a reconciliation between Uncle Butter and me. I was a kid in law school, lacking credit and credibility. Teaming up with Uncle would grant me instant access to his bookkeeping acumen and a knowledge of procedure. His presence would make my plans viable. Customers might gain confidence, banks would notice. The main thrust of our modest enterprise was servicing typewriters for corporate accounts. I had inherited a crack team of technicians who could speak neither English nor French, an office that made total mayhem seem tidy, and the most scatterbrained sales staff ever assembled. Battling incompetence, graft, and each other, I had to put that firm back together again, and for that I needed Uncle's help. Neither Barclay nor the banks were going to crown my ascendancy to the throne of ownership unless I pulled in someone of Uncle's reputation to be my counsellor.

The hardest part was broaching Uncle with an offer to become my partner. There was pride to be swallowed, recriminations to disavow. I had lunch with him and Aunt Butter, and later drove beside him on a business call, as yet unable to articulate my request. Uncle knew I wanted something, yet I had already turned down his offer of a loan, while his tender of a charitable donation to my cause had also been rejected. I quarrelled with myself. Did I honestly expect that I could condone this arrangement? I knew what he was like. The man was insufferable. His fingers in my pie would have me stuffing it back in his kisser.

Well versed in Uncle Butter's idiosyncrasies, how could I imagine for more than one second that I could tolerate him as a partner?

The older Uncle became, the slower he drove his car. The lenses on his glasses had thickened and he suffered from poor depth perception. A door on an upper balcony opened, twenty feet off the street and fifteen feet up—Uncle slammed on the brakes. A child holding a ball precipitated slowing down to five miles an hour. He stopped thirty feet in advance of stop signs, fifty for red lights, only to creep forward in increments until he was halfway across the intersection, causing gridlock. As we drove and my own exasperation increased, I was not at all certain that I could cull the dregs of my patience to work with this man. My future, as a businessman, and as a conspirator, looked bleak.

Toward the end of a block on Bloomfield Street, a souped up hotrod cruised in behind Uncle's Fairlane. The car—once a Buick—had had its hood removed to accommodate a gleaming red engine with a swirling chrome exhaust and a golden cylinder head. Revving fiercely, the driver was leaning on his horn. As these were narrow, one-way streets with parking permitted on both sides due to the absence of driveways or garages, the roadster had no hope of getting around Uncle.

I looked behind me. The idiot waved his arms, flailed a fist, punched his horn in a pantomime of fury.

Uncle reached under the dash. He flicked a switch.

The Fairlane coughed to a stop.

Uncle tried to start his car again. And failed.

Climbing out, he shrugged at the young man with the hot wheels and the horn, and lifted his hood. The hot-rodder clamoured out of his own vehicle. He virtually ripped off the air-filter cover on Uncle's car, stuck his fingers into the intake valve, and commanded that Uncle, "Start her up now!"

No luck. The stubborn engine refused to turn over.

Other cars and trucks had backed up along Bloomfield by this time. The hot-rodder directed traffic, waving and cursing at everyone. Greasestained, exasperated, he commenced the slow process of driving backwards down the entire length of the block while the cars behind him did the same. I was watching Uncle, who kept his eyes on the hot-rod. As soon as the spiffy roadster had made it to the opposite end of the block and turned the corner, Uncle put down the hood on his Fairlane.

We got back inside.

He reached under the dash, flicked a switch, and started the car. Without a word we continued on our way, both of us grinning silently to ourselves. Uncle's day had been made, while I realized that I could do a lot worse than to name a crafty codger like Uncle Butter as my associate.

When I finally put forward the suggestion, I did so nervously, fearful that he might decline. Uncle was nearly overcome with happiness. "In business with my boy? Pinch me! Am I dreaming? Yahoo! Ssssparrow! Yes! Yes!"

That was nice, seeing him so pleased.

Still, Barclay remained sceptical when I twigged my proposal. I was stronger with Uncle on side, but he continued to see me as a lost cause. My economic projections were thorough, I detailed how the company could be put right. He continued to balk. I offered to cut him in. While that had been my intention from the outset, I preferred to make it look like a concession.

Barclay consented, he sold the buy-out to the creditors at fifty cents on the dollar over two years, and I was well on my way to fabricating my disguise.

So welcome, kid, to the Palace of Deception. When you arrive, you will discover that your Daddy is not what he seems to be, that the world is a puzzle. If you intend to hang around, do yourself a favour, bring your own mask.

*

Hannah writhes in pain. Lets loose an unbridled yelp, enough to skin the hide off the most thick-skinned spouse, and sufficient to scare any foetus into refusing to be born.

Tah-boom! Tah-boom! Tah-boom!

Inside the delivery room, the amplified heart is many times louder than outside. Hannah shrieks to be heard. The shrill sound of her scares me. She makes love so quietly and in my own, male, way, I had foreseen giving birth to be a kind of lovemaking, serious thrust and lament, the push toward climax, joy unfolding into the quiet time after. It's not. It's mess and canker, screech and loathing I cannot abide. Backing off, I glare at the walls while working to stem the tide of that relentless heartbeat.

Mom, on the other hand, is a real trooper in here.

"Give it to 'em, Hannah! Give it to 'em, girl! Stick it up their arse!"

Though I don't know what she's talking about, Hannah seems to respond. "Yaaaa!" she yells, as though she's been enlisted as a marine recruit and is driving a bayonet into a sack of sand. "Aaaarrrggghhh! Yaaaa!"

Through my glimpses of blood and guts and inveterate mess, through the waves of my own nausea interspersed by Hannah's blood-curdling war whoops and my mother's obscene cheer-leading, I understand that the baby has finally gotten itself into position to prepare for entry.

If I were you, kid, I'd stay put.

"When the bastards come for thee, Hannah, sock 'em in the puss! Smash 'em in the nose! Don't let 'em get away with a damn thing!"

"Aaaarrrrggghhhh!" Hannah yelled, murderously.

"Scream at the bastards, Hannah!" My mother screams herself to be heard above the thump of heartbeat. Curls her little fists, the veins in her throat bulging with the venom of her speech. "Yell thy sweet little head off!"

"Yaaaaaa!"

"Louder!"

"Yaaaaaaaaaaa!"

"Louder than that!"

"YAAAAAAAAAAAAAAAA!"

"That's it! That's sticking it to the bastards!"

"Breathe," the doctor suggests. He's worked hard to create a certain ambience, as if this child is to be born into the dark, murky harmony of a swamp. I'm surprised mosquitoes aren't buzzing about the perimeter of the womb, so that the child's sole primal experience might seem a tad more authentic. The physician is perturbed to have had his plans rousted out by this caterwauling mother-in-law, especially as the mother-to-be clearly is in tune with such rabble-rousing techniques.

"Breathe, Hannah." I choose to endorse the doctor's standards.

"Scream!" is Mom's incantation. "Scream your liver-loving head off!"

"Mom, easy," I attempt to intervene. I hold Hannah's head slightly, keeping it in place, yet Mom clutches my wife's hands and has established the greater influence.

"See that doctor?" Mom instructs her. "See that doctor there? Tell him to go fuck himself, Hannah! Tell him to go fuck himself!"

"Ah, Mom, listen, really—"

"Perhaps this isn't such a good idea," the doctor now comes to believe in a burst of revelation. To my mother he suggests, "Perhaps you might be more comfortable outside—"

"Tell him, Hannah! Tell him!"

"Aarrrrggghhh!" Hannah yells, pushing and being pushed, stretched beyond the limit of her control.

"Tell him, Hannah! It's important!"

"Nurse, please escort Mrs. Drinkwater—"

"GO FUCK YOURSELF!" This is my wife talking, in a voice and language I've not heard. She seems possessed, so strange and powerful her indictment. Both the physician and the nurse are foiled, and the doctor nods to rescind his last command. Mom may stay.

Mom leans over my wife, and the advice is visceral and covert. She scrunches up her face and squeezes Hannah's hands and chants in riddles. "Does thou see the infidel coming? Does thou see him all in red?"

"Yes!"

"Does thou hear the enemy marching, marching with their dead?"

"Aaarrrggghhhhh!"

"Does thou see the cobras climbing, sliding on the walls?"

"Breathe, Mrs. Drinkwater! The head's visible! The baby's coming!"

"Ah! Ah! Ah!"

Mom plants her hideously composed face in front of Hannah's, which is equally unrecognizable. Nose to nose, she taunts her, "Does thou feel the breath of dragons, burning through the halls?"

"Mom. That's enough. Get off her." We have reason to fear she might crawl right onto the delivery table herself, insert her own feet into the stirrups with Hannah's. My mother possesses now a strength greater than demons, she cannot be budged by the nurse and me as we struggle to pry her off.

"Yes!" my wife calls out. "Yes, dammit!"

"Take out thy sword, O Warrior! Take out thy Sword of Light!"

"Aaaaarrrrgggggghhhhh!"

"The baby's coming. Another push, Mrs. Drinkwater. Leave her alone, people."

"Aaaarrrggggghhhhhh!"

The nurse and I both surrender, she to attend to her duties, me to witness the emergence of this new companion to our tribe.

"Strike down the fiery demon! Strike down the Evil with thy Might!"

And the whelp squiggles loose. A friendly whap of welcome and the wee one bawls. Not to worry, son, I'm weeping with you. Tears of joy, let's say. Hannah won't let go of Mom, her emotions have snagged on her coach. Both their faces have ceased their demonic initiations, at last, and shine.

Our second son is placed upon his mother's skin. I help Hannah hold her head up to look, and Mom is saying, "Oh! What a cute little birdie! Look at his little wings. Look at his cute little feathers."

"Ah, that's his hair, Mom."

"Whatever."

Place my palm on the boy's slippery back. Various emotions tangle for prominence, and I confess that I am bloated with advice. Such a tiny tyke. My hand covers his entire back. We are quiet, finally, in the room. The heartbeat gets turned down a notch. Lights dim. In the peacefulness, I am struck by the inadequacy of my meditation, I want to take more of this in, let it swim inside me forever. Poor tyke. The doctor thinks he has brought you into the world without your noticing, he had wanted you absent at your own birth. Mom figures that she has helped you stride across a dimension of heinous demons, each one grabbling for your soul. Don't be deceived! Something did happen today, and every year we'll light candles on a cake and try to figure out what. *You're born, little guy! This is it! The big leagues!* Good luck. Keep your eyes on the ball, follow through on your swing. You'll do all right. Just fine. Try not to be deceived.

On second thought, scratch that last bit of advice. That's like saying to someone, don't breathe, or don't take risks, or try not to live. You begin this life as a baby, and I am beginning my life in its adult form, a different page to the same text. What do I know? Only this, I figure we'll see each other through.

The guests at this glad tiding are being shooed on our way. I kiss Hannah. Words don't cut it, so we stare into one another's eyes, trying to cross the same realm, I suppose, that our child has just traversed. Another kiss and she is wheeled away from beneath me and I escort Mom into the dim anteroom.

"What was that lyric?"

"What lyric? What's a lyric?"

"That poem. The one you were screaming in Hannah's ear."

"What poem? What's a poem? I was not screaming."

Later I will learn that she had picked up the lines from the sect that for many years had cared for her, the same people who had influenced her to say 'thee' and 'thou' and 'thy'. Yet she would never admit that she had actually recited the verse at my son Zeke's birth. Hannah also swore no recall. Still, I was there, and being less involved, it could be argued that my comprehension of the event constitutes the true adventure of that day, though no doubt the women will laugh and mock my stance. What could a man know? Perhaps they're right. In any case, my son jumped across the great divide, to travail and frolic, to suffer and delight in this world. And given the fret and pain of the event, I am not convinced that he could have made it through a sphere of captive and vile spirits without the benefit of my mother's foray into their realm.

"*Tah-boom. Tah-boom. Tah-boom.*" The stereo heart gets switched off. As I accompany my mother down the corridors of the Royal Victoria Hospital, the echo of its percussion continues through my veins. "*Tah-boom.*"

I'd gotten used to the mess of the birthing—I didn't faint. Still, to this day, the memory scares me. What frightens the most, what chips at my confidence in the normal shape of things, was the supremacy that my mother had exhibited in that realm of unknown, unimaginable, terrifying powers.

It's her courage, her sovereignty in those mysterious quarters, that I will endeavour to emulate when passing through the unknown backrooms and boardrooms and corridors privy to my deceivers.

10.

Mountebanks and Demons

Mom's accustomed to shaky starts.

Pushing off with her right foot, she swivels, totters, shuts her eyes and prepares to crash. She's willing to die. Every time she mounts a bicycle my mother thanks God for giving her a life. She lets Him know that it's okay if He plans to abduct her now, she'll understand, she will accept the news. The first miracle is that the bike gains speed. The second is that Mom, imitating seasoned riders, settles into the leather saddle, leans forward with her face up, and opens her eyes. With the wind on her lashes and her mouth shut to keep out the bugs, she slices through the mountain air.

An aerodynamic guided missile, my mother zings down the mountainside. Her confidence springs from momentum. The faster she goes the more daring she becomes. This is freedom.

The sleeves of Mom's white cotton blouse flap in the wind her flying form creates, my way of monitoring her speed. "Slow down, Mom! Use your brakes!" In similar fashion, my ears behave as a seismograph recording the rhythmic crunch of the cinders and stones under her bike's wheels, a sound-effect reminiscent of snare drums. Skidding out, the rear tire assumes the dimension of a drum roll for a trapeze artist, and my spectator's heart performs an errant double-flip.

Imagine watching a child risking her first ride on a two-wheeler—*on an expressway*—that's an inkling of how I feel. Skinned knees, I pray, will be the extent of the damage.

Mom spent considerable time on her bicycle that summer exploring the limits of Great Cranberry Island, where we had a summer cottage. We had crossed by water-taxi to Mount Desert, and along a lengthy, ascending trail she kept ahead of me, pausing at the top to quench her thirst. My bike carried the saddlebag with the lemonade. While Mom could handle the bike well enough, this was to be her first major descent, and a new sensation. I was wary of her predilection for new sensations. Rarely was she timid about them. *Yet she's going so fast!* I lost sight of her among the trees, the path curving beyond my view in a slow arc.

Go after her!

I was stuck, fixed on the sound of her tires, our only contact.—*There!* She reappeared, out of the speckled green and bronze of the foliage, flashing through the woods like a downhill skier hellbent on Olympic gold. I seized up, and at the same time revelled in the pleasure of her sprint. *That's my mom!* Her chemise flapped like a sun-bleached Old Glory in a hurricane and her hair! her hair flew straight back, she was doing fifty. Her skin stung, the sun winked in her eyes, probably she was scared to death herself—and yet, the abandon of her free-fall must have felt awfully good to someone of her circumstances.

But she's doing fifty!

Mom, please, touch your brakes lightly. Now. Do it for me.

Now!

In a twinkling I could no longer hear her tires and the trail with its speed-drunk rider disappeared over a hill down into a glen. Nudging my bike forward, I winged my own descent.

An exhilarating flight. Mom can be a positive influence when it comes to experiencing simple joys again. I knew better than to call the air either clean or Canadian, as the locals did, yet the mountain atmosphere was fresh and tinged with the scents of moss and pine-gum and cedar, birdsong resonated with astonishing clarity, and the kick of rubber tires on the stones mimicked boyhood rhythms. Way up there, I could taste, inhale, and breathe the sea's faint fragrances.

The history of the island has always been linked to its beauty, and to the wondrous effect it has had on visitors. Samuel de Champlain, the French explorer, observing the hills rise on the horizon, dubbed them *désert*—deserted, lonely. Mythology confides that the island gained both its name and pronunciation from that remark, Mount De-zert, as though the hills were absent without leave, having abandoned their posts in the everyday world to lie moored offshore. Applying their own meaning to the pronunciation, wealthy Americans have participated in the joys of the island as their just desserts.

Promoting the island's affinity to wealth, the highest peak was named after another French wanderer, Antoine de la Mothe Cadillac, the founder of Detroit whose name would become synonymous with American industrial achievement and social status.

Ancient history. In this century, the trails on which my mother and I rode had been constructed by John D. Rockefeller as carriage paths for himself, his family, and friends. He wanted the charm of the mountains, ponds, and woodlands appreciated during buggy-rides or upon horse-back, part of a conspiracy to keep that infernal contraption, the auto-mobile—built by Ford—off his land. John D. had been developing this place to be an Eden of the new world.

Wealth can do that.

At least, it can try.

As counterpoint to his intentions, Eden is the name of the princi-pal street into Bar Harbor, the island's largest town. When it backs up with traffic on a busy Saturday night, I imagine John D. reaching for the Maalox in his grave.

The same year that my mother had been dispossessed by a flood, the playground of America's rich suffered the catastrophe of fire. After the hills were burned out in 1947, the Rockefellers donated land, bad-gered their friends to do the same, and the bulk of the great estates on Mount Desert Island, Maine, were annexed by Acadia National Park. Perhaps the Rockefellers needed the tax break that year, perhaps the rich of the island were driven by an honest sense of philanthropy and wanted to give something back to the people of America, perhaps they honoured John D. who had hated the thought of bequeathing Eden to fallen generations who might sell it to infidels in parcels or, worse, drive motorcars upon the carriage paths. The rich of that day fixed it so that no individual would own this singular patch of natural splendour again. If spite seems a sour or eccentric motivation to ascribe, consider John D.'s Last Will and Testament. By any standard his house on Mount Desert had been a palace—demolished, under the terms of his Will, upon his death. As a Rockefeller he had had the foresight and the savvy to know that you can't take it with you. He had also understood a greater wisdom—you don't have to leave it behind either.

Braking every few feet, I descended with greater caution than my mother had exhibited. Enjoying the moment and the day, I was thinking about John D. Rockefeller and the ludicrous style of wealth that he repre-sents, and I was thinking about my mother learning balance. I was think-ing about my own life. Mount Desert is hardly deserted any more, five million people visit every summer. John D. once had it pretty much to himself. Descendants remain. Their properties are rather imposing, yet the advent of children and grandchildren does tend to dilute the level of ostentation. Where once there was a castle, now a few mansions occupy choice spots along the coastline. In summers gone by I have raced International One Designs and beaten, and been defeated by, Rockefeller progeny. My interest is not to raise my standing on the Social Register, I merely point out that the family has learned to play with the riffraff now, that successive generations have grown bored with the isolation of the rich.

Old money is bound to be wrinkled. Huge piles of cash should probably be tossed in with the wash. In light of more recent events no one will want to hear this from me, but I do contend that huge wealth is not necessarily filthy or indecent, only that huge wealth is out of kilter, lacking balance. The poor in Park Extension recited their lore, that the rich were never happy because they had to worry about money. The more money they had the more they worried. An interesting proposition. We should all be so troubled. How the poor had come upon their knowledge was a mystery to me, and in any case, as far as I could see, they were the ones worrying about cash. The less they had the more they worried. These days I believe that it's a matter of balance. It's devastating to be poor, unseemly to be rich, and both conditions place impediments on the proper enjoyment of life.

I should know.

Oh? Am I pontificating again? Most summers on Great Cranberry Hannah would accuse me of the crime. When company was coming she'd cringe as I saddled up that hobby-horse.

Balance. That's what my mother was learning, and it threatened us all. We humans should not be able to walk upright, it's an asinine presumption really, an act of appalling effrontery. We do so through force of pride and the will of the mind. (I know, there's always some fool Russian bear cub who wants to ride a bike in the circus to get out of mucking berries in the woods, but *people* put the idea into its thick skull.) At the age of forty-six, my mother was learning to ride a bicycle, and in doing so she would uncover the mysteries of balance.

It's an amazing thing to ride on two wheels, each tire half the width of a heel. How do we do it? What generates this pride, this thrill? We take a sense of balance for granted, but I cannot, not after spending two weeks getting my mother upright and mobile on a bike for the first time. Not when I've experienced that human determination to get off her two feet and ride. What is this overwhelming need in us? Pick up your bed and walk. Stop loping on all fours and stride erect. Stop running and pedal. Stop pedalling and drive. Stop riding in the back seat and fly. Stop flying and blast yourself out of the solar system. Stop rocketing through galaxies—disassemble your molecules and zap yourself through time and space. Where is this new land we are searching for, and what's it like? Is it heaven or is it real estate? What is this paradise—a pristine planet with reasonable land values? Mars, let's say? We had that, we had better than Mars, and look what happened. Who's chasing us that we must rush to crawl, stand, run, pedal faster, drive faster, fly faster, rocket faster farther? Is it demons, alligators, moccasin snakes? What frightened us so much in that swamp that we can't look back? Can't slow down? Spooks, behemoths, ravens the size of priests, people? I persist in my pursuits although I could easily quit and lead a contented life. But I need to learn more, salvage more, destroy more. Just like John D. and all the rest.

Why? It is as though the act of balancing, the art of being upright, the dilemma of being human, by definition demands being subject to contrary forces. Stretched between gravity and heaven we stand erect. Caught betwixt swampland and oceanfront we settle for what we can afford, close to schools, where land values might rise. Our dreams pull us one way, and we never forget our roots. Between heaven and the primordial swamp, we scurry through our lives.

Riding a bike, my mother travelled both forward and backward in time, exploiting the miracle of balance. She recouped a pleasure of childhood that she had missed and at the same time confidently freewheeled into the future. My mother was reviving herself with the discovery of balance.

We do what we will ourselves to do, and we do what we are willed to do. Only the wise catalogue a difference.

Carrying good speed, my bike vaults down a short, steep embankment over a low stone bridge, and I cross a pastoral bubbling brook too quickly to appreciate its charms. I have enough momentum to ascend the rise on the opposite side without pedalling, and I'm wheeling down again through a meadow of wildflowers, long grasses, and bees. The slope is gradual at first, until I enter the darker woods where the path banks to the right then sweeps me left, and we drop. Gain speed. Fly through the underbrush. I emerge onto a glen and find, by the side of the trail, my mother's abandoned bicycle vertical on one wheel. The frame, supported by a bush, stands as straight as a human, while the rear tire spins freely in the breeze.

I brake hard, fishtailing.

She's nowhere in sight.

It's curious, upon reflection, that the first place I look for her is in the sky.

"Mom?"

Bushes prop the bike upright like a sapling, the front wheel planted in the soil. Who in their right mind parks a bicycle like this?

Mom might.

"Moooth-errr!"

"Will thee stop bellowing? I'm over here, Sparrow."

Following the faint trail of her voice, I ferret out my mother where the fates have pitched her, right-side-up in a blueberry patch. The concussion of her fall has not diminished her appetite, for she picks berries where she lies, spooning them into her mouth as she gathers another handful.

"Are you all right?" She must have sailed twenty feet through the air. Ass over kettle, judging by the posture of the bike. She could as easily have landed on rock, or smacked a tree.

Simply, without alarm or self-pity, merely as a matter of detail, she relates, "I'm hurt."

"Where? What hurts?"

"My bum's real sore, I scraped my neck,"—she shows me, pulling away her collar and hair. It's an ugly abrasion probably caused by striking a branch in mid-flight—"and my ankle smarts."

The injury to her tailbone I cannot diagnose, although, thank goodness, the ankle isn't swollen. I help her to her feet and she walks with a hobble. Mom's remarkably stoic with minor aches and pains, and together we amble out of the garden where she'd been tossed.

"Know what, Sparrow?"

"What, Mom?"

"That was fun. I want to try it again."

"That depends." I've learned to administer her lessons promptly, and on the spot. Rebuke delivered after the fact rarely sinks in with her.

"On what?" One arm looped through mine, she walks more easily as we go. In tandem we leapfrog a muddy patch.

"Promise me something."

"What this time?"

Extracting her bike from the plant that held it captive, I give it a quick inspection, then hand it over.

"Promise me to use your brakes."

"Oh no I won't." Unfurling her most obstinate frown.

"Oh yes you will." My eyes seize on hers. A familiar ritual.

"Nope." Doing her best to avoid my look, retreating.

"Yep."

"I like to go fast fast." Always a staunch defender of lunacy.

"You were lucky. Next time you might break your neck. Use your brakes and you can still go fast, but under control. You have to promise, Mother."

"Crum."

"Crash again and I'll make you wear a helmet."

"No way, José." Short of not allowing her on the bike, it's the biggest threat I can dish out.

"Will you brake going downhill or not?"

"All right." She drops her head. "Crashing hurts anyhow."

"Use your brakes, check your speed—we've gone over this before. You can have fun without killing yourself. You have to maintain"—the thesis has been on my mind and it's unfair to put it on her, but I do—"a balance between speed and safety."

"Okay okay already," she consents. "Is the car much farther?"

"We're almost there."

"I race thee, Sparrow! Last one to the car's a rotten apple!" And she flies off, shaky at first, gaining confidence with speed, standing to drive her pedals harder, faster, dashing through the woods like a rabbit eluding capture while I, pumping my knees as fast as they go, pursue her from behind.

"Slow down!" I shout to the vanishing form. But either she doesn't hear me or she's not inclined to listen. I am, as she informs me when I reach the station wagon, a rotten apple.

"Tell me something I don't know, Mom."

"With worms and maggots!"

"Lovely."

"A farmer polished thee up with DDT!" Where does she learn these things? "Then he spit on thee and rubbed thee on his dirty shirt. I wouldn't use thee for apple sauce!"

"Remember, dear mother, there but for fortune ..." Unfamiliar with the reference, she rambles on.

"I'd mush thee up and feed thee to the skunks and to Mrs. Raccoon!"

"Can we go now?" I finish strapping the bikes to the rear bumper.

"Step on it!" she commands in the car. "I want to get home fast fast, thou rotten apple slow-poke!"

On the ride home I reach a conclusion. I've been thinking about the matter for awhile, having had trouble crossing from speculation into action. I have protected my mother, and nurtured her, she's had time to heal. On Great Cranberry Island every summer Mom enjoys a modest facsimile of Eden, a closer approximation than Rockefeller, with his hefty allowance, achieved. She had been reared in a swamp, booted out of Eden, exiled to the wilderness of her mental dislocation, salvaged and made hale again. Now it's high time to escort her back into the world.

"You know I'm going to Geneva next week."

"Me I'll miss thee, Sparrow."

"I want you to come with me."

Mom claps her hands. "And Hannah! And Zeke and Zack!"

"No, not the whole mob. Just you and me."

"That's in Switzerland," is her initial comment. She has heard me discussing Geneva over dinner. "That's in Europe. That's across the sea."

"We'll fly," I put forward as the ultimate inducement. Strangely, she doesn't snap up the opportunity, as expected. If anything, she seems mildly dismayed.

Mother says, "Do I have to, Sparrow?"

*

Sparrow Drinkwater.

Businessman.

Sounds like a contradiction in terms.

Credit Mom with my prosperity. She's the wheel that keeps me spinning. That's another reason I invited her to Geneva, to have her strapped to my wrist as a good luck charm. A few minutes in her company would slow me down, centring me again.

I had entered a steeplechase, one hurdle followed another, and to recall the madcap sequence that led to my rise as an international financier is not easy. (Some would say, my rise as a crook—a verdict that's subject to review. I've always thought of myself as being on the side of grandmothers, the one cog in the machine trying to do the right thing. If the road to hell is paved with good intentions, I'm willing to concede that a few of mine have been mixed in with the asphalt—but I'm no crook.)

The sixties, then. My ascent to Geneva.

1. Sparrow Drinkwater goes back to school.

2. To support himself, his mother and her expensive prescription drug habit, and to pay for his education, requires funds.

3. Barclay Boisvert arranges summer employment, hiring Sparrow to manage an office equipment company that has fallen into receivership.

4. Sparrow is impressed with himself—until he steps onto the premises of "his" company. The offices are unfit for barnyard animals. Nobody knows how to answer a phone with courtesy. The bookkeeper takes hours to transcribe a row of figures with exquisite penmanship, then inaccurately tallies the column. The technicians, a talented lot from Egypt, Lebanon, Turkey and Italy, speak little English and no French. Amid the disarray, Sparrow discovers why Barclay would like to save the firm. The typewriter technicians are skilled and do good work, and the maintenance contracts, which are renewable annually, constitute a license to print money. Sparrow implements common sense procedures and saves the business.

5. Sparrow asks Barclay to let him buy the company. In return, he promises to pay the creditors fifty cents on the dollar within two years. He has plans for expansion.

6. Barclay laughs.

7. Sparrow pledges to conscript Uncle Butter to enhance his own dubious credibility, and offers Barclay ten per cent of the profits. His negotiating skills are impressive.

8. Barclay pumps his hand.

9. Young Sparrow, who continues to attend university, is a success. He's also a legend, earning a reputation for honest business practices by destroying, with Uncle's help, a system of kickbacks that had flourished among Purchasing Agents. The week he receives his law degree he hangs out his own shingle with an established client base.

10. Barclay, that bright light, is dimming fast. He's been involved with Corporation Foncière de Québec (Cofobec), a finance company with a tangled interest in an embryo known as The Bank of Western Canada. Not coincidentally, the latter corporation will

never see the light of day, although it has attracted considerable fanfare as a beacon of western aspirations and enterprise. When it's learned that Cofobec's books have been cooked, the company, and the bank, collapse. Having given the firm a healthy audit right up to the moment of its demise—when a junior associate, exasperated by Barclay's incomprehensible moves, refused to sign the statements—Barclay must account for his actions.

11. Barclay Boisvert has become expert at untracking tough loans, moving them through a daisy chain of companies until they vanish in the maze. He's learned how to ex-out entries, roll-back liabilities, and he's developed his own methods to plant mushrooms on the books. "I can make a monkey look solvent, the Royal Bank would give it a loan." He has, he claims, raised the technique of dividending-out to an art form. He explains what this means to Sparrow. "I can take a corporation's hard assets and scatter them along a trail of Chinese paper no auditor in the world can trace." As to the ethics of his performance, he's adamant that he had been out to hoodwink the Bay Street bullies, who in turn had been out to get him. "An economic union between Québec and western Canada would have crushed their monopoly on financial institutions in this country. My job was to buy Cofobec time. Another year, and this country would have enjoyed one hell of a revival. Cofobec would have emerged as a giant, the Bank as a legitimate player." He was doing it for patriotic reasons, then, personal gain had not crossed his mind.

12. Uncle Butter is delighted by this news. "Barclay Boisvert is the most moral man I know!" Barclay can impress his father and dupe the police. Hiding from the press, however, becomes increasingly difficult. "They did it to me," Uncle rants, "they tried to roust me out, the thieves. Tarred and feathered me, the blackguards! Now they're after him. Media assassination, that's the modern tar. Innuendo and rumour—the feathers. His morality and his sssuccess, it's all too much for the sssscum to bear."

13. At an official inquiry, Sparrow Drinkwater attests to the sparkling character of the defendant, Barclay Boisvert. His comments bring tears to Barclay's eyes. Uncle Butter openly weeps. They're a closely knit family.

14. Before Barclay decamps for Paris, where he decides to ride out
his disgrace, he directs Sparrow to meet a client on his behalf.

"Who?" I asked him over lunch.

"Does the name Cornelius Field mean anything to you?"

"Field!" I spoke with my mouth full, slopping soup. Each generation
churns out fresh media stars, people who have accomplished the impossible and are keen to flaunt their success. Admittedly, the name Cornelius Field did not rank with, say, the Beatles, or Timothy Leary, in
terms of front page news, yet within the decade's embattled business
world, Field was a subject of continuous speculation, gossip, and (the
litmus test) envy.

Barclay smiled. "Then you know of whom I speak."

Was this the connection I'd been searching for? Cornelius Field was
the founder, President, and Chief Executive Officer of Overseas Investment Services, a company which had, during the sixties, become the
largest mutual fund and investment service in the history of the universe. Cornelius Field. Was he my grandfather? Had he been the one
manipulating my life since the day of my birth? Why had Barclay
arranged for me to meet him?

Over lunch Barc ran through the details. I absorbed that information while expanding on the possibilities that were taking up residence
in my head. After we parted, I crossed Sherbrooke Street and headed
for the library at McGill University, where I hit the books. I learned
that Field had founded OIS in Paris in 1956. The genius of his idea
turned on the suspicion that investors would happily buy shares of
mutual funds if their profits could be concealed from the snoopy eyes of
the domestic tax man. The idea would be doubly attractive if the fund
could be based in countries where evading taxes was considered part of
the sport of being alive, and not a criminal offense.

For me, the omen was the year—1956. Prior to that time he had not
been a rich man. He was far too young to have sired my mother in the
early thirties. Field was not the man I was looking for, and I despaired.

My research continued, an interest that was professional now, rather
than personal. In 1958, Cornelius Field transplanted his operation to
Switzerland. Which made sense. The secrecy laws that governed banking in that country could prove convenient for an outfit like OIS. Later
he registered the company in Panama as a *sociedad anonima*—a fancy
title to define a secret operation—and the company grew rapidly as he
refined hard-sell techniques.

Now, Barclay had informed me, he was looking to register else-where. In the mind of the purchasing public Panama had a negative image. Who knows why. If a more suitable nation could be located, one with a reputation for financial sophistication, yet one with lax laws, Field would be interested in relocating. He wanted a lawyer and an accountant to investigate places such as the Bahamas and Bermuda, the Grand Caymans and Hong Kong. Tropical, paid vacations danced the rhumba before my eyes.

A pair of desultory notions slowly evolved and competed for atten-tion. Who had sent Field to meet Barclay Boisvert? Such a tandem may have emerged from the wealth of Barc's contacts. More likely, the men had not been matched by accident or mere fate. Someone, it struck me, remained behind the scenes, manipulating, pulling the strings. Now—finally—were my own cords being yanked?

Another thought nagged me. While embroiled in the Cofobec mess, Barclay frequently vented his anger by ridiculing Canadian law. Astonishing bluster, for whenever he circumvented a law, he blamed the lawmakers to condone his own conduct. I remained in the library through the day and well into evening—to all appearances, an eager lawyer immersed in his research.

Why, I asked myself, was Field looking to register elsewhere? I tried to anticipate his next move. Tried to think like a tycoon. What would I do in his position?

One thing to consider. Going public. It would be easier, and more profitable, to sells shares in OIS rather than investments in twenty sep-arate mutual funds. But, if he wanted to go public, who would have confidence in a company based in Panama? That's why he was looking around. Had to be.

That night, I dropped in upon Barclay unannounced. Mo's head poked out from behind the door. Seeing it was me, she opened it wide to expose an X-rated view. Net stockings supported by a garter belt, black panties, leather jacket, lips the colour of blood. Nothing here for the tame.

"Long time no see, Mo."

"How's it hanging, Bird?"

"Barc around?"

"He's indisposed."

I walked past her into the apartment. "Untie him for me, will you, sweetheart? We have to talk."

"He won't go for it, Sparrow."

"You know him better than that. In a choice between business and sex he chooses the dull stuff every time. Pack your whips and set him free."

Mo dressed and departed, carrying a discreet satchel, before Barclay emerged from the bedroom rubbing his sore wrists. (Remarkable, how he lies even to himself about his behaviour, and shows not a trace of embarrassment.)

"How deeply are you into OIS?" I needed to know.

"I'm not. I agreed to meet with Mr. Field as a favour to a friend. I am still considered an expert in the field, you know. Sorry, pun not intended. The point is, a company like OIS has to operate secretly from time to time. That's why I cannot simply hand over this job to the firm."

"As a favour," I repeated. I could have kissed him. Barclay was handing me work with which he could not trust his in-house confederates. He was admitting me into the inner machinations of his deals. Taking the stand as a character witness on his behalf had been my most brilliant move.

"That's right. As a favour to a friend," Barclay assured me.

"Then let me present this another way. How deeply would you like to be involved with OIS?"

Tough, seductive talk when aimed at a man like Barclay Boisvert.

*

Mom and me are flying to Geneva. This is how things go with her, she's happiest when she's sad. If events thrill her, sorrows pierce the skin of her mood. As though a knife made of bone whittles inside her, cutting through, hollowing out, etching the inner surface of her skull. Strange hieroglyphics, chiselled on the face of her mind. Most of us are free to revel in cheerful delusions, to sink to grief under misfortune's nimbus. Mom comes across as merely eccentric in her mature years—at her worst, as odd—yet she has never been delivered from contradictory information. That's her biggest, what she calls her hugest, problem. Life tries, but life can't kid her.

She is sleeping in my embrace. Tears have atrophied, leaving faint, crystallized tracks down to a pool at the side of her nose. My chief worry for this trip has been that Mom's enthusiasm might require my rough censure. *"Cockle-doodle-dooooo!"* she announced first thing in the morning, and I thought, "Brace yourself, Bird, here we go." So I was surprised, as we moved through the day's visits and preparations, to see her become increasingly quiet and apprehensive.

We checked our luggage at the airline counter. Mom got upset as our bags vanished down the conveyor belt. I calmed her, and for her sake didn't mention that she had every reason to be leery.

The security frisk gave her the willies.

Being herded aboard the aircraft aroused survival instincts. She held fast to my arm, not to be separated.

Mom did admire our First Class seats, although when she returned from a reconnaissance check of the aircraft she announced, "There's lots of toilets. But I can't find bathtubs no place." A few of our fellow travellers were spooked by that remark. Necks craned.

We took off, the noise and shake inspiring her confidence. She applauded as the city lights expanded below, and pointed things out to me as though she was familiar with the aerial perspective. Being served a meal aloft impressed her—she had expected food to fly about the cabin and splatter against the walls.

"That only happens in outer space, Mom." Which wasn't true either.

"Take me to outer space!" There's no satisfying this woman.

Our most troubling incident occurred while the stewardess passed out pillows and blankets for the comfort of passengers. Mom wondered, too loudly, "What happens if this here plane falls down? What if it drops out of this here sky?"

"Ssshhhh, Mom."

Not the sort of question the stewardess needed to hear while travellers were tumbling into sleep. Not the sort of company the First Class passengers had paid to keep.

Assuming that Mom had a case of the jitters, the young woman whisked her forward to meet the pilot.

Gone so long I nodded off.

She found me dozing peacefully upon her return. Mom climbed over me to reach her window seat, where she stared out at the blackness as though peering into a wretched heart. The world gone dark. We flew above a sea bereft of ships' lights. Snuggling in close for warmth, my mother pulled the blanket up to her chin, and I opened my eyes, spotting the tears dampening hers.

"What's the matter? Didn't you have a good time in the cockpit?"

Natch. She had enjoyed one of the more memorable experiences of her lifetime, flying level with the moon and stars above a few clouds, joking with the crew on the flight deck. She told me about the stars, and how the multicoloured lights on the instrument panels would blip and glow. An officer had taught her to navigate in one easy lesson. She could do it, Mom promised. She could get her license if she wanted, she knew how to fly, she could take over the plane right now if she wanted and land on Deneb. That was a star in case I didn't know.

She had charmed and entertained the crew. Unfortunately, all that good stuff had turned her sad.

Her visit had nudged various hopes, dreams, desires.

"I wish I had me a boyfriend, Sparrow. I'm sick of myself being lonely all the time."

Sometimes she speaks and my heart feels as though it's been dropped through a Pentagon shredder. "Lonely? You? Come on, Mom. You have me and Hannah and the kids." Please don't tell me you miss your street-scrounging buddies. "You have friends at home, friends on Great Cranberry, friends at the clinic—"

"Grow up, Sparrow," she told me.

"Isn't it true?"

"I wish I had somebody to love me," she cut in. "At night," she expanded, on the off-chance I didn't get it. "I wish I had me a boyfriend who was a pilot. He'd fly home and make love to me in the night."

Oh dear.

Necks were craning again.

Holding her close, I brushed her hair, kissed her forehead. "I know, Mom. I know. Every woman wants a pilot, or somebody like that. Why not? Every man wants a beautiful stewardess, or someone like that. Everybody wants someone to fly out of the sky just for them."

She slept in my arms most of the way across the Atlantic. I didn't budge, not when my arm ached, not when it went numb from the pressure of her weight. She needed rest. How was I going to keep her mind off pilots while we were gallivanting around Geneva?

*

Like an angel on leave in heaven following an assignment in the lower depths, my mother floated across Geneva. She gawked. Stared at everything, at the Alps, at the lake, at the Jura Mountains, at passers-by. In her mind, our aircraft never touched down on earth, we'd been spirited to heaven's remote quarter. Intuition told her that in Geneva her problems could be remedied. Cures lay in baskets waiting to be picked like bright red apples in Eden. Pocketing a credit card, Mom set out to recreate herself.

In my own way, I was doing the same thing.

While she shopped for sanity, I co-mingled with the maniacal.

Interesting town, Geneva. Both the seat of Calvinism and, along with Zurich, a vault of numbered bank accounts. One man's portal to paradise is another man's exit to despair. Accomplish both, is that the trick? Get rich, secretly, and while you're about your business maintain impeccable behaviour. Upon your earthly demise abandon your mansion and heaven's gate will creak ajar.

Know that Geneva is the antithesis of the swamp.

The lake is as blue as bliss. The pavement itself looks fertile. Here, in heaven, flowers must sprout from these sewers, herbal seasonings compose the dust.

Unlike being on Lake Pontchartrain, I could not row a leaky dingy upon these waters, or catch crayfish on a frayed blue line. The water reflected an enchanted azure sky.

Was this, for me, the beginning of lunacy? My approach? For my mother, could it really be the end?

Day One, we walked the ramparts of the Old Town. A glimpse of medieval Europe. Not without interest, although it lacked the mythic verisimilitude of a swamp. We took a tour bus to see the *Jet d'Eau*, the spume of water that shoots from Lake Geneva. Strange, the knowing smile that patrolled my mother's features, the elated performance of the water exactly what she had expected on an afternoon stroll through Elysium.

Hannah's advice, reinforced by my example, put the thought in her head to go on a spree. "Shop 'til I drop!"—my wife's adopted credo. Years ago, Hannah had chosen Mom's style of dress. Paisley smocks. Long skirts with feminine blouses. Pastel colours. The look clicked. As Mom thinned under our care and under the diminished burden of her medication, she became spry and attractive again, and Hannah coaxed her to diversify her wardrobe. "Try outfits to suit the occasion. The same thing day after day gets boring." Mom reneged. She was comfortable with her clothes. They fashioned a compromise between loose institutional gowns, proper dresses, and Salvation Army throwaways. Her duds possessed a natty, casual appearance. She had balked at evening wear or sport clothes or new styles. In Geneva, drifting under the city's spell, she considered a change.

My mother observed my own transformation with interest. The topaz ring. The diamond stick-pin. Clothes bedevil me. I could show up to my meeting frumpy, in effect thumbing my nose at the impeccable set. Self-confidence, individual flair, have merit as a strategic style. And yet. I needed to present myself as an alternative to Cornelius Field, at least insinuate that possibility, and he would be sure to cloak himself in the garb of the era. He'd eschew a tie to sparkle with jewellery, dispense with a suit in favour of an Indian print worn above faded jeans. Clothes may not make the man, but I had to acknowledge the possibility that they might swing the deal. Field should never see me as a threat. A grey, double-breasted suit. The silk tie. (The tie cost twice what my best trousers do at home.) A shirt collar buttoned-down by gemstones. Odd, the first garment I purchased—a black winter cape. I couldn't resist the impressive wing-span. I could not wear it to the meeting without sweating off five pounds, I'd arrive dripping, really I made the purchase for future use. And yet. Emboldened by the cape, I did feel sinister and provocative. Strolling into the OIS boardroom I'd wear my transparent black wings invisibly, I'd fly over their heads to weave my magic above the scoundrels.

Taking note of my eagerness to alter my look, Mom also chose to experiment. On a lark we commissioned the hotel's hair stylists to do their worst, and she booked an appointment with the beautician. The made-over, sophisticated woman who emerged from that session scared me, the change that startling.

"Mom? Is that you?"

She grinned. Flattered by her own appearance, delighted by my incredulity. "Who am I, Sparrow?" she asked. "Who is me today?"

Good question.

Spruced up and scented, she wore her angelic, and me my demonic, disguise.

Mom sleeps.

Oblivious to the world.

Clad only in Jockey shorts, I slump by the window, enraptured by my muse. The drapes are open a crack, a seam in the fell of darkness stitched by Geneva's sedate night lights.

Tomorrow's my big day.

Like a baseball waiting to be pitched, I pass the sad heart of my mood from palm to palm.

Too edgy to sleep tonight.

We were then halfway through 1973. The past decade had been my first as an adult, and that seepage of time, like water drained from a swamp, altered both my internal and exterior geography. Who would have thunk it? Sparrow Drinkwater. Businessman.

None of it was done purely for my own aggrandizement. Mainly, I advanced in business to help finagle my way into the mysteries of the world, and, as things went along, I also did it for fun. The latter surprised me the most. Those early days at Woodburn Office Equipment, when I circled the wagons to endure the onslaught of arrows, and defeated tribes of bankers, competitors, incompetent employees and angry clients with a quickness of mind and a steely fortitude, were fraught with endless, boundless hassles. They were days propped up by surprise, exasperation, and excitement.

Consider the time I lost my business innocence. Having coaxed a Purchasing Agent with my best lines, I learned that he was less enamoured with my promises and reforms than he was anxious about my commitment to the established practice of kickbacks. I got so depressed. I was in shock. For one thing, I had assumed that the previous administration of Woodburn had skimmed something off the top, that an end to the practice would put cash into the company's coffers. Internal jobbery I could fix, yet I was now discovering that profits had been depleted by an external system of graft. If I didn't like it, I could take my business elsewhere.

Uncle bailed me out of that mess. He taught me to sign the deals, pay the kickbacks, then to get friendly with upper management. Whacked out on the squash court, or teeing off on the back nine, I let it slip that, while I was happy to be of service to their firms, I was not crazy about buying off P.A.'s. A tempest. Purchasing Agents dropped like fruit flies in a maelstrom of DDT. Once the dailies got hold of the story, the mealy-mouthed bandits were swatted down like mosquitoes. Between us, Uncle and I restored moral procedures to Montreal business—*heady days!*

I learned the intricacies of Uncle's great lesson. Astutely played, morality's high hand won jackpots. New Purchasing Agents coming into the system knew whom to thank for their promotions, and Woodburn flourished.

My greatest challenge was putting together a sales force. The company was in no position to hire college grads or recruit IBM deserters. When I cast about, I had to form my team from among the bottom feeders in the swamp. I had drunks, I had lunatics, I had ex-golf pros, I had one guy who was too good to be true until he came down with a headache that lasted six months. Desperate at one point, I placed an ad for technical trainees, and managed to talk a few of the applicants into commencing a career in sales. These I was free to mould into a certain style and presentation. Fresh, sincere, and shy about selling, they didn't come on to my clients as institutional rejects wielding chainsaws.

That was the kind of thing—the kind of thinking—that made me successful, and commended the greater world of business to my interest and approval. I enjoyed myself. I made money. Every so often I could take a break from the pace and be proud of my achievements.

In the meantime, Mom had claimed noticeable progression, the kids slipped into my life, Hannah and I were getting along, and I was gaining Barclay's trust. Overall, life was pretty good.

What changed? Why had I come to Geneva? If Everest is there, must we humans climb it? If OIS was stuck in open view, a mountain of mismanagement, was someone obliged to either (take your pick) save it or loot it?

Apparently, yes.

Certainly, I could not resist.

My success with Woodburn was partly to blame. Once I had the company running smoothly, fewer challenges arose to arrest my interest. Problems were solved with careful attention, growth absorbed the loss of any one client, and I had employees—and Uncle—who could successfully work out glitches on their own. Efficiency bequeathed routine, routine nullified adventure. How was I going to get close to the forces that had controlled my existence? Or, would I have to retreat from my quest, admit that entry into the upper echelons had been denied for the likes of me? I had chosen time as my ally, but time had granted me no reward or encouragement. When Barclay came to me and, in effect, dumped Cornelius Field and OIS in my lap, I transformed myself into a bird of prey long deprived of a meal. I dive-bombed that squealing rat of a company.

To put a firm together, whether from scratch or as a rehabilitation project, meant something. That's why I felt both sympathetic and antagonistic toward Cornelius Field. Sympathy, because he had assembled an amazing company in a short period of time. Antagonism, for letting it flop. The fool was more interested in photo-opportunities among a bevy of bimbos than in taking care of business. So I would take care of him. He was the black knight with whom I would joust the next afternoon.

Sitting in the darkened hotel room in Geneva, listening to the gurgle of my mother's breathing, I feel nostalgic for an earlier age, a simpler, if more difficult, time. Isn't that always how it goes? Putting Woodburn right, I was often exhausted, frustrated, in despair. Now I look back and think that those were the days. Perhaps these are the days. Perhaps I will look back on my trip to Geneva and my move on OIS as wild times. At the moment, what I feel is regret, an instinctive, procured sadness, a kind of resignation to my fate. I'm being mothered by necessity, egged on by forces astride my own destiny. To penetrate the future it is often necessary to forsake the past. Actions bequeath consequences.

What's telling is this—to live the adventure, to accept a course of action, changes who and what we are, and how we think. A night-breeze off the mountains cools my skin, and I go to the closet and strap on the winter cape purchased earlier in the day. My wings. Fly above this city, Sparrow. Soar. I want to do just that, under a blemished moon, scudding along with nefarious cloud. I trek back to my chair, huddle under the warmth of my feathers.

Mom stirs, and although I sit very still, holding my breath, she awakens.

"Sparrow?" In the dark, she can scarcely see me in my black wings.

"It's okay, Mom. Go back to sleep."

She wiggles her torso upright. "Thou has a big day tomorrow. Thou must sleep." She slides out of bed. As she approaches a breeze invites her white nightie to dance.

"I'm okay. Really."

"Up, little birdie! Into thy bed with thee."

What is this? "Mom—"

"Hush!" She peels my wings and feathers right off me, then tugs on one of my ears. I get up and climb into bed. Who has a choice when ordered to sleep by a parent? My mother tucks me in.

Then she sits on the bed and watches as I attempt slumber.

"What's up, Mom-o?"

"I never was thy mom," she laments. Light from the crack between the drapes touches her face, makes it shine. "I never had a chance to be thy mom when thee was little. At Lougain there, the nurses took better care of thee, my Sparrow."

"Now you want revenge. You want to put me to bed and make sure I fall asleep."

"And make thee say thy prayers."

"Ah, wait, Mom—"

"Now I lay me down to sleep..."

I am obliged to repeat the words after her. In a way, this is more pleasant than it is strange, reciting a child's prayer with my mother on the eve of a battle with the forces of darkness. Fitting, in its own way. After our supplication, Mom loses the thread of what she's doing, she doesn't want me to fall asleep yet, she'd rather talk.

"What is it?" I say to the phantom staring down at me.

The smile crinkling on her face shows pain. "Hannah says thou art crazy." Solemn words.

"She doesn't understand what I'm doing, that's all. There's no need to be concer—"

"She says thou art rich enough."

"*Hannah* says that? She's changed her tune."

"She says thou doesn't need more money."

"Hannah? Tall girl? My wife? Pleasant personality? Mother of two boys and parent to fourteen credit cards?"

"Hannah says thee doesn't know how to set limits."

"Limits? *Hannah?*"

"She says thou will go to Geneva—"

"I'm already in Geneva, Mom."

"—because thou art nuts." Her eyes remain intent on mine throughout, seeking hints of madness.

"Mom? Do you remember the day we were kicked out of Lougain?"

She nods. "Yes I do."

"Who did that to us? That's what I want to know."

"Leaving that loony bin place was for our own good, Sparrow."

"We didn't leave. We were kicked out. We needed a miracle to find each other again. Nobody plans on miracles, but somebody wanted us to be separated, somebody out there didn't want us to find each other."

Silent awhile. The concentration of her gaze informs me that she has not been lost to a daydream in this dark night. Mom asks me, "Is that why we are here in Geneva, in Switzerland?"

"Partly. I'm searching for the people who manipulate our lives. Not just your's and mine. Everybody's."

"Hannah thinks that's crazy."

"Maybe it is. It's what I do in this world. What do you think?"

Taking my question to heart, she will sigh and cast her eyes about the room. She, too, hunts answers. Mom decides, "I don't want thee crazy like me, that's all."

"Nobody can be as crazy as you, Mom." I sit up. Squeeze her in my arms. "Now do I have to get out of this bed and tuck *you* in?"

"No." Standing. Touching her fingertips to mine. "I wish thee good luck tomorrow, Sparrow."

"That's why I brought you with me, Mom. A long time ago, me and you, we started out on a journey."

"That was not very good luck."

"This time it might be. It's the same journey, Mom. We're farther along. Time has passed. We're together. We're still travelling. That's the part about it that's lucky. Now you get to bed or I *will* tuck you in."

Mom shuffles around to her bed, crawls in under the covers. We're equally quiet awhile. I begin to believe that I might actually manage sleep.

"I love thee, Sparrow," Mom says out of the dark.

"I love thee too, Mom," I remind her. Later I will realize that we had never spoken these words to one another since my childhood, not quietly and calmly like this. I listen to her breathing, wait for her to slip into the solitude of her dreams. Then I rise. Put my wings back on. Anticipate the earth turning onto the most grandiose adventure of my life.

*

We were staying at the Richemond. I placed the hotel's brochure in Mom's purse, and repeated the address in two pockets. Plied her with lunch money, cab-fare, a credit card for her extravagances, and I wrote out a list of art galleries—she never tired of visiting these. Mom knew a smattering of rude French from her street days in Montreal. She might startle people, but I was confident that this new woman could handle herself.

"I'll shop 'til I drop, Sparrow!"

"Go easy. Visit a few galleries."

"I'll drive thee to the poorhouse now!"

God help me. "If that's what it takes to enjoy yourself, Mom, feel free. When we get home I'll find you a job."

"I'm buying tight things, and frilly things, and sexy things!"

Whoops. Warning signals. "Don't you dare model anything out-of-doors without my approval."

"To heck with that!"

Breathe in deeply. Say what must be said. "Have a good time, Mom." Most important of all, pray.

She was off to do the town, and I was bound for my illustrious appointment with destiny.

Contemporary wisdom claims that the last opportunity for true adventure resides in the boardroom. I think differently. Placing walls around the vicinity of adventure is the first of my objections. More importantly, it's been my experience that boardrooms function better as living theatre.

Contests of will are played out as psychological drama.

Buffoons perform comedies of error.

Potentates, dressed in drag, utter twaddle.

In hushed, dreary, mind-dead rooms, smoke curls from ashtrays and drifts toward the smoke-free end of the table, where bored board members are waiting for Godot.

Around other tables the circus is in town, street drama staged by colourful, rapacious C.E.O.'s. A pity that the public is denied access to these venues as they feature a marvellous theatre of the absurd.

Cornelius Field was the first man I met who instantly instilled in me a desire to grab him by the balls, hoist him aloft, and ease him down gently, tenderly, upon a picket fence. Life was an act with him, each encounter a performance. The dweeb was so damned ingratiating, a totally inane posture for someone of his accomplishments.

He snivelled, he grovelled, he *sniffed*. Bootlicking was a fetish. I wanted to scream in his face, "Idiot! *You* started OIS. From scratch. From an idea. For all your troubles, your annual sales still top three billion dollars. Your banks, insurance companies, your real estate operations *alone* are worth a hundred million. A minimum of two-point-three billion is under management in your mutual funds. You have close to one million clients. For crying out loud, don't wheedle. Quit lapping at my boot heels." That's what I wanted to say to the man, a desire shared by many. Unfortunately, no one dared censure Cornelius Field. Not even me. Until someone took it away from him, the man had power.

Field was an obsequious bully. Cast him as the villain in the piece, the scoundrel audiences would love to hate. Thespians would fear playing the role, knowing they'd be criticized for over-acting. Cornelius Field was an exaggerated caricature of his own devising. A fawning style was his strategy, one that kept opponents off-guard. He enjoyed supplicating himself. Greeting guests, he bowed like an oriental. Competitors tended to either take him too lightly, or become preoccupied with despising the rat.

Corn's thick red beard compensated for the pate harvesting curls on his head. He would pick through the undergrowth as if crushing lice between his nails, just another disconcerting habit. In truth, his international reputation as a playboy galled us lesser men. Who would kiss those thin lips, return his skimpy grin?

The curtain on our passion play will rise as I step inside the office tower in Geneva, and ascend in the elevator. I am shown to the boardroom on the top floor and enter, stage left, under a spectacular skylight of bevelled glass. The Board of Directors is seated around an oval table, looking for all the world like a gang of glum, pin-striped vultures. I come on like the Bluebird of Happiness, ruffling the feathers of their melancholy.

Natural light shines in my eyes, but confidence in my research adds the glint to my smile. In this room, on this stage, in this aviary, I breathe the rarefied air of my true destiny.

Intimate with the backgrounds, affiliations, club memberships and portfolios of these men, it's a cinch to stick names on faces. Each of the men was born to privilege, and each has maintained his station through advantage or deception. G.S. is Spanish. F.D. crossed the ocean from Brazil. An American from Mississippi, latterly of Grand Cayman Island and known to his friends as "Noseguard," W.L.M. hunkers his head between epic shoulders. He blinks rapidly. Seated beside him is the British industrialist, B.K., a resident of Bermuda most of the year. C.C. is a Swiss national, M.C.S. an Italian, and V. de M. has arrived from Paris. Not only am I the only Canadian in the bunch, I am the only bird at the table who bleeds red. Agenda and clothes aside, it would seem that I am representing the proletariat.

Neither standing on ceremony nor submitting myself to their authority, I choose the chair at the end of the table opposite Cornelius Field. A battleline drawn. As prodigiously as a slug on a leaf, Field rises from his chair, grins his thin, smarmy smirk, and bows, an annoying affectation for an occidental.

He states, "It is my distinct pleasure to welcome to the meeting Mr. Sparrow Drinkwater of Canada."

Most everyone murmurs a greeting, with B.K.'s ardent voice rising above the rest. "Here here! Welcome!"

"You will remember, gentlemen," Field continues, "that Mr. Drinkwater is a genius. He is the lawyer who successfully guided our move into Canada as a public company."

"Here here!" B.K. shouts again. I decide I don't much like the fellow.

"Mr. Drinkwater brought to our attention that Canadian regulations do not apply to corporations who undertake the bulk of their business offshore. Our Sparrow also turned up the surprising news that such companies are not subject to corporate taxes. Gentlemen, you will recall the warmth of our enthusiasm for this discovery." To illustrate that his memory remains intact, B.K. pounds the table with the heel of his palm. "Since that time our ship has floundered upon the rocks. Of course, we cannot blame our trusted friends ashore, friends such as Sparrow and his associates, for storms at sea."

"Indeed we cannot!" B.K. bellows, glowering at anyone who might presume to disagree, including me. More than the bulge of his innumerable chins, B.K.'s eyebrows dominate his features, and he has the disconcerting habit of smacking his lips together to emphasize a point.

Falling in love with his analogy, Cornelius Field, the toady, offers an effete little clap, and brightly suggests, "Perhaps Sparrow is here to return the fair winds that carried us through September! In any case, we have agreed to listen to his counsel, to learn what course he has charted for our ship."

I accept this as my cue to stand again, as my host sits down. Before speaking, I adjust the invisible cape around my shoulders. Black-robed magicians release doves and extract timid bunnies from hats—I set an unseen sparrow into the air and watch it circle the room.

Greeting each of my hosts by name effectively snubs Field for failing to introduce them. Only C.C. declines to say hello. In penalty for his rudeness my unseen sparrow alights upon his shiny bald patch, where it poops. Although impeccably Swiss, C.C. can't intimidate me now, not as long as I can imagine a purplish glob of gloop upon his shiny crown. The sparrow takes to the air again, surveying targets.

What the audience in our drama might be slow to pick up, unless the program has filled in the blanks, is that the stock offering Barclay and I had engineered for OIS raised one hundred and ten million dollars U.S., selling out immediately. For our resourceful efforts, Barc and I were jointly awarded a "loan," through OIS, for five million American greenbacks. Not bad. Although he was supremely adept at monetary intrigue, Barclay had been puzzled. "Explain, Sparrow, why I find myself in debt for two-point-five million dollars? What's the rate of interest?"

Funny how things had changed in our relationship. I had spotted the opportunity in OIS. Now I was calling the shots. He knew figures, but I knew people. He cooked books. I roasted individuals. "Dear boy, you don't pay taxes on a loan."

"You mean," he was aghast, "we don't have to pay it back?"

"You're catching on. For as long as Cornelius Field is in charge of OIS, it's ours."

"Then we have a job to do. Protect him within OIS."

"That's the point, old chum." Ascending the ladder of success, I have begun to emulate his patterns of speech.

We had something on Cornelius Field, knowledge that he was loopholing Canadian laws. In return, he needed to have something on us, so he lent us the five million, effectively putting us in his debt. Field undermined people at their roots. He made his associates dependent upon him, and upon his continued prosperity.

While we accepted his tainted generosity, we did not pooh-pooh the fiscal irresponsibility. In time, the business community also took notice. Stock issued at ten dollars soon dropped to a deuce. Trading had been halted in Montreal and Toronto, more recently in London. If the stock trades at all by the time of my visit to Geneva, it's in New York for pennies.

"Gentlemen," I begin, commencing my thrust for power, for leverage in this world, "I appreciate your presence here today. I recognize that times have been difficult for you. OIS totters on the brink of collapse. What has occurred since the stock offering is tragic. A burden, I'm afraid, that rests upon your shoulders. In one sense, you are correct if you assume that this is none of my business. Nevertheless, I do consider myself a parent of the public company. A parent frets over a child's distress. I want to help. I am here to offer my services. I believe we can turn things around. Do we not agree that OIS must prevail?"

Flicking the top of his head as though bothered by something fallen upon his exposed scalp, C.C. declares, rather defiantly, "We are confident, Monsieur, that OIS will prosper."

"Then you don't need me." In the silence that ensues, I do not flinch. To push my bluff beyond the constraints of protocol would be a mistake, so I merely stand still, making no move for the door.

This is not a discussion I have entered unprepared. Aside from the secret magic cape and the circling sparrow, I have also lugged into the room the bounty of my research. The critical aspect on which I rely turns on the singular nature of this Board of Directors. There's never been one like it. In order to prosper as its potentate, Cornelius Field deliberately selected the dumbest, the dullest, the stupidest of rich croaky frogs to splash in his pond. The pedigree of the Board is impressive, the names of the members are attached to some of the great families of Europe. What a cursory inspection does not indicate, however, is that Field chairs a committee of the witless.

I am waiting for that inherent dementia to manifest.

Happily, M.C.S. speaks up, breaking the silence. "My arthritis is bad this month. Worse than it's ever been. It's unbelievable!"

"S—! Be still!" V. de M. hisses.

"Monsieur de M.," I inquire kindly, "how has your sciatic nerve been behaving? Is it troubling you?"

Field, significantly, rests an elbow on the arm of his chair, touching fingers to his chin and lips. He's sizing me up, perhaps reevaluating his previous impressions.

"May the devil take the pain, Monsieur!" V. de M. gripes. "And now my back as well!"

"Right between the knuckles it gets me, my arthritis," M.C.S. complains. "It's killing me!"

Deciding to keep Field off-guard, I choose to walk behind Monsieur de M. "Just a second, Corn, let me help this fellow out. Lean forward, Monsieur de M. Good. Now, relax your shoulders." I whisper the rest, "Too many young girls at once, Monsieur. Your body will twist like your soul. Learn discipline. Exercise restraint. Concentrate. Or your spine will snap." I wrench de M.'s back as my chiropractor has taught me to do. "Cha!"

"Yeee-ow!" he cries. I think I may have cracked a rib.

I let him in on his prognosis. "In a few days you'll be fine. Meanwhile, remain perfectly still. Don't move!"

"Can you do something for my arthritis?" M.C.S. asks me, then poses the same question to the room. "Can he fix my arthritis?"

Satisfied that I have brought a sincere smile to the brink of Field's normally implacable visage, I return to my seat. Confirming the peculiarities, the eccentricities, and the craziness of a few of the players boosts my confidence. I have launched myself among the maniacal. Field probably assumed that these people would confuse me, or disturb me, that I'd take note of their infirmities and back off. Failing that, he would still be able to manipulate their votes to suit his wishes. He did not know how at ease, how much at home I'd feel here. In this boardroom, Sparrow Drinkwater is sovereign.

On the downside, Corn Field is beginning to understand that I am a worthy adversary. These may be his people, but he detects that I have an affinity with them as well.

"We are a curious lot, Sparrow. Please proceed with your proposal. Many at the table have travelled great distances to be here."

"No doubt a few of you are hoping that I might materialize as the Messiah," I kid. "Did I not perform miracles with the stock offering? Perhaps today I can walk on water, or at least stroll upon your sea of debts." I chuckle along with the few who can still laugh.

The British aristocrat, B.K., never cracks a grin, so I send down my sparrow to pick at his shoelaces.

"I'll settle for a Band-Aid solution," Noseguard makes known, stepping into the breech. I have expected him to be on the ball. Corruption, not infirmity, merits his seat upon this Board.

"I'll do better than that. In the wake of the public offering, OIS has been hurt by mismanagement. For one hundred and ten million dollars to be depleted so quickly without discernible advantage to the company supports this judgment. Gentlemen, we have a classic cash-flow problem. Only the scale differs from the norm. Our usual channels won't jump to the rescue. A stock collapse has a nasty tendency to make banks jittery, investors are keeping their coins in their pockets. Stop me if I'm over-stating things."

G.S., a fool but no dummy, says, "Mismanagement, is that the correct face to put on the situation? We are subject to economic forces—"

"Gentlemen, as my uncle used to preach at suppertime, when a man is mired in sow dung, it's not the job of the Good Samaritan to call it a bubble bath. It's his duty to haul him out. Mr. S., let's stick with the word mismanagement. Let's grow accustomed to the terminology. Criminal mismanagement of a company is a serious offence in Switzerland, and OIS remains registered right here in Geneva. Criminal mismanagement is the charge which everyone in this room will be facing should OIS collapse."

Out of Field's earshot, I lean across to whisper to Noseguard. "How'm I doing?"

"So far? You got us by the short ones."

Field, I notice, is curious about our exchange, but he's unable to extricate himself from his obsequious mode, he cannot presume to interrupt. I let him sweat.

"I don't think jail will do my arthritis much good," M.C.S. speaks out.

Field is fast losing control of the meeting, and his own composure comes under review. Bringing a foot up onto the table, B.K. whines, "That's the third time today my shoelace has come undone. I don't understand it!"

C.C. wipes his head with a handkerchief and laments, "We must avoid prosecution. It will spoil investor confidence if we are put in jail. Any fool knows that."

B.K. bangs his shoe on the table, shouts, "Here here!"

"At last count," I persevere with my sneak attack, dividing and conquering, pillaging their tidy compound and disturbing the peace, "more than one hundred lawsuits are currently filed against the company. How many do you expect to win? Fifty per cent? Ten per cent? Seventy-five? The legal costs will be astronomical, the repercussions for each of you personally should you lose even twenty per cent of the cases will be extraordinary."

Which finally draws Corn Field into the open, into the range of my fire. "We are aware of our somewhat delicate situation, Mr. Drinkwater—"

"More bullshit." I take him head on. "Pardon my French. The situation is not 'somewhat delicate'. You guys are fucked. I hope you're enjoying it because you're royally screwed. When this company goes down, there won't be a rock big enough to hide under. Forget about visiting America. If the Securities and Exchange Commission doesn't hunt you down, little old ladies in the streets will be whacking at you with their umbrellas."

This time, rather than supporting my cause, M.C.S. slips free from his frayed tether on reality. "My arthritis is killing me! Why doesn't anybody listen when I'm talking?"

Immediately, C.C. groans from the depths of his soul, a rich, gutteral lament. He plasters his hands over his face, and rocks himself forward and back, forward and back.

We must all stop and look. Even I'm startled. In a moment he composes himself, as though nothing at all had occurred. He sits back in his chair, and looks around at the faces staring at him.

"You sing a song of sad solution, Sparrow," Field tells me, his sycophantic style at full-throttle. "You are an extraordinary genius. Tell us what to do."

Perhaps the words are spoken silently to myself, although it is possible that they slip out from under my breath. "Mountebanks and demons, meet your master." Clearing my throat, I proceed with the content of my proposal. "Gentlemen, in exchange for a seat on the Board and the use of two private jets, I am prepared to invest, today, five million dollars in OIS. That will satisfy your immediate cash shortages. News of fresh money will interest the banks. The further bulletin that OIS will undergo a complete and thorough audit will return a measure of confidence to the marketplace. Naturally, I will assign the auditor and I am prepared to oversee the work. We will discover, gentlemen, that OIS has more money than current accounting procedures reveal. My intention is to save this company's skin. I alone, among all of you, am willing to put up cash at this stage of the game. And do not underestimate the value of outside money. A new investment will have impact beyond the mere dollars and cents."

Oh, like any family, we will enjoy our squabbles and disputes. I shall hear dissenting voices. The Spaniard, G.S., objects to having OIS salvaged with OIS money. He wants me to add fresh capital that is purely my own. He gets hopping mad when I further demand that OIS guarantee my loan. I challenge him to put up his own dough or shut up. In the end, he believes that his money is safer in a bank account than with OIS. To those who object to my level of responsibility, I note that I am putting myself on the firing line, that criminal charges are likely to ricochet off them onto me. Worried about his own hide, Corn Field isn't at all happy, and goes along with things because he has no choice. He created this company but he has no clue how to save it. The Board votes. It's unanimous. I'm in.

I spread my wings.

A gentle sparrow settles upon my tertiaries, primed for flight.

"Nice work," Corn says to me afterward. "How did you do it?"

"You were here. You saw."

"You're a magician."

"You're an ingratiating toady. Oh, lighten up. I mean it as a compliment. You have style, you have flare. I'll take care of you, Corny, rest assured of that."

From his seat, M.C.S. bellows out, "Fine! He saves OIS. What's he going to do about my arthritis? Tell me that!"

"You really ought to get the nuts and the senile wonders off your board, Corn."

"My board? For how long, Sparrow?"

Being in power is such a lark.

On my behalf, an OIS secretary contacts Uncle in Montreal, and I order the transfer of funds. I also advise him to proceed with the establishment of numbered companies in Panama. Then I call Barclay in Paris. He's been waiting anxiously, drinking the whole time.

"Sharpen your pencils, bro, we got the gig." He lets out a war whoop. "Do another one for me," I ask him. "I have to retain my composure at this end." Barclay erupts once again.

Next I put a call through to the coast of Maine.

First I get Zeke, who gurgles. Then Zack, who is silent. Hannah finally jumps on the line.

"Where are you calling from?"

"Geneva."

"How's Mom?"

"She's having a ball. How are the kids?"

"Out of control. How are you?"

"Hannah, I'm in orbit."

"Sparrow? What's going on?"

"I've just taken the biggest step of my life."

Wait for a response.

She's quiet.

"Hannah?"

Asks me, "Why?"

"I lot of people ... people will get hurt if I don't pull this one off. I have to do it, Hannah. I'm sorry. It will change our lives."

"That's what I'm afraid of. Sparrow?"

"Yes?" Our line's breaking up.

"It's okay." Something incomprehensible. Then, "Do what you have to do. Don't worry about us. We're fine. I love you, Sparrow."

"Love you too, babe."

"Hello to Mom."

"Kiss the boys."

I step out into the bright Geneva sunlight to stand by the lake below the mountains and the sky. Don't know what to do with myself, or how to celebrate. I'm not sure whom I have become. In the clear water of Lake Geneva, I'm not convinced that I recognize my own reflection.

*

Getting a grasp on my new true life was more difficult than expected. Unlike Barclay, I had never aspired to the high hills of international finance. Uncle Butter used to daydream about the three of us ruling the world—I had been too wise to take him seriously. Now, here I was. In Geneva. Messing with the strings of prosperity. For a change I was not the marionette, I had become the puppeteer.

Just trying to latch onto the spinning top of consequences that I had spun into motion was a dizzying experience.

Ever stare yourself in the face and not recognize the image?

How to commemorate the victory? How to sanction the future? How to bid farewell to a plebian past? Restlessly, I walked, jogged, sprinted, and walked some more.

Back at the hotel I looked for Mom, hoping to celebrate with her. Either she was looting fashion stores or overdosing her grey-matter on modern art. She had not returned.

Killed time in the bar.

Le Gentihomme was a landmark in Geneva for sophisticated dining and imbibing. Neither it nor the city is particularly known for licentious behaviour, so I was surprised to find myself the object of a handsome woman's attention. I was seated at one end of the bar, downwind from the breeze of her invitation. For the record, I did offer a modicum of resistance. She smiled, and crossed her legs. The lovely line of her calves and ankles a strong allure. I was not the sort of man who did this sort of thing, yet I was attracted to the way she laughed each time that I protected myself with shyness or a sip from my drink.

What could it hurt? I went over to say hello.

Just to say hello.

I said, "Hello."

She pegged me for one of her countrymen. "Let me guess. Michigan. Maybe Detroit. Am I right?"

And I had worked so hard to look New York. Was that what this was all about? She needed the company of a fellow American in this land of uppity foreigners? As I required greater meaning in my relationships, I did not reveal that I had been conceived in a Georgia swamp, born and raised in a Mississippi asylum. "I'm from Montreal."

She stared.

"That's in Canada."

"Never met a Canadian before." Note her consternation. She was hobnobbing with an inferior species, softening only when I identified the Texas lilt of her voice.

"The Lone Star State," I recited, hoping to make her comfortable. "The Texas Longhorns, the Dallas Cowboys, the Houston Astrodome. Lubbock, Texas, Buddy Holly's hometown."

Knowing the minds of men, regardless of their nationality, she cleverly established that she was not a working girl. As it turned out, her circumstances were remarkably similar to my own. This yellow rose had come to Switzerland to establish links between a Geneva bank and a Galveston investment company—instinct warned me she was laundering dirty cash—and having successfully completed her mission she had found herself in the mood for a spree.

"My associate is celebrating by taking a nap. Me, I'm just as tired. Where I come from a nap in the afternoon wastes a perfectly good bed."

And she looked at me. Blinked. Making money, closing deals, had her juices flowing.

Making money, closing deals, had my own hormones hopping.

"I'm attached," I parried. Rather weakly, that I'll concede.

She demonstrated how the bar lights refracted off her diamond ring. "Aren't we all?"

At close range, she was not the beauty she had appeared to be when seen from a distance and perched on a bar stool. The splendid legginess of her distracted the eye, nullifying various imperfections. At the risk of defeating my own excuses, I point out that my attraction was not simply for the woman, that it was also for the moment. I had become somebody else. I was teetering on the pinnacle of my extraordinary success, for which she offered a prize of blatant, come-on-to-me, Texas-style rutting.

She was waiting for my reply.

"We'll have to use your room," I hedged. If only she'd say no, then I could escape.

"We'll have to use your room," she echoed back at me.

"My travelling companion might return prematurely," I pointed out.

"My travelling companion is snoring as we speak."

Checked my Swiss watch. Turn Mom loose on art galleries and she could be cited for deserting the human race. The additional hindrance of finding her way around a strange city should slow her down as well. This woman and I might have two hours together, one to be safe.

"If we're out of the room by four ..." I let the invitation hang.

"Wham bam, thank you, ma'm." She checked her own watch, calculating if a hurried liaison was worth the trouble. "In that case,"—my heart sank anticipating rejection—"we'd better get cracking."

Know this. Adultery was a line I had not crossed. Nor had I experienced a strong inclination to do so, except in reverie. I don't mean to be boastful, I had simply never been presented with an obvious opportunity. Family and business had left me too busy and too tired to pay the pretty girls much mind. Hannah and I remained reasonably passionate (if that's not a contradiction in terms). Suddenly, I was rising in an elevator and felt the sabre of my deceit rattling my cage. Fortune had made this so easy. The woman, the opportunity, the inclination, the distance from home, my need to celebrate my new true life, my becoming somebody else, my incursion into the den of those who manipulate and decide the fate of nations—destiny had conspired to inaugurate my corruption. Kismet. What shocked me was the power, the new-born fury, of my sexual proclivity. Technically, I had a choice, but not in practice.

Wanting this woman, I was wholly intent on base, delirious, riotous sex. Call the Fire Department to douse the flames. I was wholly anxious for an illicit, no-holds-barred, anonymous free-for-all. I didn't know her name. I didn't ask.

In the midst of the fever of our tempest upon that bed I was awakened to a sexual savagery long dormant. The Texan was as mighty as her State, issuing curses and demands in a stream of wanton consciousness. When it was my turn she accommodated my surly lust.

What happened was this. This was what happened. In the midst of our fever I got up from the bed and went to the closet. I took out the winter coat that I had purchased on this trip and put it on. My cape. Black-robed, with an impressive wing-span, I returned to the laughing, writhing woman on the bed. Covered her with the full breadth of my primaries, tickling her with my tertiaries. Ravished her, and she me, according to the whims of our desires.

This is what happened. What happened was this. In the midst of our fever, in the muck of our slough, in the fecund swamp of our thrashing, my mother opened the door. She observed the gyrating black mound on the bed, and begged the question, "What art thee?"

I jerked up. The robe fell from my head, exposing the woman beneath me. Mom suffered an audible intake of breath, and dropped the arsenal of packages she had carried home. She was wearing an unusual assortment of colours, including a mauve sweater inappropriate for the climate, and a bandanna that dangled its price tag. A chronic bag lady with credit cards. The woman to whom I was fitted was the most dismayed of all, asking, "Is she your wife?"

At that most miserable moment, I was ready to defend my reputation and status. "Mother," I corrected her. The consensus being that we do not select our mothers, and cannot be responsible for them.

"You travel with your mom?" My partner sounded incredulous. Her legs wrapped around the feathers of my back and ass.

"Just this once," I told her.

Mom, as casually as you please, crossed the room, sat down with her legs tucked under her, and babbled. "I bought so many wonderful things, Sparrow. Dresses and shoes and hats and the prettiest kerchiefs thou hast ever seen. Thou art in the poorhouse now!"

Beneath me the woman resumed her grip. Her legs binding me tight. Her slippery quim gave me a squeeze.

I looked dead into her eyes.

"Who sent you?" I demanded to know. Trying to disengage heightened the fury of her pleasure. Twist and snap. To no avail. She sighed and slid and pleasured her desire. Did I have to ejaculate to wrench myself free? What game was she playing? Didn't she know my mother was in the room? *"Who sent you?"*

"Sweetheart," she chided me, "wouldn't you like to know?"

"Oh, Sparrow! Thanks for bringing me here. Geneva has made me different. It has! It's like being in heaven. I always wanted to go to heaven. There are no crazy people there. In heaven they don't have schizophrenics, not one, they cure them first before they let them in the door."

An eruption. My release clenched between my teeth.

One low, raven's groan.

"You demon!" I hissed at my mate.

"I'll take that—" and she groaned too—"as a compliment." Her back arched, her breathing came in spurts, her head flailed from side to side, she shook with the appeasement of her flesh, with the mortification of mine.

"Sparrow!" Mom shouted. "Don't you know? I'm really really really really really really really really really *really really really really* cured!"

For Mom to be so happy, she must have been feeling awfully sad. For her to be so utterly optimistic, she must have been tapping great despair.

11.

Goodbyes Now

The day's crucial hour.

A man who is feeling quite numb, perplexed by lassitude and fatigue, resurrects the slumping constituency of his body, and shuffles to the window high above the street. He looks up. Rain. A sky as dull as skyscraper cement. New York's tallest towers are decapitated by low slung clouds. Through them, lights as countless as stars, as numerous as the bright eyes of the dead, emit a sad, afternoon glow. In these headless obelisks, deals are being negotiated, minor celebrations and trivial disappointments tick by like seconds, another means of telling time.

He looks down. To the plunge of street below.

The man has never known a defeat this crushing, this absolute.

Few men have.

The dreariness of the rain is a comfort. Far below, Dinky Toy taxis and antlike humans are being soaked. If only the city would black out, if only the elevators would stop between floors or plummet, if only these monoliths would topple, one by one the buildings fall down, then he could accept the news, and embrace a destiny of ruin.

Fate has made provision for rain. His cosmic value adds up to little more than that.

A colossal ache wrenches the man's spine. The day's been a grind. A four-hour thrashing by the Securities and Exchange Commission depleted his stamina. Over lunch, his own lawyers hammered away at him, demanding that he yield. The imbeciles don't understand. To them, it's business. It used to be that for him. Now it's his life, a point he must keep to himself. Negotiations crumble if a man insists, "Dammit, this is my life! Don't take it away from me." Say that, and in a trice dignity is lost along with the corporation.

That's what's left, what keeps him in this God-forsaken hole of an office suited for no one better than middle managers, whittling away at the terms of his surrender. He must salvage dignity. Dignity will allow him to believe that once upon a time he had had a life, that once he knew success. Dignity will be the justification to keep himself alive. With his dignity intact he can succour his hatred and fashion his revenge. The others fail to grasp that nuance. They think six-and-a-half million dollars is fair. The man knows better. He knows about fairness, that the only fairness is revenge.

Seated at the large oval table behind him, a stranger awaits his response. The second man has no identity. He is an emissary from people equally unknown.

The man at the window loosens his tie. As a concession to his troubles he has worn a business suit as a last, pathetic grasp at credibility. In his heyday, he had snubbed the very world that had made him rich, he had declared his real power by choosing outrageous garb.

"That's the best that you can do?" Now he's caving in. He knows how feeble his remark must sound.

"Our price rises above market value, Mr. Field," the stranger observes.

Cornelius Field chortles. "Not so long ago my shares were worth sixty-five million."

"That's how my client arrived at his offer. He believes that ten per cent of their former worth is fair, under the circumstances."

Eleven months ago, *Playboy* magazine did a pictorial on his lifestyle. Bimbos gathered at his pool. Money flowed from taps, from artesian wells. If a mugger stabbed him, money would rupture from his spleen. In those days he was probably shitting gold coins, he just never bothered to check. Although Cornelius Field is willing to concede that he has made a few mistakes, by his estimation the cost for his errors is too severe. It's grotesque. *It's not fair.* Why must he be brought so low? How does he deserve this relentless, heartless humiliation?

"Allow me to reiterate, Mr. Field. The most important aspect of this deal is for you to extricate yourself from Overseas Investment. Your advisors have told you to get out and to get out quickly. This is the best offer to come your way. Possibly the only offer."

"I have another in hand." Sparrow Drinkwater and Barclay Boisvert put together a deal. It's complex and probably crooked. Certain liabilities and lawsuits would remain attached to him. Anyhow. He would not sell to those two bastards with a gun to his head.

"Then I must assume that mine is the preferred offer."

He knew that. Field had sent the lawyers out of the room because a single point remained to be clarified, a condition he needed to press in confidence.

"Mr.—whoever-you-are, whoever-you-represent. Last week you gave me a telephone number. An exchange in Maine."

A sign of worry? The man seemed taken aback. "Yes?"

"I checked it out. The region served by that number is Mount Desert Island."

"Yes?"

"Mount Desert is overrun by Rockefellers. Scads of Philadelphia money summers up there."

"Yes?"

"Mister, are you representing Rockefellers?"

"You know I cannot answer questions of that nature."

The few short strides back to the table demand an effort. Field feels his body rebel, the desire to toss off the stress, to return to civilian duty violent inside him. To love again, to laugh, to play a few rounds of golf. To savour a mid-day cocktail by the pool while nude beauties float under the line of his vision. All he has to do is summon depleted reserves and hang tough. The best revenge requires dignity. Otherwise it leads to another unbecoming defeat. Dignity, in turn, is the best revenge.

Coming around the table, Field notices a smudge on the stranger's shoe. "Hate this weather. How can a fellow keep his shoes polished in such a climate, mmm?" Cross-legged, the stranger turns his toe about to examine the blemish, shocked when Field is suddenly buffing the offending spot with his own handkerchief. Field looks up, his face inches away. Whispers, "Have I shown you pictures of my girls?"

The man clears his throat uncomfortably. "I never realized that you were a family man."

Putting away the blackened handkerchief, Cornelius Field chuckles and licks his thin lips. From his inner breast pocket he pulls out photographs. He arranges the bathing beauties on the table. "Take your pick," he suggests quietly. "Go ahead. Choose. Show me your favourite."

The man clears his throat again. Scans the sunny flesh. "Lovely girls," he says.

"You can't tell me whom you're representing. But you can give some indication of whom you're not representing."

"I can't do that."

"You're not representing the Pope."

"No, I'm not representing the Pope."

"You're not representing the President of the United States."

"Not to my knowledge. But stop this. I cannot entertain your inquisitive nature, Mr. Field. You might hit on the right people, then if I deny it, you would have cause to invalidate the deal later."

Field nudges his shoulder. "Tough choice, huh? Pretty girls. Don't feel you have to limit yourself to one. Make a selection."

"My clients insist on anonymity."

"Right. A Panamanian numbered company. I've had experience with those myself. Tell me straight out, are you, or are you not, representing Sparrow Drinkwater, or Barclay Boisvert? Just a yes or no. If you prefer, a simple nod of your head. Then make a selection."

"As I've tried to indicate to you, Mr. Field, I cannot entertain this line of questioning."

"Then," Field ponders, "perhaps I cannot sign your agreement."

He resumes his place on the opposite side of the table, the busty volleyball squad between them. Both men fail to look at one another. The visitor shifts his posture from time to time, self-consciously adjusts the lapels of his jacket. Field twice raises both hands to the table as if addressing a keyboard. Then tinkles imaginary ivories.

"We have reached an impasse," Field notes from the midst of his concerto. "You're in the driver's seat, buddy. Only you can solve it."

"Please, put these girls away. This is inappropriate." The stranger turns his head and waves the beach bunnies off.

"Suit yourself." Sadly, Field reaches over and collects the beauties, returning them to his breast pocket. The one card he has left to play he'd rather not deploy. There should be no bluffs in business, only threats you're willing to carry out. All he's got left to do is bluff.

"You need this deal," the stranger reminds him.

Field contends, "I need this deal like I need to suck on a loaded gun. I need this deal like I need to jump off the roof. How will your clients feel when you return empty-handed, when you tell them I spilled my brains, that my estate will be in litigation for a century?"

"Allow me to remind you that an untimely death would only open the door to Drinkwater and Boisvert. Could they wish for more?"

"Then what are you saying?" He hoped that suicide could trump his antagonist. Instead, the card is treated as a mere joker.

The guest sighs. "Perhaps this will do. To my knowledge, my clients anticipate that their first order of business will be to wrest control from the hands of Mr. Drinkwater and Mr. Boisvert. They can't do it without your block."

Bingo! "So it is someone who's already on the Board. Probably Noseguard. He's teamed up with Rockefellers before. Bragged about it anyway. Old wealth has always been jealous of my success."

"I'm not revealing that it is, or that it is not, Rockefellers. I'm merely pointing out that if it is Rockefellers, or any old-wealth family, they would want to keep their involvement in an offshore, tax-dodge company private. Think of your own best interests, Mr. Field. Never mind about the buyer."

"The identity of the buyer means everything to me! Six-and-a-half million, that's an outrage. A pittance. The only satisfaction I can take from this arrangement is the knowledge that OIS is in good hands."

"Rest assured. I represent astute business people."

"As long as that Drinkwater bastard and that mother-fucker Boisvert get theirs."

"Is that what you're worried about? Let me tell you what I overheard. One of my clients told another, 'The two rats must go.' "

Finally, success. He had broken through the facade of silence. Cornelius Field picked up the pen. "Glad to hear it. Where do I sign?"

"Please," the man indicated, "if I can have your John Hancock right here, and again at the bottom, we'll be off and running. Initial the pages. Upon receiving your block of the company, I am authorized to issue payment."

"Six point five million," Field mutters under his breath. "Peanuts!"

"Not where I come from," the gentleman argues.

Field finishes his signature with a flourish. And announces obliquely, "Revenge is mine. It's so goddamned sweet."

Standing, the stranger offers his hand. "Let's sssssshake on that."

*

Isn't it strange, isn't it incomprehensible, the lives we inhabit? What are we doing here? Anywhere? A brief interlude ago, as a sedate summer resident on Great Cranberry Island, my extra-curricular activities rarely extended beyond skipping stones across the water at sunset, or hiking at dawn. I might ride a bicycle, or challenge my mother to a game of croquet at the Claremont Inn. I might sail an International on the Western Way. Outside that summer respite, I was comfortably moored in suburbia, the captain of a modest, successful firm.

Mornings were distinguished by their ease. I'd shower and shave, dress quickly, and take myself downstairs to the breakfast nook. Orange juice and toast, boysenberry preserve. On a day that is lucid in memory, Hannah was off to her monthly power breakfast down at the Ritz Carlton (her version thereof, a female malady, a gathering of mothers who reminisce about their previous lives as bohemians), having dispatched the kids to pre-school. Before my ritual walk to the office, I stepped into the bower of my back garden to have a chat with Mom. She was lounging in a ribbon of light not blocked by the shadows of the house and trees.

"How's tricks, Mom?"

"Fine and dandy, Daddy-o. How art thee, Sparrow? Thy ugly puss is in the paper again."

The business section of *The Gazette* lay in a fold across her lap. Local media had been impressed by my hometown heroics and I had granted the occasional interview. A blossoming reputation was good for the typewriter service business, September being the month when a majority of contracts came up for grabs.

"How do you like having a famous son?" Pulling up a lawn chair I sat down beside her. The weather had been unseasonably warm. Bees pilfered nectar from the flowers. Light breezes patrolled the highest leaves. Soon, colours would appear. Then snow.

"It's okay," she decided, altogether not that impressed. "Thee looks like some other person in the papers. What makes thy eyes go small? I been thinking, Sparrow."

"What about?"

"I'm completely cured now. I'm completely cured, so I think it would be very nice to become somebody else."

"Ah, what does this mean? Sounds slightly bonkers to me, Mom." As if she had fused with the peace of the garden and expected her own colours to change with autumn's advance, my mother was in a meditative mood.

"Is not something crazy, Sparrow? I been thinking about it. Who I used to be, that happened by accident. I never had a chance to be just me. I never had a chance to turn out like I wanted. Now I can do that, me. I want to become somebody who is just me. I want to become … me, a real and a true person called—" and she lifted her chin and straightened her posture as though posing for a camera, "—Sheilagh Drinkwater."

Her ambition may have been misconstrued but I was willing to credit her resolve. "Fair enough. One thing, try not to become a stranger, okay? That's all I ask. Whoever you intend to be, make sure you're still my mother. I don't want anyone else. But this reminds me, we're overdue for a chat. This business about being completely cured— you are taking your dosage just the same?"

"I don't know. Maybe."

"What do you mean, maybe?"

"I'm cured, Sparrow."

"Do us a favour and stay that way. Take your dosage. It's so light now it hardly affects you at all."

"I don't need it any more."

"Take it anyway. Think how disappointed you'd be if you had a relapse. You're cured, so stay cured. Take your medicine, Mom. It's the only way."

"Okay, sure. Why not?"

She was being remarkably conciliatory. Maybe she really was cured.

My mother had gathered her favourite house plants around her in the back garden. She liked to treat them to a breath of freedom and fresh air. The scent of hibiscus especially enchanted her, apparently because she was the only person alive able to detect it.

"Sparrow," Mom wanted to know, "why is thy picture in the paper? I don't understand business stuff much. What's it about this time?"

"It's complicated. Barclay and me, we're working with this company called OIS? It used to do well because people like to cheat on their taxes. OIS figured out a way to help. The company was put together by cheaters, it's being run by jerks. So if Barc and I succeed, then cheaters will prosper. As will we. But. If we manage to put the company back together again, then the looters and the pirates—the lawyers, in other words—they'll be around to pick it apart. That's my dilemma. If we fail, the cheaters lose and so do we. Sometimes it's hard to see how we can win."

"I know what. Why don't thee do nothing?"

I touched the sunny spot on her forearm. "That's the big question, Mom. The answer worries me. I should warn you, it could mean major changes for us. In a way, I might have to become someone else, just like you. You might have to become someone else only you won't have much choice in the matter. We might all be living different lives soon."

"Why?"

"Things change. Let's put it that way. People can't climb out of a swamp and compose a civilization without going through changes. We could be facing a few. I don't see how to avoid it."

Covering my hand with her own, she said, "I think thee will do what's right."

I felt obliged to shake my head in the negative. "There's no clear right or wrong anymore, not that I can see. Somebody will pick OIS apart. The only question left is whom."

"Does thou know what I think?" She fixed me with her most cunning smile, and I must confess that it did not look wonky at all, that she did not look crazed.

"What do you think, Mom?"

"I think thee should stay here," she piped up, "close thy eyes, and spend a day in the garden."

"Problem-avoidance isn't the answer here, Mom."

"Works for me!" We shared a good laugh. After that I kissed her goodbye, squeezed her hand, and departed for work.

Those early morning strolls—and I preferred to walk to the office—were private moments. A time to chart flights of fancy. Scan the soul, or yesterday's sports scores. Refine a business stratagem, develop an erotic fantasy, muse—whatever's going. The beauty of those intervals I can better appreciate now. Without being fully cognizant of the fact at the time, my walks had benefited from a complete absence of demented, flying bullets. Dodging small-arms fire was never an issue. On rare occasion a truck might backfire, did I bother to duck? Never. Not once. Not back then. Bless 'em, those were the last of the good old days.

Don't all of us walk around with people in our heads who have had little effect or influence on our lives, and yet whose memories, when tripped, provoke an instant smile or a frown, or sponsor both reactions simultaneously? Romping Ron Deguire's like that. He sticks to my brain like dog-poo on a shoe. More than anyone he defines my life for me as a small businessman.

"Do you know why we call Woodburn Office Equipment, WOE?" I asked him one time after he had committed another glaring affront.

Sheepishly, knowing he'd be wrong, because he was always wrong, he answered, "'Cause that's its initials?"

"No, Ron, it's because you're here."

On that day, which was to be an auspicious day although I didn't know it yet, I had called Ron into my office to fire him. I elected to do it slowly, to inflict as much pain as possible. I figured I had a right.

A glum slug, Woodburn Office Equipment's Sales Manager sat on the opposite side of my desk and knew what was coming. He looked whipped, a sad sight given the rough-hewn, back-alley caste to the man. Romping Ron possessed the only natural talent for sales on my staff. He was tough, decisive, aggressive, energetic, innovative, a talker, gifted with an innate will to nail down the best possible price for his firm. In our business, maintenance contracts were negotiable. To establish a set price would leave us vulnerable to being undercut by competitors. Never knowing what we charged where, the competition had to guess high, or low, winning some but losing as often. Each September, in those pre-computer days, type-writer service companies played musical contracts. Overall my business was successful because we concentrated on stripping work away from IBM, a corporation committed to a one-(exorbitant)-price-for-all policy. Maintenance was the refuse side of the office equipment business, IBM was the garbage dump, and the rest of us were the maggots, flies, and creepy-crawlers. As our success increased, Woodburn was frequently subjected to raids by small companies more mean-spirited than us. We maintained our focus on IBM, but we also had to stave off the pests. When the infighting got rough, Romping Ron excelled. The rest of my staff was more likely to capitulate on price immediately, as though the very idea of a monetary transaction between supplier and client smudged their delicate sensibilities. Most of my people thought like consumers—not Romping Ron. A bona fide seller, he played these little games to win. More often than not, through a brilliant blend of brow-beating, muck-slinging, wining and dining (the whole time, of course, driving home our superior service, professional courtesy, and choice seats at the Forum—"Who'd you get last season, the Rangers? How'd you like to see the Bruins this year?"), Romping Ron would carry home the contract despite being the highest bidder next to IBM. He was my main man, my number one slimy sluggo.

But enough was enough already.

Counterpoint to his many virtues, Ron Deguire was also the most difficult challenge to my employee-management skills. His aggressiveness readily misfired. Ron's single-mindedness and savvy negotiating skills masked the disconcerting news that he was not particularly bright. His immaculate grooming and attention to attire highlighted a ridiculous sense of style. Alone among my salesmen and saleswomen, Ron possessed ambition. Among them all, he was the least likely to succeed.

What Ron didn't know, although I had done my best to get the point across, was that he had found his niche. There could be no more perfect calling for someone of his ilk than Sales Manager of an office equipment company. He needed to act like a bigshot—I gave him a title and permitted him to wear his garish suits. Being successful, he did well financially. But Romping Ron could not understand why some people jumped out in front of the pack and he did not. Ron found it galling that I was younger and richer than him, that my name cropped up in the papers. How was it that I breezed through the business world while his days were fraught with bootlicking, stress, and cold calls? Why didn't Sparrow Drinkwater, the goddamn boss with the dumb name, make cold calls? Whenever the frustration built to volcanic proportions, Romping Ron would erupt by doing something stupid.

One time he took away my best technician. Together they tried to form their own company by stealing Woodburn clients. The technician (to Ron's dismay, although I had expected it to happen) assumed that being a partner guaranteed that oil would never touch his hands again, so the real work, the greasy, messy, repetitive work, did not get done. Soon, Romping Ron was beset by a Blizzard of Bills, a Mountain of Mouths to feed, and something he had not counted on—me. Having had the good sense to respect his salesmanship, I had personally visited each vulnerable client and one way or another secured my base. Penitent in my office, Ron had returned with his shoulders slumped. I had no intention of taking him back, for all his worth he was a major headache, but above all Ron was a salesman and capable of marketing himself. He pulled out a trump card—his wife's sorry state. She was mentally ill, subject to roomy, prolonged depressions. Ron complained to me that a week earlier she had had to be hospitalized. Home again, the gal was not in a fun mood. I listened to his tale of WOE and in the end hired him back.

Something similar happened the time he went to work for one of my competitors. After the scavenger-firm used Ron's hefty sales commissions to pay off creditors, preferring to be in debt to Romping Ron instead, I found him teary-eyed at my door. Later he would embark upon a new career in pharmaceutical sales. He figured he'd have it made because his wife stocked the house with pills. At the very least, he might corner a discount. Once again, Romping Ron, the pooch with the toothless bark, found himself dog-paddling beyond his intellectual and cultural depth. Again and again I threw him a line, and always tried to impress upon him the beauty and perfection of his situation as a mutt aboard my ship.

His latest gaff was a doozy.

"Ron, it's a matter of ethics." I spoke slowly, softly, tightening the vise, watching him wince and enjoying every second. "We have standards. Like

it or not, the company's standards are your standards. We don't pay kickbacks. We don't cut corners. We charge only for what service we provide.
We guarantee our work. And number one, we don't sleep with our clients
in exchange for a contract."

He had gone further than that. A certain trust company had
eluded our grasp for years. Its management believed that IBM alone
possessed the appropriate stature to fiddle with their machines. Romping Ron Deguire, not knowing when to quit, took the obese Purchasing Agent to bed, and when that still did not elicit her signature on a
contract, he promised to marry the lady. She signed. That's when he
let it slip that he was already married. He mentioned his wife's illness,
and perhaps it would be better if they waited until her health
improved? Yeah, perhaps they ought to hold off on wedding plans until
his own marital situation was resolved.

"I fucked clients before," Romping Ron was now pointing out to
me. "This one's out of her tree, crumb. She don't know the score." He
considered it his mission to introduce me to the seamy side of life, as
though I was an innocent in need of his base instruction.

"You don't get it, do you? Saying you fucked clients before does not
excuse your action. It makes things worse."

He thought about that, and I could tell he was struggling over
whether he should pull out his you-don't-understand-how-tough-it-is-
out-there speech, or whether he should go straight to saving his hide and
speak about his wife. I knew what he would do. He chose to exploit my
weakness by detailing the horrors of his wife's malaise. He even managed
to work my mother into the conversation. I listened. Steeling myself.

Then I told him, "Ron, it's not just that you fucked a Purchasing
Agent. That alone puts you up to your earlobes in pigeon muck with me.
As it happens, the P.A. is the C.E.O.'s sister-in-law. All of a sudden he's
got the family spinster on his case demanding that your balls be shipped to
her by Christmas, in time to be hung with the mistletoe. Ron, I cannot
allow a man of his influence to be pissed off at my company. We won't get
his business, we can kiss it goodbye—I'm shredding the contract—but
there's more exposure here than that. He has friends. Friends who happen
to be clients of ours. If I don't do something about you to his satisfaction—to his sister-in-law's satisfaction, if you'll excuse the reference—
then good customers of ours, big customers of ours, will peel away."

Tears sprouted in Romping Ron's eyes, water that had not been
pumped to the surface by my gentle drubbing. Ron was frustrated by a
lifetime of screwing up. When he played within the lines and abided by

the rules, he got along. When he submitted to the discipline of my instruction he managed to succeed. Ron had concluded that everyone above him had reached their station by overstepping the bounds, and whether or not that was true, what he could not get into his ass-for-brains was that he simply did not possess the talent to freelance. Every time he tried it, like clockwork, he fucked up. As he was finding out, even when he fucked, he fucked up.

Poor Ron.

"You firing me?" he asked. Before I answered he wanted me to think about something. "How'm I supposed to tell my wife?"

The telephone interrupted my response and altered our lives, mine and Ron's both. I snapped through on the intercom to the outer office, "Helen, I asked you to hold my calls."

"It's Mr. Boisvert," she said.

"Tell Uncle I'll call him back in twenty."

"No, sir, it's Mr. Barclay Boisvert."

I took the call.

Romping Ron slumped in shabby disarray while I listened to Barclay's code. There was no need for me to reply. At the end of his monologue I said, simply, "Plan B." A judgment Barc confirmed. "See you soon."

The moment I hung up, I knew that the world had been transformed. As proof of that, rather than fire Ron, I chose to promote him. Once again, the fates had contrived to save his slimy skin. It's a wonder to me that some people are so remarkably lucky, yet remain so blithely ignorant of their own good fortune. Ron would take my news as censure, as punishment, when in fact I was offering him the opportunity of a lifetime. On a platter. No matter what road was available to him in life, he'd do no better than my offer, yet he would view this last chance as a crumb flicked from a rich man's knee.

I stepped out from behind my desk and sat next to him. Removed the watch from my wrists. My hand was trembling, I noticed.

"See this?"

"Yeah?"

"It's gold. Today it's worth maybe twelve, maybe fourteen hundred dollars retail. Hawk it, you'll get a lot less. Keep it awhile. That's my advice. When gold soars it'll be worth a mint. I want you to have it."

Ron stared at the watch above his nose as if I was trying to hypnotize him.

"Take it."

Reaching up, he accepted the watch, and concluded, "I'm fired."

"Suspended, Ron. Fifteen days. You know my uncle's been expanding our Ottawa office. Ottawa's a sedate town, up there business hasn't
been exposed to aggressive salesmanship. So Uncle's been the right
person for the job. Trouble is, I'm going to need him down here. You're
suspended for fifteen days, Ron, then I'm putting you in charge of the
Ottawa office. It'll mean a move. It'll be a change. No boss to guide you
or keep you under wraps."

"I'm only suspended?" Ron was absorbing the news slowly.

"Without pay, but you get to keep the watch."

"Then Ottawa?"

"It's not Siberia, Ron. Use the next two weeks to find a house, put
yours on the market, that kind of thing."

"I'll have to think it over."

"No, Ron. That's where you always go wrong. Take the job. If you
don't accept immediately, you're fired, and believe me, I swear on my
mother's name, I will never take you back. This is your one big chance.
Recognize it. You'll be in charge. You'll make money. Do things your
way, whatever way you want."

What bothered Ron was that others continually made up his mind
for him. He never knew when he was well off. Grudgingly, he consented to the arrangement, and Romping Ron was out of my hair.

I punched a call through to my personal accountant, then got in
touch with Hannah. "Let's have your folks over for dinner tonight,
okay? ... While we're at it, invite Uncle and Aunt along, and Miss
Plant. I'll call Nina, see if she's free ... Yeah, the whole crew. And make
sure Mom is okay for tonight. If she has something on, tell her to
cancel." Hannah had other plans, I was not giving her time to prepare,
what, she wanted to know, had gotten into me? I could not give her the
details, not over the phone, someone might be listening. "I'm not
asking you to like it ... Yes, it has to be tonight ... Trust me ... Han ... yes
... Hannah? ... please ... whatever you want to make ... I don't care.
Listen, I owe you. I'll make it up to you. In any case, you'll thank me
later ... Okay ... whatever ... eightish ... fine."

I hung up feeling angry with Romping Ron. He was probably in his
office at that moment throwing papers around the room, swearing at
me, sinking imaginary pins in my heart, muttering behind my back to
his colleagues. He didn't know that Ottawa was his first big break, or
that events on the other side of the globe had cleared the way for him.
He didn't know how close he had come to losing his job. If Barclay had
called a minute later, maybe twenty seconds later, Ron would have

been canned. Romping Ron had fifteen days to pack and move to Ottawa, a two-hour jaunt down the highway. He thought I was being unfair and unreasonable, but he was getting off lightly. The man should have compared himself to me. I had less than twenty-four hours to get the hell out of the country.

*

I had been hunting the one who had manipulated my existence. I was tracking the force that had contrived to put my mother on a journey she could not possibly complete. I was seeking the revenge of the inno-cent—reveal yourself, dark shadow, emerge from the blind night, you prick, I'm right here, take me on.

I dare you.

Everything had been accomplished according to plan. I had proven my worth in the boardroom. I'd made a name for myself. Why didn't my benefactor emerge from hiding? He had set me up with Uncle, he had set me up with Barclay, he had set me up to challenge Cornelius Field and *I'm not the one who's crazy here you can't pin that on me!* He had placed me in Uncle's care. Yet Uncle wouldn't say who. Barclay swore he didn't know what I was talking about, but the man's been con-firmed as an inveterate liar, I couldn't trust him for a minute. If Barclay had an advantage with some wealthy demagogue who finagled women to throw themselves off bridges and then plotted to have the child of such a woman raised in his own image, he was not about to reveal the bastard's identity to me.

Miss Plant, my old friend, the witch of Bloomfield Street, kept her own counsel on the matter. The poor old girl had not aged well, she had never enjoyed enough sunlight or exercise, and was often infirm. For the longest time, Mom would resist going to see her, complaining that she was the craziest person she knew. After Miss Plant began having spells, after she had become needy, the two of them forged a friendship. I suppose the therapy of taking care of someone else for a change served my mother's recovery.

"We become, Sparrow, whom we pursue."

"Fine." I was sitting in the deep cushions of the armchair kitty-corner to the foot of Diedre Plant's bed. "How about I put that one up there with 'we are what we eat', and that other golden oldie, 'we are what we think'."

"We become whom we pursue."

Her disposition did lend credibility, even authenticity, to her— remarks. Curled in the bed, her thin body scarcely creating a wrinkle in the blanket, Diedre Plant spoke from behind her aged face and clear, docile eyes. She had assumed the posture of the mystical, intractable mind, riding above the waves of compromise and indecision, her gaze deflected from the moon of illusions onto the sunrise of pure, august thought. Put another way, I was more willing to accept that she was a seer, a keeper of the flame of covert knowledge, than I was willing to admit that she was an old woman and a dear friend on the verge of dying.

"I'll bite. What do you mean by that?"

Wouldn't you know that she answered with a question, undoubtedly the most infuriating habit pertaining to oracles. "What have I become?" she asked me. I could not bring myself to utter the words, so she answered her own query. "I'm an old witch. A recluse. A hag. Ratty children call me 'Prune-Face'. I'm a know-nothing know-it-all who dispenses—" stopping to hack and wheeze—"wisdom to fools. I always wanted people to find me a trifle menacing. Now I'm merely a menace. You, Sparrow, you've been looking for your black-winged, black-robed progenitor. My reading of the situation tells me you've found him."

"Wrong. I've been looking for my mother's people. My grandparents, if you will. In any case, you're being philosophical again. Which is a polite way of saying you're being dippy."

Swinging into the room with a tray of lemonade and cookies, Mom felt the need to add her two cents worth. "She's not dippy. Thou art the one who's dippy, Sparrow. Thou art the one acting weird all over the world. Thou art the one who gets dressed up in a black robe doing those things to women thou should not do."

"That's my private business." Swift panic, to have had my indiscretion openly discussed.

"Does Hannah know?" Miss Plant wondered.

"What, are you two in cahoots? Leave me alone here. What I do is my own business."

"Men," Miss Plant sighed. Then coughed, and even that wretched agitation sounded wise.

"Sparrow's a real jerk sometimes," my mother, my own mother, proclaimed. You'd think she was a witness for the prosecution. I had not previously known that she felt this way, had hoped that the incident in Geneva had been forgotten. Apparently, Mom knew enough to be discreet around Hannah. Miss Plant, it would seem, was the one with whom she shared such confidences.

"You see what I'm talking about?" Diedre Plant pressured in her frail, squeak of a voice.

I defended myself. "I don't see anything of the sort."

Mom climbed onto the bed to sit at right angles to her patient, their legs crossing at the shins like swords.

"A black robe, Sparrow? When will you face up to it? You've become your own villain. You've become the man you're looking for."

"I'm not looking for him. He's long gone. There's somebody else I'm trying to draw out. You wouldn't understand."

"Maybe more than you know. You are in pursuit of your soul, Sparrow. I know that. You don't want to admit it. A search for the soul requires a tour through darkness. Accept your quest, and your soul may be located. Deny your quest, naturally your soul shall remain lost. 'For what shall it profit a man, if he shall gain the whole world, and lose his own soul?' "

"Give me a break. Now it's my soul I'm looking for. Finding Mom's family is tough enough."

"A man," Diedre Plant decreed, "is a sparrow. But a soul,"—she pointed her index finger to the ceiling—"a soul is a pterodactyl."

I stood. Extricated myself from this mess and company. "You pulled that cross-eyed talk on me before, Miss Plant. No. Don't bat your lashes at me. You know what I'm talking about. You had me tramping around the continent in search of Mom when you knew damn well she lived downtown. You kept us apart for years."

"I told you then. I tell you now. To seek is to become."

"He's out there!" I hurled back at her and turned to escape.

"You're kidding yourself, Sparrow." Trying to shout, her words come out with spittle, a diminished commentary on the vagaries of life. "He's not out there. He's in *there*." Pointing at me.

Perhaps she was right. In Geneva, Barclay had dipped his key into a padlock, snapped it open, and pulled the giant warehouse door across to one side. Within, I would be treated to a pavilion of booty. Is this what I had been seeking? The spoils of avarice? The world's bullion wasted on gimmicks and gadgets? In that warehouse we would find boxes of sterling silver candlesticks, Polaroid cameras, gold Dunhill cigarette lighters by the carton, electric toothbrushes by the case. That's not all. We had stumbled upon hand-tooled leather backgammon sets, Sony tape-recorders, briefcases for the rising executive, and something else—two hundred gold watches. Barclay had been there before, he'd had one of the watches appraised. Each worth more than a grand at a time when gold was pegged at thirty-five bucks an ounce.

Sorting through the goods, I did pass through a sea-change. Until then, we had been dealing with paper money, figures on a balance sheet. For the first time, the spoils were in my hands. For the first time I felt like a looter. What, in this circumstance, was the right thing to do? What was the ethical choice? The goods had been acquired by Cornelius Field or his managers, as gifts for clients and business associates. The company had coiled itself into such a spiral of incompetence it had lost track of its own warehouses, let alone their contents. Those who knew about the stuff had left or been dismissed as a cost-cutting measure (Barclay let a few of them go himself), so that the only people who knew about the warehouses in Geneva were Barclay, myself, and a number of Barclay's accountants. In all (get this), we had discovered one hundred and nineteen warehouses. Each one stuffed with surprise.

"What do we do with all this junk?" Barclay asked.

Return them to OIS control and lawyers would have the assets seized within a fortnight.

"I'm thinking." A lie. Who could think? I was begging time. The poor boy was awash. Figures and boardroom gymnastics were one thing—so much of what we were doing had seemed like sport, a game where the players were identified and the rules composed as we went along. Now, I stood amid a vast emporium of tacky, modern (to use Barc's apt word) junk. I needed a moment to breathe, a few seconds to summon my gumption. Told Barclay, "Drive the Rolls inside. We'll load her up."

Confirmation was visible in his expression. We were grown-up boys now, wending our way in the new world. True, we had already pilfered the pink Rolls Royce from another warehouse, but it had been our sense that we were borrowing it while Barclay did his work in Geneva. Now, to load it up, then to pack the jet and fly this stuff away to our holding companies, that constituted a change. Soon, Panamanian customs agents would be lighting their cigars with gold Dunhills, and we would have embarked upon a particular orientation. We did not speak further about this aspect, him and me, we simply exchanged that confirming look.

We were carting away the history of the world in the trunk of a pink Rolls Royce. All that we are is what we have been. We are gold watches and backgammon sets. We are electric toothbrushes. Take it away, take it out of here. Accumulate. Speculate. Accumulate. Transact. Accumulate. Risk. Accumulate. Accumulate.

"Look at this," Barc said. He had removed an impressive case done up in brass and alligator hide. Out of the swamp we go into the mercantile world. Barclay snapped open the case—it yawned like an alligator's jaws. Inside, two gleaming chrome Lugers.

"Take one," Barclay advised. "You might need it."

That too, was a confirmation of what we were about to do. I'm too self-conscious a bigshot to walk through the world armed. Eventually I gave the Luger to my wife so she'd feel safe on the beach with the kids.

"Derek," I said to Barc's chauffeur, our old friend and nemesis from Park Extension who had hounded me for a job, "load up the watches and cigarette lighters first. Whatever's gold."

"Gotcha."

"Let's talk, bro'," I suggested to my looter-in-arms. While Derek stocked up the trunk, Barc and I made ourselves comfortable in the plush back seat of the Rolls.

"This is how it's playing out," Barc filled me in. "I'm splitting the combine into three separate entities. The banking assets in one, the real estate and insurance interests in another, the mutual funds in a third."

"Makes sense."

"Then we take our hard assets—the banks and the real estate—and divorce them from our liabilities, principally the lawsuits."

"Understood."

"Then we put as much Chinese paper as possible between the two."

"OIS will be left as a shell," was my mild objection.

"It'll be gutted anyway. Later we can pay OIS and the shareholders dividends on the holdings. We can do that for as long as they allow."

"Which means?"

"When the sharks circle for OIS blood, we may be obliged to disengage."

"Which means?"

"We may be forced to keep what is out for ourselves, Sparrow. Otherwise, everything could be lost in the legal shuffle."

"How much are we talking about?"

"Conservatively? Four hundred million. We could go over five hundred."

I had to whistle. "Half a billion dollars. Big bucks for a couple of thugs from Park Ex."

"I was never a thug. Nor do I claim Park Extension as my ethnic origin. I will concede, however, that it is a comfortable fortune for a pair of gentlemen who are presently furnishing their trunk with gold watches."

"We'll need friends, Barc. Friends in high places enjoy gifts. Are we absolutely going to loot OIS, or is there a chance we might save the firm?"

"Should permissions be forthcoming, we will be the salvation of OIS. There's money there, too. What remains doubtful is whether or not we will be afforded the opportunity."

This was how we cooked the deal. People always ask. They want to know. Nothing was terribly onerous about our plans. We did what we had to do. Having made the decision to take the watches, the rest flowed rather easily. When you can walk off with trinkets, then it's not so hard to shuffle pieces of paper. Besides, I had prepared for this eventuality from the beginning. Both Uncle and Derek had been down to Panama on my behalf, Uncle to establish numbered companies, Derek to rent office space and install telephones. Things were hopping, yet everything seemed to be happening apace, inevitability flowering from the seed of my perception in the fecund muck of the world.

"Do we have any problems?" I asked my partner. He, of course, was on the scene night and day, while I commuted intermittently to Geneva.

"Cornelius Field, he's a problem. We have to seize power, Sparrow. I can't have him hanging around. The imbecile tries to thwart me every other minute. Something has to be done or none of this will work."

Every enterprise had obstacles to overcome. Corn Field was mine. "Not to worry. Do this. Leak tidbits of your material to the authorities. Let them put the squeeze on him. When he comes under surveillance for reckless mismanagement, he'll be inclined to sell. Give it the right push, he'll sell fast and cheap."

"Let us say, for the sake of argument, that we have the money. Which we do not, but I suppose we could move OIS funds around. Which, I confess, has its appeal, buying OIS with OIS funds. And let us say further that Field is put into a position where extricating himself from OIS becomes his only hope of avoiding prosecution. Frankly, these matters constitute the easiest part of this deal. What makes you believe that there is any amount of money, or any force of persuasion, which would make him willing to sell to us? Right now, today, Cornelius Field would slit his own throat before he sold to you or me."

I slapped the side of Barc's thigh three times. "Let me take care of that one, bro'. I'll get this problem, you take care of the next one that comes down the pike."

That's all it was. A simple conversation in the back seat of a Rolls Royce in a secret warehouse while gold watches and cigarette lighters were being stashed in the boot by a small-time hood. That's all it takes in this life to claim a piece of the world, a conversation between friends.

Derek jumped into the car behind the wheel. "All done, boss." You'd think he'd hate calling us that, but he got a kick out of it. Grant him his due, Derek was all right. He had his faults, but he was happier driving Barclay around Geneva than he had been knocking off gas stations in Montreal. He tended to be less ruled by ambition than he was by style. Hobnobbing with movers and shakers, cruising in a Rolls, was his kind of life.

"To the airport, Derek, please."

"You got it." We had to wait until he located the ignition key. He kept the passkeys to more than a hundred warehouses in his pockets.

To Diedre Plant I said, "Don't you worry about what I'm becoming. I am what I am. Sooner or later, the man who put Mom in that asylum and then put her on the road, sooner or later he'll have to show himself. I'll force him into the open. Then we'll see what I'm made of—what he's made of, too. Until then, I'm doing all right."

"Mind your back," was Miss Plant's initial advice. I thought that she meant immediately, right at that instant, and I spun. Spinning to face her again, I found her smiling, and she added, "Mind the face in the mirror too."

"Don't get smart. Listen, I came over to invite you to dinner tonight. I'll pick you up. Heaven forbid you should spend more than a millisecond out-of-doors."

Diedre Plant did not immediately respond to my invitation. She seemed intent on gazing at me. Or into me. Finally she said, "Thank you, Sparrow. I'm touched that you would want me there. Such a momentous occasion. I'm sorry, but I find myself especially weak today. I must decline. Can we settle for saying our goodbyes now?"

I just stared back at her. Absurdly dumbfounded. Only my mother was able to break that silence. "What does she mean by that, Sparrow? Goodbyes now. What does Miss Plant mean by that?"

Funny, that she would think to ask me, and not Miss Plant herself. "Don't pay any attention, Mom," I soothed her, returning my mentor's steady gaze. "Miss Plant is just an old witch talking witch-talk."

My friend appreciated that remark. She liked it so much it provoked a cackle. I guess that was her way of saying her goodbyes now.

*

I had asked Nina to arrive early, anticipating that Hannah could use the assistance of a helper and a friend, and that I could properly use a buffer between myself and my angry wife. As things turned out, Hannah was in a far better mood than I had any right to expect. She seemed remarkably cheerful about the frenzied arrangements.

"Who else is coming?" Nina called through from the dining room as she laid out the place-settings.

"My folks, and Sparrow's little extended family," Hannah shouted back. "Some big mystery why."

Intrigued, Nina came through to my study to pose the same question, adding, "Any unattached men on your guest list?"

"I've only invited people I can trust," I replied, deliberately cryptic. "Single men are less than trustworthy."

"No kidding." Nina remained sceptical about the evening. "Sounds dull. Birdie. Why have you invited me to another boring evening in Outer Suburbia?"

"How can you be so rude, Nina, when I have just confessed that you you sit at the very pinnacle of my trustworthy list?"

"Number one, try not to use words like pinnacle. Too erotic. I get hot flashes. Number two, big mistake to trust me, Bird-shot. Gegunda error. For the right price, I'd sell you out in the blink of an eye."

Later, over cocktails in the living room, Hannah and Nina got caught up, while I remained preoccupied with plans. I had reached my pilot from a phone booth, everything was arranged, but I was still sweating the details, searching for anything that might have eluded my scrutiny. After tonight, there would be no going back.

"I've never been so horny," Nina was saying, and my ears perked up. "My hormones are way out of whack. Doorknobs look virile to me. The other day I made a pass at a bicycle that had these really sexy handlebars, with hot red grips? My grocer's at a loss. I can't buy enough turnips, fat carrots, cukes—and bananas! My landlady thinks I'm feeding monkeys. I got bananas coming out of my ears!"

"Not to mention other orifices," Hannah added.

"Not to mention. Hannah, sport, pal, cousin-first-class, won't you *please* put me out of my misery and lend me your husband for a fortnight? I'm so weary, and so *dissatisfied*, with vegetable love."

"Sorry, sweetpea. I've got first dibs on his next moment of free time, provided he's got the energy."

"Sounds like wifely complaints to me, Birdman. Are you being less than attentive to your devoted spouse?"

"Still no steady guy, Nina?" I asked. She tended to binge on lovers, then retreat into celibacy and the blues for months.

"You know what they say, 'A hard man is good to find'. I haven't had much luck lately. What about your chairs, Hannah?"

Innocently, my wife asked, "What about my chairs?" In the living room, we were seated on comfortable, big cushioned sofas and arm-chairs, so the object of her lust was not obvious. Nina was looking through to the dining room, lit by candlelight.

She strolled through to the other room and proceeded to provoke one of the tall knobs that rose from the backs of our chairs with a slow, tantalizing hand-job. "I love the patina of dark wood, don't you? It's smooth. Hard. The right size, with interesting ridges. I love the varnish. Hannah, you little devil. You have very erotic furniture. Can I take a chair home with me?"

"On the bus? Nina! Stop that!"

"Come on, Han! One chair! You have so many. Now I know why you're happy with your lot. Raising children doesn't give you that glow. It's polishing all this furniture."

"God, you're crude. Get a man, girl. Quickly. Before you lose the rest of your marbles."

I was watching the slow, expert hand, rise and fall and squeeze the smooth, deeply varnished mahogany.

Nina, in turn, kept an eye on me.

Even Hannah seemed mesmerized, as if expecting the wood to ejaculate.

Thank God for the doorbell, ringing in our guests.

Somehow we had never managed to have those particular people together in the same room at the same time. Either the Boisverts or my in-laws, or Nina or my mother or the kids, had been absent in the past, and the moment I was pointing this out to everyone the doorbell jin-gled again. Who could be calling at the dinner hour if not Interpol or their Canadian lackeys? Opening the door, I expected handcuffs, and discovered instead a walking miracle—heaven's emissary on leave from sick-bay. Diedre Plant glowed under the porch light. "I wouldn't miss this for the world," she stated, walking past me as straight as a pencil, and just as thin.

So we sat down, one large, unbridled, happy family, and as usual Mom improvised grace.

"We thank thee Father for the food on the table. We thank Thee for, ah, for, ah, we thank thee for the dishes on the table. We thank thee for ... the people at the table. We thank Thee for the children at the table, and, and that's all for now." Not her best rendition, and lifting her head, snapping open a napkin, Mom explained, "Hannah told me don't make it so religious, so I didn't. I hope it was okay for thee." She had singled out the Morgansterns for this overture.

What might have been an awkward moment, for the religious orientation of their grandchildren was a sensitive issue with my in-laws, was diffused by Hannah's father, Zachariah. "Fine, Sheilagh. It was fine. A lovely prayer."

His wife was less than helpful when she thought to add, "Very nice. It's nice to learn about *other people's* religions, but." Fortunately, everyone had the good sense to allow the insinuation to fly by.

Indeed, we drifted through the evening rather well. The dinner party was animated, and even my own misgivings failed to cast much of a shadow. Miss Plant was quiet, as was her wont in company away from her hovel. Seated as still as an icicle in her prim white dress, she melted as the warmth of the night was prolonged. I do believe she had to concentrate to keep from keeling over, that's how weak she had become.

Mom and Nina made jokes between themselves all evening. Invariably a bad influence on her, Nina's naughty whispers incited Mom's ribald instincts and piqued her penchant for mischief. Mom chortled, and mocked my mannerisms, and did a command performance of my habits. Not that funny, really, I don't know where she got those facial tics and judgmental expressions, but she and Nina had a ball.

In a different, and more formal way, Mom also got along with Mrs. Morganstern. My mother-in-law was neurotic. Washing, ironing, and shrink-wrapping her folding money was just one manifestation of that. She was a neat freak. Whenever Mrs. Morganstern pulled one of her house-cleaning stunts, such as holding her breath while the cat strolled through the room, or smuggling her cutlery out to the kitchen to practically scrub off the silver plate, my mother followed her moves with interest, wonder, and a curious sense of pride. Some bee buzzed in her bonnet. Mrs. Morganstern was convinced that my mother was a loony-tune, and every so often Sheilagh felt called upon to put her straight.

"I'm completely cured now, Mrs. Morganstern. Ask anybody."

"How lovely for you, dear. I'm sure you're very happy, but." Probably due to Mom's breathless voice and her quaint 'thees' and 'thous', Mrs. Morganstern tended to address my mother as she did the children.

Although ignorant that this was her last chance, Mom did gain the upper hand that night. "Maybe it will give thee hope."

"Pardon me, Sheilagh, dear?"

"If I can get cured, so can thee!"

I am unable to vouch for what went on around the table over the next few minutes. Nina lay in convulsions on the floor, and I had had to drop down beside her. I was pretending to clean up the children's mess. "It's okay, Mother Morganstern! I saw that noodle fall! We'll get it!" I was on the floor for quite awhile hoping to keep my paroxysm out of view while trying not to look at Nina who would only get me started again.

Zack Senior, Hannah's father, had decided from the outset to behave coolly toward me. Over dinner he concentrated on his grandchildren, while he answered cordial questions from the rest of us with grunts worthy of King Kong. I gathered that he had been studying the newspapers and foolishly reading between the lines. Perhaps he had been engrossed in secrect communications with Diedre Plant. She was on to me, too, although in her case her sources could only have been witchcraft.

Uncle, who had shown up in unusually high spirits, was soon miffed that I had not seated him at one end of the table. He felt usurped by Zachariah. "You're my right hand, man, Unc," I whispered to mollify his funk. "This is where you belong, at my right hand." I gave him a wink and he perked up after that. What a job he had done in New York! Without saying so, he had convinced Corn Field that he was dealing with Rockefellers. What fun he'd had inscribing a cheque for six-point-five million for Field's block of OIS. Peanuts! What a joy it had been for Uncle to have participated in his boys' big move. We were on the go now. We were making our mark now, just as he had always prophesied.

After dessert, I got to my feet to dole out the remnants of my estate. My old life was rapidly coming to a close. Heaven awaited. In more ways than one, I had the impression I was presiding over the reading of my own will.

"As you know, or suspect, this has been a prosperous year for me. Today I would like my family and friends to share in that prosperity. I wish to share not only the bounty of my table, but also the blessings of my life."

"Oh goodie!" Nina exclaimed. "Presents."

"Since we are so amused, I'll begin with you, Nina. It's not a Rolls, it's only a Mercedes, but here are the keys to our car. The papers are in the mail. Enjoy."

I dropped the keys into her astonished palm. Even Nina was momentarily speechless, although it did not take her long to resuscitate that mordant wit. "Hey, Sparrow, this is serious transportation. I couldn't. You know how it is. I have my reputation as a n'er-do-well to consider."

"Even deadbeat scientists need to commute. Drive safely."

Hannah was nodding quietly. "He gave away the car. The car. The Mercedes. Gave it away. Just like that. Has he found religion?"

"Miss Plant," I continued, "Uncle's been working on this one for awhile. The swine's been holding the paper on your house for some time, and he has finally come through." Crossing over to the buffet I pulled out a manila envelope. "You have hereby ceased to be a tenant, Miss Plant. Whether or not you get kicked out is entirely up to you, as you are now the sole proprietor of your home. Woodburn Office Equipment Company has contracted to pay the taxes and utilities on your behalf. Here's your title."

Diedre Plant craned her neck for my kiss as she accepted the deed. Her eyes were moist. "Such a cost," she said. "Such a cost. But thank you, Sparrow, I'm touched by your consideration."

Placing my hand upon his shoulder, I reminded Uncle Butter of our history together. "When I was a child, your home, Aunt Butter's home, became my home. Hannah and I have always tried to make our house your house as well. Now, today, my house, *is* your house. Here're the keys."

"Ah, Sparrow," Hannah interrupted while Uncle dumbly stared at his prize, "can I see you in the kitchen a minute?"

"It's all right, love, bear with me a minute longer." Hannah sat down again. She was trembling. Nina tried to buoy her up with encouraging looks. "Do you understand, Auntie?" I inquired. "This is your house now. You will live here."

"I don't want to put anyone out ..." Aunt suggested sweetly.

"I think Sparrow's gone a little nuts," my mother put in.

"Not to worry, Auntie. We'll be fine. Please keep your opinions to yourself, Mom. Who are you to talk?"

"I know something about it. I know all about going nuts."

"You're the expert on coo-coo-ness, Sheilagh," Nina confirmed, patting her hand. "I always defer to you. You put me to shame."

"That's right."

"Mother and Father Morganstern! Now what can I give you?"

"The kids?" Zack Senior suggested. He may have been serious.

"Sorry."

"That's something anyway," was Hannah's comment. "Whew. We're keeping the children. *Where* we keep them, that's another question."

"Will you settle for my legal practice, Zachariah? Plus I'll throw in the country house in Maine."

"No," Zack Senior stipulated. "Thanks."

His wife contradicted him. "Yes," she said. "Please."

"Done! The deed's in the mail. Here're the keys, Mother Morganstern. Now! Is everybody happy?"

"I didn't get nothing," Mom pointed out.

"I saved the best for last. To you, Mom, and also to you, Hannah, and to you, Zeke, and to you, Zack, I give you paradise. An extended tropical vacation, beginning tomorrow. The jet leaves at six."

"Zowie!" Mom exclaimed, and clapped her hands. Otherwise the room was silent, and soon Mom was objecting to the implied rebuke. "I think paradise is very nice. Doesn't nobody else think so?"

"It's not that simple," Miss Plant mentioned quietly. "We won't be seeing each other anymore, Sheilagh. Sparrow is taking you away with him. That's nice. I think that's very nice. We're sad because we know you won't be coming back."

The disclosure furled Mother's brow.

Hannah had not yet spoken. On occasion she'd sneak a glimpse my way, then return her gaze to the fingers tying knots in her lap. What else could I have done? There had been no easy way to break the news, and I had had to be discreet. We could not have managed this final dinner had I said something sooner. She'd have been too distraught. This way, we had had the chance to say goodbye to everyone. That is, Hannah could say goodbye if she chose to come with me.

"Best of luck!" Uncle Butter belted out. "I know how it is. The blackguards and the vermin, out to get your hide because you tried! You and Barclay *dared* to put OIS under proper management! Those of us who fight for the ethical ssssolution, we're the ones the rabble despises."

Of course Uncle was impressed by his familiar rhetoric, but I was mildly surprised by his grasp of the situation. When I looked up, it was into the gaze of my livid father-in-law.

Zachariah Morganstern stood. By virtue of his girth and bearing, he summoned the attention of the room. "Sparrow Drinkwater," he began, and proceeded to launch into an expurgated version of my life story, "you came out of a swamp and a nuthouse, or so you're fond of saying. You were separated from your mother early. You found her again."

"I found him," Mom corrected.

"Pardon me, Sheilagh. You're right, of course. Sparrow, you were located by your mother and you cared for her, you nursed her back to health."

Mom was glad to have her own diagnosis confirmed. "I told you I got completely cured, didn't I?" she asked no one in particular.

"You married my daughter. Established yourself in business and in the legal profession. You have begun to raise a family, never an easy task, but you've been involved, you've contributed as much as the next guy. Everything has gone along smoothly. Real smooth. Eh, Sparrow? Maybe too smoothly." He paused to stuff his hands in the pockets of his sports coat, to suck on his lips, and finally to shake his head in raging despair.

"Come on, Zachariah," I put in, "it's only business."

"It's business, Zack!" Uncle supported me.

My father-in-law wagged his legal finger at me. "There is business, Sparrow, and there is business."

"I agree. This is business."

"No no no. Your business," Zack Senior stipulated, "that's not business. Your business, I know, I can smell it, is business."

"Sheilagh," Nina put in, "don't you just tingle all over when you're in the company of articulate men?"

"Oh yes I do," Mom agreed.

Zachariah had not stood on his feet to be easily dismissed. "What's the matter with you, boy? Don't you know right from wrong? *What's the matter with you, boy?*" he positively yelled at me, bearing down on me in my own house. "You made me proud of you!" he stormed, as if my life had become a personal affront. "Now look what you have done. You have brought shame, my God, *shame* onto yourself, shame onto my daughter, shame onto my grandsons. Shame onto me. Shame onto all our good names."

"Uncle Zack," Nina tried to interject, "could we ease up a little on the melodramatic throttle, it's too—"

"Shut up, Nina." Just like that, he blew away my one good chance at rescue. "Sparrow, I don't know what the hell it is you hope to accomplish. Just don't include me in your scam." He picked up the keys to the house on Great Cranberry Island and tossed them back in my face. His aim was poor, they hit me in the chest. "You think we're fools? You're giving away your assets, your non-liquid assets, because they'll be confiscated soon anyhow. I don't want your house. My daughter, she doesn't want your paradise. Your sons don't want your legacy." Zachariah sat down again. "Why don't you just take your stuff and get the hell out of here, Sparrow?"

"Ah, it's my house, Zack."

"Actually, it belongs to me now," Uncle Butter reminded us both. "Don't worry. From where I ssssit, you can both sssstay."

"Hannah," Zack Senior said, "your mother and me are leaving now. Your husband is into bad business, Hannah. Take Zeke and Zack, and come with."

That, then, was the crucial moment. All eyes veered across to Hannah. Perhaps if her father had left it alone, perhaps if he had minded his own business and not challenged her, perhaps if he had not forced a choice between my offer of paradise and her father's bid to take her back to Cote St. Luc with Mommy and Daddy, Hannah might have stayed behind. Who knows? Certainly she did not give me a full vote of confidence when she told him, "I'm sorry, Daddy. I'm Sparrow's wife. You know that. He's the father of my children. We're a family. I'll be going with him."

I guess the shock for me was realizing that Hannah, too, had seen this coming. She had already prepared herself.

Funny, how my first thought was to look at Nina. I exhaled relief. Nina conferred a wink of reassurance. That was nice, to learn that I still had a friend in this sorry world.

Zachariah had done it. He had gone and provoked reminders of my past. I had been nurtured in a swamp and been kicked out of Eden. I had journeyed through life. Now I had concluded my last supper as a free man. In the old days, after a last supper, some men got hung on a cross. In modern times it's the electric chair. But I had faith. As always, I knew, the future lay in front of me, my true adventures were waiting for me there.

All but one of our guests had bundled themselves off home, Hannah had put the kids to bed, and in the midst of her fury she had forcefully closed the bedroom door with nary a word, indicating that the intrusion of a husband on our last night at home would be unwelcome. That was okay. I was too pent-up, would never sleep, and I was happy enough to pass time drinking with Nina in my study.

"You've done it now, Bird."

"Win or lose, it's big time."

"Neat trick. Inviting us along to defend yourself from Hannah."

"Ironic, isn't it? The family was here to buffer me from Hannah, and Hannah turned out to be my best defence against the family."

"As long as things work out, huh, Sparrow?"

Since I would have no time to pack the bottles, we were plundering single-malt scotches. Our discourse was fraught with prolonged silences during which we concentrated on the Knockando, the Laphroaig, or Isle of Skye's Talisker. There were times when she was asleep in her chair and on occasion I woke myself up with a snore. As the night waned, we were both more comfortable side by side on the small sofa, arms interlinked, adrift on the malt in an eerie light.

"I guess you know this is it," Nina said.

"What's it?"

She thought about things some more. "After tonight, you'll be cut off from the world. You might be on top of the heap, but you won't have any friends there. More than likely you won't be at the top either, you'll just be another whiz-kid on the run. I mean, this is really heavy. You're cut off, Sparrow. It's like being cut off at a bar, only it's permanent, and it's every bar everywhere, only it's not only bars, it's every human estab-lishment, it's every human organization in the entire world. Wow, man."

"You're drunk."

"You better hope so. Because if I'm not, what I'm saying is true. You've done it, Bird-breath. You're a fugitive now."

"At least I can count on you."

"In a pig's eye."

"Come on, Nina. You'll visit?"

"Send me down the fare. Buy some place with a beach, okay? I know what! Hire really hunky armed guards, don't let them off the grounds for months, then give me a bunk in their barracks."

"Nina, come on, it's not going to be that bad. Someday I'll be back, you'll see, cleared of all charges."

"Think so?"

I had another sip. I was too far gone to distinguish what brand presently occupied my glass. "No," I admitted, "I don't think so. What's the difference where I live?"

"Maybe nobody will have you. You're on the run, Sparrow."

I put my head back. Breathed. The future was all so hard to imagine. I was being severed from my past, utterly and irrevocably, and that was hard to fathom. I was getting kicked out of Lougain all over again, only this time I was a big boy and no one had pinned instructions to my coat. "Yeah," I said. "I'm on the run. But aren't we all, really, ultimately?"

"Good, Sparrow. Be philosophical. That's about all that's left of your true self now."

"You're cheery."

Returning from a trip to the toilet, I spotted the keys to the house on Great Cranberry sparkling under the dining room table. I retrieved them and tossed them to Nina. "Have a house," I said.

"Don't mind if I do. I'm not proud."

"Ask Uncle to send you the papers."

Later, Nina placed a blanket over me. She was going home in her new Mercedes and she bent down to kiss me goodbye. "Do me one more favour? Take care of Hannah. I know you will the children, and Sheilagh. But be good to Hannah, too. It's going to be hardest on her. For as long as she lasts with you, be good, Sparrow."

My eyes did water then, my lower lip did tremble, and we held onto one another for a time. When we broke it off, she was crying too. "Thanks for the wheels," she said, but at the doorway she couldn't be flip. She had to say it. "You know, you bastard, you're the goddamn love of my life. You know that, don't you?"

"Yeah, I know. Right up there next to your cockroaches."

"I'm into centipedes at the moment. A centipede strolling across an erect nipple. There's nothing quite like it. Tell Hannah to give it a try."

"Insects don't turn her on."

"She's lucky. She's had you to distract her."

"Will you get out of here? And drive safely."

She flipped the car keys into the air, catching them again. "So long, Birdbrain. Take care of yourself. Let me know where you go into hiding. I could always trade that information for a tank of gas."

"Goodnight, Nina."

She shook her head slowly. "Wrong, Sparrow. This is goodbye. But I won't say it, okay?"

We couldn't see each other for the water in our eyes, and she was gone. I heard the car mutter away from the driveway, then in the middle of the road, in the middle of the night, Nina blared the horn. She sped away. That moment was my worst. I felt severed, cut off, denied, and I had to grip the blanket between my teeth.

I was thinking of country, of place. Of what was familiar. What did it matter where I lived? I would never see snow again. Never again walk the old streets of Park Extension or the forested avenues of Mount Royal. Never again see a big league game or bar-hop along Crescent Street.

I hadn't asked to come into this world, or this country. Of late, I had come to think of the planet, and of Canada, and of Montreal, as home, and all three constituencies were about to declare me unwelcome.

12.

Chinese Paper

How well we thrived under the brilliant Bahamian sun!

Bending at the waist, Mom squinted her eyes, stuck out the tip of her tongue, and with the head of her mallet lined up the gaily striped wooden ball and knocked it through the hoop, irrevocably squashing Barclay's faint hope of mounting a comeback. More than defeated, he had been crushed.

In a pantomime of disgust, Barclay tossed down his mallet and stomped on it, and Mom got a giggle out of that.

What a perfect day! Caribbean sea breezes loitered across the lawn. Under the canopy, descendants of British pirates and the dispossessed royalty of European nations fanned themselves, sipped margaritas, and lingered in the lassitude of their beautiful, tanned limbs. What Paradise was this? Arise! Out of the swamp we go and ascend to a tropical garden. Mother remained Queen of the Lawn and this week's croquet champion, Barclay was pickled, the children revelled in the comfort of their mother's attention, while I surveyed my commonwealth of adventures.

I had been summoned to the tropics, I knew that then. My life in the north a petty abduction. Perhaps the notion had remained dormant in me all these years. Emerging from swamp-mud I must have known my kismet. Damming tributaries and shaping lakes I must have known my true landscape, the true adventure of my geography. Delivering *Montreal Stars* in sub-Arctic temperatures conditioned the reflex in me—I'm a child of the sun-belt, a bird of equatorial climes.

Know that. It might help to understand.

Can anyone know this? My wife, abandoning the children to the frolic of their nanny, sauntered under the bright blue brim of the Bahamian sky, one leg crossing the path of the other, a sultry sashay that ignited my mood. Do many men lust after their own wives this way? I was fortunate in paradise. Hannah sat alongside me. With the back of her wrist she dabbed droplets of perspiration from her lip.

"The Prime Minister has arrived," she let me know.

"I didn't see him."

"He came with the Ashfords. He asked me how you've taken the news."

"What news?"

Hannah's gesture was a cross between a shy smile and a smirk. "Funny, Sparrow, that's exactly what I said. 'What news?'"

I was sipping lemonade, and gave warning, "I'm not prepared for more shocks."

"Maybe you already know this one, Sparrow. Maybe you didn't bother to tell me. Maybe it's one of the kazillions of details you neglected to mention to your own good wife, who ends up following you to the ends of the earth for who knows what reason."

"What news, Hannah?"

"The SEC is celebrating. Someone discovered that you were born in Mississippi. Apparently you told one of the former OIS board members that you were born in Mississippi. That means—correct me if I'm wrong—if you did not take the trouble to renounce your citizenship, you're an American."

"I'll renounce." Gulp lemonade.

"Oh? You're going to return to Canada and get arrested just so you can renounce being a Yank? Sparrow, if you're an American, they have the right to subpoena you."

"They don't have the right to piss in the sea. They don't have the right to shit on the shore."

"Sparrow. Please. Don't get like this."

"Like what?"

"Vulgar." Hannah was bewildered, poor girl. Which was not surprising. The pace had been frenetic. Who ever would have thought that things would move so quickly? She's adjusted well, sheltering the children from the storm, nursing her own wounds without calling attention to her pain.

"Barclay and I divested ourselves of OIS three days ago. I'm high and dry. The SEC won't want to talk to me any more."

"Get serious. The *New York Times* says you and Barclay stole between two- and five-*hundred* million dollars."

"Stole? *Stole?* Where do they get off using language like that?"

"Auntie called this morning. She's heart-broken."

"We didn't steal, Hannah. Who're you going to believe? The *New York Times* or your own husband? What does Aunt know? She's been reading the papers too. Where's her faith? Where's Aunt's confidence in her own children? In her own husband? I can't believe she doesn't know any better."

Under the sedentary sun, Hannah nibbled the tip of her ring finger meditatively. In a different temper, the gesture might have come across as seductive. "Aunt was raised poor. She believes that no one can make that kind of money honestly. Sparrow, I was raised rich and I'm inclined to agree."

"What money? I'm barely scraping by."

Everybody wanted to know how and how much. Everybody wanted to know why. Nobody asked for the truth. I told reporters that we did what we had to do, that the idiots and numbskulls foiled our best attempts. They kept after us with their tired questions. How much did you embezzle? Will you give yourself up? What're you going to spend it on? How much does one person need? Nobody understood. I was supposed to go back and face a trial when nobody understood?

Never. Not me. I was staying put.

What happened was both simple and necessary. Cornelius Field fell under the scrutiny of the Swiss authorities for reckless mismanagement, a serious crime in that country. He had to relinquish his stake in OIS. Barclay and I put in a bid. The best we could offer. We negotiated, and upped the ante. We had to insist that some of the lawsuits remain with Field, but otherwise we were fair, given the ruthless judgment of the market place. Field, the scoundrel, accepted a bid inferior to our own. He snubbed us at his own expense. He sold out for a meagre six-point-five million. We had offered eleven. Unfortunately for him, we were also the principals behind the other offer, and what he didn't know really hurt him when he found out.

Way to go, Unc!

After we had dispensed with Field, which was for the good of the company, Barclay reorganized OIS assets as we had planned. We had to take control of a failing enterprise. We also had to divorce the company's operations from the firm's considerable liabilities. If we didn't do that, the lawsuits would have looted OIS down to nothing. We had to protect the shareholders, the grandmothers and the fathers saving and slaving for their children's education. Barclay was very clever at placing reams of Chinese paper between us and OIS. Naturally, we controlled the new holding companies, what were we supposed to do, give them away? We had every intention of paying dividends to OIS shareholders. Had they given us time they wouldn't be in this pickle. It's the media again. The alarmists and the nincompoops, screaming *fraud!* Screaming *theft!* Screaming *grand larceny!* Like we were a couple of punks heisting Camaros. We knew what we were doing. They forced us out. Sure, some of the assets remained in our holding companies, we couldn't very well return them to a firm that clearly was bankrupt, that clearly was on the verge of being looted by litigators. What would be the good of that?

We did what we had to do.

Barclay even went back to OIS the day after we had divested ourselves of our interest and talked the new board into investing in one of our companies that was holding former OIS assets. (I admit, that took a lot of gall.) The thing is, the new OIS board agreed. They plunked down twenty million Yankee dollars. They did. They recognized a good investment when they saw one. Now, does that suggest that people in the know think we're thieves? It's just how things go when you're on top. Money flows your way and everyone resents your position in charge of the taps.

One morning you wake up, and there's your destiny staring you in the face. Grinning, right in your puss. It's revelation. What do you do? Ignore fate?

"Where's the Prime Minister now?"

"He's having a drink with Mom."

Imagine that. Discreetly stretching forward, I spied them down by the big tent, Mom in her billowing white dress and floppy-brimmed hat to protect herself from the blazing scrutiny of the sun. Once upon a time the sun would disorient her. Now she entertained heads of state under its light. She was doing a good job too. Several times Hawking reared back to issue a mighty guffaw.

"Sparrow," my wife, quite rightly, wanted to know, "will we be able to stay here?"

She meant in the Bahamas. "I'm working on that. Hawking's the key."

"Another deal? Another scheme?" Now she was cross. She had a short fuse in those days and who could blame her? Anxious times for us all. Barclay and I had agreed upon one thing above all else—we were not going back. We would not answer to the charges against us. We would not surrender what we had rightfully earned. We would not become anybody's scapegoat.

"When someone achieves a certain level of influence, it becomes incumbent to use whatever powers of persuasion he or she may possess, and to use those powers wisely."

"Now you're giving speeches to your wife? Sparrow, are you totally off your rocker or just pretending?"

"What do you mean?"

"You talk to me as though I'm holding a microphone to your lips. Are you practising for the press?"

"Sorry. The pressure gets to me once in awhile. The bastards are everywhere. Don't you feel them too? It's like they're listening in. Like our clothes are bugged. I wouldn't put it past them."

Hannah fanned the heat from her face. Posed her worry again. "Will we be able to stay here, Sparrow?" She feared another night flight, a demotion to Uruguay among Nazis. She, the Jewish exile, feared midnight arrest.

I caressed the lovely tan of her forearm, promised, "I'll fix things with Hawking. Count on it."

My wife threw up her hands, laughing, and I had to agree that, overall, she had been a good sport about the swift changes to our lives. "I don't want to know the details. Just get it done, Sparrow. Please, get it done."

Together we walked across the croquet lawn to visit with the Prime Minister.

What's adventure, really, without a soupçon of danger?

Our lives get funnelled by routine, and for good reason we shy away from the eroticism of violence. The civilized among us tend to disapprove of the contradiction, that we never feel so wickedly alive as when bullets bark, yap and snap around us like a frenzy of wild dogs. Danger buffs life's lustre, it can polish every nuance. These latter days I'm hip to danger. Infidels aspire to serve my head on a platter, what's my response? I take superior care with my grooming.

My enemies will want to see my skull roasted, my hair garnished with lotus petals. No doubt they will prefer that my ears be lopped off to float as wontons in a soup, that my nostrils be plugged with the fattest turnips they can grub, that my mouth generously be stuffed with offal. A base, vile lot, my enemies. A society of larcenists. Mere words fail to suit their description. These people kidnap mothers.

Distinct in memory is the moment of hesitation, of shock, that instant miracle of disbelief. Glass at our backs has shattered before we have heard the gun's retort. A dog—this I remember—a dowager's Corgi, yipped before his arrogance imploded. Where the head used to be we were stricken by blood, gore, brain-ooze. The pathetic sack of its body tumbled to one side. Within the moment we have heard the gun's follow-up burst.

This time we got the message.

And still the world was fragile, unreal, dreamlike. I had observed these occurrences as though they were common tropical phenomena. How could this be happening to me on such a fine and sunny day?

We hit the dirt. After the fact we screamed at one another to do the same. Crawled and scrambled and scraped for cover. So much was instinct. Hannah and the children crouched behind the patio furniture, which wasn't much use. Guessing that I was the primary target, that going back to them might attract gunfire their way, I stayed put. It was Hannah who could think despite the delirious moment. She tipped over a table, hiding her infants and herself behind that plastic shield. The table's white surface and circular shape reflected the sun, forming an ideal bull's-eye for target practice, so I made a low-to-the-ground dash to the stunted stone wall, drawing fire, and crouched there. Barclay lay with his face in the sand, his chubby form partially screened by the same abutment. His shape lay squandered under the shade of a coconut tree. Much exposed, Barclay was too substantial a target to presume to move.

This was the amazing part. To this day it gives me pause. Hannah, my wife, devoted mother of our two children, a lawyer's daughter, a former *artiste*, calmly reached into her purse and extracted a Luger. She tossed it like a frisbee over Barclay's prone, petrified body to me. I had never been so impressed with the changes to my life as I was at that moment, watching, transfixed, as my wife threw me her German pistol. A spinning chip of the sun. A shining example of our progress in the world.

I caught it.

My wife was expecting me to return our attackers' fire.

I took a peek over the low wall. Shots struck stone, a volley went *peetu!* past my left ear. Mortified by the taut velocity of the wind, I ducked.

Scratched that approach.

Hannah was miming. She encouraged me to perch the pistol on the ledge and, with my head down and more or less out of the way, return the enemy salvo.

I lay on my back and rested the barrel of the gun above me on the stone. Even my fingers were not exposed. Blindly, desperately, I shot.

Prayed that the innocent had long since ducked for cover. How, I begged with each squeeze of the trigger, had I ever—*blam! blam!*—wormed my way into this mess?

What a life. Look at me there, then. A scruffy, northern sparrow vociferously bickering with birds-of-a-feather, shooting it out with assassins in the tropics.

In the distance, sirens proposed rescue.

"Barclay!" I shouted to my companion, whose chin was imbedded in the white sand of the Bahamas, while the rather robust protrusion of his rear served as an inviting target to snipers. Why had he not been picked off? Like Romping Ron, the man was born with a horseshoe wedged up his rectum. The child prodigy, the accounting whiz, the crack administrator was sprawled out behind a palm tree not thick enough to shelter his waistline. He was positioned so that only blind marksmen could miss that flesh. Blind marksmen—how lucky could he get? The gunmen must have mistaken him for a shadow.

"What?" Barclay whispered hoarsely. He was anxious that our assassins not hone in on the sound of his voice. As he turned to me, putting one ear on the ground, I detected the sandy colour of fear floating across his eyes. Beads of fright perspired on Barc's brow, dripping as shiny amulets off the glistening tip of his nose. To so acutely identify Barclay's terror, pixilated under the high sun, was to spy my own dread in a mirror. I realized in a second that I, too, was mush, a wrung-rag of sweat, a sopping doll awaiting the further abuse of my benefactors.

"Get us out of this jam!" was my terse command.

"You got the gun, dumbhead!"

"I mean permanently, you Neanderthal! We need protection here. We need a haven, Barc."

"I told you already. I'm working on it."

"Not fast enough!" There we were, under assault. The bullets had ceased and we had taken advantage of that temporary boost in our life-expectancy to bicker.

"These things take time. You know that, Sparrow."

"It's your job, Barc! I don't need your fucking excuses." I knew that political negotiations took time, and under the circumstances Barclay had been making reasonable progress. Still, at that moment, I possessed a compelling argument of my own. "Time's a luxury we don't have. We'll be dead before then. Make arrangements, Barc."

A waggle of police sirens descended. Sneaking a peak might kill me, so I kept my head down, content to gaze at the sky and to imagine the livery of black-skinned constables in their pressed white shirts and spiffy blue trousers flushing out, if not snuffing out, our interlopers.

Privy to a view different than my own, Barclay shouted, "The cops are here! Hey! Hey!" An ironic glee, really, considering that police forces throughout the world were on the lookout for us, that composites of our faces decorated the offices of interested financial investigators around the planet.

"Keep your head down."

"Think you have to remind me?"

Hannah. The kids. As relief staggered through her, I observed her attitude change. With the kids safe, defence of her children was no longer Hannah's paramount concern. Her maternal instincts were neatly supplanted by rage against her husband for inviting this danger upon us all.

"Barclay," I repeated, while remaining attentive to the police voices and the running feet, "find an answer."

Some say that we are the authors of our own misfortune. Some say that that aphorism is particularly true of Barclay and me. I have resisted the charge. Everyone is manipulated by happenstance, and over the past few hectic months incidents had joined forces with destiny to bear down upon us. Our endeavours had been ambitious, granted, but we were not the purveyors of greed attested to by the press, nor were we culprits of wrong-doing. Barclay and I subsisted, I say, as the abused servants of our best intentions.

In the Bahamas, for instance, we had wished to live in peace, to imbibe in restaurants and enjoy an afternoon of croquet without inviting an armed attack. We wanted to make a deal with the government of the day to insure our peace and prosperity. Was there something wrong with that? Were we committing a crime simply because we wished to benefit from a decent level of protection?

I think not. And yet anyone paying attention to the press would conclude that we were messing with internal Bahamian politics. What balderdash.

To be left in peace—that was the height of our ambition.

The brilliant Bahamian sun was suddenly eclipsed by a massive black skull. A different face in the mirror. My soul? If this shadow was my attacker, I was dead meat.

"It's all right now, suh," the policeman stated, and *oh!* how I revelled in his extraordinary confidence. "Whoever was shooting at you, suh, he run away a long time ago now, suh."

I could stand again. Walk tall. Albeit shakily. Hannah's eyes were scorched with anger, although for the moment she had to hug me, as did Barc, and the boys each clutched a kneecap. Our relief and love abounded in this tight clasp of bodies.

"What's going on outside here?" Stepping from the club restaurant and slurping a strawberry ice cream cone, Mom posed the question. She had missed the commotion and was surprised by our intimate connection and the circle of police. Her companion was the Prime Minister of the Bahamas, Milton P. Hawking, and I saw less surprise in his eyes than I had read in my mother's—less surprise, and the germination of deceit. Right then I knew why he had kept my mother behind in the club, why he had offered her an official escort home. He had spared her the attack. Not my children, not my wife—he had allowed the rest of us to take our chances. The only person he was not willing to risk to a gunfight was my mother. He was looking at me, knowing that I had him figured out.

"Barc?"

"Yeah?"

"This is your deal to make."

"Our haven, you mean? Yes, old man. We agreed. This is my turn."

"I want in on it. It's going to take both our brains."

"I have no difficulty with that."

I was looking at Hawking, then at the dead dog with it's snout blasted off. So. We had not been attacked by nervous or embittered shareholders who had failed to shoot straight. We had been set upon by sharpshooters. Marksmen. Their job had not been to hurt us, only to scare us.

Which they had done. Poor Barclay had soiled his trousers.

He was mightily embarrassed. Smelly, too.

*

Always we were charmed by the Prime Minister of the Bahamas, he was a card. At one time I believed that he deserved my gratitude for keeping Mom behind that day, after tea, preventing her from becoming a target for snipers. The thought of her dancing amid the bullets, or charging the gunfire, made me flinch. For a long time I honestly appreciated the gesture. On the other hand, if my recent past had taught me anything, it was to look for the schemes within the plots, the motives within the actions. Had my mother been involved in the shooting, her reaction might have been unpredictable. The Prime Minister had recognized that. Today I believe that he had kept her behind because she might have called the gunmen's bluff. She might have attacked the bullets, or performed a jig, she might not have chosen to hide like the rest of us. Then we would have learned conclusively that the hired guns had been under orders to cause us no harm, an opinion Hawking could ill afford.

We had to become serious about protection. Our villa became a compound, the compound a fort. Guard dogs patrolled the perimeter. Whenever Hannah took the kids to the beach, she packed the Luger in her picnic basket. Anyone attempting to abduct our children would pay a price. Even Mom had to learn to go shopping with a bodyguard. That was all right, until I spotted the two of them rising behind the hibiscus where the hummingbirds flew. The dolt had taken his job description too literally. So had Mom. After Mom's bodyguard remembered that he had a pressing engagement on the continent, his replacement taught each of us how to effectively discharge a pistol at close range.

In those early days in Nassau, our best friends were the Ashfords. Mercedes and George were about my age and sensitive to the troubles faced by exiles under duress. The Ashfords had been kind enough to clear a path to Milton P. Hawking, the new leader of the Bahamas, a necessary introduction given that he was being pressured to return Barclay to Canada and me to the United States. The Ashfords understood the value of a well-chosen political contact, and in consideration of our status as fugitives prominent in the international media, they had gone right to the top.

As the daughter of the Canadian robber baron Sir Henry Ashford, who had helped to develop the islands both as a tourist attraction and as a haven for socially-advantaged, dislocated buccaneers, Mercedes had come to her diplomacy and wisdom through an honourable line of descent. In his heyday, Sir Henry centred a convivial gang of Russian princes, dispossessed English monarchs, American gangsters, and European gentry noted for their quick fingers and sewn-in pockets. Sir Henry had been a scoundrel, an elite modern-day rogue, and thanks to his good works, Nassau had begun to challenge Zurich for its secret bank accounts and nimble transactions.

This was to be expected, of course. The lovely, bejewelled necklace of the Bahamian islands had long enjoyed a colourful history as a haven for pirates. In this century, that heritage of putrid plundering scoundrels, knives clenched between their teeth, tattoos of the skull and crossbones splayed across their filthy chests and biceps, dicks dipped in the tender rumps of cabin boys, had been gentrified by a new class of expatriate. An elegant decadence was bestowed upon the community when King Edward abdicated his crown in favour of an American divorcee who had learned extraordinary sexual prowess in Asian brothels. Exiled to paradise by being named Governor General of the Bahamas, the Duke of Windsor presided over the colony's elite social whirl. He gave the community its perverse prestige, while Sir Henry was its economic and political engine. The dispossessed monarch and the banished financier were not always on the best of terms, and the Man-Who-Would-Not-Be-King remains one of a glut of suspects in Sir Henry's unsolved murder. Mercedes, an inheritor of island intrigue, a font of lore and insider knowledge, dispensed both political and personal advice with an acute sense of caution. She was good to know.

She and Hannah became fast friends. For my wife's sake, I was glad of that.

Now it was not difficult to reason that the interest Mercedes Ashford expressed in my little entourage stemmed from her position as a major shareholder in The Ashford Bank. Barclay and I were reported to be travelling with bags of lucre. (Gold watches! *The New York Times* said we stole gold watches. As if we were a couple of punks from the old neighbourhood. As if we visited bars and peeled back our trench coats, saying, "Psst! Buddy! Wanna buy a watch?" Believe me, journalists are the locusts of the modern era. We didn't *steal* those watches, we merely expropriated them for the good of the business. Yes, dammit! There is a difference.) To Mercedes we were pirates who had plundered the bounding main of international finance. Fair enough. Good business requires an eye for opportunity and an aggressive disposition. She befriended us, helped us settle. Her bank was managed by her husband, one George Crowley, a Harvard grad and a financial swashbuckler himself before that dogged bloodhound, the SEC, barked regulations and nipped at his heels. He fled to the Bahamas rather than deal with the hassle, much like me. Mercedes hired him, then married him, and his association with his wife and with her bank led to his being known by her surname. He's given up trying to identify himself as George Crowley—or, as seems to happen on the islands, he was quite happy to be known by a name other than his own. George had been invaluable assisting Barclay and me to establish a corporate presence in the Bahamas.

Barclay had opened a bank in Nassau, International Finance Corporation. (He insisted on devising dull names for our companies.) He had assured the Ashfords that we were not in domestic competition with them, and he and George explored joint projects. I had not known this about Barclay—he was obsessed by peculiar ambition. He wanted to be a Bay Street boy, to sidle up to a club bar in Toronto and have everyone know the extent of his influence. He wanted to be Chairman of the Board of a company listed on the Toronto exchange. A pipe-dream, given the way the world was treating us, but he figured that George (Crowley) Ashford might have been able to provide him with the necessary access.

As thanks for his help, Barclay and I presented George with a sensational gold watch.

We were trying to establish ourselves on the Bahamas, to settle down in peace. Was something wrong with that? I needed to see to the well-being and future education of my children, and to the safety of both my wife and my mother. We had to get on with our lives. What the hell was wrong with that? True, I was not a pauper, but I did have expenses. That's what the bloodhounds never took into consideration. I had expenses. Being rich did not mean that all problems were solved. Problems were merely of a different magnitude, solutions had to be discerned on a higher plane.

To be introduced to the Prime Minister, for example, was one hurdle, to secure his confidence quite another. Mark Hawking down as nobody's fool. He elected to take time to weigh his options. American political persuasion was no trifle, and the Canadian government was fond of offering aid to the Bahamas, which could be used as a political weapon against us. Hawking was allotting Barclay and me time to demonstrate our value to his country, to prove we were worth the aggravation.

He was also hoping that we might move elsewhere on our own accord, and at the same time consider the Bahamas an investment and banking paradise. He wanted our money but not our friendship. Principally, that's why he had tried scaring us off.

We had in a roundabout way broached the matter of financial leverage. Hawking had been chatting poetically about a lovely piece of property. Within the Prime Minister's earshot, I openly suggested to Barclay that we ought to acquire the land for the new leader of the Bahamas as a way to commemorate his election.

Hawking had laughed at that, as if I had recited a dirty joke, one that he found both humorous and embarrassing.

"Here in The Bahamas, we have embarked upon a new era of home rule matched by democratic tranquillity, Mr. Drinkwater. It is imperative, at this early stage, that our officials not only *be* ethical, but are *seen to be* ethical in every respect. It is important that we retain the confidence of the Bahamian people."

Ethics. The appearance and presumption of ethics. My bailiwick. The facade in which I had been reared. I assured the Prime Minister that I understood his position completely. I also reminded him that I was a creative thinker. To which he nodded. To which he tapped the tip of his nose. To which his left eyebrow arched ever so slightly. Ever so ethically.

*

Shunted off to the Bahamas, eclipsed from the world, we were being treated to a tropical rain in winter.

There are sounds that soothe the nerves.

The thrash and chatter of palm fronds.

The prattle of rain on the roof.

The murmur of streams carving sand from banks, rushing to the sea.

Sounds of rain calmed this disparate soul. My mother had been misbehaving at night, would the weather dampen her wayward impulse?

Outside the window where my desk was positioned, our German Shepherds had been whimpering on the front porch. Rain bored them, and reduced their territory. Taking a cue from Mao Tse-Tung who was fond of calling Americans running dogs, I had named mine after Presidents. Every ten minutes or so, Eisenhower lumbered across the steps, barked at the rain, and returned to his pallet on the porch. Mission accomplished, he felt he'd done his duty on the night patrol.

My mother had mastered the dogs. They adored her, they hunkered down for a sniff of her footprints, prostrated themselves for a pat from her hand. My mother had been misbehaving at night, adventuring beyond the wall of our compound. Frequent nocturnal habit. And the dogs knew, they saw, they sniffed, not once did they raise an alarm. These beasts who growled if a salamander twitched were mute to my mother's forays in the volatile depths of our darkest tropical nights.

Damn mutts.

Minutes earlier a call had set my nerves on edge. Which was why I concentrated on the rain and its engine of diverse sound. I was trying to relax, to transcend the stress of challenge and grim report.

Uncle Butter had telephoned. His plane had put down in Florida pending dawn and a break in the weather, and his tone made it obvious that he was coming specifically to see me, rather than Barclay. I presumed that his message would not be cheerful. Whatever was on his mind could not be uttered or even alluded to over the phone. Honestly, I could have done without the suspense, the endless waiting for more bad news.

Sometimes the wind was strong. Then rain took a swipe at the rooftop and sullied the shutters. Palm fronds created a mob's racket, like the fists of the infidel hammering upon my doors.

More often, the rain was steady, intense, relaxed. Cascading straight down from heaven. Contact with the earth invoked jungle smells, vegetation's rich dung. History's sludge took shape, assumed form, sauntering through the oligarchy of darkness.

My mother went over the wall most nights. In search of spirit lovers. She fell into the arms of young black men who prized the submission of rich white skin.

She repeatedly thwarted my best attempts to keep her in.

I'd hear her creeping in the corridors. Moving with stealth, and stepping softly through the shadows. I'd hear her fingertips explore a map of cracks splayed across the walls. The caress of her dry hands moistened stone. My mother ran through the gauntlet of dogs as though she was a wraith in a kingdom of the sane, her scent seducing them into silence.

Of course, I had locked her in her room. She must not enter this pitch blackness, or flee to the downfall of cool, abiding rain.

Hannah meandered through to my office. She felt bound by the rain, rather than protected. She was fearful of the nights, the scrutiny of unknown eyes, the impenetrable dimension of the omnipresent black void. Hannah was waning under the long wet tropical winter confined to quarters. Perspiration marked her upper arms, signs of her duress in the humidity of this place.

"Kids down?" I inquired.

"One story and they were out. They're both exhausted."

"Good."

She sat in the way I adored, her legs sprawled across the arms of the chair as she flipped through magazines, *Life*, *Newsweek*, for images of the outside world. Since retreating to the compound our lives had been fixed on one another, the slightest gesture invoked my lust, the most casual remark triggered frustration and rebuke.

"We have to talk," Hannah said, a certain signal of where this night was headed.

"So talk."

She sat up. Also not a good sign.

"This life we're leading, it's nuts."

"It's temporary."

"You always say that. I'm losing my mind. I need a holiday."

I've made the suggestion in the past. Hannah had always turned down the notion because I'm not free to travel to many places. In the summer things were better. The wet season had become more difficult to endure.

"Sure. Leave the kids or take them, it's your choice. I'd be happy to take care of them for a few weeks."

"This isn't any easier on them!" she practically ranted at me, as if I was missing something. "I'll take them," she added more quietly.

"Suit yourself. Where will you go?"

"Home," she said.

We both mused about that awhile, struck, I guess, by the remoteness, the mystical dimension to the idea. I was jealous that she could even speak the word.

"That might not be such a hot idea," was my advice. "Reporters will hound you. Angry people might seek you out, shareholders, that sort of thing."

Hannah looked right at me, the scent of her attitude a whiff away from scorn. "*I* was never part of your scam."

It's hard to know where to strike back first. If at all. I let the matter of the "scam" drop, and reminded her, "Guilt by association. If people can't get at me, they might go after you. Not to mention Zeke and Zack."

Hannah noticed for the first time that her arms were damp. Perspiration had broken the surface of her skin when she was playing motorboats with the kids in their bath. She gave her wrists a brisk rub, and announced, "I'll be careful."

There was more to the conversation than she had managed to broach. Hannah was emotionally equipped for war. She wanted to thrash things out. What stopped her was the strange sounds from down the hall.

"What's that?"

In the tropics we had grown accustomed to weird intrusions. A cricket in a drawer can keep a family awake through many nights. Rats slink around.

We had learned to listen first and panic later. Assassins, or mere thieves? Animals washed in by the flood or through a leaking roof? Then I knew. "It's Mom."

She was on the floor in her bedroom. Mom had stuffed socks into her mouth, which was foaming with froth, and she had frizzed her hair in a ludicrous style. Like a dog excavating bones from the earth she aggressively pawed the carpet.

"Mom." My heart hammered wildly, catching at life's breath.

She ceased her rapid, rabid two-handed dig to look up. It was shaving cream that she had smeared across her mouth. She erupted into a word salad, a tossed dictionary of language knowing no sense or rhythm, complicated by the socks in her mouth. She was basking in gibberish and rolling her eyes up into her head. In unison, Hannah and I pulled her up off her knees. Her body distended, mounting a seizure. She shook in our arms and we pulled the socks out of the froth of her mouth to help her breathe.

And she declared, "This is what thee gets when thou locks me up."

I just stood there. Hannah recovered first. She burst out laughing. I was less amused.

"What do you think you're doing?"

"What does thou think *thee* is doing?" she shot right back. "Thou locks me in my room like some kind of crazy old woman—fine! Thou treats me like I'm crazy, I'll act like I'm crazy."

"You can't go out tonight."

"Thou can't lock me in my room!"

Hannah attempted to intercede. She wiped Mom's foamy mouth clean with a facecloth. "Sparrow? Did you lock Mom in her room?"

"She can't go out tonight. It's raining, dammit!"

"You locked her in her room?" She looked ready to hit me.

"Yes, he did! He's really mean to me, Hannah. He's bad to me and not nice!"

"Listen, Mom, this has gotten out of hand. You're climbing over the wall at night—"

"So give me a key to the gate!"

"It's her business."

"Shut up, Hannah!" Sorrow, rage, frustration informed my words, and more. I knew, and I suspect she knew, that I was referring to her hidden agenda for our marriage.

"Don't tell me to shut up, Sparrow Drinkwater. What are you going to do, lock me in my room too?"

"I'm tired of being in this place like a jail," Mom wailed. "It's like living in an asylum. It's like I'm back in a nuthouse."

"You can't go out at night."

"Thou can't make me stay in!"

We were screaming at each other and waking the kids, and Hannah wisely got between us. To me, she said, "Mom has a point. You're not her keeper. This isn't an institution." Just as I was about to object, she switched to Mom. "It's raining hard tonight. We do worry about you when you go out alone. You know it's dangerous. No one should be out on a night like this."

"I won't live in a locked room, Hannah. Sparrow locks me in my room, I will go crazy for him. I will do it. I will go crazy for him he locks me in my room. He wants to treat me like I'm schizophrenic? I show him what it's like to be schizophrenic."

She began to oink and bark, bray and hiss, carving her face into hideous, surreal creatures.

"All right! Stop it. I won't lock you in your room. But I did it for your own damn good. You have to start behaving yourself." Stabbing at her with my righteous index finger.

"That's what the nurses used to say." She nearly took a swing at me, and might have, had Hannah not caught her.

"You're not taking your medication! Don't lie to me, Mom! You're skipping and this is what happens. I don't believe you're taking your medication."

"Take my medication thyself!" was her retort. "Take it thyself! Thou art the one who's crazy, Sparrow! Thou art the one crazy all over the world! What happened to our own good life? Look what thou hast done! Cooped up here like a bunch of crazy people in the loony bin going crazy."

"All right. You want to go crazy, go crazy. See if I care. Go on. Climb over the wall. Go fuck the whole damn town. See if I care." And I stomped from the room.

"If thou says so!" Mom was screaming after me. "If thou says so, Sparrow! I'll fuck the whole damn town if thou says so!"

I wouldn't put it past her.

I was alone for awhile. Hannah saw to the boys, they'd been awakened by the fight, and Mom fumed in a style not terribly dissimilar to my own. What could I do? If I didn't lock her up at night, should I allow her to roam the island? In the dark? In the rain? Misbehaving?

Pouring myself a drink I felt a lassitude extend from my toes to my soul, knit my mind to my spleen. I had become my mother's keeper, our love had been reduced to institutional wrangles about freedom of movement and pill-taking. She was sensitive to environment, I knew that, and the changes of the last months had eroded her rehabilitation. There were matters that had to be resolved, so much rested on the outcome.

"I can't believe it," Hannah said, returning, and my back stiffened, my hackles reared up. "Locking Mom in her room. She says she's not fucking anybody, Sparrow. She's just visiting friends. What's gotten into you? Are you losing it or what?"

"She goes out at night," I endeavoured to explain calmly, but Hannah wasn't listening. She just shook her head, so I shut up.

Hannah answered the ring from the front gate, and the voice over the intercom was Mercedes Ashford's. I'd been expecting her visit. At the window, waiting, I noticed that the dogs had vanished. Either they'd heard the car and intended to do their job, or—and there, *there!* a wisp, a quick glimpse of white dress. My mother had vanished again, she had slipped into the night.

The brick of my heart weighed heavily upon the chipped, cracked stone of my soul.

Mercedes looked like she'd been drowned, resuscitated, and fed bad food, all in the same half-hour. Hannah let her in, but she must have been told that the visit was business, for my wife had not followed her into the room.

"Mercedes. Good to see you. Can I get you something? A drink? A towel?"

This was a night for ill-humour, and she declined.

"What's up?"

"Don't you know?"

"Sit down. Fill me in."

She was tall, slightly heavy, made attractive by angular bones and green eyes. Mercedes had always known how to dress. We were attracted to one another and I had considered slipping. In this instance it would have been a double betrayal, as Mercedes was Hannah's only confidant and pal on the islands. So we had circled around one another from a distance, choosing the safe habits of protocol.

Life-long training eased her into this difficult conversation. "You must know," Mercedes began, "about Secure Financial and Great Lakes Capital?"

"Can't say the names ring any bells, no."

She resorted to a cigarette. I had never seen her quite so perplexed or nervous.

"Don't you and Barclay confide in each other?"

"He has his ventures and I have mine. When they're separate, we keep them private. Tell me what's up, Mercedes. How can I help?"

Behind me, outside, the wet bedraggled dogs returned to the porch. They were miserable, soaked through after escorting my mother over the wall. They whimpered and scratched at the door to be let in. Mercedes had come through the electric gate, driven her Land Rover up the long drive, dismounted and entered the house without rousing a bark, so intent had the dogs been on my mother's safe passage.

"I guess I'll have that drink now, please. Scotch." While I was decanting, she went on with her problem. "The Ashford Bank is controlled, through a network of companies, by Secure Financial, one of my father's old firms in Toronto."

"I see. I always considered you to be the principal owner."

"I am. The majority shareholder, at least. But when the bank needs cash, we go to Secure. I'm not—" she brushed back her wet locks, "—in an exciting position at the moment."

"Secure wants to buy you out."

"That's not it. You really haven't heard this?"

"Not a word."

"God. I came here expecting to chew you out."

"What's Barclay's involvement?"

"Barclay knows, even if you don't, that The Ashford is not in great financial straits. To save ourselves, we were planning to help Secure buy out a company called Great Lakes Capital. It's complex, but Barclay promised us five million dollars—"

"Hmm," I noted, and sat back in my chair. "I see."

"What?"

"I'll explain later. Go on."

"Barclay was supposed to have the five million in front money on deposit with the Bank of Nova Scotia, ready for the closing of the deal." In a trice she lost her composure, her voice suddenly strident and accusatory. "At the last minute, at the very last minute, Barclay pulls out. This is my life we're talking about here! This is my family's bank!"

Her fists were poised and deadly. Tears reddened her eyes. "Okay, Mercedes, hold on now. I want to understand the damage."

"The damage? The takeover has collapsed, which has its own repercussions for me, and more important than that, The Ashford has to pay penalties for failure. *I can't pay those penalties!* I'm finished. My bank is finished. All because Barclay screwed me over."

Picking up my drink, I moved to the sofa beside her. "Okay. There are ramifications to this, of which you may be unaware. Barclay and I have a silent partner in many of our deals. He lives in Canada, and I suspect he can shed light on the situation. Right now, he's stuck in Florida until the weather shifts. What I can tell you," I said softly, hoping to ease her distress with comfort, "is that Barclay's five million dollars was seized by the Royal Canadian Mounted Police yesterday."

"Oh God."

"I asked him what the hell it was doing there, he said it was a long story. He spent the rest of the day trying to get another five million into the country safely. Obviously, he failed. I'm sure that this is devastating for him, letting you and George down."

"Great. That's just great. He's devastated, I'm wiped out, the world is in ruins. This is just peachy. I don't suppose he's so devastated that he wants to make my failure-payments?"

Mercedes remained enough of a businesswoman that I needed only to give her a look to answer that.

"Exactly. Silly of me to ask."

"Maybe there's something else we can do."

"I could drown myself. There's always that possibility." Not bothering to stand on ceremony, she finished her glass and refilled it herself.

"I was thinking of something less extreme."

"I'm listening."

"I could buy The Ashford."

Quick to laugh. I have found that so many people now assume the worst of me. "You bastard. Find somebody in trouble, skim the cream from their operation, take no prisoners. I wasn't born yesterday, Sparrow. I know how you do business, and frankly, it stinks."

"For now I'll pretend that I didn't hear that. Listen to this, Mercedes. I buy The Ashford. I'll give you more than fair market value for a company that is on the verge of bankruptcy. I could use my own bank in the Bahamas. You will benefit financially, and the debt in the Secure Financial fiasco will be paid."

The offer was worth considering, and Mercedes did just that. "I guess if I'm going to be out on the street, I could use the cash. What exactly do I have to deliver for this deal?"

"All the shares. Sell me yours, and see that Secure sells me theirs. Can you deliver?"

"In a pinch."

"Good. There's an incentive."

"I'm listening."

Hannah, perhaps as a grievance for being left out of my negotiations once again, ventured outside to feed the dogs. They instigated racket, bickering over the spoils of their laziness. To my mind, the mutts should be starved until they do their job with a modicum of ferocity and meanness. The night they prevent mothers from slipping over walls at night,—*then* they may be fed.

"After I have purchased all the shares, you can buy back Secure's portion of the shares for yourself, at the same price that I will pay."

"The same share price?" she needed confirmed.

"No. The same price."

She had to think about that one. "Hold it. You will end up as the majority owner of The Ashford."

"Correct."

"Wait. I sell you my majority share, then you turn around, and for the same price, sell me the *minority* share for the same amount of money? You make a profit off me, which reduces the cost of buying Secure Financial's stake. You get the bank for less than the cost of the minority holding."

"I admit, it's clever. But you end up with a continuing stake in The Ashford, which I think you will find more comfortable than bankruptcy. Plus you now have an interest in a bank that will be profitable."

"It's not fair. You're buying The Ashford for next to nothing."

"From what you tell me, it's not worth much more. Once Barclay and I refinance it, your minority stake will look awfully good."

"But I won't have any say."

"What say will you have once The Ashford is bankrupt?"

"Sparrow, why do you want my bank?"

I sipped my Grand Marnier. "I don't, Mercedes. I just want to help out. As a banker you know that business is business, it can't be charity."

"What if I don't buy back the minority shares? What if I just take the money and walk away?"

"Then the deal's off."

"That cinches it. Don't kid me. You want to buy The Ashford Bank for next to nothing. You could wait for it to go bankrupt. But who wants a bankrupt bank? Besides, you might have to deal with competitive bids. You're very bright, Sparrow. In a perverse way, I admire that."

"We'll be partners. That's sounds like fun to me."

Mercedes eyed her reflection in her scotch, then swilled it around. "In a perverse way," was her contention, "that sounds like fun to me too."

"Then it's a done deal?"

"I wish I knew all that's going on here."

"Going once," I announced.

"You're up to something. I can feel it in my bones."

"Going twice." Keeping the pressure on.

"Sold," Mercedes conceded. And we drank to our new alliance. "On one condition," she thought to add.

"What's that?"

"I'm going to check on Barclay's five million. If he didn't lose it—"

"Believe me, that money's gone. Investigate to your heart's content. Barclay's broken-hearted. I might have to let him participate in our venture, just so he feels he got something for his cash."

Clinking glasses, we drank again.

She laughed, in that full, throaty graininess of hers.

"What's so funny?"

"I'll probably find out that you and Barclay tipped off the R.C.M.P. yourselves. You probably lost that money on purpose."

I laughed too, and escorted her to the door. Naturally, I did not tell her that that's exactly what we had done. I preferred to bask in the praise that she proffered to my wife at the door. Then she dashed outside to her vehicle, pelted by the rain.

*

Mercedes was correct to assume that I had my reasons to acquire her bank, and she was the sort of woman who might have appreciated the need to do so with some measure of deception. Later that night, over Hannah's objections, I crossed by speedboat back to Nassau for an audience with the Prime Minister. The worth of The Ashford lay not in its reserves, which were slight, or in the quality and quantity of its loans. The Ashford's value lay in the sensitivity of many of its loans to political matters. Mercedes had always made a point to court the business of politicians. It never hurts to have persons in power also in your debt.

To Hawking that night I waxed poetic about Barclay's ability to make loans vanish without a trace. I referred to his mortgage on his present house, and to his family's loan on a building that once housed the family bakery. Both could disappear. The bakery building could be purchased, and I suggested a price. Barclay was looking to buy a house, and I suggested an amount that he might be willing to pay for Hawking's current dwelling. And I discussed the matter of a loan on the property that he had long coveted, repeating again that loans at The Ashford might evaporate beyond the ability of anyone to notice the loss.

Prime Minister Hawking shook my hand as I stood in the rain upon leaving his house. The last words he said to me that night were, cordially, "I hope that you enjoy your life in the Bahamas, Mr. Drinkwater. You will always be welcome here."

Haven. I did not mind walking through the rain to my taxi. For the first time in many months I felt high and dry. All I had to do was shore up the remnants of my family, and life would be grand again. When I arrived home in the wee hours, Hannah met me at the gate with her Luger in her hand. Inside the compound, the dogs, bless them, had run down and chewed an intruder. The man lay pinned against an orange tree, watched over by Roosevelt, Nixon, Truman and Coolidge, who snarled when he twitched or moaned. Blood leaked from his calf. He held a savaged wrist in his free hand. Eisenhower panted next to him as though he expected the intruder to proffer a biscuit for running him down.

"The police say they're coming. But they're not here yet," Hannah cried. She hated this. She hated this place, this life. In the streaked light through the rain, she looked ghostly white.

"What you want here, Mister? What you doing at my house?" I demanded of our terrified captive.

"Nuthin', Mister. I don't want nuthin'."

"He had a hammer," Hannah told me. "When the dogs first caught him, he had a hammer."

"What were you going to do? Smash my windows?"

"No, suh."

"Coolidge! Attack!"

The dogs were never that obliging, but this man didn't know it. He screamed, hollered for mercy. The dogs had him in a state. "Coolidge! Back!" Coolidge looked at me quizzically, wondering what I was about. The only words he understood were "dinner" and "sit."

I knelt down near the black man. Brandished the Luger. "You came here to kill me. That's why you're here."

"No, suh."

"Maybe I should shoot you on the spot, coming in here to kill me and my children." I raised the gun to his temple. "Bang!" I yelled at him.

"I brung you a note!" he shouted. "Don't know what it is!"

We figured out part of what this was about, and dug the note from his jacket pocket. He had come to tack the news to the front door, and he showed me the proof of the nails. He had lost the hammer fighting the dogs. I left him in the care of the canine presidents, went back to the house, and read under the foyer light.

The ransom demand was for twelve million dollars. In exchange I was being offered the safe return of my mother.

13.

Sheilagh's Elf

My mother lies flat, unbent, uncurled, on a bed that moves. She's sore all over. She opens her eyes to find that it's not the bed that's in motion, the whole room rocks gently from side to side. Stale vomit travels across the floor and back again, crusting into a map of barren yellow planet. Stinks. The air is distasteful, it suffocates. Under the low ceiling on a wall, light shines through a circular mirror. She shuts her eyes. My mother feels sore all over, and twisted up inside.

She can handle it. And when she opens her eyes a second time she can handle the braided nylon line that binds her wrists together. It's strange, she tries to jerk her hands apart and cannot. She has been bound before. She has been tied up and dumped in a strange bed before. It feels like a dream this time. What does not feel like a segment from a dream, and is therefore more pressing, is the bearded, balding, nattily-attired gentleman perched cross-legged on the wooden post at the foot of her bed. He hums off-key while giving himself a manicure—a dandy who cannot be more than six inches tall. That fellow looks awfully peculiar to her.

Hunching her head into her shoulders and crouching into the corner of the bed and wall, Sheilagh peers at the creature with a guarded mixture of panic and morbid fascination. She's terrified, prays she's dreaming. And yet, when the elfin being glances up from his labour and spots her—promptly realizing that he has himself been sighted—it is the wee one who comes across as the more confounded and perturbed. Exclaims, "Crikey!" as if caught out after curfew, or with his lilliputian pants down. The miniature man promptly leaps right off the bedpost, which in a landscape of human scale is tantamount to a grown man springing from the rooftop of a five-storey building.

Reacting as she would to the spectre of an average-sized mortal leaping into an abyss, with revulsion and terror and an instinctive longing for supernatural powers to catch the falling friend, Sheilagh bounces from her prone position to the foot of the bed. Gazes over that sheer cliff into the whirlpool of a blue and white hooked rug swirling on the floor below. She spies her sneakers, the socks fluffed inside like jaunty sails, bobbing on the waves as white-hulled yachts. As she gropes to remember who she is and where she is and what's going on, it is all that my mother can do to muster her own name.

Like a seasick voyager on a pitching deck, Sheilagh grips fast to the baseboard, and she's caught in that position when the steward swings open the door to the stateroom carrying her mid-day snack.

"Afternoon, ma'm."

She does not know what compels this behaviour, or why she has regressed so quickly into an odd attitude and compulsion. One part of her reacts with vile loathing as she leaps to the food tray and, working her lashed hands, stuffs sliced fruits into her mouth. These are old habits, old routines, dusty old dreams. She would rather not holler at the man in the prim white suit who backs away from her, she would rather not bare this duress inside her, but Sheilagh hears herself yelling, "Doctor, shit! Doctor, shit! Get out my face, Doctor, shit!" He leaves the room and she hears the lonely click of the lock and my mother wails, cries out in her misery, and slumps upon the untidy floor.

Perhaps she sleeps again. In a twinkling she bounces to her feet— *it's a window*, a window!—the flash jarring into her realm. What she had perceived as a mirror is indeed a window emitting light, a porthole. She rushes to it so quickly that the line that binds her wrists—knotted also to the bed—snaps her back to the floor. For the first time she has discovered this restraint. Rises. Steps toward the oval of light. And can't stretch her head high enough or far enough to see. *I'm tied up!* She tries to think, she tries to imagine what she has done to deserve this contempt, what she has done to be sent back to an asylum.

On her knees, Sheilagh weeps. Falls over as her body is racked by spasms of sadness and regret. She cries out for her boy to forgive her, she's sorry, she didn't mean it—*Sparrow! Don't do this to me! Sparrow!* And curled, shaken, defeated by despair, my mother tightens into a little ball on the floor that rises, rises, and sinks.

She is thinking about her elf. He must have been an elf. A fabric-cutter, or a machinist in Santa's workshop, retired. Sweet little guy. Cute little face. She's glad he's gone because it's dangerous and it's sick and it's *schizophrenic* to see an elf and she doesn't want to be that way, except he had been nice. She wonders about his name. What's a suitable name for an elf?

Yitsak. Yatsik. Kwill. Juke.

A long time ago she had fallen from a bridge and floated down a river where she landed on a shore as barren as Ararat. There she had lived with a family where the man had control over a book of names and every once in a while everybody got a new name. People names. But what do you call an elf?

Oolig. Oblong. Blink. Blotter.

She was probably right to be interested in him. Blessed with an indigenous charm, the little man had shown an infectious personality, and anyone who could unselfconsciously use a word like "crikey" as a spontaneous expression harkened back to a time of innocence. Any self-respecting contemporary pixy would have shouted, "Oh shit!" Or something much worse.

Besides, what man manicures his own nails these days? Execs prefer pretty girls in barber shops to stoop to the task, or they absent-mindedly rip them off themselves while their eyes are glued to the tube. Clippings accumulate on the arm of their favourite chair, awaiting maid service. Definitely, the little guy had shown a keener sense of style than that. What was his name?

How about Flith, Hark, Scrim, or Peetha?

Or do elves have names like Ed, Tom, Mike, and Bill?

Or Francis?

My mother is lying on her side on the floor, her hands bound at the wrists and by a rope to the stationary bed. Her eyes snap open. Out loud she says, with recognition, with understanding, with a modicum of hope, "Crikey! That's his name! His name is Crikey!"

She sees him again, as if she has called him forth, crawling onto the top of her hip like a mountain climber. He uses ropes and spikes in his shoes and my mother panics and screams, screams with all her being, and as she thrashes and kicks she remembers kicking, remembers the abduction and the hands forced on her and being tied up and gagged and then nothing, blackness, the absence of memory, waking into the presence of the elf. The elf is on her face now and she doesn't want to see this, yells, bucks, and on the bed eighteen demons sit watching, stone-faced, watching, they're not breathing, like faces in a photograph, watching, eighteen miniature demons and she's terrified of them, terrified of this, why can't she be released and the little hand of the elf is touching her cheek, caressing her cheek, soothing her—oh! it feels nice, making her calm, letting her close her eyes again. The little hand of Crikey is upon her face like a dream and the demons fade, they vanish, and my mother is permitted to swim into sleep.

When my mother awakes there are splotches in her vision. The elf rests upon her shoulder. She opens her eyes and looks at him. He lies on his side with one knee up and one hand supporting his head. He's munching on an apple. The tiniest little apple anyone has ever seen. She almost panics, almost stops breathing, until Crikey puts a finger to his lips, cautioning her to be quiet.

My mother relaxes. The next time she looks up, the wee creature has departed.

There's a pot in the room. Mom uses it. She lies down on the bed.

Feels such terrible fatigue. Such unworthiness. Shackled to the bed means she's shackled to her illness, it's come back, her illness has captured her one more time.

Remorseful, penitent, Sheilagh suffers these moods believing that somehow she is responsible for her own demise. *Sparrow! I'm sorry! I won't go out at night!* When a fierce hammering assails the door, she cringes against the far wall, convinced that she has brought this bedlam upon herself. She does not know if the assault will be on this plane, or upon another, or if she will know the difference. *Crikey! Help me!* The door breaks open and men dressed in skins like black fish jump into the stateroom. This can't be real. My mother screams at them and furls her little fists and strikes at them but she's no match for their ruthless strength. This can't be real. Two of them drag her out of the room. Down a narrow corridor. "*Agggagghhhhagghhh!*" she's saying. Through a narrow companionway. "*Nnnnooooo! Sssooorrry!*" More men in black fish skins. Up a short ladder to the sky. On deck, men are lying face down, their hands above their heads. One man bleeds.

A fish man shakes her. This mustn't be real.

"Okay, Sheilagh. Okay now. You're all right. Ever worn a mask before? Yes you have. We heard you have. I'm going to put it over your eyes." There's water on the lens and suddenly the world has an oval view. "Breathe through your mouth. That's it. Now, put this in your mouth and keep breathing." It works. "We're going for a swim. Come to the side of the boat. We're going to swim under the water." She hears noise, then shots blast her mind apart. "We will take care of you. Do you understand?" The water washes beneath her. A sun shines in her eyes, eyes that had become accustomed to the dark. The sun hurts. "Do you understand?"

Somebody yells, "Go! Go! Go!"

"Oh Crikey!" she cries into her mouthpiece. After she says it, she is able to nod her head in the affirmative.

Suddenly Sheilagh is in the air, then she is in the water.

My mother swims below the sea. The clear blue water. Above her, the sunlight dances on the surface. Coloured fish sail by. She feels cold, and something else, she feels ... dark. She moves through the water in the grip of the frogmen and one time she stops breathing, and chokes, and swallows water. They put her mouthpiece back in and she begins to breathe. She's all right. She is in the water and there was another time, she remembers that time, when she had fallen through a hole in the darkness and entered upon a different world. She is in the water again and something about that makes her want to cry. Then she's lifted up! Lifted right out of the sea as if by the hand of God and she's grabbed and put in a small boat with a blanket wrapped around her. The men with the slippery black fish skins slide up beside her and the boat rears ups and roars away, the bow high, making huge waves as it roars across the bright blue sea.

Everything's real. It must be. I alone can hear her, as I am the one she clutched as she bolted upright out of the sea. My mother repeats out loud, several times, "I thank thee. I thank thee very much." She speaks in a wee voice, making a small sound, as if speaking to tiny and sensitive ears. Then she begins to wail.

*

That's her own true version, as close as I've been able to make it out, following her escapade among her captors.

14.

Soufrière

"Cockledoodledooooooo!"

Scrunched tiny fists poised at her side, my mother likes to deliver her morning wake-up call perched on the balls of her feet. She rarely gets it right, usually her voice breaks in mid-screech, inevitably she comes off sounding more like a churlish, frightened hen than any barn's rooster. Though she does put her heart into it. By the time she's concluded her cracked-trumpet blast, she will have rocked back onto her heels, her fists will have risen to the level of her neck—subtle changes which nevertheless prove the fervour of her sunrise petition.

"Cockledoodledoo, Sparrow!"

She will stand in my doorway and cackle until my eyes snap open and my head moves to acknowledge the light of a new day. At times I feel as dormant as the volcano upon which my head lies, as sleepy as rock, so I suppose that my mother's morning rituals do have value.

We live these days on the island of St. Lucia, in the British West Indies. My mother has many activities to keep her busy. I have none. She fishes with her friend, Finnbar, and plays games with schoolchildren. She takes food and cigarettes to inmates at the Prison for the Criminally Insane. She bathes in the sulphur springs, becoming young again in the hot, black water. I'm more hard-pressed to occupy my time. I play football with palm trees for linebackers. Climb Gros Piton for a mystic's view of the Caribbean Sea. I chat to tourists and banana-pickers. Overall, I take my pleasure in the poignancy of reminiscence, in pontificating upon the state of the world to my political friends, in writing this memoir, and in being involved in the developmental process of thermal energy. Do you know, there is enough energy beneath this volcanic isle to power the Caribbean? If only we can find the means to harness that source. I assist the project with my cash, and it's a thrill. Ever since I was a boy I had wanted to be involved in engineering, in moving water around, in building tunnels or bridges, so in a way I have found my niche with underground steam.

I feel it sometimes, when I sleep, damp in my dreams, that sulphurous cauldron, mother earth's brew, boiling beneath the slant of my bones.

In the remote home of my boyhood, a man I had known dug deep, intricate tunnels below his house. That's what we're doing here, in our own way, tapping the energy under our feet. I could never figure out why that man dug tunnels—in part to disprove his wretched history, to escape it, and in part to claim it, to never forget. I have come to accept that, each in our own way, we all do similar things. My own trench was dug through the minefield of international finance. While not necessarily a subterranean realm, it was serpentine and genuinely hazardous. This memoir is a tunnel, if not a real tunnel then one that is true to my life, and true to the chaotic adventure of life. One that seeks to both celebrate the true life adventures of Sparrow Drinkwater while serving also, if possible, as a disclaimer. In short, as usual, I want to make the impossible possible, that's the miracle that attracts me. I want to make the insane sane, the foolish wise, the sad happy. I want to make the schizophrenic clear and calm and cogent. I want to make the real true and truth a reality. Isn't that why we all dig tunnels? Or tap steam? Or make love? Or have babies? Live?

Days go by. Communism is on the run, I see. You know what that is. You know what I tell my political friends. What it takes to govern is moral authority. Humph. Moral authority. That and an economic plan. Lose it, count the days before you're heaved out of office. It's a mercantile world, but business doesn't work without a moral stance. Tiny England had an empire because her people believed themselves to be on the side of grace. The Japanese and the Germans are successful today because their people celebrate, and do not doubt, the moral imperative of capital and the nationalist ethic. The exhaustion of the United States, the cynicism of her people toward their own institutions, is a prophesy for economic demise. Economies don't work without conviction. Watch your back, America. As I do mine. Forget about hunting me down. You've got much bigger worries.

They laugh, my political cronies, these tender black fellows with their Ivy League educations. They wonder where I'm coming from with my moral authority. Me. They walk away chuckling amongst themselves, they're amused when I talk about an economic plan. Me. The swindler extraordinaire. An economic plan!

Money, that's my moral authority as far as they're concerned.

Theft, that's my economic plan.

For many years, in the mornings, under the coconut palms and the mangroves, I would pontificate—it's a sport, a pastime—while my mother went fishing. Blacker than pitch, her boyfriend took her out in his rickety boat. When she was sixty-four years old her pal had reached eighty. Mom fished and in the afternoon shopped for our food in town, both in the stores and in the street markets. She had learned to cook the local delicacies. (I could never bring myself to tell her that I was sick to death of stewed green bananas. Have been for years.) Needless to say, it did my heart glad to see her content, although "happy" was never a word I'd reserve for her.

Sheilagh never fully recovered from the kidnapping. She incurred changes to her disposition that, while superficially subtle, were actually telling and incisive. The trauma of the event, for someone of her beleaguered defences, had been distressing enough. Added to her disquiet, she had to live with the knowledge that the world can be a dangerous place. I had not made it safe. On the contrary, I had placed her in jeopardy. Her son had enemies. As crazy as it seemed, as insane as things had become, her boy had enemies who, if they could not manage to strike at him, might choose to retaliate against her. She was scared, a hard aspect to counteract. Mom became frightened of the dark and for awhile she was afraid of water. She'd go loony in small rooms. A panic had infected her, and it took some time to rout it out. The wee nub of a miracle which would help my mother overcome a portion of her fear was the grim knowledge that she had every right to be afraid, that there was nothing remotely crazy or schizophrenic about her feelings.

The worst of it was remembering, being unable to forget, what had happened to her mind. Spying an elf and all that stuff. Believing in him. Sheilagh could no longer tell herself that she was cured. As a sad corollary, she no longer believed that she was curable, a battering to her self-esteem that ruptured her recovery. No use explaining that anyone in those circumstances would have been traumatized and subjected to nightmare. Mom believed that she had failed herself, and consequently she diagnosed herself as unworthy.

In my own two-bit attempt to release her from this tyranny, I endeavoured to tap the feelings and tangled motives motoring within her. We were thwarted by a sadness, by a shifting mood which took the form of a presence, like some miserly, grudge-bearing lodger who had taken up residence in her life, never to move away. Sadness had come home. Joy, to all appearances, had departed.

Surely, that was the cruellest irony. Now that my mother, at long last, could discriminate between happiness and sorrow, without sifting one in with the other, she experienced only sorrow. She was sad, and for the first time in her life she could find nothing redemptive about that mood.

For the longest time, even when my mother was happy she was sad. Even when she laughed, she felt regret.

Her trauma would find companionship in grief. The night that Mom was taken hostage, Uncle Butter had landed in Florida waiting for the weather to clear. The next morning he flew in with bad news, only his had to wait, as mine was much worse.

"What do you mean, kidnapped?" His face visibly paled. Perhaps he feared being next.

I passed him the ransom note.

"Mmmm," he muttered. "Interesting."

A curious response. The blood returned to his cheeks. "Why are you here?" I asked him just as my man was entering the room with Uncle's tea and crumpets.

"It can wait," he replied. In his old age Uncle was looking quite distinguished, at least from a distance, with his white brush moustache and thin grey hair. He had never been inclined to put on weight, and while he would not dare thwack his stomach and boast that he had the physique of a soldier—"Ssssstand me in the trenches!"—which had always been a lie anyway, he did look trim and wiry. (Up close, pancake make-up sabotaged his look. It gave me the creeps, as though he had prepared his own death mask.)

Uncle took two sips of tea, and one bite of his crumpet lathered in a fine marmalade from London, then promptly headed for the door. Whether his pretence was business or sightseeing, clearly he had neither the time nor the sinew for family crisis.

"What can wait?" I called after him. "Wait until when?" Why had he come? What dreaded news had he brought with him this time, at once so urgent that it required the hurried flight, yet so secretive and disturbing that the words could not be conveyed over the phone? Who was after me now, I wondered, what circling net closed in?

"Until we find your mother!" Uncle stipulated. What shocked me was the rider attached to his news. "Sssshe's the one I came to sssssseeee."

Startled, I followed him outside, where he commandeered my driver. "Take me to the goddamned docks! Be quick about it, you insolent galoot!"

I decided not to count on him when things got rough. Remembering how he had panicked on the day we'd met, the day a mad cowboy bandit had pressed a pistol to his cheek, I concluded that nothing was new. Frankly, I was just as glad that he would no longer be underfoot, wishing only that he had not chosen to abduct my chauffeur for his escape.

Turning back into my house, I was met by the emptiness, and by the shrill aloneness of the rooms. Since receiving the ransom note I had not slept, nor had I been left to my own company. Hannah had been with me continuously, then she had taken advantage of Uncle's arrival to deliver our children to the care of their nanny and to pop a sleeping pill, shutting life's door for a few hours. Things were brewing between Hannah and me, and neither of us had the wit or the strength for that rampage just yet. Adventure was one thing, being hounded by the authorities had its covert pleasures, but danger to our boys was chilling. Poor Hannah. I'm sorry for the grief I caused her. God knows she was stalwart, hanging in there when first the police and later the political emissaries came calling, but she was not difficult to read. She was seeing herself gone from this place. Perhaps, at that point, she hadn't thought things through to a decision, yet my wife was making up her mind to decamp. Lovely Hannah would see this debacle through to its end, that's the sort of woman she is ... later she would pack her bags. I recognized that I had left her no alternative, and suspect that I knew Hannah's next move before she had herself reached that decision.

That, perhaps, was the loneliness I confronted. Alone, alone, alone in the main body of my house. I was consigned to the prejudices of my solitude. Police inquisitiveness had instigated a particular, indigestible line of thinking which gave rise to a pair of questions. Who was behind the kidnapping? And this—upon whom could I depend now?

Indeed, who was behind the kidnapping? I could wish for an enemy who bore me no personal grudge, a professional criminal out to make a buck, or an embittered terrorist intent on political statement—such options might signal the good news. A negotiation, a payment, and my mother could be set free. Uppermost in my suspicions, however, and the police rallied behind a similar viewpoint, was the prospect that the kidnapping constituted an act of vengeance. A shareholder made savage by the loss of his life-savings—as if the residue of a life could be stored away, as if anybody's life could lay claim to a surplus.

More cruel in my deliberations was the healthy possibility that the conspirators were people close to me. Mere kidnappers and terrorists tend to abduct children or wives. Mothers? That someone had the sense to take mine indicated knowledge of my situation. Someone knew how to strike at my heart. Only an intimate would know both my greatest weakness, if love for a parent can be construed as a weakness, and how best to exploit that gap in my defences.

Who had done such a terrible thing? Mercedes Ashford? Had her visit that night been intended to defray suspicion? I knew a great deal about the elements of conspiracy. I could write the book. The first ploy is always to establish a position with the target contrary, or at least askew, to one's actual intentions. Like the time Uncle had purchased Corn Field's shares. Daily, Barclay and I had been calling with offers, offers better than the one he'd ultimately accept, continuously upping the ante in order to deflect from the notion that Uncle might be representing us. Had Mercedes dramatically stormed into my house in the rain, ranting about the collapse of her bank while planning this raid upon my family all along? Mercedes could have used twelve million right about then. Once the news had gone around in the morning she had called with condolences and expressions of support, but how the hell did I know who sounded sincere?

I couldn't trust anyone.

If not Mercedes, then Hawking? Politically, we had remained a liability to him despite proving our worth in matters personal. Had he seen this gambit as his last chance to kick us out, while leaving our deals and corporate holdings behind? Or had the game been in progress before I had paid him a visit? I had helped him out, but I had not offered support to the tune of twelve million dollars. *Was there no limit to people's greed?* Hawking and Mercedes went back a long way together, probably they were itinerate lovers, so it was not hard to affix an alliance between them designed to destroy me.

My meditation grew more ghastly, more dark. I wondered if Cornelius Field was back for another kick at the can. I might never be able to shake off his pursuit. As I had spent a lifetime in search of my unknown relations, I envisioned Field dedicating himself to revenge against me. And finally, as I despaired, I considered one more name. That of the ambitious, avaricious Barclay Boisvert. Now that he had looted OIS, did he intend to loot me? Was my best friend an enemy? It was a thought.

I count myself lucky. I recognized that I was coming unglued. Isolation was dictating my paranoia. The best that I could do for myself was to stop thinking.

When my mother and I first came to St. Lucia we lived in the idyllic community of Marigot Bay. Palm fronds bend to the water's edge and such is the design of the harbour that it is virtually invisible from the sea. You have to sail right into it to make out the homes and the yachts behind the curve in the bay. In 1778, a British admiral tucked his fleet into Marigot and the pursuing French sailed right on by, a vanishing act so astonishing that the incident gave rise to an eighteenth century legend similar to modern tales about the Bermuda Triangle. The bay is more reminiscent of the South Seas than of the Caribbean, and in the long-term perhaps the prettiness of the place undermined my senses. An expatriate population of Europeans and Americans grumbling in paradise made me uneasy. Castries was not to my liking either, cinder block and rusting iron, I felt I was in some shabby Med' seaport. Since I preferred to be near the volcano where we do our research on thermal energy, my mom and I moved down to Soufrière.

It's a poor town. Dirt-floor shacks line the water's edge and men and women stare at you with the stale, oppressed eyes of the helpless and the lost. This is Third World stuff and it's not a fond sight, nor do I wish to diminish the despair of the situation by pointing out that the town is sustained by a good spirit. I like it because it's real, a town true to the life of this place. Western influences are ingrained here, they're not a veneer. I love walking through Soufrière. The name means, literally, under the volcano. I'm treated well, although with curiosity, and the sight of small barefoot girls in their blue tunics and braided hair carrying their school books never fails to bolster my morale. Levels of education are improving, as are employment prospects. That said, progress in a place like this must be measured in increments.

Mom took a lover when first we came to Soufrière. His name was Malcolm Childress and he was a rich man's son, a banker's boy, from Toronto. He had come to St. Lucia as a young man and the old codger was fond of saying to me in his English colonial diction, "A man has not lived until he has helped to develop a Caribbean island." He was much older than my mother, having come here either after the First World War, or, as I suspect, in lieu of that conflagration. In any case, he liked to call himself 'Colonel'. He'd regale me with stories about banking in Toronto, how the head office for the Imperial once maintained a whore house in the basement, that sort of thing. He was either a superb story-teller or a superior liar, and he had made a decidedly modest fortune in the hotel and yacht-charter business. The Colonel had retired to an ancient sugar cane plantation to make his own (delicious) rum.

Malcolm had put together a few dollars, and yet his old age was sustained by the affection of the local people. They liked him, they were amused by him, they made jokes about him behind his back which conveyed how silly they thought the old man had become, and also how much they loved him.

When Malcolm asked my permission to have my mother over for dinner, I consented. Late in the evening, he sent a messenger asking if it would be all right if she stayed the night. I declined. Mom came home fuming. One punch and she bloodied my nose. "If you think she did damage to you, dear boy, you should have seen the impression left upon my chin. She appears to have a delicate constitution, yet she definitely knows how to brawl. She's my kind of woman. Where did she learn to fight like that? Dear boy, your mama seemed rather upset that I sought your approval. I shan't do so on future occasions. I'm too old. My constitution cannot sustain another drubbing."

And so my mother had chosen a lover once again. Their affection and our friendship helped the years to pass, and did much to dissolve the sense of banishment I had experienced after life in the Bahamas had become untenable, after Hannah had left me.

I had been in my Bahamian house, frayed, desperate, thoroughly whacked out—I can still bring to mind that desolate spirit—when a message came through from Uncle. I am waiting for a call from the kidnappers, but Uncle is insisting that I must see him first. I was to get my ass down to the docks and charter a speedboat across to Nassau.

"I have my own boat," I told my chauffeur who had telephoned with the communiqué.

"No, please, sir, you don't have that boat. Your uncle, he took that boat. He stand up on it right now, please, sir. Come to Nassau, please, sir."

When I arrived I managed to find Uncle without difficulty, partly because I recognized my own boat, partly due to the flurry of activity in the vessel's vicinity, and partly because my chauffeur was jumping up and down on the deck desperately waving to me as though his life, please, sir, hung in the balance.

Frogmen sat on the bow. A stranger in the cockpit received communications on a radio slung across his back. Apparently my boat's radio was considered too public for this covert operation.

"Uncle—what's going on?"

"You're late!" he hollered at me. The temerity of the man. "Get aboard." I was angry enough to do as he asked, intending in my fury to heave him into the drink. "You! Driver! Get off!"

My chauffeur was so willing to obey that he literally flew through the air from one boat to the other, then he pummelled the charter boat's captain's shoulders to get going. In the same instant our mooring line was cast off, the boat fell away slightly, and I collapsed into the cockpit at Uncle's feet as the bow lifted into the air and we rampaged through the crowded anchorage. Crawling to my knees, I could see the other boaters in our disruptive wake hurling curses upon us.

"What're you doing?"

"Sssssssshut up and sssssssit down," Uncle said.

"I will not sssssshut up. Where are we going?"

I had mocked his speech impediment for the first time ever, and I suppose that that was what had garnered his attention.

"We know where your mother is," he told me simply.

"Where is she?"

Defiantly, stressing his sibilant ess more than usual, he repeated, "Sssssssssssshut up and pay attention."

So I did. For about twenty seconds. "Who are these men, Uncle?"

"They're frogmen," he answered, as though designating their species. "They're mercenary soldiers. Their hands are deadly weapons."

That description may have been intended to make me feel secure, but I took it as a threat. Said nothing. I could now guess that we were headed for the anchorage in the lee of Paradise Island. As we approached, the boat's skipper, the man with the radio slung across his back, finally eased the throttle. We had the sun right at our backs and that was part of it, I'm sure, a tactic encoded in the strategy. People watching us from the harbour would need to protect their eyes to decipher our activities. The frogmen back-flipped into the emerald sea while we were still underway, one, two, three, four of them, like black depth charges dropped upon a submarine. Then the world went very quiet, the engine had been cut, we drifted, and when the breeze thwarted our forward progress, Uncle said, "Throw out the anchor, Sssparrow."

I did. Dropped the Danforth and got a good bite. Waited under the glare of the sun. I felt myself spinning, going dizzy, afraid that I had caught the illness of my mother's youth, that I was allergic to light. I lacked sleep, I was stressed beyond my limits, perhaps I was hyperventilating. I looked over the side into the mirror of the water, at the clouds adrift upon the sea, at my own face rippling on the surface. How long did I wait? I know that at one time I felt Uncle's hand sympathetic upon my shoulder. He removed it when shots were fired. I flinched then too, and searched for evidence of disaster. But noise travels easily across the water and we were on the distant periphery of the harbour. There was nothing to see, and the echoes of the gunfire reverberated off the coconut trees on Paradise Island.

I stared back into the water, tense and afraid, trying to hold on. After an eternity I spied movement below the surface, rising, like dolphins breaking for air. And then, straight up out of the water, her arms upraised as if to catch the sun, my mother ascended before me. Huge and rapt and as holy as an angel, standing right on the water before me.

We grabbed each other before this miracle dissolved.

I fell back with her on top of me and clutched hard, in the shock of the moment instinctively hanging on, as if the sea that had spewed her into my arms might wash over us again and in the next instant claim us back. Sounds were vented from her, words of thanks, then a rising wail like police sirens and I wasn't certain if she knew who was holding her, all I knew was that I would not let her go.

We never weighed anchor. Someone just cut the line.

The bow was high and the boat was pounding through the light chop, travelling faster for our escape than it had for our attack. We had dropped off four frogmen, we were returning with eight. Rather than incur casualties our forces had multiplied. All these images, even the spinning sun, abetted my confusion. I had reached a point where I could not cope. What brought me back into this world was the voice of my mother questioning the body that enclosed her.

"Sparrow? Sparrow!"

I let her see that it was me. Witnessed her happiness in recognizing that she had guessed right, that I was real enough.

Uncle came over. Mom was delighted to see another friend, as if each sighting restored her sense of reality.

Now to rely on recollection, as I have been discovering, is an imprecise art. To conjure a situation where the emotional swings had been extraordinary, risks allowing a distorted view to prevail. So be it. I became conscious of being watched, I felt the bore of another's scrutiny. That may not be so. What occurred next might have been more simple. I may have looked up and to one side, accidentally engaging the eyes of a frogman who sat on the gunwale of the craft with his feet pointed aft. I may then have recognized those eyes to be my own. Or, upon reflection, akin to my own. The head of the man was covered by the protective black skin of the wet-suit, with only the oval of the face revealed. His mask had been lifted onto his forehead, and his mouthpiece dangled freely just below his nose. So I really had very little to go on. I had the eyes, and their striking familiarity. They were the eyes that glanced back at me in every mirror. I had his black costume. And I had the interest and intensity of the man's stare. At that time, under those wild conditions, that was all that I required to confirm that this man and me had to be connected.

I stared back at him and his look did not waver.

"Do I know you?"

A gesture of his chin signalled me to come closer, away from the earshot of my mother.

"You're Sparrow?" he asked.

"Yeah."

"How do you do?" He extended his hand, which I did not accept. "I'm your father."

If he had ever had wings, he had lost them. Although he was a white man, he was wearing a skin as black as a crow's, consistent with my mother's description.

The boat heeled as it veered sharply into a cove south of Nassau. Another launch awaited our arrival, begging the conclusion that it was intended for the frogmen.

I had been looking for my mother's people. I had assumed her lover, the man or bird whose seed had stimulated my existence, had been itinerant. I had never guessed that he had shown enough interest to guide us through our lives.

The shock of my mother rising from the sea, the astonishing aspect of what I had assumed to be my other-worldly father, intimidated familiar speech.

Our boat slowed down dramatically, moving our bodies around. We rounded up against the other vessel.

"This makes us even," my father said to me. Not Hello, or How's the family? but, "This settles the score."

I didn't know what he meant for a second, until I remembered my litany of grievances. "You sonofabitch. You're the one. My mother fell off a bridge because of you. You got us separated. You bastard!"

Frogmen, clutching their flippers, stepped from my boat onto the awaiting launch.

"I didn't know she'd fall off a bridge, for Christ's sake. I made a mistake. Your mother fell off a bridge into a river and you and she got separated. Okay. I'm sorry about that. Okay? Today I rescued her out of the sea, I brought you back together again, so we're square. Now maybe you can give it a rest."

My father's first and final advice to me. Give it a rest. He leapt onto the launch and that vessel sped away, leaving me with my fists clenched and nobody left to strike.

He had a point, of course. He had just rescued my mother. But who the hell was he? Why had he finally come? Why had he so swiftly departed again?

"*Bastard!*" I shouted into the wind and loud outboard motors. "*Come back here! You have to talk to me! YOU HAVE TO TALK TO ME!*"

What I appreciated most when I came to St. Lucia was that it was not necessary to bribe anyone to stay. For someone in my circumstances, that's as good as a welcome. The Americans and the authorities in Canada have never put undue pressure on the government here to have me extradited. I'm not sure what mollified them. Most likely there was a connection to the monies Barclay paid to have Nixon elected, and while the discovery of our relationship was an embarrassment to the President, I think he managed to live up to his end of the bargain and yank a few strings. Not the strings of amnesty, unfortunately, yet the pressure eased. The Americans, who have always been poor geographers, probably deduced that St. Lucia was sufficiently remote and underdeveloped that it represented adequate banishment for the likes of me.

Barclay and I had already departed company before I came here. He fell in love with a woman in Nassau, an American, who was familiar with Costa Rica, and she enticed him to go to that country. (Unlike me, he had had to pay his way in.) He maintains a splendid, well-guarded estate in the hills near San José, raises thoroughbred horses, and dabbles in enterprises with which I have no links. Exile has not always been an easy lot for Barclay. His heavy drinking led to the rupture of his pancreas. He was dead on an operating table in Panama for a minute and thirty-seven seconds. Fortunately for him, his wife had had the sense to have flown him to Panama for the operation, where he benefited from the skills of a superior surgeon who restored him to life. Had he had the operation in Costa Rica ... well, the possibilities don't bear contemplation.

Not much of his pancreas remains, and the remnant is unable to manufacture sufficient insulin, so Barc's a diabetic. It's all for the best. One of life's pet accidents that, if we survive, work in our favour. Nobody recognizes him any more, he's trimmed down, he keeps fit, he's no longer a drunk. Once a year or so Barc and I get together. Often he urges me to join him in Costa Rica. I admit, he has a nice set-up there.

It's just that I like being of some use, and the thermal energy project keeps me where I am.

For Hannah's sake, I don't think it's necessary to detail the termination of our marriage. We had some spats, she and I, and some good cries. In the end things were amicable. We went through the motions, she forgave me I think, and we parted. She's my ex-spouse now, which is different than being a friend, and we remain connected and cordial because of the kids. Both Zeke and Zack come down to St. Lucia for Thanksgiving, and again after Christmas to enjoy the tropical sun over the New Year's break. They've developed faint British accents because we sent them to a private school in Wales. (One that made a point of being secure from kidnappers.) Now Zack's at Harvard and doing well. He's intent, geared, ambitious. Zeke is struggling a bit at the University of Toronto, although I'm confident he'll come around once he decides what he's willing to do. He's very intelligent, just dreamy. What he'd like to do is play baseball, and he's had a hard time accepting that, no matter how ferociously they hustle, Canadians who can neither hit *nor* field attract zero attention from the scouts. Like everyone else, even baseball players, Zeke will learn that life requires accommodations to be made. In the meantime, he lives with his mother, swings a bat in the backyard, and neglects his studies.

I miss the boys. I love it when they visit. We get along. They've reached an age when they question their old man's past, and I can't dissuade them with easy assertions. Their curiosity was one motivation to commence this memoir. Boys, if you've read this far, what can I say? The world surprised me and I surprised the world. The point of any adventure is to survive intact. Beyond that, we cannot predict how the experience will mark or change us. I, for one, can scarcely believe that I am whom I have become.

After Hannah left, and then Barclay, I felt desolate on the Bahamas. The luck of my life was that Nina telephoned from Montreal. "Sparrow-bird. How's it hanging?"

"Nina! It's great to hear your voice."

"Any voice I bet. Does anyone on the face of this planet stoop to talk to you?"

"With my money? Are you kidding? People line up for interviews."

"That's why I'm calling. Money."

She had me off-guard for an instant. I had assumed that I could count on Nina to be herself, not to be defrayed by the trappings of my wealth.

"Sparrow?"

"I'm still here. How much do you need?"

"You sound like you have indigestion. Listen, Bird, I need ten million bucks, but there's a hitch."

I coughed into the phone. "Yes, I would say there's a hitch."

"You have to be part of the deal."

"Nina-poo, you've done it again. You've lost me."

"You used to be swift. Sparrow, you're slowing down in your old age. You're rotting down there, baking in the sun. You need something to do. You need a challenge, Bird. I'm calling to provide it."

The sound of her voice was soothing. Like being slipped into an alternate reality. Hers was the voice of home. As if I had ever known one.

"It's your dime, Nina. You can tell me what you're talking about or you can babble on. Either way, I'm perfectly content to listen."

"Sparrow, the way I figure it, we're related by divorce, if you know what I mean. Anyhow, I saw you first. I introduced you to Hannah, so just because you and my cuz are splitsville, that doesn't mean you and me can't be pals, right?"

"Of course not. I'm glad you called. It's great to hear your voice."

"You keeping saying that. Look. This is what I'm into. Earth orgasm. I've got this government grant to study the possibility of thermal energy on the island of St. Lucia? Okay, so I'm going to do that. But you know studies. They get put on the shelf. So I said to myself, 'Self, maybe Sparrow would like to invest.' So, would you?"

"Earth orgasm?"

"Think of it as several ice ages of foreplay. What we want the earth to do is ejaculate, but not mess the sheets like in a volcano, but be a really tender, considerate lover and come slowly, over a hundred years, let's say. Earth orgasm. Thermal energy. I've had some bad reports about you, Sparrow. You need a change. Sheilagh does too. Let me show you a real Caribbean island, not that sandbox you're living on now. What do you say? I figure ten million should cover our start-up costs. Not much to help save the earth and get the Third World out of a jam."

The rest is history.

After my mother's rescuers had sped on their way, I took her into Nassau for medical attention. I figured there had to be something wrong with her because she did not object to being admitted to a hospital. Once she was safe and comfortable, and I had hired armed guards to ensure her security, I took a helicopter from the roof back to my compound. Yanked Uncle out of bed. "Come on. We have to talk."

I waited under the palm trees while he dressed. Cleared everyone, including Hannah, out of the way.

Uncle wore a silly, sheepish grin.

"You have a lot of explaining to do," I said.

"Didn't we do a job? Didn't we get things done? Sssparrow, we sssaved your mother! Wasn't that exciting?"

I had to check myself to keep from punching him out. "Don't talk to me about excitement. What do you know?"

"Ssssparrow? What do you mean? I knew some people. Pals from the war. We put together a rescue team."

"Shut up. My father was on that boat."

I don't know what he had been planning to tell me, what spiral of lies would support his explanation about being able to find my mother in a country that was foreign to him, and then brilliantly effecting her rescue as if he was a trained commando. Telling him that I knew the identity of one of the frogmen wrecked his rehearsed performance, and Uncle shifted into a quieter, more honest, gear.

"I ssseee. I didn't know you knew that. Was that what you were sssssscreaming about, on the boat? Ssso. What do you want to know?"

"For God's sake, Uncle, tell me who he is. Tell me what's going on."

He wiggled his moustache, the habit that used to irritate me so much when we first met, and he sat himself down on the garden bench beside me. "Your father, Sssparrow, is an adventurer."

Those were his first words, and I'm not sure that he had to say more. I didn't go dizzy exactly, it's more like losing my sense of equilibrium, remaining upright while forsaking balance. He would talk on and I would absorb every word, question some, and yet feel as though I had been cast out a great distance, listening to him as though I dwelled on a faraway shore. "He hunted alligators, in those days." The tale wove through swampland and war zones, histories and circumstances. "By day, one of the schoolteachers had been his lover." So that, when my mother became pregnant, one of the staff at her school knew whom the father must be. She had confronted him, and told him that the girl he had impregnated, the child who had made a habit of running out after dark to pee in the swamp, was crazy, an orphan, and destitute. Irresponsible with his zipper, this father possessed a grain of integrity imbedded in his marrow. "You were always looking for your mother's people, Sssparrow, but sssshe had been cared for only by her lover in the sssswamp, the alligator-poacher." Later Uncle and the poacher would meet during the war. Uncle had been a valet. He admitted that to me at long last and without blinking, as though he had no recollection of his boasts about life in the trenches. Uncle's General refused the courtesy of a valet, didn't believe in them, and was about to make a foot soldier of Gerald Boisvert. That's when my real father intervened. A sergeant, he assigned Uncle to his platoon, and became the only sergeant in the forces with his personal servant. The Army never knew. After the war, my father had Uncle help him with his private obligations.

"He was an adventurer. I thought I had talked him into letting me adopt you. I know better now. That had been his idea all along. He was a conniver, like you. Like you he could manipulate people."

"Why has he never shown himself to me?" I suppose that that was the crux of my complaint. I forgive everything except his absence.

"Why would he?" Uncle asked me back. "Look who you've become. Did you think he'd be impressed, do you think he'd be pleased to know that his ssson is ssssupposed to be ssssome kind of a crook? Do you think he's proud of you? Do you think he's proud of himself to have ssseen what you've become? I guess he thought I'd raise you to be a decent sss-sort of fellow. He never imagined you'd turn out a whole lot more like him than like me. He's not exactly proud of his conduct in your life—or in your mother's life. He doesn't want to have to atone."

"But he came! He rescued Mom!" I don't know. I suppose one part of me wanted to elevate him as a hero.

"I think he's hoping that that's enough."

"Enough?"

"Ssssparrow, leave the guy alone. He wants you off his back."

"How can I be on his back when I never knew he existed?"

"What he did once nearly cost Sssssheilagh her life. He's a robust ssort of a man and he thought that he sssshould make things difficult for both of you, that that would help you in life. His mistake. Ssshe plunged into the river and the two of you were ssseparated. Now he's plucked her out of the sssea and presented her back to you. He thinks you're even. He wants you to sssstop pursuing him."

"I didn't know I was." But, of course, I had been. I had been pursuing the idea that somebody had to be out there manipulating our existence, and that Uncle had been filling him in on our progress. He hated thinking that one day I might find him.

"What man wants to be known?" Uncle continued, more philosophically than I had ever observed him to be, and more calm and rational. "Who wants to be discovered—least of all by ssssomeone with questionable motives. He sssaved your mother, now let him be, Ssssparrow. Let yourself be too."

Uncle didn't know what he was asking. Or, on second thought, maybe he did. To surrender my quest for my secret guide meant that I had to take responsibility for the construction of my own life. I couldn't blame everything on him, or on my quest. I am whom I have become—that's a difficult realization. That's sobering knowledge.

"He's a rich man?" I asked.

"Not particularly. He moves in sssstrange circles. That's how he was able to find out who had taken your mother sssso fast. He's an adventurer, not a businessman."

"He's a mercenary?" Uncle allowed that question to remain unanswered. "But Barclay told me, when we were kids, that you had a big client."

Uncle continued to be still. When he did speak again I could detect the edge of contrition in his voice. "Barclay was wrong. But that was my fault. He ssssstarted to ssssay that I was a ssssmall-timer, a sssssmall-fry, sssso I made up the idea that I had one big client. I did have a sssssecret client, ssso it wasn't hard to perpetuate the notion that he was also rich."

"But once, I don't know if you know this, Barc broke into your safe one night, a long time ago. What did he find?"

Uncle needed even more time to formulate his confession. "Sssso that was Barclay? I figured. Alone or with you?"

"I put him up to it. But Barc took the contents of the safe. What did he find?"

Uncle shifted his weight, as though dissatisfied with his posture, the seat, his life. "He would have come across an extra sssset of books. He would have come across an accounting process—just a hobby of mine really—an accounting process that would, sshall I ssssay, have facilitated his ssstudies."

I thought about that for a minute. "You cheated on your taxes? Barc learned to ex-out entries and spread paper trails through you?"

"It was only theory. I didn't do it. I mean—no, I don't mean that. I had developed methods of cheating—just ssssso I could catch people at it, you understand. And, of course, to test my theories, to ssssssee if they worked—"

"You cheated on your own taxes."

He shoulders slumped further. "I guess so."

"Barclay learned his tricks from you."

"Yes. But give him credit. He developed them to new heights."

"He put them into action, you mean."

Uncle was sitting staring into the floral garden, wringing his hands. "Yes," he confessed, as if I alone could give him absolution. "That's what I mean."

"Uncle, why are you here? How did my father happen to be here? Everything's going so fast. I don't get it."

"I have news, Ssssparrow. I came to tell Sssssheilagh, and also your father, because they're both involved."

"Hold it. Other than being lovers a long time ago, what possible connection, what ongoing connection, could my mother have to this man that you would want to share information with both of them?"

"Your father's ssssister is Diedre Plant. Ssshe's your Aunt. Miss Plant is your mother's best friend. This isn't coincidence or anything. He had brought his sister to Montreal and charged me with ssseeing to her welfare. Then he figured to bring your mother to Montreal, too, once you were old enough and maybe she was well enough. When it was obvious that your mother couldn't live in the house and raise you, he gave it to his ssssister, who was also needy but had made a lot of progress. He's a man who takes care of the people in his life. You and him are alike that way."

"Uncle, what did you come to tell them?"

"Miss Plant is dead."

"Oh God," I remembering saying, panicking. "Don't tell her now. Don't you dare tell Mom that now."

"I'll leave it," Uncle informed me, "in your hands."

Several years ago, Mom scared me half-to-death. Her boyfriend's name was Finnbar, and she took his fishboat out onto the bay. Enjoying an evening coffee and liqueur, I had a plain view of her from the small balcony off my study. I was thinking about fetching my pistol to take potshots at the rats. I've learned to treat the rats here as city dwellers do squirrels back in Canada. We co-exist, they are essentially benign. The palms on my property wear girdles of tin partway up their trunks to discourage rats from harvesting coconuts prematurely. I have screens on my doors and windows primarily to admit no bugs, but also to keep the chameleons and the white rodents away. Still, on any human scale of pests, they are quite minor. Every so often, however, I slink back into my upper class North American mode, and reach for my gun to blast away at the intruders. When people in town ask me what I'd been shooting, and I answer "Rats," it's as though I'd been firing salvos at coconuts, or blasting clouds. They really don't see the point.

Anyhow, I did not step inside for my pistol. My mother sustained my attention. Finnbar's boat is narrow with shallow freeboard aft and a very high bow. Oddly enough, it bears some similarity to a Venetian punt. Mom was not travelling fast. She kept one hand on the outboard and steered a careless, meandering course out of the bay. I was watching her from the balcony, sipping coffee, enjoying a Drambuie, when I heard her motor die out. Not a rare occurrence on Finnbar's boat, and Mom was as adept as anyone at getting the damn thing started again. I was intrigued when she did not make the attempt. Out there on the water, as still as an angel in prayer, she seemed from a distance perplexed. That's when I went inside to fetch the binoculars.

The next time I spotted her she was standing in the boat. I've never been impressed by the stability of the local craft. They're reasonably sound underway, especially at high speed, but walk around on them or set them adrift in the waves and they appear as tipsy as canoes. Mom was standing precariously, and reaching into her handbag.

As she was pointed toward the sea and my view was from one side, I could not make out her face in the binoculars. Her grey hair fell across her visage as she rummaged in her bag. Yet her motion, particularly as she spread an upraised hand slowly above the bow, seemed rapt. Her movement ceremonial, even reverential. She made another sweep with her hand from one side to the other, and this time flakes fell from her fingers to drift upon the water. I had no idea what these specks could be—until it was suddenly obvious.

When I had moved in haste to the Bahamas, and later to St. Lucia, a mere portion of my personal belongings came with me. Once settled in St. Lucia, I sent for my stuff, and thanks to Uncle's meticulous industry everything that might possibly be of interest (other than furniture, which Hannah claimed) arrived. This included my mother's belongings, both what she had accumulated since our reunion and also what had been stored away in Uncle's attic—along with her son—for so many years. Going through the artifacts had been a thrill for her, and together we had reminisced. Now, something was wrong.

My mother, with great ceremony, cast floating hearts upon the waters. The flowers that she had salvaged at great personal risk from a Georgia swamp were set adrift.

What did this mean?

I had no knowledge of my mother's intentions, or what she meant by this display, yet I was convinced that she was about to follow the floating hearts, the dried bits of flowers, into the sea.

I ran down the mountainside. Stopped to train the binoculars on her once. My mother had sat down in the boat. Thank God! She's thinking about it first. She's hesitating. I ran along the muddy road that lines the southern shore of Soufrière, watched by citizens from their sheet metal, wood and plastic shacks. I heard the engine fire. She had successfully restarted the motor. She had changed her mind! I kept running, a distance beyond my normal endurance, and met her as she returned to the shore.

Swept her into my arms. The enthusiasm of my greeting startled her, and I was the one obliged to explain myself. "I was worried about you."

"How come?"

"You were standing in the boat."

"So?"

"So! It's dangerous to stand in a boat!"

"Oh, Sparrow, thou art so dumb. I do it all the time."

Later I had the courage to ask her about the floating hearts. It seemed to me that she had been casting her life away, at least her past, which made me apprehensive about what she might be thinking or planning. Mom told me that she had not been allowed to do anything on her own for Miss Plant or for Malcolm, except cry. "When I die the angels will speak to me. They will understand me because I say 'thee' and 'thou' and 'thy'. When they hear me say, 'How art thee today?' they won't think I'm schizophrenic." I had listened to this catechism before, once when I had skirted around the possibility of returning her to normal patterns of speech. Mom, quite rightly, had stuck to her religious guns—religion she had learned from the people who first cared for her in Montreal, until they went out of business. She maintained the few archaic phrases she had acquired. And why not? I'm convinced that any angel would cheerfully bend an ear to her speech. If saying certain words convinces Mom of the same thing, what can be the harm in that?

Miss Plant had been buried in Montreal, and we had been unable to return. Much to our surprise, Malcolm's body had been claimed by relations in Toronto, and while I fought like hell to get the poor fellow laid to rest on his beloved Caribbean island, his family stuck it to their black sheep, bullying him in death as they had been unable to do in life. They got back at him by taking him back. They hauled him home. Malcolm had failed to anticipate such a horrific gesture. His will had distributed his property among St. Lucians, but he had not made requests regarding his burial. And so, Mom missed that funeral as well.

"The floating hearts are mine and thine," Mom said. "They're part of me. So I sent them on the water for Miss Plant and Malcolm to enjoy in heaven. To let them know I'm coming."

This is what I mean by her inherent sadness. It is with her always.

Later that evening, to the music of a tropical shower, percussion tapped by the palms in the wind, we were talking about the floating hearts, the swamp, and her early days. "My father had wings," I said. This was gospel. This was lore. This was the true life adventure on which I had been weaned.

"Yes," Mom said. She appeared submerged in thought. When she surfaced, she qualified our mythology. "Or maybe it was a tent."

"A tent?" This was sacrilege. Between us, at least between us, my father had been a huge black raven.

"Maybe a man took me inside his tent, Sparrow."

"A tent! You told me he had big wings!"

"But Sparrow, I'm schizophrenic. Not everything is real like it seems. Men don't have big wings. Birds don't make people-babies. So maybe a man took me in his tent and his tent in the wind was like wings."

I appreciated how much figuring out she had had to do to unravel that episode and locate its logic. She was winding a strand of her grey hair in a finger, over and over again until it hung in a ringlet, and I was mute with pride. Then she startled me again.

"I thought I saw him again that time. Remember when I got res-cued? One of the men with skin like a fish, he looked like that man. He was looking at me with eyes like that man, with eyes like thine. I thought it was thee every time I looked at him. If he was a bird he would have looked a lot like that man. Except he was a fish, except I know he was not really a fish, and he was not really a bird either."

"How did that make you feel?" I wondered. Often I had contemplated telling her the news, connecting the apparition of the frogmen to us.

"It made me feel very sad."

"Why sad?"

"Because it was a crazy thought, Sparrow. I don't like to have crazy thoughts. They make me feel so bad." I had puzzled over this one for a long time. Do I risk telling her that her first lover had revisited, that he had rescued her from danger? How would she react? My mother did not learn things casually, the news would tap another wellspring. How would she absorb the news that this old friend had not identified himself, had not said hello, had simply done his duty and gone on his way. I could not explain his actions to her, because I did not fully understand them myself.

"Maybe it wasn't such a crazy thought. One of the frogmen—fish-men, you call them—one of those guys looked a lot like me."

Should I tell her?

Fortunately, Mom answered that question for me, and perhaps said more about the floating hearts than she had meant to reveal. "I don't want to have old thoughts. I want the past to leave me alone, I want it to be like it never happened. That's my dream. I want it to be so I can just go on now, so I can live like any person. I want to get myself ready for heaven."

To live like any person. A great wish. A noble endeavour. For all my prosperity, I cannot. For all my mother's progress, she is also denied an ordinary life. In a way, this is how my mother and me truly found one another, and came to share one another's deepest wish—to live like any person. What we have shared emerged from our diversity. My mother had a past she wished to deny, while embracing the present and yearning for heaven. My deepest past had been honourable, yet it was my present that required mending. She is a fugitive from the pernickety distinctiveness of her mind. I'm on the run from angry nations and hot-heads, not to mention the recriminations of my mistakes.

I do not speak from remorse. I cannot request forgiveness. I did what I did. At the time I thought that I had to do it. I was younger than I knew. Somebody was going to take that money, as things worked out it was me. I was not a crook. I merely accumulated money that had once belonged to other people. There's a difference. Thievery is action. Accumulation is circumstance, it's fate, it's destiny, it's practically unavoidable. Investors lost their shirts—I say this, had I never been born they would still have lost their shirts. Their quarrel should not be with me. But—a man with X million dollars (exactly how much is my business) would be a fool to request, and absolutely he will not receive, the sympathy of anyone.

All I can do now is do good, and probe the earth's bowels for polyps and thermal energy. All I can do now is sit on this volcanic isle and be good company to my friends. All I can do now is join the search for my soul. Some nights Nina drops by, out of her steam-spewing crater, down from her mountaintop, away from her young St. Lucian lovers. Ours is a tangle of regrets and whims, sadnesses and joyful noise. The shame of it is that Nina requires absence and tension in her relationships, she's not about to stay for long.

Click!

We connect though. In our own haphazard way. And in fairness I should add that she does not admit to having young St. Lucian lovers.

In her very own words, "At least not so often, Sparrow." I accept my portion, I endure my lot, I take solace that I defy the anticipated end of villains. In the movies the bad guys get theirs. If the truth be known, I not only live well, I live harmoniously. I even get to enjoy the tantalizing prospect of future adventures, for I know from Uncle that Cornelius Field was the one who kidnapped my mother. The swift punishment inflicted by my father's incursion taught him to disavow violence. But I have heard that in the capitals of the world he has pledged vengeance of some kind. Over the years I have come to expect that he has mellowed, that he seeks a more sophisticated satisfaction than assassination. We shall see.

So, in the end, I have it all—even hope for further adventure. I shall not rot here. (Although, God knows, that would be the most cunning trick of all if Field has the wit to play it, simply ignoring me. Do you think he is such a master of this game? I doubt that he has the patience.) I have my hobby—earth orgasm—and I have my politicians to berate. St. Lucia is blissfully short of beaches, therefore it will never be over-developed as a tourist attraction. To compensate, the Prime Minister plans to legalize gambling, believing that a casino will attract the construction of a megahotel. I'm fighting him all the way, but of course, I am no fool. If I lose this argument, as I expect I shall, I am prepared to invest.

Beneath my feet then, the volcano. An image of molten rock, the fires of hell. My mother, with one foot in heaven, pinned her hopes on a redemption where schizophrenia is cured as easily as popping a pill. I hope she's right. There is, however, a downside to her prophecy. If she is astute in these matters, and she might well be, and the spiritual realm is governed by competing kingdoms, then I guess it's hell for me. And if she's wrong, if there is no heaven, no hell, then I am exalted upon this earth as a rich man, and her life portioned to its sadness and her earthly malaise. Either way, we win, we lose. I suppose that's why I feel comfortable living here. Mom and I returned full-circle to Eden. She, comforted on this idyllic isle by the prospect of heaven, while I am reminded of the lava flowing in its rage through eternity below.

The floating hearts cast upon the waters, and her persistent talk of heaven, gave me a few anxious nights. Despite her cogent, and poignant, explanations, I was concerned that she was preparing to die. My mother was shedding aspects of her past and memory. In a peculiar way, this constituted a continuation of the process of recovery, except that she could not recognize her own good health, she kept on "curing" herself, passing beyond recovery into what I feared could become an equally psychotic state.

Contrary to my mom, I attended to my baggage, drawing my memories close around me, writing of my adventures in this world, and in many ways shielding myself behind the cloak of prosperity. I did many good works. I wanted to teach the young men of St. Lucia how to play baseball, for I consider them to be superior athletes to the Dominicans who have so dominated the middle infields of the Major Leagues. Hey, it's one way out of poverty, and there are so few choices. Here we produce the occasional boxer who, if he can acquit himself well in the Caribbean tournaments (before getting whupped by the Cubans), can manage the down payment on a house and set himself up as a windsurfing instructor or buy a cab.

Mine were good intentions, but clearly misguided. There's not enough flat land on St. Lucia, and none around Soufrière, for baseball diamonds. More importantly, British and French colonization ruins a people for the American game. So I developed a form of touch football. I'm better at it, and we don't really need open fields. Our fun is not oppressed by the hope of a future career. Instead, we merrily run amok in the congested streets of Soufrière or in the banana groves, having added new meaning to the old touch football pass pattern, "Banana right!" Instead of a pigskin we play with hollowed-out, smoothed-down coconuts, and instead of being a wide-receiver, age, gimpy knees, and clipped wings have transformed me into a quarterback. I have tried to teach these gallant boxers to tag and not to fight, and to throw perfect coconut spirals, which they insist on calling "sparrows." We have fun. They keep me in shape. When the assassins come, they'll be my early warning system and my first line of defence.

Sometimes I play in Castries while waiting for Sheilagh to come down from the mountain where she visits crazy people.

Sheilagh had always enjoyed the street life of Soufrière and Castries, and I encouraged her participation. Maybe I was guilty of reliving my brief and glorious gridiron past, but she was suspected of far worse— living in a heavenly future. I kept fearing that she wanted to discard her life too soon. One night I had taken her to the Prime Minister's residence high in the hills that steep down to the harbour of Castries, and it was on the drive away that she first noticed the Prison for the Criminally Insane. She made our driver stop.

"Mom, let it go."

"Say nothing, Sparrow."

We gazed at the sad-eyed, wretched men behind the fence and barbed wire in their hovel of a jail. This is the tropics, so prisons are largely open-air. This is also the third world, so prisons and sanatoriums are not tucked out of sight for propriety's sake.

"They don't look insane," Mom observed.

I argued that they were not like her. "They committed terrible crimes, Mom. Murders and rapes. They're not like the people you used to live with."

"Thou has committed crimes, Sparrow. Thou art not living there."

"Ah, Mom. That's not fair."

"That's right. It's not fair. Always they put schizophrenics in with real crazy people. Bad men in there. Not nice men. But I bet thee, I bet thee anything they got nice men locked inside there too. Nice men got stuck in there. They can't get out. People always put crazy people in the same place they put bad people. People always think crazy people are bad."

Probably she was right. In any case, I permitted her to become an angel of mercy for these wretched souls. It was not merely that the project gave her something to do, for she had always found something to do, but she now had a cause, a devotion, a passion. My mother needed her passions. So she brought the men food, and she tried to bring them treats. In the beginning, when she was not allowed inside, she'd toss chocolate bars over the fence. Chocolate fights escalated into riots, which obliged the authorities to regulate her activities. She was granted limited, and supervised, access.

Mom arranged for hot meals during the rainy season, and provided the men with cigarettes, chocolate, beef, chicken, and quality vegetables the rest of the time. My mother also brokered their sorrow with dances. She'd set a ghetto-blaster against the fence and play the latest Caribbean hits while the crazies behind the wire would gyrate and work themselves into a psychotic frenzy. She also taught them to play croquet, and loaned mallets.

She conversed with the inmates. She was on a first-name basis with most of them. They learned to love her and they flocked to her whenever she dropped by. Mom, we would all discover, was shrewd. She figured out who should not be inside, and she'd buffalo me into talking to the Prime Minister. Once we managed to have one young man transferred to a proper prison, away from the insane, and another time we actually engineered an inmate's release.

Heady stuff.

So I was pleased with her and proud of her and I have no regrets.

I say this. I have no regrets.

For I am awake the night that my mother chooses to slide from her window down the outside wall of our house. She may use the front door, it's not locked from the inside, but Sheilagh does not surrender her idiosyncrasies easily. My mother steps softly through the shadows. While her eyes adjust to the darkness, her fingertips explore a map of cracks splayed across the walls.

The caress of her dry hands moistens stone.

Stillness attracts. A seduction of silence as volatile as the grief of sunrise. Any rupture of sound will startle her, alter her shape, align her against the day.

She moves so as not to awaken her son.

She need not bother. I'm awake already. Watching her go.

As my mother steps into a clearing, shards of moonlight gash her skin.

She heads down the road, walking at first, then running, toward the harbour.

I see her go. Wonder what she's up to now. Wonder, at her age, who her new lover can be. Wonder if Finnbar knows. I'm also curious why she has chosen to wear a dark shirt and pants, her gardening clothes, rather than one of her usual cotton dresses.

My mother does not choose her best friend's boat, which is rickety and dangerous in the open water. For once she chooses my speedy launch, and in the still of the night spirits out across the water toward the city of Castries.

My mother is sixty-seven years old. She docks at a rickety old wharf in Castries, removes a bag she must have previously hidden in the hold, and minds her footing stepping ashore. Holes in the wharf resemble shadows at night, and her eyesight is poor.

In the tarnished silver of moonlight, my mother moves through the darker shadows. She climbs through tropical forest and muddy back streets, avoiding the stairs and the proper streets on the long high climb to the Prison for the Criminally Insane.

In the deadfall of night, Sheilagh rests her bag outside the fence. In the moonlight, in the starlight, the white eyes of black men peer out at her. Mouse-quiet, a few gather where she squats. They do not speak.

"Does thou see the infidel coming?" my mother chants in a covert whisper as she removes the wire-cutters from her bag. The men look from one to another. "Does thou see him all in red?"

The men breath more heavily, in rhythm to her words, to the music of their conspiracy, and to the *snip, snap* of the wire.

"Does thou hear the enemy marching, marching with their dead?" Having created a door in the outer fence, Sheilagh begins to cut at the furls of barbed wire. More men, seven in total, squat silently, and expectantly, by the fence. An eighth hovers off to one side, perhaps on guard. "Does thou see the cobras climbing, sliding on the walls?" she taunts them. "Does thou feel the breath of dragons, burning through the halls?"

They don't know if they should reply. Or what that reply should be.

Mom's own breathing accelerates with the exertion of her effort. I have had to worry about her health. She's supposed to wear glasses to support her failing eyesight (usually she doesn't bother), and of late she tires easily. Broken down from a lifetime of drug-taking, her heart has lost its efficiency. She perspires in the moonlight, and must put down her wire-cutters after every few bites, to rest.

Her incantation revives her. Pushes her on. The men are silent. Watchful. Expectant. They are, all, madmen.

"Take out thy sword, O Warrior! Take out thy Sword of Light!"

I am standing on my balcony, gazing at starlight, and at the few reciprocal lights of Soufrière. This is a dark night. I sense shadows moving through the tropical air. My own dark shadow stirs in my belly. "A man is a sparrow," Miss Plant had taught me. "A soul is a pterodactyl." I feel my own flying in the darkness of this night. My soul preens its feathers, seeking to be reborn. At least now, in this grim world, I know what I'm looking for. A prehistoric shadow moving across an eternity of night.

Mom is finished with the barbed wire. Her gloved hands and her wire-cutters push it out of the way. As she positions her tool against the inner fence, the eighth man edges closer. She sees the bright, moonlit whites of his eyeballs in the night.

"Thou has to stay," she tells him, speaking both sternly and quietly. "Thou art too crazy. Only nice men escaping tonight. Thou needs thy meds. I'm sorry, thou must stay here for thy own good."

Almost reverentially, the hunched man moves back. Then everyone scatters, and my mother seeks shelter in the ditch. The rooftop guards pass by overhead, and my mother hunkers down under the hibiscus plants. Hiding feels like being oppressed by a drug, and she imitates old memories of being numbed. When the guards with their rifles have passed, cigarettes glowing, she crawls forward and resumes her travail upon the inner fence.

Breezes and the palm fronds chatter.

As the inmates return, curled and frightened in the shadows, battling the stress of escape and as well the circulation of their private nocturnal demons and angels alike, Sheilagh urgently whispers her final instruction, "Strike down the fiery demon! Strike down the Evil with thy Might!"

Snip. Snap.

She's through.

One by one the men come out, squiggling through the wire as if through tunnels carved in the air. They lift their eyes to the heavens as though starlight knows a different course, or speaks an alternate decree, on this side of life's fence.

Mom lines them up in single file. She will take them down to the boat, then spirit them across to another island. We cannot say for sure where she intended to drop them off, but she and I had often ferried across to the French-speaking, crowded, impoverished island of Martinique to shop in the street bazaars, and that's my best guess. If not there, then St. Vincent. She gives the men their orders. "Follow me and stay in line." Then she stops.

The eighth man has moved to the fence.

Mom is quietly insistent. "No. Thou must stay. Stay!" She talks to him as if he is a Black Labrador Retriever. She knows him. Understands that this is the only speech he will comprehend.

This is one of the times the man does not obey.

He charges through, barrels through quickly, pulling a strand of barbed wire with him that rips off a chunk of his flesh, which makes him howl like a freight train in a dark Missouri night. My mother steps forward to stand in his way. She puts her hand up in the attitude of *Stop*, and she says to him, "Stand there!" She is careful to keep her voice low, not to compromise the escape of the other men. But the man is howling from his wound, and with the delirium of escape. She says, "Stop! Thou must stop!" He rushes right through her, knocks her down and runs on through, into the refuge of the black night.

The only sound is the hurry of his sprint, a dog's objecting bark, and wind in the fronds.

My mother listens to the error of his escape.

Where she has fallen, she lies perfectly, peacefully still.

Shards of moonlight gash her skin.

She's as silent as the blossoms of hibiscus bending low for a glimpse of her face.

Accidentally, I place my hand upon a chameleon. The rubbery wee fellow shoots away. Breathing in, I smell banana and coconut, and the human abode of Soufrière in its slumber. The wings of the pterodactyl were supported from its fourth digit, the wing-finger. I spread my own arms wide, and feel the scent and the breezes in my feathers, lifting me higher. I fly. Soar under the moon and look down upon the earth where the freed inmates are circling around my mother. One touches the blood at the back of her head. She does not move. Another stoops to listen to the silence of her heartbeat. They do not abandon her. They will not. They alone see her spirit flee into the night. They alone stand, and run alongside her, her guardians of this world escorting her into the hands of angels.

My mother's frail form lies alone and still in the moonlight. God bless her, God speed her journey into the twinkling night sky, my good, my lovely mother is gone.

15.

Hibiscus

I was walking with my mother through a tropical garden on the cusp of spring. Some long while ago. Foreign to the season and latitude, olean-der, hyacinth, and magnolia spilled sharp fragrances under the glass roof of the greenhouse into the mossy air. Once upon a time all the earth had been a garden, now only this imported loam stank like swamp mud. It was the olfactory seductions of another epoch that lured my attention, soil composed of the decomposed. Mudpies baked with sand, blood, and myth, sifted together in history's clay oven.

Having been house-bound throughout a long winter, Mom wel-comed this harbinger of a new season, this remedy of another cli-mate, and we were both the beneficiaries of an additional bonus. The assault of scents, colours, and the unfamiliar humidity tweaked mem-ories of our legendary sojourn in the south. "Thou was a boy," she criticized, harshly, and her eyelids fluttered as they did whenever her anger was genuine, "what could thee remember?" So I rattled on about Lougain, and surprised her by digging up the mythological tales on which I had been weaned, excavating stories about the girls' school abutting the swamp. My mother relaxed, she smiled, and only when I broached New Orleans did she stiffen again, only then did she scoff.

"Those women never nice to me," Mom declared. Her scowl was shaped in a curious pattern, as though the venom was current. "Made me eat terrible awful food, I didn't like it, with hot sauces. Burn my tongue. Anytime they wanted to be not nice to me they did it—went ahead and slapped me on my face."

"They didn't slap you. I never saw anyone hit you."

"Slapped me hard on my face! Sparrow, they did, they hated me! I didn't do nothing wrong, they called me 'mush brain'. I never hurt them, they called me 'coo-coo clock', they called me 'pussy-face'. They called me 'crazy white whore.' Why does think they were nice? Why does thou always think people are good? What's the matter with thee, Sparrow? The man was okay. I forgot his name."

"Sturgess Rawlins. See how well I remember?"

"The women were meanies, Sparrow. Why do I make that up?"

"Please, try and forget it. I'm sorry I upset you."

"Singing! Never went around singing. When did thee hear those meanies singing?"

"I didn't. I was just trying to imagine what your days must have been like."

"Thou can't do that. Nobody can imagine my days. Nights neither."

Scratch the Broadway show tunes. I had been six, my memory of the time was bound to be faulty, and even my perceptions were conditioned by my age. I did not remember people who were not nice, that's all that I could say. My mother refuted that version, but the question begged to be put forward, how reliable was hers? One problem with knitting our lives back together again, each of us used different threads. The mind of the child and the mind of the schizophrenic combined to recreate the adventures of our true lives, but we could not always distinguish between what was real and what was merely feared, between what was witnessed, or experienced, and what was desired. Privately, I stuck to my account about New Orleans. If that was not the precise adventure we lived, it remained the escapade that I recalled, the distillation of memory. If not confirmed by historical veracity, the events remained the true adventures fermenting in that dank cask of mind usually inebriated with recollections.

In that botanical garden, my mother buried her face in the hibiscus. Call it inspiration, call it intuition, but in a flash I reached right inside her and pulled out a plum of an idea. I had identified something germane to the particular nature of her schizophrenia. In circumstances where our common minds—I shall refrain from declaring them 'normal'—caved into fear, my mother submerged herself in an attitude of awe. Awe. A state of grace, perhaps. Conversely, when conditions commonly provoked a sense of awe in the rest of us, my mother succumbed to a hybrid fear. Walking in the greenhouse, the thesis grew inside me like an exotic tropical bloom. It occurred to me that my mother's brain made her a liability to herself in this world, yet her crossed switches favoured her with a threshold into other dimensions. Staggered by evidence of nature or a momentary lapse into awe, we celebrate those occasions with cocky pleasure—a faint approach. In contrast, my mother would stand fearful of her Maker. When the rest of us were sore afraid, my mother shrugged off the illusion of our predicament and was awed by the moment. Walking in that garden, I begged a deeper cognition. Are mortals, comfortable with our strategies on this earth, viewed from heaven as a tribe of astral schizophrenics? I began to wonder. Perceived from above, are we not the ones in the reverse mirror, doing everything, even gauging our own sanity, backwards? These were notions that I did not shake off easily, as my mother's influence had obviously undermined my logic.

She buried her face in the hibiscus. Unlike the others strolling though the greenhouse she did not timidly sniff the flowers. Mom implanted the whole of her face in the petals, breathing in so sharply and deeply anyone would think that the scent was oxygen to her. Consumed by the flower, she allowed the colour and the perfume and the delicacy to transform her. What was really crazy, there is no scent to hibiscus. She was inventing the fragrance. Mom would emerge from this intimate embrace invigorated and restored.

"Smell, Sparrow," she'd say to me.

"Aw, Mom."

"Smell."

So I'd do it. Bow my head. Inhale deeply. And sense nothing.

Mom would have been delighted, and certainly I was pleased, that her funeral reunited our far-flung family for the first time in many years. Barclay flew across from Costa Rica with his wife, three children, and four armed guards. Hannah accompanied Zeke down from Toronto, while Zack made his own way from Boston. I had not seen Auntie Butter since our last supper. The moment she stepped from the plane, my heart splintered. She was my other mother, old and frail and I hugged her fiercely. Uncle pried us apart before I did one of us an injury. Hobbled, Auntie panted for breath in the humid tropical air. She found the treacherous mountain journey into Soufrière a great trial, our Jeep heroically bucking on the steep cliffs of goat-track that passed for road. We made it, and at the end of her journey she was glad to be there, happy to have travelled for the first time in her life. Auntie was relieved to see me before she, too, passed away. We talked, and ate, and often tears bubbled in our eyes when someone recalled something that Sheilagh had either said or done, and then we'd remember something else about her and we'd break into laughter again. Mom would have liked that. We missed her much. Out of our laughter we would weep again. Mom would have understood that, too.

Uncle embarked upon a tirade one night. He regaled the forces of the world that had conspired to exile his sons. Barclay and I listened. We did not concur, nor did we contradict. Uncle knew better, but he still seemed able to convince himself. If Barclay's thinking was any-thing like my own, our reaction was one of sadness, of wonder, of mis-giving, of comprehension. We allowed Uncle his rant. Who were we to deny anyone access to lunacy?

At the funeral, more than a hundred girls in school tunics showed up on their lunch hour. They had loved Sheilagh's gentle spirit. They missed her batty conversation. Remembering her great fondness for them, they needed to say goodbye.

In the latter days, I often told my mother how much I loved her. We had become naturally, perhaps notoriously, affectionate with one another. Unfortunately, and this is my one great regret, I never got around to saying how damned proud I was of her. Proud of her, right up to the sharp instant of her death. Each of the recaptured inmates told the same story. She had held out her hand for the brute to stop. I mean, holding up her hand as a stop sign to this demented, fullback-sized pris-oner, that was so *nutty*, so *batty*, it was so downright *crazy*, and I love her for it and I'm proud of her. Proud of her life. Of her simple, every-day accomplishments and victories. I'm even proud that three of the seven men she let escape have not been located. May they continue to enjoy their freedom in peace. More than anyone else, I'm convinced, Mom knew what was best for them.

I trust her judgment.

The man who killed her, who flew right through her like a huge black raven, was apprehended. He was too crazy to remain out of sight for long. The Prime Minister wanted to know if I would have some-thing done about him, as if I was entitled to a claim on his life or something. I don't know what he had in mind. I said no, leave him alone, don't add to his miseries, for I guess that that's what Mom would have wanted.

A stop sign. Mom. Really.

"I'm proud of thee, Mom," I said, when I kneeled to toss dirt on her coffin. Scores of schoolchildren leaned around me, anxious for a glimpse of what was down there. Her coffin was better made than most of their homes, maybe that was part of the attraction, although, like all of us, they were wondering about her change of residence. I whispered, "Talk to your angels now, Momma. Thou knows their language. They will listen to thee." My mother knew her soul. Angels would speak to her.

The schoolchildren had brought flowers, hibiscus and cinnamon blossom.

Nina assisted me in walking away from the grave site. She helped get me through. After the funeral, and after everyone had left for their widespread homes, I kept a promise to her and visited the volcano for a week or so. We lolled around in the mud and mineral water that flowed black from the lava pools and sulphur springs. We have our private spots. Mom loved them. She had enjoyed making herself beautiful by covering herself with mud, the concept was nutty enough to keep her entertained. Nina and I recuperated in the mineral-laden baths.

I made the decision, that week, to carry on with Mom's work among the criminally insane. It's no big deal. On weekends, I hire reggae bands to play outside the compound, and the inmates dance and the people on the streets join in. The best food on the island is delivered to the gate. Some say the prison is the best hotel on the island too, with bargain rates besides. I don't know about that. The most important work, for which I continue to nurture my political connections, is to see that the mildly disoriented are segregated from the hopelessly, violently insane. Society does tend to bunch the two together and nothing made my mom more angry. I also see to it that those who are disturbed beyond the pale receive a higher level of care than what is usually granted in the developing world.

This is it then. I cannot ask for sympathy, beg mercy, or lean upon my good works from the paradise of exile. Instead, after great consideration, what I must ask is something very different (the last wish of a doomed man, perhaps), for these are the thoughts which plague my contemplations, these are the matters which adorn my days and remain unresolved after a lifetime of adventuring. Is it true that human life ascended from a swamp? I'm fifty-plus years old and I would really like to know. I ask the Prime Minister this question, and he shrugs. After eons, did amoebae, weary of the muck and slime, yearn for a succulent breath above the fetid air, desire a new address? Think about it. Can it be true? I mean, did I do right or did I do wrong? That's the issue suspended in the balance. The answer depends solely on the truth of our suspicions about this planet. Are such pursuits—accumulating funds, let's say—merely the occupations of the fallen, of heaven's rejects? Or, as measured on a different scale, is all human endeavour ultimately a quarrel about real estate? Is this the true path? Is it okay, you know, with God, with the cosmos, with the powers that move the universe and dance the stars in the night sky, is it all right with them if I build a casino? "Have you talked to God about your casino?" I have asked the Prime Minister. He assures me that it is none of God's business, also that God is not interested. He wants to know if I talked to God before looting OIS. I tell him that that was something I neglected to do. Is this it then? I argue. Is any quest more significant that the scramble for power, fame, possessions? I'm asking the question. Can we honestly accept that humankind emerged from the swamp, pursued by alligators and demons and moccasin snakes, running terrified as spirits mocked from seats high among the trees? And if we do, what then? And if we don't, what then?

What was the point of that crusade?

Some days, on rare occasion, I play the Russian sport. Some days I can't resist. I ask my questions. Take aim. I will hear the trigger—*click* and the hammer snap or I will hear nothing at all. The game does focus the mind so well. One time, Nina came upon me sitting in a dry tub, fully clothed, on the off-chance there'd be a mess. "Sparrow?" An abject day all around.

She was furious with me and grabbed the gun. She was hysterical and screaming at me and I followed her out to the main room and she was wailing and saying, "You can't do this to me! You can't, Sparrow!" And she pointed the pistol at her head.

"Nina. Don't. Stop."

"How do you like it, Sparrow? How do you like it?"

"I don't. Please. Nina. Stop. It's just a game but there is one bullet."

She said, "I want to try one." As though we were children with a new toy. She pulled the trigger.

Click!

Then we were weeping in one another's arms. And after we calmed down we did the dirty on the floor and who cares if the servants watched? I won't let Nina play anymore, and try not to play myself.

Some call this life.

Great insanities pervade the world. My life has been touched by a few. To view a mind in disarray is a grim experience. Tragic, in the rotten, miserable sense of the word. And yet, how equally sad it is to witness the madness of the sane. It's a wonder that we do so much, accomplish so much in this mercantile world, when we don't have the first inkling as to why we are here. St. Lucia, as one star in a galaxy of examples, can portend to be paradise. If we can harness the hellish energy beneath its skin we might spare it from casinos. But only for a few years, and then the island, like every island, like every nation, like every noble thought, like every person, will wreck on some foreign or internal strife. And the wonder of it is that we are all so busy *doing*, doing, doing, when we don't know what it is we've done. Are we angels or swamp-bugs? This is what we must find out. This is what holds us back. Not knowing is killing me. What are we?

Click!

My sole contribution to the debate is to admit that I, for one, emerged from a swamp. I stand below the prudence of starlight, in the night air endowed by the fragrance of hibiscus which the humming-birds probe throughout our tranquil days. The scent, of course, is non-existent, although Mom always assured me that it was lovely and sweet. "Thou don't got the right nose for smelling, Sparrow." But she was crazy and I choose not to quarrel with her, I prefer to argue with starlight. I, for one, was conceived by a poacher (but aren't we all?), born to an angel (but aren't we all?), and having come this far, so far, I must let it go at that (but don't we all?).

My mother prayed to be visited by reason, to possess a serene, sane, composed mind. I plead the opposite. *Oh God, I beseech Thee, spare me the insanity of reason*. Grant me my search for my soul.

Click!

We quest after riches with greater fervour than we imagine harmony. That's where our reason gets us. We imagine power more potently than we desire love. Which is reasonable. We desire fame more than we nurture humility. Thanks to reason. We nurture self-interest at the expense of pursuing peace. Perfectly reasonable. Pursue an edge, an in, an advantage with greater relish than we quest for wisdom. Power, fame, possessions compel our imaginations and corrupt our ethics. This is what I say to my political friends. They laugh. They find me amusing. Nina says I'm forever a romantic, puke, snort, that that's what she loves about me. Love, wisdom, peace are undermined by our ethics, I tell them. But our ethics are good for business. A casino, they insist, will be good for business. People will be fed. I can't deny that. Not only do I not deny it, I am willing to invest. Oh God! Our imaginations have grown so dim! Corrupted by good business and shallow ethics, we have done our worst. The worst we could ever do. We have lost our sense of adventure. When we act we do so for economic gain. Searching for our souls we sit on the sofa. To find a soul, surely we must adventure.

Pick up thy bed and walk, run, fly, disassemble thy molecules and zap thyself through time and space.

Nina repeats again that I'm a romantic.

I vow to retaliate by romancing her.

She shudders. She says, "Ugh! Puke! Snort!" And we laugh. We laugh and make love and squeeze no triggers.

Early in my life I had misinterpreted my lineage. My father was a bird, I thought, or something like that. My mother and I were guided by my rich and powerful grandparents—so I believed. These were not the facts. Yet I believed them, and because I believed them and acted according to my misconceptions and because I did not recognize that I was searching for my soul but made my choices based on incorrect assumptions, my life has been skewered and scarred.

If anyone, acting alone, can make weird choices, what do we hapless humans do as a gang? If humankind cannot ascertain its lineage—beast or fowl, swampbug or ditched angel—if we cannot know conclusively whether or not our dim past is swamp or ethereal air, what can we know, how can we choose, which way do we turn when the next choice challenges us? What is the structure of our reason, I ask myself, when the foundation of our reason has been constructed upon a mystery?

Oh God. I protest. *Spare us the insanity of reason.* And my mother says, in the voice that wakes me every morning, a voice that I will always hear, "Cockledoodledoo, Sparrow. Cockledoodledoo."

And you know, when all is said and done, she might be right, even if she does sound more like a churlish hen than a rooster. She's beginning to make sense to me, that woman.

Each morning I wash, I shave, I dress. Before I eat I venture outside into the garden. The last time we were separated, I used to piss on the flowerbeds as my way to remember my mother. Now I sniff the hibiscus which grows wild around my house. New blooms are produced daily. I snip a few and carry them down to the sea. I will always do this, a ritual preferred to my nocturnal pee in search of her memory. Mom taught me to do it when she had performed a remembrance for her missing loved ones. Perhaps that had been her motive, teaching me a signal with which to greet her in her dwelling on the other side of life. I cut the red blossoms into shapes and set these floating hearts adrift upon the sea. They will let her know I'm coming. I watch the hearts bob upon the surface for as long as they are visible, then scan the ocean and sky for a glimmer of her presence.

I wait. I remember. I say, "I'm proud of thee, Mom."

Pause for a moment. Try to see the world through her eyes.

And through the eyes of my black-feathered soul.

Time passes.

Before leaving the shore, it is always prudent for me to train my binoculars on whatever boats occupy the harbour, to check for assassins. I carry no guns outside my home, and keep no guards, my wits alone must guide me. Then I hike up the mountainside in the rain or in the sunshine and sit down to a breakfast of delicious green-skinned oranges and eggs spoon-fried in coconut oil. Honestly, I rarely feel alone. It's not an issue. For we are travelling still, my precious mother and me, we are travelling still, from this day and this world and this adventure into the next.

"Cockledoodledoo, Sparrow. Cockledoodledoo."

THE END